W9-AFX-746

The Orchid House

THE ORCHID HOUSE

A Novel

LUCINDA RILEY

ATRIA PAPERBACK

New York London Toronto Sydney New Delhi

ATRIA PAPERBACK
A Division of Simon & Schuster, Inc.
1230 Avenue of the Americas
New York, NY 10020

This book is a work of fiction. Names, characters, places, and incidents either are products of the author's imagination or are used fictitiously. Any resemblance to actual events or locales or persons, living or dead, is entirely coincidental.

Originally published in Great Britain by Penguin Books.
Published by arrangement with Penguin Books.

First Atria Paperback edition February 2012

Manufactured in the United States of America

ISBN 978-1-61793-683-8

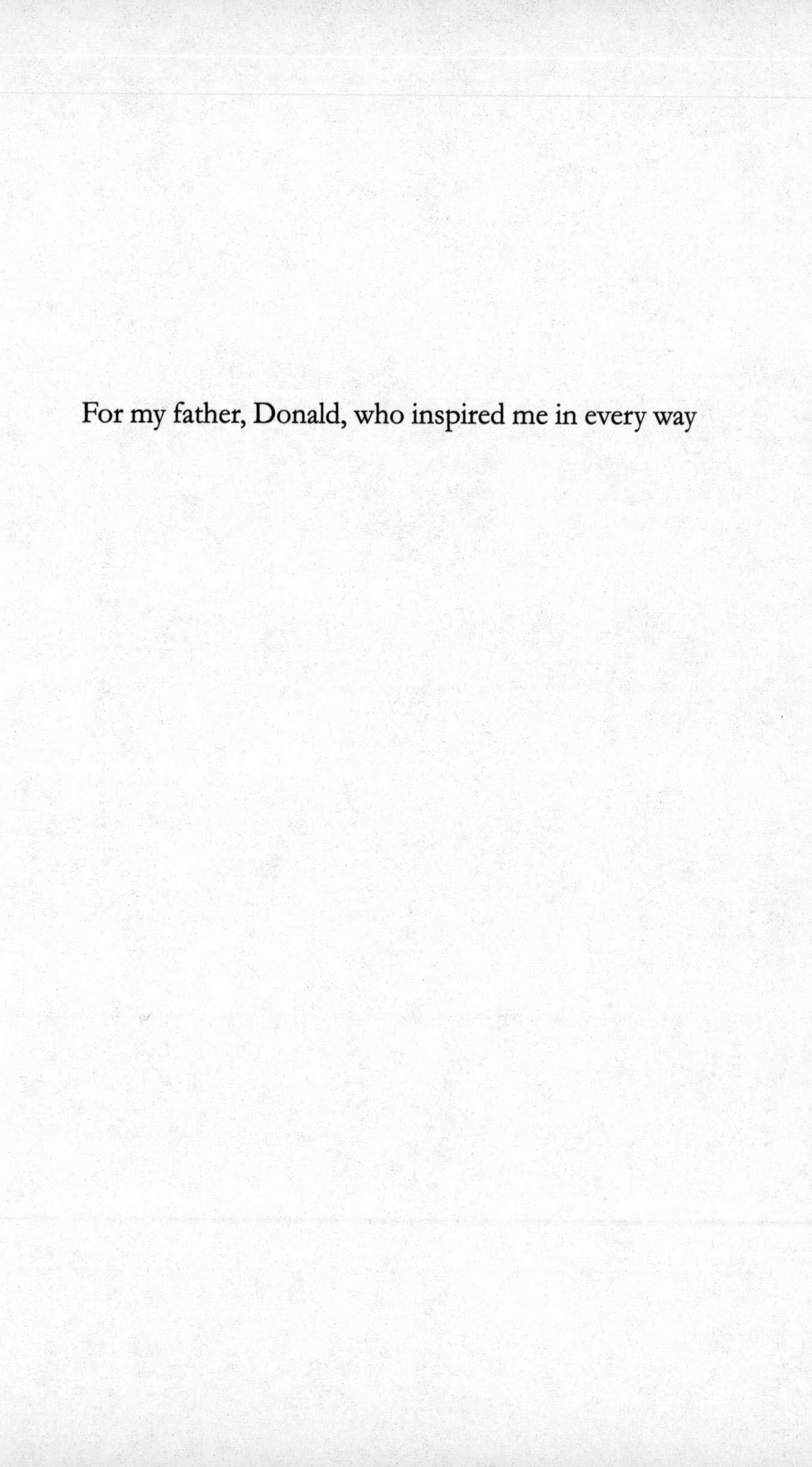

For my father, Donald, who inspired me in every way

Siam, Many Moons Past . . .

It is said in Siam that when a man falls in love with a woman—deeply, passionately, irrevocably—he will be capable of doing anything to keep her, please her, to make her value him *above all others.*

And once there was a Prince of Siam who fell in love this way with a woman of rare beauty. He pursued and won her, but yet, only nights before their wedding, a celebration that would include a nation feasting, dancing, and rejoicing, the Prince felt uneasy.

He knew he must somehow prove his love to her with an act of such heroism and power that it would bind her to him for all time.

He must find something that was as rare and beautiful as she was.

After much thought, he called his three most trusted servants to his side and told them what they must do.

"I've heard tales of the Black Orchid that grows in our kingdom, high up in the mountains of the North. I want you to find it for me and bring it here to my palace so I may give it to my Princess on our wedding day. Whichever one of you brings the orchid to me first, I will reward with the kind of treasure that will make you a rich man. The two who fail will not live to see my marriage."

The hearts of the three men, bowing in front of their Prince, were filled with terror. For they knew they were staring at death. The Black Orchid was a mythical flower. Just like the bejeweled golden dragons that adorned the prows of the royal barges, which would carry their Prince to the temple where he would take his vows to his new Princess, it was the stuff of legend.

That night, all three of the men made their way home to their families and said their good-byes. Yet one of them, lying in the arms of his weeping wife, was cleverer than the others and wished to die less than they did.

By morning, he had hatched a plan. He set off to the floating market, which sold spices, silks . . . and flowers.

There, he used coins to purchase an exquisite orchid of deepest magenta and pink, fulsome with dark, velvety petals. Then he walked with his plant along the narrow klongs of Bangkok until he found the Scribe, sitting among his scrolls in his dark, humid workroom at the back of his shop.

The Scribe had once worked at the palace, which was how the Servant knew him, but his work had been deemed unworthy due to the imperfections in his lettering.

"Sawadee krup, Scribe." The Servant placed the orchid on the desk. "I have a task for you, and if you help me, I can offer you riches you can only have dreamed of."

The Scribe, who had been forced to scratch a living since his days at the palace, looked up at the Servant with interest. "And how might that be?"

The Servant indicated the flower. "I wish you to use your skill with ink and color the petals of this orchid black."

The Scribe frowned as he stared at the Servant, then studied the plant. "Yes, it is possible, but when new flowers grow, they will not be black and you will be discovered."

"When new flowers grow, you and I will be many miles away, living like the Prince I serve," answered the Servant.

The Scribe nodded slowly as he thought about it. "Come back to me at nightfall and you will have your Black Orchid."

The Servant returned home and told his wife to pack their meager belongings, promising that she would be able to buy whatever her heart desired and that he would build her a beautiful palace of her own far, far away.

That night he returned to the Scribe's shop. And gasped in delight as he saw the Black Orchid sitting on the desk.

He studied the petals and saw that the Scribe had performed an excellent job.

"It is dry," commented the Scribe, "and the ink will not rub off onto a pair of inquiring fingers. I have tested it myself. You try."

The Servant did so and saw his fingers were clean of ink.

"But I cannot say how long it will last. Moisture from the plant itself will dampen the ink. And, of course, it must never be subjected to rain."

"It is good enough," said the Servant, nodding, picking the plant up. "I am off to the palace. Meet me down by the river at midnight and I will give you your share."

On the night of the Prince's wedding to his Princess, and after he had shared his day of joy with his kingdom, he stepped inside their private quarters.

The Princess was standing on the terrace outside, looking down on the Chao Phraya River, which was still alight with the reflections of fireworks set off to celebrate her union to the Prince. He came to stand beside her.

"My only love, I have something for you; something that signifies your uniqueness and perfection."

He handed her the Black Orchid, set in a pot of solid gold, bedecked with jewels.

The Princess looked down at it, at its black-as-night petals, which seemed to be struggling under the heavy color its species had produced. It looked weary, wilted, and malevolent in its unnatural darkness.

However, she knew what she was holding . . . what it meant and what he had done for her.

"My Prince, it is exquisite! Where did you find it?" she asked.

"I searched the kingdom, high and low. I am assured there is no other, as there is no other of you." He looked at her, with all the passion he felt alive in his eyes.

She saw the love and stroked his face gently, hoping he knew it was returned by her and always would be.

"Thank you, it is so very beautiful."

He grasped her hand from his cheek and, as he kissed her fingers, was overcome with a need to possess all of her. This was his wedding night and he had waited a long time. He took the orchid from her, set it down on the terrace, then took her in his arms and kissed her.

"Come inside, my Princess," he murmured into her ear.

She left the Black Orchid on the terrace and followed him into their bedchamber.

Just before dawn, the Princess arose from their bed and went outside to greet the first morning of their new life together. She saw from the shallow puddles that it had rained during the night. The new day was stirring into life, the sun still partially hidden by the trees on the other side of the river.

On the terrace stood an orchid of pink and magenta, in the same solid-gold pot that her Prince had presented to her.

She smiled as she touched its petals, now cleansed and healthy from the rain, and so very much more beautiful than the same Black Orchid he had given her the night before. The faintest hint of gray tinged the puddle of water surrounding it.

Finally, understanding everything, she picked it up, smelling its heavenly scent as she mused on what to do: was it better to tell the truth to wound, or a lie to protect?

A few minutes later, she wandered back into the bedchamber and curled herself back into her Prince's arms.

"My Prince," she murmured as he awoke, "my Black Orchid has been stolen away from us in the night."

He sat up abruptly, horrified, ready to call his guards. She calmed him with a smile.

"No, my darling, I believe it was given to us only for one night, the night we became one, when our love blossomed and we became part of nature too. We could not presume to keep something so magical only to us . . . and, besides, it would wilt, then die . . . and I could not bear it." She took his hand and kissed it. "Let us believe in its power and know that its beauty blessed us on the first night of our lives together."

The Prince thought for a while. Then, because he loved her with all his heart and because he was so very happy she was now completely his, the Prince did not call his guards.

And as he grew older and their union was successful and blessed with a child conceived on that very night, and many more to follow, he believed for the rest of his life that the mystical Black Orchid had lent them its magic, but was not theirs to keep.

The morning after the Prince's wedding to his Princess, a poor fisherman sat on the banks of the Chao Phraya, a few hundred yards downriver from the royal palace. His line had been empty for the last two hours. He wondered whether the fireworks of the past night have sent the fish to the bottom of the river. He would not get a catch to sell and his large family would go hungry.

As the sun climbed above the trees on the opposite bank to shine its blessed light on the water, he saw something sparkling amid the detritus of green weeds that floated along the river. Leaving his rod, he waded into the water to retrieve it. Grabbing it in his hands before it floated past, he hauled the weed-covered object to the bank.

And when he had removed the weeds, what a sight met his eyes!

The pot was made of solid gold, inset with diamonds, emeralds, and rubies.

His fishing rod forgotten, he stowed the pot inside his basket and set off for the gem market in the city, knowing—with joy in his heart—that his family would never go hungry again.

PART ONE

Winter

I

Norfolk, England

I have the same dream every night. It's as if my life is thrown up into the air and all the pieces are sent down . . . back to front and inside out. All part of my life and yet in the wrong order, the view fragmented.

People say that dreams are important and they tell you something, something that you are hiding from yourself.

I am hiding nothing from myself; I only wish I could.

I go to sleep to forget. To find some peace, because I spend the whole day remembering.

I am not mad. Though recently, I've been thinking a lot about what madness actually is. Many millions of human beings, each one an individual, each with their own DNA profile, their own unique thoughts—their personal perception of the world from inside their heads. And each view is different.

I've come to the conclusion that all we humans can really share is the flesh and bones, the physical matter we were born with. For example, I've been told time and time again that everyone responds differently to grief and that no reaction is wrong. Some people cry for months, years even. They wear black and they mourn. Others seem untouched by their loss. They bury it. They carry on exactly as they had before. As if nothing had happened to them.

I'm not sure what my reaction has been. I haven't cried for months. In fact, I have barely cried at all.

But I haven't forgotten either. I never will.

I can hear someone downstairs. I must get up and pretend I am ready to face the day.

• • •

Alicia Howard pulled her Land Rover to the curb. She switched off the engine and walked up the shallow hill to the cottage. Knowing the front door was never locked, she opened it and stepped inside.

Alicia stood in the still-darkened sitting room and shivered. She moved toward the windows and drew back the curtains. Plumping up the cushions on the sofa, she swept up three empty coffee cups and took them into the kitchen.

She walked over to the fridge and opened it. A solitary, half-empty bottle of milk stood in the door. One out-of-date yogurt, some butter, and an aging tomato sat on the shelves. She closed the fridge and inspected the bread bin. As she had suspected, it was empty. Alicia sat down at the table and sighed. She thought of her own warm, well-stocked kitchen, the comforting smell of something cooking in the Aga for supper, the sound of children playing and their sweet, high-pitched laughter . . . the *heart* of her home and her life.

The contrast with this bleak little room was not lost on her. In fact, it was an apt metaphor for her younger sister's current existence: Julia's life, and her heart, were broken.

The sound of footsteps on the creaking wooden staircase told Alicia she was approaching. She watched as her sister appeared at the kitchen door and, as always, was struck by her beauty; while she was blonde and fair-skinned, Julia was dark and exotic. Her thick mane of mahogany hair framed her fine-featured face, the weight she had recently lost only serving to highlight her luminous, almond-shaped, amber eyes and high cheekbones.

Julia was inappropriately dressed for the January weather in one of the only outfits she currently possessed: a red caftan top, gaily embroidered in colorful silks, and a pair of loose, black cotton trousers, hiding the thinness of her legs. Alicia could already see the goose bumps on Julia's bare arms. She stood up from the table and pulled her reticent sister to her in an affectionate hug.

"Darling," she said, "you look freezing. You should go and buy yourself some warmer clothes, or do you want me to bring you over a couple of my sweaters?"

"I'm fine," Julia replied, shrugging her sister off. "Coffee?"

"There's not much milk, I just looked in your fridge."

"That's okay, I'll have it black." Julia walked to the sink, filled the kettle, and switched it on.

"So, how have you been?" asked Alicia.

"Fine," replied Julia, pulling two coffee mugs down from the shelf.

Alicia grimaced. "Fine" was Julia's stock reply. She used it to swat away probing questions.

"Seen anyone this week?"

"No, not really," said Julia.

"Darling, are you sure you don't want to come and stay with us for a while again? I hate thinking of you here by yourself."

"Thanks for the offer, but I've told you, I'm fine," Julia replied distantly.

Alicia sighed in frustration. "Julia, you don't look fine. You've lost even more weight. Are you eating at all?"

"Of course I am. Do you want coffee or not?"

"No, thanks."

"Fine." Julia slammed the milk bottle back into the fridge. As she turned round, her amber eyes glistened with anger. "Look, I know you're only doing this because you care. But, really, Alicia, I'm not one of your children. I *like* being by myself."

"Nonetheless," Alicia said brightly, trying to stem her rising impatience, "you'd better go and get your coat. I'm taking you out."

"Actually, I've got plans for today."

"Then you'd better cancel them. I need your help."

"How?"

"It's Dad's birthday next week, in case you'd forgotten, and I want to buy him a birthday present."

"And you need my help to do that, Alicia?"

"It's his sixty-fifth, the day he becomes a pensioner."

"I'm aware of that. He is my father too."

Alicia struggled to keep her composure. "There's a Sale of Contents at Wharton Park at noon today. I thought we might go and see if we could both find something for Dad." She saw a flicker of interest in Julia's eyes.

"Wharton Park is being sold?"

"Yes, didn't you know?"

Julia's shoulders slumped. "No, I didn't. Why is it?"

"I presume it's the usual story: inheritance taxes. I've heard the current owner is selling it to a man with more money than sense. No family can afford to keep up a place like that. And the last Lord Crawford let it fall into a dreadful state of disrepair. Apparently, it requires a fortune to fix up."

"How sad," Julia murmured.

"I know," agreed Alicia, glad to see that at least Julia seemed engaged. "It was a big part of our childhood, especially yours. That's why I thought we should see if we could pick up something from the sale, some kind of keepsake or memento for Dad. It will probably be all the rubbish, with the good stuff going off to Sotheby's, but one never knows."

Surprisingly, without need of further persuasion, Julia nodded. "Okay, I'll go and get my coat."

Five minutes later, Alicia was maneuvering the car along the narrow high street of the pretty coastal village of Blakeney. Turning left, she headed east for the fifteen-minute journey to Wharton Park.

"Wharton Park . . . ?" muttered Julia to herself.

It was her most vivid childhood memory, visiting Grandfather Bill in his hothouse: the overpowering smell of the exotic flowers he grew in there, and his patience as he explained their genus and where in the world they had originally come from. His own father, and his father's father before him, had all worked as gardeners to the Crawford family, who owned Wharton Park, a vast estate comprising a thousand acres of fertile farmland.

Her grandparents had lived in a comfortable cottage in a cozy, bustling corner of the estate, surrounded by the many other staff who serviced the land, the house, and the Crawford family itself. Julia and Alicia's mother, Jasmine, had been born and brought up there in the cottage.

Elsie, Julia's grandmother, had been exactly as a grandmother should be, if slightly eccentric. Her welcoming arms were open, and something delicious was always cooking in the oven for supper.

Whenever Julia thought back on the time she had spent at Wharton Park, she remembered the blue sky and the lush colors of the flowers blossoming under the summer sun. And Wharton Park had once been famous for its collection of orchids. It was strange to think that the small, fragile flowers had originally grown in tropical climes, and yet there they had been, flourishing in the cool Northern Hemisphere, amid the flatlands of Norfolk.

When she was a child, Julia had spent all year looking forward to her summer visits to Wharton Park. The tranquility and warmth of the hothouses—sitting snugly in the corner of the kitchen garden, sheltered against the cruel winds that blew in from the North Sea during the winter—stayed in her memory all year. This, combined with the domestic certainty of her grandparents' cottage, had made it a place of peace for her. At Wharton Park, nothing changed. Alarms and timetables weren't in charge, it was nature dictating the rhythm.

She could still remember, in a corner of the hothouse, her grandfather's old Bakelite radio playing classical music from dawn until dusk.

"Flowers love music," Grandfather Bill would tell her as he tended his precious plants. Julia would sit on a stool in the corner by the radio and watch him, listening to the music. She was learning to play the piano and had a natural ability for it. An ancient upright piano was in the small sitting room of the cottage. Often, after supper, she would be asked to play. Her grandparents had watched appreciatively, and with awe, as Julia's delicate young fingers sped across the keys.

"You have a God-given gift, Julia," Grandfather Bill had said one night, his eyes misty as he smiled at her. "Never waste it, will you?"

The day on which she turned eleven, Grandfather Bill had presented her with her very own orchid.

"This is especially for you, Julia. Its name is *Aerides odoratum*, which means 'children of the air.' "

Julia studied the delicate ivory and pink petals of the flower sitting in its pot. They felt velvety beneath her touch.

"Where does this one come from, Grandfather Bill?" she had asked.

"From the Orient, in the jungles of Chiang Mai in northern Thailand."

"Oh. What kind of music do you think it likes?"

"It seems particularly partial to a touch of Mozart," chuckled her grandfather. "Or if it looks like it's wilting, perhaps you could try some Chopin!"

Julia had nurtured both her orchid and her gift for the piano, sitting in the drawing room of her drafty Victorian home on the outskirts of Norwich—she had played to it, and it blossomed for her time and again.

And she had dreamed of the exotic place from which her orchid had come. No longer was she in a suburban drawing room, but in the vast jungles of the Far East . . . the sounds of geckos, birds, and the intoxicating perfumes of the orchids growing all over the trees and in the undergrowth beneath.

One day she knew she would go to see it for herself. But, for now, her grandfather's colorful description of Far-Away Lands fired her imagination and her playing.

When she was fourteen, Grandfather Bill had died. Julia remembered the feeling of loss vividly. He and the hothouses had been the one certainty in her young and already difficult life—a wise, kind influence with a listening ear—perhaps more of a father to her than her own had been. At eighteen, she had won a scholarship to the Royal College of Music in London. Grandmother Elsie had moved to live in Southwold with her sister for company, and Julia had visited Wharton Park no more.

Now here she was, at thirty-one, returning to it. As Alicia chattered about her four children and their various activities, Julia relived the anticipation she had felt every time she'd driven in her parents' car down this road; staring out of the rear window, waiting for the Gate Lodge to appear as they reached the familiar bend in the road.

"There's the turning!" Julia said, as Alicia almost overshot it.

"Gosh, yes, you're right. It's such a long time since I've been here, I'd forgotten."

As they turned into the drive, Alicia glanced at her sister. She could see a glimmer of expectation in Julia's eyes.

"You always loved it here, didn't you?" Alicia said softly.

"Yes, didn't you?"

"To be honest, I was bored when we came to stay. I couldn't wait to get back to town to see all my friends."

"You always were more of a city girl," offered Julia.

"Yes, and look at me now: thirty-four, with a farmhouse in the middle of nowhere, a brood of children, three cats, two dogs, and an Aga. What the hell happened to the bright lights?" Alicia smiled ironically.

"You fell in love and had a family."

"And it was *you* who got the bright lights," Alicia added, without malice.

"Yes, once . . ." Julia's voice trailed off as they drove down the drive. "There's the house. It looks exactly the same."

Alicia glanced at the building in front of her. "Actually, I think it looks rather better. I must have forgotten just how beautiful it is."

"I've never forgotten," murmured Julia.

They followed the line of cars slowly down the drive, both lost in their own thoughts. Wharton Park had been built in classic Georgian style for the nephew of the first prime minister of Great Britain, although he had died before the house was completed. Built almost entirely in Aislaby stone, the house had mellowed into a soft yellow over its three-hundred-year existence.

Its seven bays and double staircases, which rose in front of the basement to the piano nobile, forming a raised terrace overlooking the park at the back, added an air of French glamour. With a domed tower on each corner, its vast portico supported by four giant Ionic columns, a crumbling statue of Britannia perched jauntily atop the apex, it had a majestic but rather eccentric air.

Wharton Park was not large enough to be termed a stately home. It did not have the perfect architecture to complement it either, having had a couple of odd additions from later generations of Crawfords, which had compromised its purity. But for that very reason, neither did it have the daunting starkness associated with other great houses of the period.

"This is where we used to turn left," indicated Julia, remembering the track she had taken around the lake to reach her grandparents' cottage on the edge of the estate.

"After the sale, would you like to go to their old cottage and take a look at it?" asked Alicia.

Julia shrugged. "Let's see, shall we?"

Yellow-coated stewards were marshaling the cars into parking spaces.

"Word must have got round," commented Alicia as she swung the car into the space indicated and brought it to a halt. She turned to her sister and put her hand on her knee. "Ready to go?"

Julia felt dazed, suffused with so many memories. As she stepped out of the car and walked toward the house, even the smells were familiar: wet grass, freshly cut, and the faintest hint of a scent that she now knew to be jasmine in the borders that lined the front lawn. They followed the crowd of people slowly up the steps and inside the main entrance.

2

I am eleven again. I'm standing in an enormous room that I know is really an entrance hall, but looks to me like a cathedral. The ceiling is high above me, and as I study it, I see it is painted with clouds and fat little angels with no clothes on. This fascinates me and I'm staring so hard at them I don't notice that there's someone standing on the stairs watching me.

"Can I help you, young lady?"

I'm so startled that I nearly drop the precious pot that's in my hands and is the reason I'm here in the first place. My grandfather has sent me especially to deliver it to Lady Crawford. I'm not happy because I'm scared of her. When I've seen her from afar, she looks old and thin and cross. But Grandfather Bill has insisted.

"She's very sad, Julia. The orchid might cheer her up. Now run along, there's a good girl."

The person on the stairs is definitely not Lady Crawford. It's a young man, maybe four or five years older than I am, with lots of curly, chestnut hair worn, I think, far too long for a boy. He's very tall, but painfully thin; his arms look like sticks, hanging out of his rolled-up shirtsleeves.

"Yes, I'm looking for Lady Crawford. I brought this for her from the hothouses," I manage to stammer.

He saunters down the rest of the steps and comes to stand opposite me, his hands outstretched.

"I'll take it to her, if you'd like."

"My grandfather said I was to give it straight to her," I answer nervously.

"Unfortunately, she's having a rest just now. She's not terribly well, you know."

"I didn't know," I reply. I want to ask who he is, but I don't dare. He must be reading my mind, for he says:

"Lady Crawford is my relation, so I think you can trust me, don't you?"

"Yes, here." I proffer the orchid, secretly relieved I don't have to deliver it myself. "Can you tell Lady Crawford that my grandfather says

this is a new"—I struggle to remember the word—"hybrid, and just flowered?"

"Yes, I will."

I stand there, not quite sure what to do next. Neither does he.

Finally he says, "So, what's your name?"

"Julia Forrester. I'm Mr. Stafford's granddaughter."

He raises an eyebrow. "Of course you are. Well, I'm Christopher Crawford. Kit, to my friends."

He extends the hand that isn't holding the plant and I shake it.

"Good to meet you, Julia. I hear that you play the piano rather well."

I blush. "I don't think so."

"No need to be modest," he chides me. "I heard Cook and your grandmother talking about you this morning. Follow me."

He's still holding my hand from shaking it, and suddenly he pulls me with it, across the hall, and through a series of vast rooms filled with the kind of formal furniture that makes the house feel as if it is a life-size dollhouse. I can't help wondering where they sit and watch television in the evenings. Finally, we enter a room that is bathed in golden light, coming through the three floor-to-ceiling windows that overlook the terrace leading to the gardens. Large sofas are arranged around a huge marble fireplace, and in the far corner, in front of one of the windows, is a grand piano. Kit Crawford leads me to it, pulls out the stool, and pushes me down.

"Come on then. Let's hear you play something."

He pulls up the lid and a shower of dust mites fly into the air, sparkling in the afternoon sun.

"Are . . . are you sure I'm allowed?" I ask.

"Aunt Crawford sleeps at the other end of the house. She's not likely to hear. Come on!" He looks at me expectantly.

Tentatively, I place my hand above the keys. They are unlike any that my fingers have ever touched. I don't know it then, but they are finished in the finest ivory and I'm playing a 150-year-old Bechstein piano. I strike a note lightly and yet the echo of it resonates through the strings, amplifying the sound.

He's standing waiting by me, arms crossed. I realize I have no choice. I begin to play "Clair de Lune," a piece I've only recently learned. It's my current favorite and I've spent hours practicing it. As the notes appear under my fingers, I forget about Kit. I'm carried away by the beautiful sound this wonderful instrument makes. I go, as I always do, to another place far, far away from here. The sun shines across my fingers, it warms my face with its glow. I play perhaps better than I ever have and am surprised when my fingers touch the last keys and the piece is ended.

I hear the sound of clapping somewhere in the background and I bring myself back to this enormous room and to Kit, who is standing with a look of awe on his face.

"Wow!" he says. "That was brilliant!"

"Thank you."

"You're so young. Your fingers are so small, how can they move across the keys so quickly?"

"I don't know, they just . . . do."

"You know, Aunt Crawford's husband, Harry, Lord Crawford, was apparently an accomplished pianist?"

"Oh, no, I . . . I didn't."

"Well, he was. This was his piano. He died when I was a baby so I never heard him play. Can you play something else?"

This time he looks genuinely enthusiastic.

"I . . . I really think I should be going."

"Just one more, please?"

"All right."

And I begin to play "Rhapsody on a Theme of Paganini." Once again, I am lost in the music and I'm halfway through when I suddenly hear a voice, shouting.

"STOP! Stop that now!"

I do as I'm asked and look across to the entrance of the drawing room. A tall, thin, gray-haired woman is standing there. The look on her face is one of fury. My heart begins to beat fast.

Kit goes over to her. "Sorry, Aunt Crawford, it was me that asked Julia to play. You were asleep so I couldn't ask your permission. Did we wake you?"

A pair of cold eyes stare back at him. "No. You did not wake me. But, Kit, that is hardly the point. Surely you know I forbid anyone to play that piano?"

"I'm truly sorry, Aunt Crawford. I didn't realize. But Julia is so wonderful. She's only eleven years old, yet she plays like a concert pianist already."

"Enough!" snaps his aunt.

Kit hangs his head and beckons me to follow him.

"Sorry again," he says, as I skulk out behind him.

As I pass Lady Crawford, she stops me. "Are you Stafford's granddaughter?" Her cold, blue, gimlet eyes bore into me.

"Yes, Lady Crawford."

I see her eyes soften slightly and it looks almost as if she might cry. She nods and appears to be struggling to speak. "I . . . was sorry to hear about your mother."

Kit interrupts, sensing the tension. "Julia brought you an orchid. It's a new one from her grandfather's hothouse, isn't it, Julia?" he encourages.

"Yes," I say, also trying hard not to cry. "I hope you like it."

She nods. "I'm sure I will. Tell your grandfather I said thank you."

Alicia was patiently waiting in the line for a sales catalog.

"Did you ever come into this house when you were a child?" she asked.

"Yes," replied Julia, "once."

Alicia indicated the ceiling. "Rather tacky, those cherubim, aren't they?"

"I've always rather liked them."

"Funny old house this," Alicia continued, taking the proffered catalog and following the crowd through the hall, along the corridor, and into a large, oak-paneled room where all the sales items were on display. She handed the catalog to Julia. "Sad it's being sold, really. It's been the Crawford family seat for over three hundred years," she mused. "End of an era and all that. Shall we wander?" Alicia took Julia's elbow and steered her toward an elegant but cracked Grecian urn—from the telltale moss lines around the inside edge, obviously used as a planter for summer flowers. "What about this for Dad?"

Julia shrugged. "Maybe. It's up to you."

Sensing Julia's fading interest, and her own irritation, Alicia said, "Well, why don't we separate, and that way we can cover what's available faster? You start this side, I'll start that, and we'll meet in ten minutes by the door."

Julia nodded and watched as Alicia made her way over to the other side of the room. Unused to crowds recently, Julia felt uncomfortably claustrophobic. She made her way toward the emptier end of the room. In a corner was a trestle table, with a woman standing behind it. Julia approached it because she had nowhere else to go.

"These items aren't included in the actual sale," said the woman. "It's general bric-a-brac, really. You can buy them now, they're all individually priced."

Julia picked up a dog-eared copy of *The Children's Own Wonder Book*. She opened it and saw the date inside was 1926.

To Hugo, from Grandmother, with love.

There was also a 1932 copy of *Wilfred's Annual* and a copy of *Marigold Garden* by Kate Greenaway.

These books had a poignancy: over eighty years of Crawford children reading the stories inside as they grew up in the nursery somewhere above her. Julia decided to buy them for herself, preserve them for the lost children of Wharton Park.

A battered cardboard box full of prints was to the left of the table. Julia leafed through them listlessly. Most were pen-and-ink lithographs, depicting the Fire of London, old ships, and ugly houses. In among them was a worn brown envelope. She removed it from the box.

Inside the envelope was a set of watercolor paintings, each one depicting a different type of orchid.

The cream vellum on which they were painted was spotted with brown marks, and she surmised that the paintings were by an enthusiastic amateur, rather than a professional. Nevertheless, she thought, framed and mounted, they might look rather special. Each one had the Latin name of the orchid penciled in below the stem.

"How much are these?" she asked the woman.

The woman took the envelope from her. "I don't know. There doesn't seem to be a price marked on them."

"Well, what if I gave you twenty pounds, five pounds for each of them?"

The woman looked at the tatty paintings. She shrugged. "I think we should say ten pounds for the lot, don't you?"

"Thank you." Julia took the money out of her purse, paid, then walked back through the room to rendezvous with Alicia, who was already waiting for her.

Alicia's eyes alighted on the envelope and the books under Julia's arm. "Find something?"

"Yes, I did."

"Let me see?"

"I'll show you when we get home."

"Okay," agreed Alicia. "I'm going to bid for the urn we saw earlier. It's Lot Number Six, so hopefully we shouldn't be here too long. The auction's starting any minute."

Julia nodded. "I'll take a walk while I'm waiting for you. I need some fresh air."

"Right." Alicia dug in her handbag for her car keys and gave them to Julia. "Just in case I'm delayed. Otherwise, I'll see you by the front door in half an hour. You might have to help me carry my trophy down the steps."

"Thanks." Julia took the keys. "See you later."

She wandered out of the room, along the corridor, and into the entrance hall, which was now deserted. She stood and looked up at the cherubim on the ceiling. She glanced at the door that led toward the drawing room, housing the grand piano on which she had once played. It was standing open on the other side of the hall.

On a whim, she walked toward it, hesitated for a few seconds, then stepped through it. The vast room was shrouded in dim January light. The unused furniture was still exactly as she remembered. She walked on through other rooms until eventually she arrived at the door to the drawing room.

No sun was shining today through the long windows. The room was bitterly cold. She walked past the fireplace and the sofas, an unpleasant smell of mildew emanating from them, and toward the grand piano.

Only then did she notice the tall figure, standing with his back to her, staring out of the window beyond the piano. Half of him was shrouded by the damask curtain—the outer fabric of which was now so delicate it was reminiscent of innards through paper-thin skin.

She froze where she stood, knowing immediately that she recognized him. He didn't move; standing, statuelike, in repose. Obviously he hadn't heard her.

Understanding she was trespassing on a moment of private contemplation, Julia turned round and attempted to leave the room as quietly as she could.

She had reached the door when she heard him:

"Can I help you?"

She turned back. "I'm sorry, I shouldn't be in here."

"No, you shouldn't." He stared at her. Then his eyebrows furrowed into a frown. "Don't I know you?"

A good thirty feet of drawing room was between them, but Julia remembered the thick, curly, chestnut hair, the slim body—which had filled out and grown by at least a foot since she had last seen it—and the same crooked mouth.

"Yes. I . . . that is, we met many years ago," Julia stuttered. "I apologize. I'll go."

"Well, well, well." His face melted into a smile of recognition. "It's little Julia, the gardener's granddaughter, now world-renowned concert pianist. I'm right, aren't I?"

"Yes, I'm Julia"—she nodded—"though I'm not sure about the 'world-renowned' bit . . ."

Kit raised his eyebrows. "Don't be modest, Julia. I've a couple of your recordings. You're famous! A 'celebrity'! What on earth are you doing here? You must spend most of your life living in five-star hotel suites across the globe."

Julia realized he obviously hadn't heard.

"I'm . . . visiting my father," Julia lied.

"Well, we are honored." Kit feigned a half bow. "You're my claim to fame. I tell everyone that I was one of the first ever to hear you play 'Clair de Lune.' Rather fitting we should meet back in this room, at a time when this house is about to be sold."

"Yes. I'm sorry about that," she answered stiffly.

"Don't be. It's all for the best. Aunt Crawford let it go to rack and ruin while she was living here, and my father hadn't the money or the interest to sort it out. To be honest, I'm lucky I've found someone prepared to take it off my hands. It's going to cost a fortune to restore."

"The Wharton Park estate is yours, then?"

"Yes, for my sins, I'm afraid so. With Aunt Crawford and then my father dying recently, I'm next in line. The trouble is, all I inherit is a shedload of debts and a shitload of hassle. Anyway"—he shrugged—"sorry to be so negative."

"I'm sure there must be a part of you that's sad?"

They were still standing thirty feet apart. Kit dug his hands into his trouser pockets and walked over to her. "To be frank, on a personal level, no. I only came here for holidays when I was a kid so there's no big emotional tie to the place. And playing lord of the manor isn't really my thing. However, being the one who's had to make the decision to sell three hundred years of family history has admittedly given me a few sleepless nights. But what choice do I have? The estate's in serious debt and I have to sell it to pay the creditors off."

"Are you selling the whole lot?"

Kit swept a hand through his unruly hair and sighed. "I've managed to negotiate the old stable quadrangle where some of the workers used to live, plus a few meager acres. There's a separate path out to the road which I can make usable, so I won't have to use the main entrance to get in and out. My new home is a rather shabby cottage that has no central heating and a bad damp problem." He smiled. "But it's better than nothing and I am renovating it. I think it'll be okay when it's finished."

"That's where my grandparents lived and my mother was born," Julia said. "I never saw the cottages in the Quad as shabby or noticed the damp, but I suppose they were, really."

Kit reddened. "Sorry to be patronizing about them. Actually, the reason I fought to keep the Quad out of the sale is because I think it's a very beautiful spot. Really," he emphasized, "I'm looking forward to living there. And hoping that, when I've finished renovating the rest of the barns and cottages around me, I can rent them out to provide some income."

"Don't you have anywhere else to live?"

"Like you, I've been abroad for a long time. I never quite got round to sorting out a home, somehow . . ." Kit's voice trailed off and he averted his gaze to the view out the window. "And this neck of the woods doesn't hold particularly good memories for me. I spent some pretty miserable summers here during my childhood."

"I used to love it here at Wharton Park."

"Well, it's a fine old house, and the setting is magnificent," Kit agreed with reticence.

Julia studied him. She could see he had a deep tan but looked drawn and exhausted. Not knowing what else to say, she replied, "Well, I hope you'll be happy in your new home. I'd better be going."

"And I suppose I must come and lurk at the back of the salesroom."

They walked side by side through the darkened rooms toward the hall.

"So," asked Kit companionably, "where are you living these days? Some vast penthouse overlooking Central Park, I shouldn't doubt."

"Hardly. I'm staying in Blakeney, in a small cottage I bought years ago, when everyone told me I had to put some money into property. I've been renting it out for the past eight years to vacationers."

"Surely you must have another home somewhere else?" Kit frowned. "Celebrities don't appear on the pages of glossy mags sitting in damp cottages in North Norfolk."

"I don't do 'glossy mags,' " Julia countered defensively, "and it's a . . . long story," she added, realizing they were approaching the main entrance hall. She needed to ask an urgent question. "Are the hot-houses still here?"

"I don't know." Kit shrugged. "To be honest, I haven't been into the kitchen garden yet. There's been rather a lot to do elsewhere."

As they entered the hall, Julia could see her sister standing by the door with her urn, looking impatient.

"There you are, Kit!" A large woman with chestnut hair and deep brown eyes just like his accosted them. "Where have you been? The auctioneer wants an urgent word with you about a vase. He thinks it might be Ming dynasty or some such, and you should pull it out of the sale and have it valued by Sotheby's."

Julia saw a hint of irritation appear on Kit's face. "Julia, meet Bella Harper, my sister."

Bella's eyes swept Julia up and down without much interest. "Hi," she said absently as she tucked her arm through Kit's. "You need to speak to the auctioneer now," she told him firmly, and pulled him off across the hall.

He turned back and gave Julia a fleeting smile. "Good to see you," he called, and was gone.

Julia followed in his wake and walked across the hall to Alicia, who was staring at the departing figures.

"How do you know *her*?" Alicia asked curiously.

"Who?" questioned Julia as she took the other end of the proffered urn and they carted it down the steps toward the car.

"The ghastly Bella Harper, of course. I saw you talking to her just a few moments ago."

"I don't. I only know her brother, Kit."

They had reached the car and Alicia opened the trunk to stow the urn inside. "You mean Lord Christopher Wharton, the heir to all this?"

"Yes, I suppose that's who he is now. But I met him years ago in this house and bumped into him again just now."

"You're a dark horse, Julia; you never said you'd met him when we were kids." Alicia frowned, moving an old mac to swaddle the urn and wedging it into the side. "Let's hope this makes it home," she said, slamming the lid. They both climbed in and Alicia started the engine.

"Fancy a quick drink and a sandwich at the pub?" Alicia asked. "You can tell me all about how you met the delectable Lord Kit. Hope he's more pleasant than his sister. I've met her a couple of times at local dinner parties, and she treats me as though I'm still the gardener's granddaughter. Thank heavens the closest male heir inherits the title. If Bella had been a man, there'd have been no stopping her!"

"No . . . I don't think Kit's like that at all," said Julia softly. She turned to her sister. "Thanks for the offer, but if you don't mind, I'd just like to go home now."

Alicia read the exhaustion in her sister's eyes. "Okay, but we're stopping at the shop on the way back and I'm buying you some supplies."

Julia acquiesced, too weak to argue.

Alicia insisted that Julia sit on the sofa while she lit the fire and stowed away the food she had bought from the local supermarket. For once, Julia didn't mind being fussed around. The trip out—her first in weeks—had drained her. And returning to Wharton Park and seeing Kit had unsettled her.

Alicia appeared from the kitchen with a tray, which she placed in front of Julia. "I've made you some soup. Please drink it." She picked up the brown envelope that Julia had placed on the coffee table. "May I?"

"Of course."

Alicia drew the paintings out of the envelope, laid them on the table, and studied them. "They're lovely, and the perfect gift for Dad. Will you frame them?"

"If I can do it in time, yes."

"You are coming to us for his birthday lunch next Sunday, aren't you?"

Julia nodded reluctantly as she picked up her soupspoon.

"Darling, I understand it'll be hard, that big family gatherings aren't quite your thing at the moment, but I know that everyone's looking forward to seeing you. And Dad would be devastated if you didn't come."

"I'll be there. Of course I will."

"Good." Alicia looked at her watch. "I suppose I'd better be off, back to the madhouse." She rolled her eyes, walked over to Julia, and squeezed her shoulder. "Is there anything else I can get you?"

"No thanks."

"Okay." Alicia planted a kiss on the top of Julia's head. "And listen, please keep in touch and try and remember to keep your mobile switched on. I worry about you."

"The signal's almost nonexistent here, but I will." Julia watched Alicia as she walked to the door. "And thanks. Thanks for taking me back to Wharton Park."

"My pleasure, really. You just call and I'll be here. Take care, Julia." The door slammed behind Alicia.

Julia felt sleepy and lethargic. Leaving the half-drunk bowl of soup on the table, she walked wearily up the stairs and sat on her bed, hands folded in her lap.

I don't want to get better. I want to suffer the way that they suffered. Wherever they are, at least they're together, whereas I'm here alone. I want to know why I wasn't taken with them, because now I'm neither here nor there. I can't live and I can't die. Everyone wills me to choose life, but then, if I do that, I must let them go. And I can't do that. Not yet . . .

3

At two minutes to one the following Sunday, Alicia marshaled her family into the drawing room.

"Lissy, have some wine, darling." Her husband, Max, pushed a glass into her hand and kissed her on the cheek.

"Grandpa's here," shouted James, her six-year-old, excitedly.

"Let's go and get him," shrieked Fred, the four-year-old, and he headed for the front door.

A few seconds later, George Forrester was pulled into the drawing room by his grandchildren. At sixty-five, he was still a handsome man—slim, with a full head of hair just graying at the temples. He had an air of authority and confidence, gleaned from years of addressing an audience.

George was a renowned botanist—professor of botany at the University of East Anglia—lecturing often at the Royal Horticultural Society. When he wasn't sharing his knowledge, he was off to foreign parts, searching out new species of plant life across the world. Which was when, he readily admitted, he was at his most content.

George had always told his daughters that he had walked into the hothouses of Wharton Park expecting to be overwhelmed by the famous collection of orchids that grew there, but had instead instantly fallen in love with the young beauty—his future wife and mother of his two daughters—who was in the hothouse with them. They had been married only a few months later.

George advanced toward Alicia. "Hello, darling, you're looking as beautiful as ever. How are you?"

"I'm well, thanks. Happy birthday, Dad," she said as he hugged her. "Drink? We have some champagne in the fridge."

"Why not?" His eyes creased into a smile. "Bizarre really, celebrating the fact I'm one step nearer the grave."

"Oh, Dad!" Alicia chided. "Don't be silly. All my girlfriends are still in love with you."

"Well, that's always nice for a chap to know, but it doesn't change the facts. Today"—he turned around to face his grandchildren—"your grandfather is a pensioner."

"I'll go and get the champagne," Max said, winking at Alicia.

"So"—George perched himself on the arm of the couch, stretching his long legs out in front of him—"how's everything?"

"Hectic, as usual," sighed Alicia. "What about you?"

"Same. Actually, I'm rather excited. Last week I had a call from an American colleague of mine who lectures at Yale. He's planning a research trip to the Galápagos Islands in May and wants me to join them. It's one place I've never been to and always intended to go—Darwin's *Origin of the Species* and all that. I'll be away for a good three months, mind you, as I've been asked to give a couple of lectures while I'm in the States."

Max came back in with the champagne uncorked and poured it into three glasses.

"Well, cheers, everybody." George lifted the glass of champagne to his lips. "Here's to the next sixty-five." Taking a sip, he asked, "Is Julia coming?"

"Yes, she said she would. She's probably running a little late."

"Such a terrible thing." George sighed. "I feel so . . . helpless."

"We all do, Dad," said Alicia despairingly.

"First, losing your mother when she was eleven, and now . . ." George shrugged. "It seems so unfair."

"It's dreadful," Alicia replied, "and very difficult to know what to do or say. Julia took Mum's death so hard then, as you know, Dad. It's like she's lost the three people in the world that have meant the most to her."

"Has she mentioned if she's going to return to the South of France?" asked George. "I would have thought she'd be better off in her own home, rather than sitting in that depressing cottage all day."

"No. Perhaps she can't face the memories there. I know I'd struggle if this house was suddenly"—Alicia bit her lip—"empty."

Alicia saw Julia's car snaking slowly up the drive.

"She's here, Dad. I'll go and greet her, see how she is."

"Right-ho, darling," George agreed, sensing Alicia's concern.

Alicia went to the front door and opened it. As she stood waiting for Julia to climb out of the car, she mused on how, even though it was over twenty years since her mother had died, George had never done what most men did and looked for a replacement for his wife. Alicia remembered the eagle-eyed divorcées circling her still young and attractive father, yet he had never shown the least bit of need or interest.

Perhaps having a passion as her father did had helped fill the hole of losing his beloved wife.

But then, surely, that should be true of Julia too?

Julia emerged from the car, shrouded in a cardigan several sizes too big, and walked up the path toward her.

"Hi, darling. Dad's here already."

"I know. I'm sorry I'm late. I lost track of time," Julia answered defensively.

"Never mind, come in." Alicia indicated the rectangular present under Julia's right arm. "You managed to get the pictures framed, then?"

"Yes."

"Julia!" Max walked toward her as she entered the room. "Lovely to see you." He smiled as he put his arms around his sister-in-law's painfully thin shoulders. "Can I take that from you?"

"Thanks." She handed Max the package for her father.

"Hello, Dad. Happy birthday." Julia bent down to kiss him.

"Darling, thank you so much for coming." George reached for Julia's hand and squeezed it.

"Right, now we're all here, shall we open the presents?" suggested Alicia.

George started removing the wrapping paper, helped by a small pair of hands that had appeared, like magic, from under the coffee table.

"It's a very big pot, Grandpa," announced Fred as the urn was unveiled. "Do you like it?"

George smiled. "It's wonderful. Thank you, Alicia, and thank you, kids." He looked up at his daughter. "Did you say you got this from Wharton Park?"

"Yes." She looked at Julia. "Are you going to give Dad your present now?"

"Of course." Julia indicated the package on the coffee table. "Why don't you open it?"

Julia couldn't help but look expectantly as her father opened the present. The framers she had taken the paintings to had done an excellent job, mounting them with a fawn-colored border and advising Julia to use a simple black wooden frame around their edges.

"Well, well, well . . ." George's voice trailed off as he looked at each one. Eventually he said, "These were from Wharton Park too?"

"Yes."

He sat silently, trying to work out something that was puzzling him. The whole family was watching him. Finally Alicia broke the silence. "Don't you like them?"

George looked up at Julia, not Alicia. "Julia, I . . . love them, because you see"—he smiled and surreptitiously wiped a tear from his eye—"I'm positive that these were painted by your mother."

The conversation over the lunch table was full of ideas as to how Jasmine's paintings could have ended up at the Wharton Park Sale of Contents.

"Are you absolutely sure they were Mummy's paintings?" asked Alicia.

"Darling," George said as he tucked into the perfect roast beef Alicia had cooked, "I'm convinced of it. The first time I clapped eyes on your mother, she was sitting in a corner of your grandfather's hothouse with her sketchbook and her tin of watercolors. And later, when we traveled together, and we'd find a species of interest, I'd take down the notes and she would paint the flowers. I'd recognize her style anywhere. When I get home, I'll study them again and compare them to some of your mother's other paintings. But, Julia"—he smiled warmly at his daughter across the table—"you really couldn't have given me anything better."

After coffee back in the drawing room, Julia stood up.

"I'm off, Dad."

George looked up. "So soon?"

Julia nodded. "Yes."

George reached for her hand. "Come and visit me someday, will you? I'd love to see you and have a chat."

"Okay," agreed Julia, but they both knew that she wouldn't.

"Thank you so much for those paintings, darling. They really do mean the world to me."

"I think we'd better thank serendipity," said Julia. "Bye, kids, see you soon." She waved.

"Bye, Auntie Julia," they chorused.

Alicia caught her hand just as she was walking out of the door. "Coffee next week?"

"I'll give you a call. And thank you very much for lunch." Julia kissed her sister on the cheek. "Bye."

Alicia shut the door behind her sister and sighed. A pair of arms snaked round her waist from behind and held her tight.

"I know, Lissy. She's still in a pretty bad way," sighed Max.

"She is. But she doesn't help herself, sitting in that miserable cottage alone all day long. It's been over seven months now."

"Well, you can't force her," Max sighed. "At least she uttered a few words today. Anyway, Grandpa's staying on for tea and I'm in charge of the washing up. Go and put your feet up, darling, and talk to your father."

Alicia went back into the drawing room and sat down.

When their mother had died, tragically young, of ovarian cancer, Alicia—being the elder of the two and, even at fourteen, already a nurturer—had done her best to "mother" her younger sibling. George was often away lecturing or specimen-collecting; it seemed to Alicia he spent as little time at home as he could. She understood it was her father's way of dealing with the loss of his wife and never complained about his absence.

After Jasmine's death, Julia had withdrawn into herself. Alicia had seen the pain of loss written on her face. Yet, try as she might to help and comfort, from the start Julia seemed to resent Alicia's well-meaning protectiveness. As she grew through the difficult, teenage years, she had been unwilling to open up to Alicia about school, friends, or boyfriends, building a wall around her private thoughts and spending all her free time perfecting her technique on the piano.

Alicia had actually come to view the "set of teeth," as she called the upright piano in the study, as her rival for Julia's affections. Her sense of responsibility to take care of Julia—it was the last thing her mother had asked of her—overrode her own wants and needs. At eighteen, Alicia had won a place at Durham University to study psychology, but Julia was still at school. Even though a housekeeper took care of their domestic needs and stayed overnight when George was away, Alicia didn't feel she could leave Julia alone. She'd gone to university in Norwich instead, and subsequently, in the year Julia had won a place at the Royal College of Music and moved to London, she'd met Max.

Her unnatural, often lonely childhood had made Alicia dream of a husband, a large family, and a comfortable home to put them in. Unlike her sister, who suffered from the same wanderlust as her father, Alicia craved security and love. Max proposed and they were married within six months. She was pregnant within the year with Rose and, since then, had concentrated on giving her children all the things she had never known during her own formative years.

If her horizons had been narrowed because of her past, Alicia accepted them. What she found harder to accept was her younger sister's continued antipathy. As Julia's career had taken off, and she'd become a celebrity in the classical music world, Alicia had rarely heard from her. Seven months ago, Julia had needed her again, and Alicia had been there for her immediately, to bring her home to Norfolk, to try to comfort her. Yet Alicia still felt the same distance and undercurrent of tension between them.

Just as twenty years ago, Alicia simply did not know how to reach her sister.

4

When Julia awoke the following morning, she lay there, waiting for the dark thoughts to assail her mind as they always did—the feeling of hopelessness that insidiously consumed the first few positive seconds when she was too sleep-ridden to remember.

They didn't arrive.

And so, rather than rolling over and clapping her hands to her ears, as if to uselessly block out the thoughts, she decided to get up instead.

She walked over to the bedroom window and pulled open the curtains.

Today, the sun was shining its crisp January light on the frost-covered hillock. Below was Blakeney harbor, and beyond that the sea. She opened the latch on the small window, flung it wide, and breathed deeply. Today, Julia thought, it was actually possible to believe that spring might come again.

She closed the window, shivering suddenly in her thin T-shirt, pulled on her cardigan, and went downstairs to make some tea.

By lunchtime, Julia was aware that something *had* shifted. Try as she might to remember what she had been doing here in this cottage every day for the past few months, she could not. Time was dragging; she felt restless, bored even. She searched her mind fruitlessly for the path back to the comforting torpor, but it steadfastly refused to take her there.

Feeling claustrophobic, Julia realized she needed to get out of the house. She threw on a jacket, scarf, and wellies, opened her front door, and marched across the grass and down toward the sea.

The harbor was deserted. The small boats brought in safely to land during the winter sounded restless too, their rigging making a tinkling sound, as if to remind their owners of their usefulness to come. Julia left the harbor behind and continued walking along the long spit of land, at the far end of which seals basked on the sand, to the delight of the tourists who took boat rides out to see them.

The chilly wind nipped at her face and she pulled the collar of her jacket up higher to protect herself. She kept going, relishing that she was so completely alone, now with water on both sides of the diminishing strip of land—as if she were walking away from the world.

She stopped, then turned and made her way down one side of the spit toward the water lapping below her, just inches from her feet. It was deep here, deep and cold enough to drown in, especially with the strong outgoing current that would swiftly sweep her away from the shore. She looked from side to side, reassuring herself she was truly alone.

If she threw herself in, there would be no one to stop her . . .

. . . and the pain would be over.

At worst, she would go to sleep forever. At best, she would see them again.

Julia dangled one tentative boot out past the land's edge.

She could do it now . . .

Now . . .

What was to stop her?

She looked down at the gray water, willing herself to take the final plunge into release, but . . .

She couldn't.

She gazed up hopelessly at the wintery, white sun, then threw her head back and let out an enormous scream.

"*WWWWWHHHHHYYYYYY!!!?*"

She sank to her knees on the melting frost. She howled and beat her fists into the ground in fury and pain and anger.

"*Why them?! Why them?!*" she repeated over and over, until, through exhaustion, she had to stop, so she sobbed instead.

She lay flat, spread-eagled, her tears mingling with the wetness of the grass, crying with the full force of seven months of not doing so.

Finally, she ran out of tears and lay there; still, silent, and empty. After a while she sat up, rose to her knees as if she were praying, and spoke to them.

"I have to . . . *live*! I have to live without you, somehow . . . ," she whimpered. Her hands went out to the side, palms stretched upward to the sky. "Help me, please help me, help me . . ." She sank back down, put her head in her hands, resting it on her knees.

All Julia could hear was the rhythmic lapping of the water surrounding her. She concentrated on it and found it calmed her. She felt the weak warmth of the sun on her back and was suffused with a sudden and unexpected sense of peace.

She had no idea how long it was before she stood up. Wet through from the thawed grass, her legs like jelly and both hands numb from the cold, she staggered back along the spit toward home.

She arrived at the cottage, shaking from the exertion of the long walk and the release of emotion. She was just turning the handle to open the front door when she heard someone calling her name.

"Julia!"

She looked down the hill and saw Kit Crawford striding up the narrow path toward her from the High Street.

"Hi there," he said as he reached her. "I came to see you, but you weren't in. I put a note through your letter box."

"Oh," she said, feeling disoriented, and hardly ready to cope with speaking to the living.

Kit was staring at her. "You're soaked. What on earth have you been doing?" He looked up at the sky for an answer. "It hasn't been raining, has it?"

"No." Julia pushed open the front door, her boots treading on the folded piece of paper that Kit had pushed through the letter box. She leaned down to pick it up.

"I left my mobile number." He indicated the note. "But as I've caught you, do you think we can have a quick chat?"

Julia knew she was looking less than enthusiastic and her teeth were starting to chatter. "I think I need to get straight into a hot bath," she said, hoping this was enough to make him leave.

Not to be dissuaded, Kit followed her inside the cottage. "Yes. Those precious fingers of yours are virtually blue. We can't afford to have Britain's most famous young concert pianist getting frostbite, now can we?" He shut the door behind him, then shivered involuntarily. "Blimey, it's freezing in here too. Listen, why don't you go upstairs and have a hot bath while I make a nice fire and some coffee?"

Julia turned round and eyed him. "I might be some time. I need a good soak."

"I'm in no rush," Kit answered amiably. "Off you go."

Julia lay in the bath, taking time to thaw out both her feet and her brain, wondering at the timing of Kit's appearance. She wasn't used to having visitors turning up unexpectedly on her doorstep, and she wasn't sure she liked it.

Yet . . . out there alone, she had known she couldn't stay in the place she'd been any longer, that she *had* to do what everyone told her she must and try to move on.

Pulling on her jeans and her old woolen cardigan, she walked back down the stairs. Kit was sitting on the sofa, a small package resting on his knee. The fire was merrily burning in a way she could never quite achieve, however hard she tried.

"So, how did you find me?" she asked Kit as she hovered by the fire.

"My sister, Bella, of course. She knows everyone. Or should I say, she makes it her business to know everyone, and if she doesn't, then she'll know someone who does. In this case, it was your sister, Alicia. I did try to call, but your mobile seems to be permanently switched off."

Julia thought guiltily of the seventeen messages she hadn't listened to last time she switched it on. "There's very little signal here."

"No problem. Firstly, I wanted to apologize for the other day."

"Why?"

Kit studied his hands. "I didn't know about what had happened to you. As I said, I've been abroad for years. I only came back to England a few months ago."

"Who told you?"

"Bella, of course. Apparently it was in all the newspapers here. I'm sure most of the information was inaccurate, as these things usually are."

"I . . . don't know," Julia sighed. "As you can imagine, I didn't read them."

"No, obviously you didn't." Kit looked uncomfortable. "I'm sorry, Julia. It must have been . . . must *be*, terrible for you."

"Yes." For both their sakes, Julia swiftly changed the subject. "So, what was it you wanted to see me about?"

Kit's face brightened. "I've found something that you and your family might be interested in."

"Really?"

"Yes. You remember I mentioned that I was renovating the cottages in the Quad?"

Julia nodded.

"Well, it turns out my new home *is* your grandparents' old house. The plumbers were taking out the floorboards and they found this." Kit indicated the package on his knee.

"What is it?"

Julia watched Kit unwrap the package carefully to reveal a small leatherbound book. He waved it at her. "It's a diary, beginning in 1941. I flicked through it briefly and it's an account of life as a prisoner of war in Changi jail."

Julia's brow furrowed. "That's in Singapore, isn't it?"

"Yes. A lot of British soldiers who were fighting in Malaya at the time ended up in there for a while as guests of the Japanese. Do you know if your grandfather was a prisoner of war?"

"Grandfather Bill talked a lot about the 'East,' but mostly of the beautiful flowers that grew there." Julia smiled. "He never mentioned Changi."

"I don't suppose he would talk of it to a young child, but it certainly seems a possibility this diary is his," said Kit. "And I can't imagine it being anyone else's, seeing as your grandfather lived in the cottage for the whole of his life."

"May I?" Julia reached out her hand and Kit gave her the diary. She opened the first page and saw that the leather had protected the thin paper from too much aging, and the writing on it was quite legible. A beautiful hand had written these words, the writing elegant, scripted in black ink.

"Do you recognize that as your grandfather's writing?"

"To be honest, I can't ever remember seeing anything he wrote. It was my mother who used to record his notes on the many different types of orchids he grew in the hothouses," said Julia. "Perhaps my father would know his writing. Or, of course, my grandmother, who's in her eighties, but still hale and hearty, from what I've heard. The question is, if it *is* his," Julia pondered, "why on earth did he hide it?"

"Having read a little about the experiences of POWs at the hands of the Japanese, they had a pretty grim time of it. Perhaps your grandfather hid it not wanting to upset your grandmother. When your family has read it, maybe I could borrow it? A firsthand account of a piece of history is always fascinating."

"Yes, I suppose it is," said Julia, feeling guilty she knew so little of Grandfather Bill's past.

Kit stood up. "And . . . I was going to ask you a favor." He wandered over to the shallow bookshelf that stood on one side of the fireplace and pulled out a book. "This, I believe, is mine."

He was holding *The Children's Own Wonder Book*, which Julia had bought for one pound at the Wharton Park sale.

"It's actually *my* grandfather's book. So would you call it a fair exchange for the diary?"

"Of course."

"Thanks. Look, Julia." Kit seemed suddenly awkward. "I'm starving and I was wondering if maybe we could go and get—" He was interrupted by his mobile. "Excuse me, I'd better take it." He put the phone to his ear. "Hello? . . . Hi, Annie . . ." He listened, then shook his head. "I can't hear you, the signal's dreadful here. . . . What? No good, can't hear. I'll leave now and see you there. Thanks, bye."

"Sorry, Julia, I've got to go." Kit stood and walked toward the door, then turned back to her. "Let me know what happens with the diary, won't you?"

"Of course I will, and thanks, Kit, for taking the time to bring this over."

"No trouble. By the way, I checked on the hothouses; they're still standing, although God knows what kind of state they're in, judging by the mess in the kitchen garden. Come and see them soon if you'd like to, before the new owner takes up residence. Bye, Julia." He gave her a weary smile and shut the door.

5

"Julia, what a lovely surprise!" Alicia's face lit up as Julia entered through the kitchen door. "Look who's here, kids—Auntie Julia!"

"I was meaning to tell you that Bella Harper had called for your number. Actually, she was quite chatty." Alicia went to the table to clear the bowls away and presented the children with a yogurt each. "I presume she's worked out exactly who you are. I've been elevated in her estimation, due to the fact I have a famous sister." Alicia raised her eyebrows. "Anyway, enough of that silly woman. How are you?"

"Kit Crawford visited me today. He found something at Bill and Elsie's old cottage and he wanted to give it to me," Julia replied.

"Really? What?"

"A diary, which was presumably written by Grandfather Bill. It's an account of being a prisoner of war in Changi jail in Singapore. I'll let you know more when I've read it."

"How fascinating," breathed Alicia. "How old was Grandfather Bill when he wrote it?"

"Well, it was 1941, so he would have been in his early twenties. Did you know he was held captive there?"

Alicia shook her head. "No, but that doesn't mean he wasn't. The person to ask is Grandmother Elsie. She would know."

"Have you seen her recently?"

Alicia looked guilty. "No, I haven't. I never quite seem to find the time to go and visit her, what with the kids . . . I should have made more of an effort."

"Is she still living in Southwold?"

"Her sister died a year or so ago, so she lives there alone now. Do you remember the way she was obsessed with doing our hair? Up, down, plaits, ponytails, curls . . ." Alicia giggled. "And that strange collection of wigs she kept in the back room of the cottage. She used to spend hours styling them, like a child playing with her dolls. She always wanted to be a hairdresser, didn't she?"

"Yes, and she hated my hair because it was too heavy to curl, even when she put it in what she called 'rags' overnight." Julia smiled fondly at the thought. "I will go and see her. I'd like to anyway."

Alicia walked over to the cabinet and opened one of the drawers. She pulled out an address book and flicked through it. "This is Elsie's telephone number and her address. Do go, Julia. What with you living in France and me up to my neck in kids, we haven't exactly been model granddaughters, have we?"

"No, we haven't. And when I see her, I'll decide whether or not to give her the diary. As Kit said, it might have been hidden by Grandfather Bill because what it contained was so distressing."

"Good point." Alicia walked over to the table to clear it. "Wash your hands and faces. Then you have half an hour's TV before Rose comes home and it's bathtime. Go on, off you go."

The children didn't need to be told twice. They ran from the room, and Julia helped Alicia stack the dishwasher.

"So, you and Kit had a good chat?"

"Yes, I swapped him *The Children's Own Wonder Book* for the diary." Julia smiled. "He's been away for years, abroad somewhere. He didn't know anything about . . . what's happened to me. Until his sister told him, that is."

"Maybe that's a good thing," said Alicia. "He's very . . . attractive. Don't you think?"

"I don't 'think,' no. Anyway, I must be going."

Alicia could see by Julia's sudden change of expression that she had overstepped the mark and inwardly kicked herself. "Listen, let me write down Elsie's telephone number." She scribbled it onto a piece of notepaper. "There," she said, handing it to Julia. "Let me know what happens, won't you?"

"Yes." Julia was heading for the door already. "Bye."

Julia got into the car, slamming the door much harder than she needed to, and set off at a fast pace for home.

She ground her teeth in frustration at her older sister's unerring habit of upsetting her. She understood Alicia was only trying to help, to look after her, just as she had when they were younger. But her protectiveness only made Julia feel patronized and small.

Julia had grown up in her shadow, simply struggling to organize *herself.* She had been a loner, with no regard for her appearance, and only managing to scrape through her exams at school, due to the countless hours spent instead on the piano. She'd always known she couldn't begin to compete with Alicia's perfection. Added to that, Alicia had always been closer to their father, whereas Julia was attached at the hip to their mother. Everyone used to comment how alike Julia and her mother were—not just physically, but in their otherworldliness and artistic nature.

Her childhood had ended on the day their mother had died.

When Julia arrived home, she stoked the fire aggressively, trying to return it to some of its earlier glory, still unsettled. The problem was that Alicia genuinely cared—Julia couldn't fault her. Which made her feel even more inadequate and guilty. She knew how hard Alicia had tried to fill her mother's shoes when she was younger, and how difficult she'd been in response. But *no one* could fill her mother's shoes . . . *ever.* And she'd only wished Alicia had stopped trying, had understood she needed a sister with whom to share the grief, not a "stand-in"—albeit well-meaning—who could never replace what she'd lost.

She sat down on the sofa with the diary in her hands, determined to focus on something else. She opened it at the first page, but couldn't concentrate on the words. She sat instead staring into the fire.

He's very attractive, don't you think?

Julia sighed, Alicia's comment and her own exaggerated reaction to it forcing her to focus on why.

Yes . . . this morning, out on the Spit, she had accepted that she must move on, that she really had no choice. But even a hint that "moving on" would almost certainly at some point include a *man* was a step too far. The half-lit world she'd inhabited for the past few months had held no thoughts of the future.

How could it when the future was gone?

Julia stood up and meandered into the kitchen. She opened the fridge, which was now brimming over with all sorts of foodstuffs that she had picked up that morning, and pulled out a pasta ready-meal. She wondered meanly whether she should take a photograph especially for Alicia, to stop her nagging.

As she carried her supper back into the sitting room, she acknowledged the source of her anger with her sister. She felt . . . *guilty.* Guilty because, despite herself, when Kit had been here, she had enjoyed his company. And, *yes*, she did find him an attractive man.

After supper, Julia picked up the diary, but felt too distracted to tackle it. It had been a long and emotional day. She made her way up the stairs to bed, and for the first time since her world had been blown apart seven months ago, Julia slept without having nightmares.

The next morning, she was awake and downstairs by eight. A cup of tea, this time with milk, and a bowl of muesli stiffened her new resolve to face her life once more. She dug her mobile phone out of the drawer, switched it on, and went upstairs to the bathroom, the only place in the cottage with a proper signal.

She now had nineteen voice mails, some of them stretching as far back as two months ago. The most recent were from Alicia, her father, Kit, and numerous messages from Olav, her agent.

Her housekeeper in France had also contacted her, asking her to call back immediately. There was some problem with the house, but Agnes spoke French so fast, Julia couldn't work out where the leak was. She sat on the edge of the bath and made a list of the other callers, her hand shaking with the fear of speaking to people from her past.

Today, she would tackle her housekeeper and her agent. Everyone else could wait.

She went back downstairs, threw herself onto the sofa and closed her eyes. She forced herself to picture the vine-covered terrace of her beautiful home, perched high up on the hill in the ancient village of Ramatuelle, with the deep blue waters of the Mediterranean sparkling far beneath it.

She sighed, knowing the memories she had avoided with such determination could no longer be ignored if she was to start on the road back to life. And, besides, perhaps she needed to begin to remember those precious moments and treasure them, not resist them. . . .

The sun is on its descent as I watch it, its lustrous red-gold colors making the blue water beneath it look as if it is on fire. The sound of Rachmaninov's Piano Concerto No. 3 drifts across the terrace, reaching a zenith as the sun plunges gracefully into the sea.

This is my favorite moment of the day here, when nature itself seems to be still, watching the spectacle of the King of the Day, the force it relies upon to grow and flourish, make its journey into sleep.

We are able to be here together far less than I'd like, so the moment is even more precious. The sun has gone now, so I can close my eyes and listen to Xavier playing. I have performed this concerto a hundred times, and I'm struck by the subtle differences, the nuances that make his rendition his own. It's stronger, more masculine, which is, of course, how it should be.

I am "off duty," with no engagements until the middle of next week, but Xavier must leave for a concert in Paris tomorrow, so this is our last night here together. When he's finished playing, I know he will appear on the terrace with a glass of rosé from the local cave, *and we'll sit together, talking of nothing and of everything, and luxuriating in the tranquillity of our rare solitude.*

The heart of our life, the energy that binds us both together, is inside the house. When I bathed our son, Gabriel, and put him down for the night, I knelt quietly alongside his cot, watching as the tension fell from his face and he drifted off into sleep.

"Bonne nuit, mon petit ange," *I whispered, tiptoeing out and closing the door softly behind me.*

I'm glad that I am able to share a further week here with him. Some mothers have the pleasure of watching their children twenty-four hours a day, catching each smile, each new skill they learn on the path to adulthood. I envy them that, for I don't have that luxury.

As I stare at the darkening sky, I contemplate the question that has turned around in my mind since the day that he was born, wondering whether I should put my career on hold to watch him grow. I can't develop my thoughts, however, for here is Xavier with the promised glass of rosé and a bowl of fresh olives.

"Bravo," I utter, as he kisses me on top of my head and I raise my hand to stroke his face.

"Merci, ma petite," *he replies.*

We speak in French together, his bad English verbs deemed worse than my dreadful French accent.

Besides, it's the language of love.

He sits in the chair next to me and swings his long legs up onto the table. His hair, as always after he's been practicing, is standing on end, which gives him the appearance of a gigantic toddler. I reach across to him and smooth it down. He grabs my hand and kisses it.

"It is sad I must go tomorrow. Perhaps next year we could plan to take the whole summer off and be here together."

"I would love that so much," I reply, watching out of the corner of my eye as the moon unveils itself, taking the place of the sun and becoming Queen of the Night.

Xavier's already pale skin is bleached whiter in the moonlight. I never tire of looking at him. He is so extraordinary. If I'm a creature of the day—of the sun—with my dark skin and dark eyes, then he is of the night—the moon.

His dramatic, aquiline features, inherited from his Russian mother, could never be described as classically handsome. His nose, for a start, is too long, his eyes—glacial in their blueness—set too close together. His forehead is furrowed and high, his thick black hair of a strawlike texture. His lips are the only perfect thing on his face, girlish in their fullness—pink, plump pillows—which open when he smiles to reveal a set of large, white, strong teeth.

His body is out of proportion: legs that could double as stilts they are so long, carrying a short upper torso, which makes the length of his arms and his elegant, talented fingers seem as though they've been grafted onto the wrong body. He towers over me, a good foot taller than I am. There is not an ounce of fat on him and I am sure he will stay that way for the rest of his life. The nervous energy that even in sleep will not let him rest, as he tosses and turns next to me, twitches and fidgets—shouts out loud at some imagined foe—will eat up any middle-age spread his hormones care to produce.

And I have loved every millimeter of him, body and soul, since the day I listened to him playing Schubert's Piano Sonata in B-flat Major at the Tchaikovsky piano competition in Leningrad.

I won.

He came second.

I look at his beloved face, so familiar to me and yet ever fascinating, because there are so many depths still to explore. I'm so much less complex than he is. I can play the piano, quite brilliantly, so I'm told. Just because I can. Equally, I can walk off the platform and return to being a normal human being. Xavier, however, carries his music with him everywhere, always thinking about how to perfect the next piece.

I truly believe that if they turned all the pianos in the world to firewood, he would throw himself on top of the bonfire.

We have laughed together about how I am famous, not him. But we both know that I look much prettier in a dress than he does, that I play much more photogenically . . . I am a "girl," and therefore more marketable.

But I know that he is the genius, that he can take the Chopin Études and add a touch of magic, a spark, that makes them definitively his own. I also know that one day the world will recognize this. And I will be happy to take second place.

I'm sure my playing has gone from strength to strength because of him.

And I adore him.

He is my piano. He is my bonfire. And if he were no longer there, I would throw myself on top of that fire willingly.

6

Julia found her face was wet with tears. She knew many more were to come, as she continued to force herself to remember.

"Xavier." She spoke his name out loud for the first time. "Xavier, Xavier . . ." She repeated the word again, and again, knowing that when she spoke to her housekeeper and her agent, they were sure to speak it too, and she wanted to be practiced in controlling her emotions when she heard it.

She went upstairs to take a shower, dressed, and sat on the edge of the bath once more, steeling herself to press the numbers that would launch her back into her life.

Agnes, her housekeeper, did not answer her mobile, and Julia was grateful for the stay of execution. She left a message and asked Agnes to call her back.

Next: her agent, Olav. She checked the time on her mobile—it was ten thirty. Olav could be anywhere in the world; he had offices in New York, London, and Paris. As she dialed his number, she hoped she would get his voice mail too, but it was rare that he didn't answer his phone to her, even if it was the middle of the night for him.

The line rang and she waited, holding her breath. He answered after three rings.

"Julia, honey! How wonderful to hear from you. At last," he added pointedly.

"Where are you?" she questioned.

"In New York. I had a client playing with the New York Symphony Orchestra at the Carnegie tonight. Jeez, it was uninspired. Anyway, honey, let's talk about you. I've a hundred unanswered e-mails currently sitting on my desk; requests for your presence from the usual suspects in Milan, Paris, London, et al. I've told them you're taking a sabbatical, but, Julia, baby, they won't keep asking forever."

"I know, Olav," she replied apologetically.

"These guys are working eighteen months to two years in advance. If we don't accept a booking soon, it could be three years before you're back on the platform. Any thoughts as to when you'll be ready to give me a yes?"

Even though Julia was grateful that Olav had not taken the sympathy route and had got straight down to his greatest love—business—it did not give her a solution as to how to respond.

"No. To be honest, I haven't given it a lot of thought."

"Do you have e-mail there, honey? I can send the requests through to you, you can peruse, and see if any of them appeal."

"No, I don't. My laptop is still in my house in France."

There was a pause on the line. "You still in Norfolk?"

"Yes."

"Well then, baby, I've gotta better idea. I'm in London next week. We can meet for lunch at Claridge's, and I'll give you the file myself."

Julia could hear pages being turned at the other end of the line. Eventually he asked, "How would next Thursday suit? I can also hand you over the bunch of checks that have arrived here over the past seven months. As I said on the voice mail, it's a substantial sum. I didn't bank them with you, as I normally would. I wasn't sure what you were doing with your old joint account."

Julia swallowed. "Next Thursday will be fine."

"Great! It'll be good to see you, honey. Now, as it's four thirty in the morning here and I'm flying to Tokyo tomorrow, I'd better get some shut-eye. Let's make it noon in the bar by the restaurant. See you then, baby. Can't wait."

The line went dead.

Julia sighed in relief that initial contact had been made. She knew she could always cancel next Thursday, but her newly hatched, still fragile shred of optimism had not allowed her to turn him down point-blank. Besides, she had to be practical. She had been living on the money in her English account, on the rental checks from her cottage that she had deposited there over the past eight years. Last time she'd looked, which had been over a month ago, only a few hundred pounds had been left. She hadn't been able to face calling the bank in France where she and Xavier had held their accounts and into which the majority of her earnings were poured. There would be forms to fill in to change the accounts into her sole name. So far, she had not been ready to accept that Xavier was gone.

She knew she must return to France to sort out her life. But making a call was one thing, physically confronting the facts was another.

Not wanting to cloud the progress she had made so far this morning—one step at a time—Julia decided to go for a walk. Just as she was pulling on her jacket, there was a knock on her door.

"Hi, darling, it's me, Dad," said a voice through the wood. Surprised, Julia opened it.

"Sorry to barge in," George said, as he stepped over the threshold. "Alicia said you were usually here. I can come back some other time if this isn't convenient."

Julia thought how incongruous her father looked in the tiny room; like Gulliver in the land of Lilliput. "No, it's fine," she said, removing her jacket as he sat down. "Want some coffee?"

"No thanks, I've just had some. I've been out on the marshes at Salthouse taking a cutting of an unusual plant that one of my PhD boys found there. So, I thought I'd drop in on the way home." George studied her. "I won't ask how you are, I know from experience it's irritating. But I will say that I think you look better than I've seen you in a while. Not quite so drawn. Alicia keeps telling me she's worried you're not eating. Are you?"

Julia grinned. "Dad, you can check my fridge if you want. I went food shopping only yesterday."

"Excellent. You know, I . . . do understand. I've gone through similar myself, although at least I didn't have to suffer the pain of losing one of my children as well as your mother. And Gabriel was such a sweet little thing. It must be unbearable for you, darling."

"It has been, yes." Julia's voice caught in her throat.

"All I can say, without sounding patronizing, is that things do improve, but it takes time—not to 'get over it,' because of course you never really do, but to"—George searched for the right word—"adjust."

Julia studied him silently, knowing he had more to say.

"And at some point, you do get over the 'hump,' " he continued, "when you wake up one morning and the dark isn't as dark as it was, if you understand what I mean."

"Yes. I think . . . well, something happened yesterday, and today—this morning, anyway . . ." She struggled to voice what she felt. "You're right. The 'dark' isn't quite as dark as it was."

"What say we get out of this godforsaken cottage and walk across the road to the White Horse for a glass of wine and some freshly caught fish?"

Julia overrode her immediate knee-jerk negative response. "That sounds like a good idea, Dad."

Ten minutes later, they were ensconced at a cozy table by the fire. George ordered two plates of fish and chips and carried the glasses of wine back from the bar.

"Great pub this," he commented, "a real 'local.' Anyway"—George cleared his throat—"what I wanted to talk to you about was those orchid paintings you gave me. I've compared them to some of the other watercolors your mother did, and there is absolutely no doubt they were painted by her. More than likely when she was much younger."

"I'm so pleased I found them, Dad. It was obviously meant to be."

"Yes, but there's something else interesting about those paintings, or at least, one of them." George took a sip of his wine. "I know that, as a child, your mother would spend hours in the hothouses with your grandfather, just as you did after her. To pass the time, she'd sit and paint the flowers. Now, I've identified three of the orchids, which are all commonly cultivated in England and could have been grown by your grandfather; all three of them are genus of *Cattleya.* William Cattley, a man whom one could call the 'father' of British orchids, was the first horticulturist successfully to grow epiphytic orchids here in the early nineteenth century, and most of the orchids we see here are descended from them. But the fourth orchid your mother painted, well now, that's another story altogether."

"Really?" said Julia, as their lunch arrived.

"Yes. If her painting is accurate, and having worked with her for fifteen years, I have to assume it is, then the orchid she has drawn is a *Dendrobium nigum.*" George broke into the thick beer batter on his fish. "Now, either your mother copied the picture from a book, which is of course a possibility, and to be honest the most likely scenario—or," he added between mouthfuls, "it was growing in her father's hothouse at the time."

Julia began to eat too. "So, if it was growing in the hothouse . . . ? "

"Well, put it this way: the last specimen of *Dendrobium nigum* sold at auction for almost fifty thousand pounds. It's an unbelievable bloom. Only a few were ever found around the hills of Chiang Mai in Thailand. It's the closest thing to a black orchid there is, even though its true color is deep magenta. Botanists have never been able to reproduce it out of its habitat, which makes it very valuable. I'd be amazed if this plant had found its way to the Wharton Park hothouses in the 1950s."

"Didn't Grandfather Bill have Mum type up all his notes, and then weren't they passed to you when he died?" Julia asked. "Surely there might be something in there?"

"That's what I thought too. I've spent most of my time since Sunday scouring through them, but as far as I can see, there's no mention of it." George placed his knife and fork together on the side of his empty plate. "Your grandfather had over two hundred different species of orchids growing in his hothouses. I haven't found this one recorded yet, but I'm going to keep looking."

"Changing the subject for a moment," said Julia, "did Alicia mention the diary that Kit Crawford found under the floorboards in their old cottage?"

"Yes, she did, briefly. Apparently, it's an account of being a prisoner of war in Changi jail. If you're going to ask me whether Bill was in Changi during the war, I'd have to tell you I've no idea. The only person who'd know would be Elsie, your grandmother. I received a Christmas card from her and she's still going strong at eighty-seven. Why don't you go and visit her?"

"I'm going to, Dad. Alicia's given me her number and I intend to give her a call."

"Good. So what else is new?" asked George. "Apart from perhaps thinking whether you really want to stay for much longer in that depressing cottage of yours."

"I know," Julia agreed. "But it's only in the last couple of days I've actually realized how ghastly it is."

"And no room in it for a piano . . . ," added George softly.

"I don't want a piano," Julia said vehemently, "but if I'm going to be here for a while, then I might get Agnes to ship a few of my things over from France."

"That's the spirit, darling. Right"—George banged the table—"I must be off. I've a pile of e-mails to answer and a lecture to write before tomorrow morning."

Julia waited for him at the entrance to the pub while he paid, and they walked companionably across the road and up the hill to the cottage.

"Darling, this has been an unexpected pleasure." George enveloped Julia in his arms and hugged her. "Take care and please keep in touch."

"I will, promise."

Her father nodded, then ambled off in the direction of his car.

7

The following morning, Julia called Elsie. The old lady was delighted to hear from her, making Julia feel further guilt that she hadn't made the effort to get in touch. She arranged to drive to Southwold for tea the following Saturday. After that, she dressed, threw on her coat, and set off for the hothouses of Wharton Park, glad to have a positive destination rather than face a long day of solitude at the cottage.

She turned right into the entrance of Wharton Park, admiring the copper beeches that fringed the edges of the parkland on either side of the drive. And the old oak, under which, legend had it, Anne Boleyn had once kissed Henry VIII.

Five hundred yards later, she turned right again and drove down the bumpy road that would eventually take her to the Quad. Beyond that lay the kitchen garden, in which the hothouses nestled. Feeling a shadow of the excitement and anticipation she had experienced as a child, she realized it mattered hugely to her that they were still there.

She parked her car in the Quad and stepped out into the chilly air. She remembered this as a place of high activity and recalled the families who lived around it. The stables had also been here. There had been horses clopping in and out, bales of hay constantly being transferred and dumped in the barns from the tractors, narrowly avoiding the workers' children playing football in the center of the Quad.

It had been a world within a world . . .

Which now stood silent and deserted.

Julia left the car and walked along the overgrown path toward the kitchen garden. The blue door was still there, albeit covered in ivy. With effort, she pushed it open and walked through.

The carefully cultivated, long lines of carrots, peas, and parsnips were no more. In their place was a tangle of weeds and nettles, interspersed with the odd, mournful face of an overblown cabbage. Julia walked toward the small orchard that stood at the bottom of the kitchen garden, shielding the hothouses from view. The many apple, pear, and plum trees, some of them extremely old, were still there, their crooked branches stark and naked, windfalls from the previous autumn lying uncollected and turning to mulch beneath them.

Julia walked through the trees and saw the roofs of the hothouses peeping above the bushes that had spurted up unchecked around their sides. She stepped along the now barely distinguishable path toward the first door.

It was no longer there. Instead, it lay at her feet, a heap of rotting wood and broken glass. She picked her way through it and entered the hothouse. It was empty, bar the old trestle tables that used to line it, and the row of iron hooks hanging from the trusses above her head. The concrete floor was covered in moss, and weeds were encroaching underneath the frame and inside it.

Julia walked slowly to the end of the hothouse. There, in the corner where it had always been, was the stool she used to sit on. Underneath it, its metal components heavily rusted, was Grandfather Bill's old Bakelite radio.

She knelt down and picked it up. It was beyond repair, but she had to take it with her anyway. She cradled it to her breast like a baby and twiddled the knobs in a fruitless attempt to resuscitate it. . . .

"Orchids love music, Julia. Perhaps it replaces the noises of nature they hear in their native homelands," Grandfather Bill tells me as he shows me how to mist the delicate petals with a spray gun. "And warmth and moisture, to imitate the humidity they're used to."

Everyone else finds the hothouses unbearably stuffy, with the strong sunlight pouring through the glass windows. Which added to the lack of natural breezes, raises the temperature far above that of a humid English day.

I love it, for I hate wearing lots of clothes to keep me warm. It feels like my natural habitat, and Grandfather Bill doesn't seem to notice the heat either.

Besides, it allows the beautiful smells of the flowers to permeate the air.

"This is a Dendrobium victoria-reginae, *sometimes listed as the Blue Dendrobium, but, as you can see, it's lilac," chuckles my grandfather. "A true blue orchid is yet to be discovered. This one grows on trees in Southeast Asia. Can you imagine? Whole gardens in the air . . ."*

Grandfather Bill would get that "look," as I call it, and even though I ask him to tell me more, he never does.

"Dendrobia like to rest in the winter—I think of it as hibernating, I do—and not be fed and just misted with enough water to prevent them shriveling."

"How did you learn what they like in the first place, Grandfather?" I asked him once. "Did you go to Orchid School?"

He shook his head and chuckled. "No, Julia. I learned a lot from a friend of mine who lived in the Far East and had grown up surrounded by them. And the rest by trial and error, watching them closely to see how they responded to what I tried. Nowadays, I know what I'm getting because it says what the flowers are on the packaging, but when I was a lad, I used to get crates sent from far away and we never knew till it flowered what sort we was growing." He sighed. "It was exciting in them days, it was, even though I lost more than I grew."

I know that Grandfather Bill is famous in the orchid world for managing to grow something called hybrids. His are unusual, and often well-known horticulturalists will come to see his latest bloom. He's very modest, doesn't like to talk about it; says his job is about growing flowers, not boasting about the flowers he grows. Grandmother Elsie doesn't feel the same—I hear her saying sometimes how much money Bill has brought into Wharton Park, what with all the day-trippers coming to see the hothouses and buying the plants he has for sale, and that he should get a bigger slice of it.

I don't listen when she says these things. I don't want anything to disturb the peace of my special haven. When I'm away from here and feeling sad, I go back to it in my mind and find comfort.

Julia brought herself back to the grim reality of what had been and wasn't anymore. She realized she was shivering with cold and didn't want to be here any longer. Turning on her heel, she walked swiftly out of the hothouse and hurried across the kitchen garden to her car. As she was climbing inside, she saw Kit emerge from one of the stables. He waved to her and walked over.

"Hi, Julia. I presume you've been to view the sad demise of one of the former glories of Wharton Park?"

Julia sighed. "I feel so depressed. The hothouses are completely empty—there's nothing left." She shook her head in despair. "You don't happen to know where all the orchids went, do you?"

"No, I don't. I only wish I did. My father was an absentee owner here for far too long. And Aunt Crawford, for some reason, seemed to shudder at the thought of the plant. You remember that day you brought her the orchid? Well, when you left, she handed it straight back to me and told me to get it out of her sight." Kit raised his eyebrows. "Don't ask me why. I haven't a clue. You'll be pleased to know I kept it in my bedroom and took it back home with me when I left. It bloomed for years afterward."

"How strange," Julia mused, "and sad."

"Absolutely. And God knows what else has gone missing from the estate, along with all those orchids. The sooner I hand this place over now, the better. Anyway"—Kit brightened—"want to wander over and see your grandparents' old cottage? I'm heading there now."

"Why not?"

They made their way across to the cottage, tucked away in its own small quarter-acre garden just behind the Quad. Julia could already hear the sound of crashing and banging emanating from within its walls.

"I hope that you won't feel this has been ruined too, but it really wasn't fit for human habitation. And while I still have the last vestiges of the estate workers in my employ, I thought they might as well do something useful."

"What will happen to them once the new owner takes over?" asked Julia.

"They will be reemployed, most of them, and probably far more content working for a hands-on employer than they've been for the last twenty years. Shall we step inside? I'm warning you, it's very different."

As Julia did so, she expected to see a dark, narrow hallway and a flight of steep stairs straight ahead of her. Instead, she found she was standing in a vast empty space.

"I'm allergic to low ceilings," he apologized, indicating his height. "I am six foot three, after all. So I took them out."

The ceilings were not the only things Kit had taken out. The whole interior layout, which had previously housed all necessities such as the kitchen, bedrooms, and bathroom, had gone. She looked up to what had once been the bedroom ceilings and in the apex saw four newly fitted skylights. The only surviving interior feature was the large inglenook fireplace, which she had warmed herself in front of as a child.

"I . . . it's certainly . . . changed," she managed.

"The upstairs is yet to go in. I've used the loft space to raise the level of the ceilings, providing more height downstairs. And I'm converting the old lean-to next door into a kitchen and bathroom. I know it's radical, but I think it will suit me when it's finished."

"You've certainly brought it into the new millennium," Julia murmured. "It's difficult to think this is the same cottage."

He looked down at her. "You're upset, aren't you?"

"Of course not."

But they both knew she was.

"Look, Julia, why don't you come up with me to the house for a sandwich? I feel I owe it to you, having desecrated your heritage."

"Hardly *my* heritage. But, yes, I—"

"Hi, my darling. Sorry I'm late."

An attractive, auburn-haired woman appeared behind them. She kissed Kit warmly on the cheek and smiled at Julia.

"Julia, this is Annie," said Kit. "She's been helping me design my cottage and is drawing up plans for turning the rest of the Quad into rentable homes—while she's waiting for her own project to come to fruition." Kit indicated Annie's swollen stomach and threw an arm round her shoulder. "Not long now, is it?" he said affectionately.

"No, only four weeks to go, thank God." Annie's clear green eyes twinkled at Julia. She spoke with a hint of an American accent. "I'll be glad now when it's hatched. You have any?"

Julia's eyes filled with involuntary tears and she stood silently, saying nothing. How could she answer?

"Julia's a very well-known concert pianist." Kit came to the rescue, understanding instantly. "We met at Wharton Park years ago, and I was one of the first people she ever performed for. Isn't that right, Julia?" His eyes were full of empathy.

The respite had given Julia a chance to recover. She managed a nod and cleared her throat. "Yes. I've got to get off home. Nice to meet you, Annie, and . . . good luck."

"And you, Julia."

"Yes. Bye, Kit. I'll see you soon." Julia turned tail and almost ran to her car before he could stop her.

8

The following Saturday, the forecasters were predicting snow. Julia decided to ignore the warnings—she wanted a day out of the cottage—and set off just after lunch toward Southwold to her grandmother's bungalow.

She turned on the radio to break the silence and instantly recognized the haunting notes of the middle section of Rachmaninov's Concerto No. 2. Julia immediately switched it off. Some things, even after her epiphany of the past few days, were still unbearable. Annie's innocent pleasantry had torn her to her core. She'd cried for two hours on returning home. That reaction was the reason she'd hidden away for so long; being alone was a better alternative than facing a world full of sights, smells, and people who, however well-meaning, were bound to say or do something to remind her of her tragedy.

As Julia neared the outskirts of Southwold, she reassured herself that the very fact she was here, sixty miles away from the sanctuary of her cottage, was testament to her radical improvement over the past few days. Julia knew that seeing her grandmother would not cause her pain. Instead, she would be hurtling backward over the past few years of her life to a time that held only comforting memories. It was "safe" territory and she was genuinely looking forward to seeing Elsie again.

Julia consulted the directions she had scribbled down. She followed them and found herself turning into a tree-lined cul-de-sac, and then into the drive of an immaculate bungalow.

She picked up her bag, which contained the Changi diary, and walked to the front door to ring the bell. The bell played a tinny, electronic tune, and within seconds her grandmother was at the door, throwing her arms open to welcome her.

"Julia!"

She was enveloped in the fulsome breast, which smelled of Blue Grass perfume and talc.

"Let me look at you." Elsie took Julia by the shoulders and stepped back, clasping her hands together with pleasure. "My! You've turned into a beauty," she exclaimed. "You're so like your mother was at your age. Now come in, my love, come in."

Julia followed Elsie inside. The bungalow was tiny, but everything was as neat as a pin, fresh, and bright. Elsie led her into a small sitting room, furnished with a pink Dralon three-piece suite, crammed around a gas fire.

"Now then, let's take your coat, and you sit and warm yourself by the fire while I go and make us a nice hot drink. Coffee or tea?"

"A cup of tea would be lovely thanks, Granny."

"Righty-ho then, and I baked you some of those scones you used to like as well." Elsie eyed her. "You look as though you could do with some of Granny's feeding up."

Julia smiled. "You're right. I probably could."

Elsie went into the next-door kitchen and switched on the kettle. Julia sat back in her chair and succumbed happily to the familiar cocoon of security her grandmother had always provided for her. "So," said Elsie, returning with a laden tray and placing it on the small coffee table, "how has my famous granddaughter been?"

"I'm okay, Granny. And it's really lovely to see you. I'm sorry I haven't visited before. I haven't been out much lately."

"You've been through a lot, my love, and I knew you'd turn up when you were ready." Elsie patted Julia's hand in sympathy and understanding. "Now then, I'm putting plenty of sugar in your tea. You could double for your grandpa when he turned up back from the war; like a skeleton he was. There now." She passed Julia a cup, then began the task of thickly buttering some scones and adding jam. "It's my special homemade damson. Do you remember how you used to love it? I managed to grow a damson tree in that tiny patch of fresh air they take for a garden round here"—Elsie indicated the small lawned area visible through the window—"and it does lovely, it does."

Julia looked at Elsie's twinkling eyes. Whatever she had been expecting in terms of her grandmother's aging, it just hadn't happened. Perhaps when someone was, in the eyes of the young, "old" to begin with, the passing of the years seemed much less obvious. Julia took a bite out of the scone and savored the familiar taste.

Elsie watched her approvingly. "I haven't lost my touch now, have I? I bet they're the best scones you've tasted, for all your fine Frenchy food."

Julia chuckled. "No, Granny, you haven't lost your touch." She saw Elsie was frowning as she studied something on the top of Julia's head.

"I can tell you haven't been eating, miss. Your hair's lost all its shine." Elsie reached a hand across to Julia and picked up a lock of her hair, rubbing the ends between her fingers. "Dry as a bone. You need a good trim and a bottle of conditioner on that. And some decent food inside you," she clucked. "It's what I tell all my ladies: what you put in your mouth ends up on your head."

Julia stared at Elsie in surprise. "Your 'ladies'? Are you hairdressing now?"

"Yes, I am," she confirmed gleefully. "Only at the old people's home on Thursday mornings, and they've hardly got much hair left between them all," Elsie chuckled, "but I love it, I do. Finally got myself the career I always wanted!"

"Have you still got all your wigs?"

"No, I don't need them no more, now I have the real thing." Elsie glanced at her. "You must have thought me odd, the way I used to spend hours fiddling with them, but they were better than nothing. It was all I ever wanted to do," she sighed, "and I used to be right good at it, I did. Her Ladyship used to have me style her hair and do the same for her guests who came to stay at Wharton Park. Ah, well, funny how life turns out, isn't it?"

"Yes, it is, Granny. And are you well in yourself?"

"As you can see"—Elsie surveyed her substantial waistline—"still enjoying my own cooking. Bit more of a struggle now though, as it's only me to feed. Your great-aunt died at the beginning of last year."

"I was sorry to hear that, Granny." Julia finished her scone and took another one from the plate.

"Well, at least she didn't suffer. She went to bed one night and just didn't wake up. That's the way I'd choose for me too." Elsie was sanguine, as old people often were about death. "She left me the bungalow, seeing as she didn't have kids of her own. These modern buildings are so much better than those poky, damp cottages I used to live in.

Always warm, with hot water for a bath whenever I want one, and a lavvy that flushes every time."

"So, you don't get lonely?"

"Lord, no! I'm rushed off my feet. I've got my hairdressing, and there's not a day goes by when I'm not off to one of my social clubs or out visiting some of my friends. We was so isolated at Wharton Park, Julia, with just the other estate workers to choose friends from. Here, I've got a whole town full of Old Age Pensioners!"

"I'm glad to see you're so happy, Granny. You obviously don't miss your life on the estate."

Elsie's face darkened. "Well now, that wouldn't be the truth, my love, cos I miss your grandpa something rotten. But, no, I don't miss the life I had there. Remember, I went into service when I was fourteen at the Big House; up at five, bed by midnight if I was lucky and they didn't have a dinner or no guests staying. I worked like that for over fifty years of my life." She shook her head. "No, Julia, I've enjoyed my retirement, make no mistake. Anyway, enough of me, now you know I'm well and happy. How are your dad and your sister?"

"The same as ever. Dad's still working far too hard and just about to trek off to the other side of the world on a research project. Alicia's got her big family to look after, so that keeps her busy too."

"I should bet it does, she sends me pictures sometimes. She's always saying come over for a visit, but I don't like to be a bother. And besides, I can't drive and I don't like them trains. Maybe one day, when they've got time, they'll come and visit me here, like you have today."

"I promise I'll try and come to see you more often from now on. Especially now I'm back in the country."

"You're staying here, are you? Permanent, like?" Elsie asked.

"I don't know," Julia sighed. "I've got some decisions to make, but up to now, I haven't wanted to make them."

"No, my love." Elsie looked at her with sympathy. "I'm sure you haven't. So, you told me you'd got something you wanted to ask me."

"Yes. I don't know whether you've heard that the Wharton Park estate is being sold?"

Elsie's face remained impassive. "Yes, I had heard."

"Kit Crawford, the heir, is keeping the Quad and moving into your old cottage."

Elsie threw back her head and laughed, a deep, rich sound that resonated throughout her body and made it shake. Finally she wiped her eyes. "Master Kit, or should I say, his Lordship, moving into our old gardener's cottage?" She shook her head. "Oh, Julia, you aren't serious, are you?"

"It's true. He's had to sell up because the estate is in bad debt and needs a lot of money spent on it. Besides, it was a lovely cottage," Julia added defensively.

"That's as may be, but the thought, in my day, of Lord Crawford moving into our basic place makes me laugh." Elsie found a hankie from her sleeve and blew her nose. "Sorry, my love, carry on with your story."

"Well, the thing is that, when the plumbers were putting in some new pipes, they had to pull up the floorboards." Julia dug into her bag and pulled out the diary. "And they found this."

Elsie stared at it and immediately Julia could see she recognized it.

"It's a diary," Julia said, stating the obvious.

"Yes" was all Elsie could manage.

"Of being in Changi jail in Singapore during the war."

"I know what it's about, Julia." Tears appeared spontaneously in Elsie's eyes.

"Oh, Granny, I'm so sorry. I didn't mean to upset you. You don't have to read it or anything. I just wanted you to confirm it was written by Grandfather Bill. He was there, wasn't he? Out in the Far East during the war? I've been thinking that some of the things he used to say to me in the hothouses when I was younger probably indicated he was. Although he didn't ever tell me where or when," she added hurriedly, seeing Elsie's face paling.

Finally Elsie nodded. "Yes, he was there," she said slowly.

"In Changi?"

Elsie nodded.

"So, this *is* his diary?"

There was a pause before Elsie asked, "Julia, have you read it?"

She shook her head. "No, I keep meaning to, but somehow"—she sighed—"the truth is, I thought it might be painful, and right now, selfishly, I've had enough pain."

"I understand." Elsie nodded. She heaved herself up and walked slowly to the window, where fat flakes of snow were covering the grass on the small patch of garden outside. The sky was darkening already, even though it was only just past four. With her back to Julia, she said, "Weather's coming in fast now. Will you stay tonight?"

"I . . ." Up to that moment, Julia had not thought of staying. She looked at the snow, thought of the drive home, her bleak cottage, and her grandmother's obvious discomfort. And nodded. "Yes, I will."

Elsie turned round. "Good. Now, Julia, I'm going to go and prepare us a bite of supper. I'm best to think while I work. And I need to think," she added, almost to herself. "Why don't you watch some telly while I do it?" She indicated the remote control and left the room.

Forty-five minutes later, after Julia had watched some bland Saturday-night talent competition and enjoyed it more than she thought she would, Elsie came back into the sitting room with a tray.

"It's almost six and I always treat myself to a Noilly Prat on a Saturday." Elsie indicated her tumbler. "I've got some red wine that a friend brought round. Don't know if it's any good, but would you like a glass?"

"Why not?" said Julia, glad that Elsie had a little more color in her cheeks.

"Shepherd's pie's in the oven and we're all set to eat it later." Elsie nodded, passing Julia a glass and taking a swig of her own drink. "I've had a think too, while I was chopping, and I feel a little bit calmer now."

"I'm so sorry, Granny, I really didn't want to upset you. I should have realized it was painful." Julia took a sip of her wine. "I've spent too long thinking about myself recently and I need to start remembering the feelings of others."

Elsie reached across to Julia and patted her hand. "Course you've been thinking about yourself. You've had it tough, my love, and there's an end to it. You haven't upset me, really. Seeing *that*"—she indicated the diary—"was just a bit of a shock, that's all. I thought Bill had chucked it onto the fire. I told him to, said that one day someone was bound to find it and it would lead to no good. . . ." She stared into the distance.

Julia sat patiently, waiting for her grandmother to speak.

"Well now . . ." Elsie collected herself. "I suppose you're wondering what the matter is, what I'm thinking. The truth is, Julia, that diary has been found and given to you. I could lie to you, and believe me, I've thought about it, but I don't think that's right. Anymore, at least."

"Granny, please tell me. If it's a secret, you know I can keep it. I always did when I was younger."

Elsie smiled at this, then reached across and stroked Julia's cheek. "The problem is, it's not quite as simple as that. It's one of them secrets, you see, family secrets, that if it were told, would upset more than a few people."

This made Julia even more intrigued. "There's hardly anybody left to upset," she said. "Just Dad, me, and Alicia."

"Well," mused Elsie, "sometimes these secrets affect more than just one family, don't they now? Anyways, I think the best thing to do is start the story at the beginning and see where it leads, don't you?"

Julia nodded. "Granny, you do what you think is right. I'm happy to listen."

Elsie nodded. "I'm warning you, it might take me some time to remember, but—well now, I suppose this story starts with me, when I was learning to be a lady's maid in 1939, up at the Big House. You wouldn't have recognized Wharton Park, Julia. The whole place was so alive, buzzing with the Crawford family and their friends. They had house parties almost every week in the shooting season. And one weekend, some friends of theirs came up from London, and I was put in charge of looking after their eighteen-year-old daughter, one Olivia Drew-Norris. She was my first 'lady.' " Elsie's eyes brightened with the memories. "Oh, Julia, I'll never forget until my dying day, the moment I walked into that Magnolia bedroom and saw her for the first time. . . ."

9

Wharton Park
January 1939

Olivia Drew-Norris walked over to the window of the large bedroom she had just been ushered into and looked out of it. She gave a heavy sigh at the grayness of the scene that presented itself.

It was as if, since she had docked in England two months ago, someone had decided to wipe the bright, warm colors from her visual palette and substitute them with a blurry, sludgier version painted in brown and gray. The starkness of the view, with the mist already skimming the tops of the fields, even though it was only just past three o'clock, made her feel physically cold and mentally depleted.

She shivered and walked away from the window.

Olivia knew her parents were both glad to be back in England. They could accept this horrid, damp island because its memory was stored in their brains as "home." For Olivia, it was different. She had never set foot outside India since the day she had been born. Having finally arrived here, she couldn't understand how all the talk she had heard—at the club or over dinner at her parents' house in Poona—tended to lean nostalgically toward England. As far as she could tell, it had nothing to recommend it whatsoever. Everyone complained about the heat in India, but at least they didn't have to retire for the night in six layers of undergarments and then lie freezing in sheets that smelled of damp, waiting for the circulation to return to their toes. Olivia had suffered from a permanent cold since she had stepped off the ship.

She craved the scents and the sounds of her birthland . . . ripe pomegranates, incense, the oil her ayah had used on her long, black hair; the sweet noise of singing from the servants in the house, children laughing in the dusty streets of the town, the traders in the market shouting out their wares . . . it conjured up a colorful, noisy picture in such contrast to this silent and bleak land.

After all the buildup, the excitement of coming "home," Olivia had never felt more dejected or miserable in her entire life. The worst part was, she could have stayed behind when her parents left to return to England. If she had paid more attention to the advances of that ruddy-cheeked colonel and allowed him to woo her, she could still be in Poona now. But he was so jolly old—at least forty-five—and she was just eighteen.

Besides, she had survived the searingly hot nights, when sleep was rendered impossible, by reading a miasma of English novels by Jane Austen and the Brontë sisters. They had served to fire her belief that "true love" would one day be found.

In the next few months, she was to do the Season in London, where she would be introduced to suitable young men. And from them, she fervently hoped, she would find her own Mr. Darcy.

It was the only bright spark in a haze of bleakness. And, Olivia thought brutally, unlikely. The young British chaps she had met so far did not fill her with confidence for the future. Their pasty complexions, immaturity, and apparent lack of interest in anything other than shooting pheasant had not endeared any of them to her. Perhaps it was because she had spent so much of her life amid adults, unluckily being one of only a few young ladies and gentlemen in Poona's social circle. She had mostly grown up with her parents' friends, attending dinners and parties, riding and playing tennis. Her education had been unusual too, although Olivia saw this as a bonus. Her parents had employed the tutorial services of Mr. Christian, a Cambridge graduate who had been wounded out of the army in the First World War, but had decided to settle in Poona. Mr. Christian had studied philosophy at Trinity and, finding a willing young mind, had taken the opportunity to fill it with a breadth of knowledge Olivia would not have found in an all-girls' English boarding school. He had also taught her how to play chess to a near-professional standard *and* cheat at bridge.

However, in the past few weeks Olivia had come to realize her cultural sophistication would be no help to her here in England. Her wardrobe, which had seemed modern in India, was hopelessly out-of-date. She had insisted her mother's dressmaker take up her hems, allowing them to fall nearer her knee rather than her ankles, as all the young ladies she had recently seen in London were doing. And when she had taken a shopping trip to Derry & Toms with her mother, she had secretly purchased a bright red lipstick.

The shortening of her skirts and the lipstick were not because Olivia was particularly vain, but rather because she didn't want to stand out from the crowd more than she already did.

And now here they were, in another freezing, damp mausoleum of a house for the weekend. Papa had apparently been at school with Lord Christopher Crawford, their host for the weekend. As usual, Papa would spend the days shooting, and Mama, or *Mummy*, as she was learning to call her, would sit in the drawing room drinking tea and engaging her hostess in polite conversation. Olivia would sit by her, feeling like a spare part.

There was a light knock on her door.

"Come," she said.

A sweet, freckled face containing a pair of sparkling brown eyes appeared around it. The girl was dressed in an old-fashioned maid's outfit, which looked rather too big for her.

"'Scuse me, m'um, my name's Elsie and I'm to help you while you're here. Can I unpack your suitcase for you?"

"Of course."

Elsie stepped over the threshold and hovered nervously. "'Scuse me, m'um, it's a little dark in here. Can I put on some light? I can hardly see you over there." She giggled shyly.

"Yes, please do."

The girl scuttled over to the lamp by the bed and switched it on. "There we are. That's better now, isn't it?"

"Yes." Olivia stood up from the bed and turned to the girl. "It gets dark so early here." She felt the maid's eyes boring into her. Finally she said, "Is there something wrong?"

The maid jumped. "Sorry, m'um, I was just thinking how beautiful you are. I've never seen a girl as beautiful as you. You look like one of them actresses from the flicks."

Olivia was rather taken aback. "Thank you. It's awfully kind of you to say so, but I'm quite sure I don't."

"Well, I think you do. And, m'um, you must forgive me if I don't get things quite right for you, it's the first time I've been a lady's maid, you see." Elsie heaved Olivia's case onto the bed and unlocked it. "Now, if you can tell me what you'll be wanting to wear for afternoon tea, I can lay it out for you. And then I'll take your dress for dinner down with me for a press and a freshen." Elsie looked at Olivia inquiringly.

Olivia pointed to her new pink dress with the Peter Pan collar and large white buttons placed in a row down the front of it. "That for now, and then the blue brocade for later."

"Right you are, m'um." Elsie nodded, unfolding the dresses carefully and laying them out on the bed. "I'm sure that blue'll look beautiful with your complexion. Shall I hang the rest of your clothes in your wardrobe for you?"

"You're very kind, thank you, Elsie."

Olivia sat uncomfortably on the tapestry-covered stool at the end of the bed as Elsie bustled around the room. She had hardly been aware of her staff in India; just accepted their position as servants. But she was unnerved by this girl, who was probably about the same age as herself, and English.

Her father had vigorously complained when they had arrived back at their old Surrey home about how difficult it was to find staff these days. Far fewer girls were going into service, he said, preferring to take jobs as secretaries in offices and in the new department stores that were opening up all over the country.

"Girls don't want to *serve* anymore," he had muttered.

Although, from their recent visits to the country estates of her parents' friends, Olivia had observed that female emancipation was far further ahead in the big cities.

"Right, m'um, I'll just be nipping downstairs to give your evening dress a press, and then I'll be back up after tea to draw you a bath and light a fire. Is there anything else I can get you?"

"No, thank you, Elsie." She smiled. "And by the way, please call me Olivia."

"Thank you, m'um—I mean, Miss Olivia." Elsie scurried to the door and closed it behind her.

• • •

That evening, before dinner, Elsie proved to be a rather fine hairdresser. "Would you let me put it up for you, miss?" she said, brushing Olivia's thick, golden waves. "I think it'll suit you, make you look sophisticated, like Greta Garbo. I've practiced on my sister before, so I know how to do it."

Olivia sat on a stool in front of the mirror and nodded. "All right, Elsie, I trust you." After all, she thought to herself, she could always take it down.

"I love doing hair, wanted to train properlike, but the nearest salon's fifteen miles away and I haven't got no transport. There's only one omnibus a day that leaves from the Gate Lodge at eleven o'clock. That's no good for me now, is it?" Elsie confided as her expert hands brushed and curled and pinned Olivia's hair up into a sophisticated pile.

"Would you not think of moving into the city?"

Elsie looked horrified. "What! And leave my ma with all my brothers and sisters? She needs my help and the money I bring in. There." Elsie stepped back to admire her handiwork. "What do you think?"

"Thank you, Elsie." Olivia smiled. "You've done it very well indeed."

"Don't thank me, Miss Olivia, it was a privilege. Now, can I help you with your corset?"

"You're a darling, Elsie," Olivia said shyly. "To be frank about it, I've no idea how it goes on. I've never worn one in my life, and I'm bound to get into an awful muddle with it."

Elsie picked it up off the bed and studied it. "This is the new 'wasp waist' corset," she said admiringly. "I've seen them in *Woman's Weekly*. It gives you a perfect hourglass figure, so they say. Right, I think I know how it goes on. We'll do it together, Miss Olivia, don't you worry."

With the corset on and Olivia utterly convinced there was no room for an olive, let alone a four-course dinner, Elsie slipped the new midnight blue brocade dress over Olivia's head and fastened it at the back.

Olivia smoothed down the skirt, which frothed out below her newly nipped-in waist, and gazed at her reflection in the mirror.

The hair, the corset, and the dress had achieved a transformation. It was no longer a young girl who stared back at her from the mirror, it was a woman.

"Ooh, Miss Olivia, you look so beautiful. That color matches your eyes perfectly. You'll be turning a few heads tonight and that's for sure. Hope you get to sit next to Master Harry, his Lordship's son; all us girls are in love with him," Elsie admitted. "He's so handsome."

"Knowing my luck, I shan't. I'll almost certainly get the old major with the paunch that I met downstairs during afternoon tea." Olivia smiled and raised her eyebrows, and the two girls shared a moment of understanding that crossed their social barriers.

"Well, for your sake, I hope not, Miss Olivia. Enjoy yourself."

Olivia turned at the open door. "Thank you, Elsie, you've been awfully kind. I'll report back later." She winked and left the room.

Olivia was not the only member of the household who was dreading dinner that night. The Honorable Harry Crawford had already decided that when he took over Wharton Park from his father, there would be no more shooting parties. The whole sensation of killing a defenseless, living thing made him sick to the stomach.

Struggling to put his cuff links in—his man had been sent to assist the elderly major with dressing—Harry straightened his bow tie in the mirror. And wondered how many other human beings felt they had been born into the wrong life. In his, "duty" was everything. Although the many who served him at home and in his future regiment might look on with envy, Harry thought he would swap with any of them in an instant.

He knew no one was really interested in how he felt; his life had been mapped out for him long before he had even been conceived. He was a mere vessel of continuity, and the situation could not be altered.

At least the two years of hell at Sandhurst were over. He was on two weeks' leave before joining the Fifth Battalion Royal Norfolks—his father's old regiment—for his first posting as an officer. Having attained the highest rank, Lord Christopher Crawford was now working at Whitehall in an advisory capacity to the government.

There were rumblings of war . . . the thought made Harry break out in a cold sweat. Chamberlain was doing his damnedest and all were hoping for a peaceful resolution, but given that his father was privy to the actual facts, rather than the gossip on the streets, Harry knew this was unlikely to be the case. His father had said there would be war within the year, and Harry believed him.

Harry was not a coward. He had no problem with the thought of giving his life for his country. However, the gung ho attitude of his fellow officers, who were relishing the thought of giving the Krauts a jolly good thrashing—a thoughtless euphemism for death and destruction on a grand scale—was not an emotion he shared. He kept his pacifist views to himself—they didn't go down awfully well in the officers' mess. But often, he would lie awake in his narrow bed at night, wondering whether, if faced with a Kraut on the end of a long gun, he would actually be able to pull his trigger to save his own skin.

He knew plenty of others thought like him. The problem was, they didn't have a high-profile, high-ranking general as their father, or a history of two hundred and fifty years of family heroism behind them.

Harry had acknowledged a long time ago that his father's genes had obviously given him a miss. He resembled his mother, Adrienne, far more in personality—gentle and artistic—but also in the way that he was prone to sudden, abrupt fits of depression, when the world turned black and he struggled to see the point of living. His mother called these moments her petit mal and would retire to bed until she had shaken it off. As an officer in the army, Harry did not have that option. His lack of prowess with all things military had remained undiscussed with his father. In fact, their conversation was limited to a cheery "Good morning" or a "Day seems fine enough" and an occasional "Get Sable to pour me a scotch, will you, old chap?"

His father could have been any one of the commanding officers Harry had dealt with at Sandhurst. His mother knew, of course, how Harry felt about his life and his future, but he understood she was powerless to help. So they did not discuss it.

Yet, at least she had managed to provide the one thing that gave him solace, and for this he was eternally grateful: when Harry was six, and against his father's wishes, Adrienne had employed a piano teacher to tutor him in the basics of the instrument. Sitting with his fingers on the ivory keys, Harry had acquired some sort of meaning to his life. He had since become a very, very good pianist. Partly because, both at school and at home, he could hide either in the music block or the drawing room and keep himself busy and out of harm's way.

His music tutor at Eton, hearing his talent, had suggested he audition for the Royal College of Music. His father refused to countenance it. The boy was going to Sandhurst. Playing the piano was for dilettantes and not a career for the future Lord Crawford.

And that had been that.

Harry had continued to practice as much as he could, although his playing at Sandhurst was limited to entertaining the mess with modern pieces by Coward or Cole Porter, and Chopin was not on the agenda.

When the bouts of blackness hit him, Harry sometimes hoped for reincarnation, to be in a world where he could utilize his talent and his passion. Perhaps, he sighed, if he bought it in the war to come, he would be one step nearer his goal.

10

As Olivia entered the drawing room, she had the new and not unpleasant feeling of her arrival being noted approvingly. Lord Crawford was the first over to her.

"Olivia, isn't it? My, my, how that Indian sun nurtures buds into full bloom. Snifter?"

"Thanks awfully," she replied as she took a gin from the tray proffered by the hovering butler.

"Rather glad you're my neighbor at table tonight, my dear," Lord Crawford commented, throwing a discreet nod in the butler's direction. He answered with an equally discreet nod back. Even if Olivia hadn't been beside him for dinner, she was now.

"So, how are you finding Blighty?" he asked.

"It's thrilling to see the country I've heard so much about," Olivia lied smoothly.

"My dear, I'm delighted that you should take the time to visit us in our rural Norfolk backwater. You're doing the Season, so your papa tells me?"

"Yes." Olivia nodded.

"Jolly good show," Christopher chuckled. "One of the best times of my life. Now, let me introduce you to my wife. She was indisposed this afternoon, but seems to have recovered for this evening." He guided Olivia over to a slim, elegant woman. "Adrienne, do meet Olivia Drew-Norris, whom I'm sure is going to break many chaps' hearts this Season, just like you did years ago."

Adrienne, Lady Crawford, turned toward Olivia and extended her delicate white hand, and in a parody of the male handshake, their fingers touched.

"Enchantée," said Adrienne, smiling at her approvingly. "You are indeed a heartbreaker."

"It's awfully kind of you to say so, Lady Crawford." Olivia was beginning to feel like a prize heifer being paraded around a showground, waiting to be judged. She hoped this wasn't a precursor of the Season to come.

"Please, you must call me Adrienne. I am sure we will be great friends, *n'est-ce pas*?"

Lord Crawford looked down fondly at his wife. "Good show, good show. I'll leave Olivia in your capable hands, my dear. Perhaps you can give her a few tips." He strode off to welcome two new arrivals.

Olivia took the moment to enjoy Adrienne's own beauty. Although mature, in her early forties at least, Adrienne had the body of a slim young girl. And a beautifully sculpted face, with high, chiseled cheekbones underneath a flawless, ivory skin. Her quintessential femininity reminded Olivia more of a delicate Indian maharani, rather than the usual female English aristocrat, built as they were to withstand the harshness of the British weather, with wide hips to engender the brood of children they needed to continue the family line.

Adrienne was so elegant, so fragile, Olivia felt she would be more suited to a salon in Paris than a drafty English country house. Indeed, Olivia's mother had told her that Adrienne was French. Judging by the way she wore what was a simple black cocktail dress, adorned only with a string of creamy pearls, she had the effortless chic of her native land.

"So, Olivia, you are back in this dreadful country, with its filthy weather and its lack of natural sunlight, *n'est-ce pas*?"

Adrienne stated this as a matter of fact and Olivia was taken aback by her bluntness. "I am certainly finding the change is taking rather a lot of getting used to," she answered as diplomatically as she could.

Adrienne's tiny hand rested on hers. "*Ma chérie*, I too was brought up in a place full of warmth and light. When I left our château in the South of France to come here to England, I did not think I could bear it. You are the same. I can read how much you miss India in your eyes."

"I do," Olivia whispered.

"Well, I can only promise you it will get easier." Adrienne gave an elegant shrug. "Now, I must introduce you to my son, Harry. He is of your age and will keep you company while I play the hostess *parfaite. Pardon, chérie,* I will go find him and bring him to you."

As she watched her hostess glide across the room, Olivia felt disarmed by Adrienne's empathetic assessment. She was, on such occasions, used to only making small talk, never delving below the surface to discover more. Any form of inner thoughts—or worse, emotions—was frowned upon by British society. That much she *had* learned from the club in Poona. Her conversation with Adrienne, albeit short, had comforted her. She allowed herself a secret smile.

Harry had been ordered by his mother to go and keep the young "Indian" girl company. Dutifully, he made his way toward her across the room. A few paces away from her, he saw her lips open wide as she smiled.

Her cool, blonde beauty was suddenly animated, filled with a radiance beneath her creamy skin. Harry, not usually particularly aware of the physical charms of women, realized she was what most of his fellow officers would term a stunner.

He approached her. She saw him and said, "You must be Harry, sent to make polite conversation with me by your mother." Her turquoise eyes were filled with amusement as she spoke.

"Yes. But I assure you, it will be my pleasure." He glanced at her empty glass. "May I find you another drink, Miss Drew-Norris?"

"That would be just the ticket, thank you."

Harry summoned the butler, and as Olivia placed her empty glass on the tray and took a fresh one, she said, "I do apologize if you think me forward. I don't mean to be. I feel rather sorry for you, that's all, having to speak to endless people you've never met before."

Olivia was surprised at her boldness and blamed the particularly potent gin. She looked at Harry, "handsome" Harry, as Elsie had described him, and decided that Elsie was right. Harry had garnered the best physical qualities of both his parents; he had the height of his father and the fine bone structure and luminous brown eyes of his mother.

"I can assure you, Miss Drew-Norris, coming to talk to you isn't a chore. You are, at least, under the age of seventy, which always helps. And, to be frank, around these parts, pretty unusual."

Olivia laughed as Harry responded to her glibness. "Touché, although wearing that dinner suit, you could be taken for your father."

Harry shrugged good-naturedly. "Why, Miss Drew-Norris, I do believe you are making fun of me. Do you not realize that war is coming to these fair isles and we must all make some sacrifices? For me, that's wearing my father's hand-me-down suit, even if it is three sizes too big for me."

Olivia's face darkened. "Do you really believe there will be war?"

"Without a doubt." Harry nodded.

"I agree, but Daddy refuses to countenance it."

"I'm sure that after a day's shooting with *my* father, he may well have begun to." Harry raised his eyebrows.

"I very much doubt that Herr Hitler can be pacified," sighed Olivia. "He's intent on world domination, and his youth movement seems to be as passionate as he is."

Harry stared at her in surprise. "If I may say so, Miss Drew-Norris, you seem awfully well informed. Rather unusual in a young lady."

"Do you find it unbecoming, women discussing politics?"

"Not at all. As a matter of fact, I find it extremely refreshing. Most girls simply aren't interested."

"Well, I was fortunate to be tutored in India by a man who believed women had as much right to an education as men." Olivia gazed past him, her eyes suddenly sad. "He brought the world alive for me and made me aware of my relevance in it."

"Gosh, your chap sounds wasted in Poona. Wish I'd had that kind of inspiration at Eton. Couldn't wait to finish and get out of the damned place." Harry lit a cigarette, fascinated. "And will you be taking your education further?"

Olivia shook her head ruefully. "I can't imagine what Mummy and Daddy would say if I suggested it. They would be horrified: 'What! A *bluestocking* in the family?!' No, I'm to be married off, assuming someone will have me, that is."

Harry looked at her with genuine admiration. "Miss Drew-Norris, I assure you that will present no problem at all."

She glanced up at him. "Even if it's not what I want?"

Harry sighed as he stubbed his cigarette out into a nearby ashtray. "It occurs to me that most of us don't have what we want. But do try not to be too downhearted. I believe there are changes coming, especially for women. And perhaps the only advantage of the prospect of war is that it will alter the status quo even further."

"I can only hope it does. And what of you?" Olivia asked, suddenly remembering that the golden rule, taught from the cradle, was never to dominate the conversation, especially with a gentleman.

"Me?" Harry shrugged. "I'm a mere soldier, on leave at present, but I fear not for long. We've just received orders to double the numbers in my new battalion, recruiting through the Territorial Army."

"I find it quite impossible to understand how life here can go on as normal." Olivia indicated the other members of the drinks party, guffawing loudly at some joke.

"Well, it's the British spirit, isn't it? The world may be coming to an end, but in houses such as these, everything goes on as it always has done. And in some respects, I thank God for it."

"Ladies and gentlemen, dinner is served."

"Well, Miss Drew-Norris," said Harry, "it's been a pleasure. By the way, mind the shot in the pheasant. Cook's not terribly careful." He winked at her. "Perhaps we'll meet again before you leave."

Olivia spent dinner responding to Lord Crawford's dreadful jokes and behaving like the young lady she had been brought up to be. She risked the odd glance down the table at Harry, who she could see was doing his duty too, entertaining the wife of the army major. Later, as the men retired to the library and the women to the drawing room for coffee, Olivia feigned tiredness and excused herself.

Adrienne appeared by her side just as she was mounting the stairs. "*Ma chérie*, are you ill?" she asked with concern.

Olivia shook her head. "No, just a headache, really."

Adrienne held her by the shoulders and smiled. "It is this cold English weather that has chilled your tropical bones. I will ask Elsie to relight your fire and bring you some cocoa, and we will see you tomorrow. Perhaps you will take a walk with me in the garden and I can show you something that might remind you of home."

Olivia nodded, appreciating Adrienne's genuine concern. "Thank you."

"*Je vous en prie.* You enjoyed speaking to my son, Harry?"

"I did, awfully, thank you." Olivia could feel the heat rising in her cheeks and hoped Adrienne hadn't noticed.

Adrienne nodded approvingly. "I knew you would. *Bonne nuit, ma chérie.*"

Olivia climbed the stairs wearily. She genuinely had a headache, probably brought on by her still being unused to alcohol, but more important, she wanted time alone to think back and relish her conversation with Harry.

She changed into her nightgown in double-quick time, an art she had perfected since arriving in the cold English climate. As she hopped into bed and snuggled under the covers, there was a knock on her door.

"Come."

Elsie's bright face appeared round the door. She was holding a tray with a mug of cocoa on it. "Only me, Miss Olivia." She walked across the room and placed the tray on the night table next to Olivia. "Made to my ma's special recipe"—she smiled—"with a dash of brandy for the cold."

"Thank you, Elsie." Olivia picked up the warm cup and nursed it in her hands as she watched Elsie rekindle the fire.

"So, did you have a good evening, Miss Olivia?"

"Oh, yes, Elsie, I did." She smiled.

Elsie turned from the fire and caught the smile. Her eyes twinkled. "And did you meet young Master Harry?"

"Yes."

"And what did you think of him, then?"

Olivia knew that another golden rule was not to gossip with servants, especially when not one's own, but the temptation of discussing Harry was just too great.

"I think he was . . . a very unusual man."

"And as handsome as I said he was?"

When Olivia didn't answer, Elsie cast her eyes down. "Sorry, miss, I'm forgetting myself. I mustn't ask personal questions."

"Elsie, I promise you're doing marvelously well. And after tomorrow, we'll probably never see each other again. And"—Olivia took a deep breath—"if you want to know the truth, I thought Harry was . . . a darling!"

Elsie clasped her hands together. "Oh, Miss Olivia! I just knew you would! I knew you'd like each other."

Olivia took a sip of her drink. "Elsie, this is the finest cocoa I've ever tasted."

"Thank you, miss." Elsie headed for the door. "I'll be here in the morning to draw back your curtains. Sleep tight."

When Elsie had left the room, Olivia lay back on the soft pillows sipping the cocoa. Then she closed her eyes and began to relive her conversation with Harry from start to finish.

11

The following morning, Olivia took breakfast alone in the dining room as the shooting party had left early, and both her mother and Adrienne were taking breakfast in their rooms. Afterward, for want of anything better to do, Olivia made her way into the library to choose a book. With reading material in Poona a precious and rare commodity, she was overcome by the supply on the floor-to-ceiling shelves.

She pulled off Virginia Woolf's *To the Lighthouse* and settled down in a comfortable leather chair by the fire to read.

The sound of music, distant but audible, attracted her attention. Someone was playing the piano, and as she concentrated, Olivia realized she recognized Chopin's "Grande Polonaise." She stood up and left the library, following the direction of the music, letting her hearing lead her eventually to the doorway of the drawing room.

She stood where she was, listening to the exquisite rendition of one of her favorite pieces, closing her eyes as the sound emanated from the piano at the other end of the room. As the last notes drifted across to her, she opened her eyes and peeped round a tall Chinese vase filled with flowers, which had blocked her view of the player.

Olivia gasped in astonishment when she saw it was Harry. Feeling like an interloper, she watched him as he sat, hands in his lap, staring out of the window and to the park beyond. Finally, he gave a sigh, stood up, and saw her.

"Miss Drew-Norris! I didn't realize I had an audience." He walked toward her, embarrassed, hands in his pockets.

"I was in the library and I heard the music and"—she shrugged—"followed it."

"You're fond of classical music?"

"Oh, yes. Especially when it's played like that. You're really terribly good." Olivia flushed slightly. "Where did you learn?"

"My mother had me tutored when I was younger and I continued at school. But . . . rather like you and university, the old ivories can't feature in my future plans. More's the pity," he added morosely.

"Well, they should," said Olivia stoutly. "I'm no expert, but you sound just as good as the recordings I listened to in India."

"It's very kind of you to say so." He turned away and looked out the window, then asked, "Fancy accompanying me on a walk? The sun seems to have managed to struggle out from behind the clouds today."

"I think I was supposed to be taking a walk with your mother, but I haven't seen her so far this morning."

"No, and I doubt you will. She's almost certainly in bed with a migraine. She suffers awfully from them, especially after late nights. What say you, you find yourself a coat, and we'll rendezvous outside on the terrace in five minutes?"

Olivia ran upstairs to find the only coat she had brought with her—far more suitable for the city than stomping across a country estate.

Harry was waiting for her, smoking a cigarette and leaning over the balustrade that led to the gardens. She came to stand next to him shyly. He pointed to one of the trees. "Can you see underneath? There's actually a sign of life: snowdrops."

They walked down the wide stairs and into the garden.

"How do you like our miniature Versailles?" Harry indicated the immaculate and beautifully laid-out formal garden around them. Manicured topiary hedges surrounded the edges, and in the center was an elegant fountain, topped with a statue of a young boy. "Mother wanted to create something of her French homeland. She's done a marvelous job. You should see it in high summer when all the flowers are out. It's a riot of color."

"I can imagine," breathed Olivia as they walked toward the fountain.

"You've just missed the mimosa by a few days," said Harry, pointing to where the bushes sat, protected, under the terrace. "It flowers anytime between January and March and really does smell heavenly. Our gardener doubted it could be grown here—it's normally a plant that likes the temperate weather of the South of France, but, sure enough, Mother won and it flourishes."

"She obviously has a talent for gardening. And the design is simply perfect." Olivia turned around to take everything in, then followed Harry along one of the many paths that led away from the fountain.

"Your mother told me that she might have something growing in the garden that would remind me of India," Olivia offered, breaking what seemed to have been rather a long silence.

"Oh, she most certainly means the hothouse. Our gardener, Jack, who was more used to nurturing turnips than exotic blooms, has spent the past few years trying to grow the bulbs that Mother gets sent to her from Kew Gardens. We can take a look at it if you'd like to."

"Rather," Olivia accepted eagerly.

"It's a bit of a hike, but we'll make it brisk. Sun might be out, but it's jolly nippy. So you're returning home tonight with your ma and pa?"

"No, not directly. First, we're off to London to discuss my Season with Grandmother. She's rather keen to be involved and, as Mummy's been out of the country so long, will be able to offer advice on the protocol."

"It may not be as bad as you think, you know, Miss Drew-Norris."

"Olivia, please," she insisted.

"Olivia," Harry corrected. "I went to a few dances a couple of years back and they can be quite enjoyable."

"I do hope so, although I can't say I'm very eager to go to London. There's a horribly tense atmosphere there—everyone's waiting for something awful to happen." She looked up at him for a reaction and saw that he was nodding in agreement. "And you will have read about the unemployment and the unrest on the streets?"

"Of course. It's a damned unsettling time to be living in. To be honest, I'll be relieved when we all know what will happen."

"Well, one never knows one's luck; the war might get me out of the Season," chuckled Olivia. "They can't hold it if there's a war on, now can they?"

"Horrors!" said Harry amiably, lighting a cigarette and offering her one, which she refused. "Not even a war could stop that!"

They both smiled in comfortable acknowledgment.

"Well, if war does come, I, for one, am not going to sit around and drink tea," she replied fiercely. "I shall sign up for something. I'm not sure what yet, but Mummy and Daddy can hardly stop me from helping to save my country, can they?"

"That's the spirit, Olivia! Now step in here." Harry opened the blue-painted wooden door that led into the kitchen garden. They walked through rows of immaculately planted cabbages, carrots, potatoes, and turnips, across to a hothouse nestling in the corner of the garden, sheltered by a high redbrick wall. Harry opened the door to the hothouse and they both stepped inside.

The pungent smell of flowers, combined with the heat, sent Olivia spiraling back to her former homeland. She inhaled the evocative scents and surveyed the burst of color in front of her.

"Oh, Harry," she said in ecstasy, as she began to walk down the long rows of plants. She turned to him. "It's simply heavenly!"

Harry could see tears in Olivia's eyes. She leaned forward to grasp a delicate yellow plant, held it in her hands, and smelled it. "This is frangipani, which used to grow outside my bedroom window in Poona. I lay there every night breathing its scent." She buried her nose in the flowers again. "I had no idea you could grow them here."

Harry was moved by her emotional reaction and realized then what a shock it must have been for her, landing here in England after years of living among plants like these, abundant in their natural climate.

"Well now, you absolutely must take it with you, mustn't she, Jack?" Harry turned to the middle-aged gardener, whose face was weathered and lined from years of outdoor work.

"Of course she must, Master Harry," he replied, smiling. "I've plenty more where that came from, managed to get the hang of them frangipani now, I have. Grand job," he muttered. "You wander around as much as you like, miss. It's a pleasure to have someone in here who appreciates them."

Olivia strolled up and down the rows of flowers, dipping her nose into the blooms and stroking the velvet petals.

"You've done a simply marvelous job, Jack," she commented. "These flowers can't like the English climate any more than I do."

"Well, I've been growing them now for fifteen years, and I might be no trained botanist, but I understand what they all like and dislike. And my son, Bill, here," Jack said, indicating the tall, handsome young man watering some of the pots farther down the hothouse, "has a real feel for them, don't you, Bill?"

The young man turned and nodded. "Suits me far better than cabbages." He grinned. "The best part is when we get a new bulb in and we've no idea what's going to grow out of it."

"He'll be good to take over, Master Harry, he's a natural," Jack confirmed. "As long as he don't get called up. They say they're recruiting from the Territorials already round here." Jack eyed him. "Is that true, Master Harry?" he asked, concern in his eyes.

"I really couldn't tell you, Jack," Harry answered diplomatically. "I think all of us are rather in the dark at the moment."

Jack turned to Olivia. "At least the hothouse will be safe with me if the war does come, miss. The Hun blew my leg to pieces last time, so they won't be wanting me again."

"Well now, Jack, Bill . . ." Harry nodded at them both. "You really are doing the most marvelous job in here. Well done."

"Tell her Ladyship from me she's to come down when she's got the time. One of the new bulbs she gave me has just flowered and I want her to see it." Jack touched his cap. "Good day to you, Master Harry, and you, miss. Enjoy your frangipani."

"Thanks awfully, I will," said Olivia. "It really is very sweet of you to give it to me."

"Grand job," said Jack, as Harry led her out of the hothouse.

"You're an absolute darling for taking me in there, Harry," Olivia enthused. "I feel uplifted."

"It was my pleasure, really," Harry remarked amiably. "It is rather special, isn't it?"

They walked back through the kitchen garden toward the house in silence. Harry lit another cigarette, took a few puffs, then stubbed it out with his foot. He sighed. "I was just thinking, if war does come, every bally family on the estate will be affected. Take Bill, for example. He's currently courting Elsie, one of our maids up at the house."

Olivia smiled. "I've met Elsie. She's a bright young spark and she's got herself a good-looking chap there."

"Won't be so damned good-looking if he gets half his face blown away by the Krauts," Harry muttered as they made their way back up the steps to the terrace. He turned to Olivia. "Sorry to be so mis, but I rather wonder what will happen to the estate if all our young workers are called up."

"The women will have to take over." Olivia grinned.

Harry smiled genuinely at this and offered her a half bow. "Well, there we are then, Mrs. Pankhurst. It has been my pleasure to show you around our humble gardens. And now, I suppose I'd better go and search out the guns before anyone notices I'm missing."

"Why weren't you out at the crack of dawn with the rest of the men?"

"I said I had some business to attend to, but if I'm truthful, any excuse will do. Not really my thing." He held out his hand. "I may not see you before you leave. Take care, Olivia, and safe journey back to the Smoke. It's been an absolute pleasure meeting you."

She shook his hand and smiled back. "And you, Harry."

Harry nodded, stuffed his hands into his pockets, and disappeared off inside the house.

12

It had been agreed between Lady Vare, Olivia's grandmother, and her parents, that Olivia should move to London for the duration of the Season. Her Surrey home was not an appropriate location from which a debutante should be launched, as it was too far from the glitz and glitter of the London scene. So, two weeks after leaving Wharton Park, Olivia arrived with her suitcases at her grandmother's house in Cheyne Walk.

The house was from another era: stuffed full of Victorian furniture and laden with heavy brocade curtains, the walls covered in highly patterned William Morris wallpaper. Olivia found it oppressive and was glad to be billeted high up on the fourth floor in her own small suite of rooms, where at least there was some light. In the morning, she would pull back the curtains, open the windows, and look across to the river Thames to stem her feeling of claustrophobia.

The first thing that had to be done in becoming a debutante was to register at St. James's Palace. Girls could only be presented at court if they were sponsored by a lady who had been presented herself. As Olivia's own mother had been a debutante, she could quite easily have acted as Olivia's sponsor. But Lady Vare would have none of it. In the end, Olivia's mother gave in to her *own* mother's determination to take charge and retreated to her Surrey home, leaving the arrangements for Olivia's Season entirely to her grandmother.

Between the endless dress fittings, Olivia was left much to her own devices. Which meant she had far too much time to think about Harry Crawford and her time at Wharton Park. The two days spent there had become almost miragelike in her memory. She relived her conversations with him, relishing that Harry had treated her as an intellectual equal. This was in stark contrast to her current life in London, where she felt she was little more than a doll being dressed up. She knew that, at least once the Season began, her timetable would be full as she embarked on the grueling round of dances, lunches, and late suppers that were all part of launching her into Society and finding her a suitable mate.

The injustice of so much opulence—the whole jamboree—set against a backdrop of unemployment, poverty, and unrest was not lost on Olivia. As she was chauffeured around London in her grandmother's old Bentley, Olivia would glance out the window at the poor souls living on the streets, warming their hands on paltry fires; at the men who marched past Parliament, holding their banners, which asked the government to help feed their children because they were starving.

She felt isolated by her privilege; she was trapped in the Old World when she wanted to belong to the New. She would sometimes take a walk along the Embankment, throwing coins at the homeless men and women shivering under the bridges, feeling embarrassed and uncomfortable in her warm, expensive clothes.

One afternoon, having just been to Lenare, so the famous photographer could capture her in her traditional white presentation dress, Olivia heard a knock on her door. It was her grandmother's maid.

"Her Ladyship has asked if you would be kind enough to take tea with her in the parlor downstairs."

When Olivia entered the room, Lady Vare was sitting stiffly in a high-backed leather chair placed by the fire.

"Please sit down, Olivia. As your presentation is now so close, I wanted to talk with you about the people you might meet during the Season. In the old days, it was not necessary to be wary of anyone. But"—Lady Vare wrinkled her nose in distaste—"unfortunately, standards have slipped and there is a certain . . . *element* that is no longer suitable company for a young lady such as yourself. The foreigners, for a start, but also, I have recently talked to another mother whose daughter is being presented and discovered there is a set who are considered *fast.* Olivia"—she wagged her finger sternly at her granddaughter—"you are to stay clear of them."

"But, Grandmother, how will I recognize them?" Olivia's eyes were round and appropriately innocent.

"They wear lipstick and smoke cigarettes."

Olivia tried not to giggle. From the look on her face, Lady Vare could well have been saying that these girls carried knives in their evening purses.

"I'll keep on the lookout, Grandmother, I promise, and I hope to make you proud."

Lady Vare nodded graciously. "I'm sure you will, Olivia. And now, you must excuse me, I have some business to attend to."

Olivia went to bed that night, willing the next three months to be over quickly, so she could finally begin to get on with her life.

The Presentation Night itself passed smoothly enough and was actually far more enjoyable than Olivia could have imagined. As she was driven down the Mall toward Buckingham Palace, crowds of well-wishers lined the road, and hundreds of people surrounded the gates to the palace. The crowds blew kisses at her, asked her chauffeur to switch on the interior lights of the car so they could look at her dress and cheer Olivia on her way. She was amazed that they didn't seem to disapprove of her or envy her privileged situation.

Her own car followed the long line that drove into the inner courtyard at Buckingham Palace. Her main concern, as she walked up the grand staircases and past the palace servants wearing their powdered wigs, was that she might dirty her white dress and kid gloves. Even though she deemed her presentation a relatively unimportant moment in her life, she could not rid herself of the small butterflies in her stomach as she stood in the anteroom waiting to be presented to the king and queen.

"This is a hoot!" said a striking young woman with jet black hair standing behind her. She was thin as a rake and wearing what Olivia's grandmother would call unsuitable lipstick. "What number are you?"

"I'm number sixteen."

"I'm in after you. Isn't this a yawn?" number seventeen drawled, looking suitably bored. "So completely passé."

Olivia wanted to agree, but as she was due into the Throne Room within the next two minutes, she ignored the girl and tried to concentrate on what she needed to do.

Afterward, everyone was much more relaxed. Olivia's presentation had gone smoothly. She had not tripped or fallen at the king and queen's feet or stumbled on her walk to and fro. The girls were chattering and tucking into a feast provided by Lyons. They all seemed to know one another, and Olivia stood on the sidelines, feeling awkward and out of place.

"Buck up, almost over," whispered a voice beside her. It was number seventeen. "We met earlier, I'm Venetia Burroughs. And you are?"

"Olivia Drew-Norris."

"I'm dying for a ciggie. When do you suppose we'll be released?" Venetia flicked back her long black hair, which was noticeably not styled in a bouffant, unlike Olivia's and most of the other girls'.

"I've really no idea. I'd look at my watch, except it's such a palaver to take off these kid gloves."

Venetia raised her eyebrows. "Oh, heavens, yes." She looked around the room and indicated the girls. "We all look rather like brides of Dracula, don't we?"

Olivia giggled. She knew that Venetia must be one of the "fast" girls her grandmother had warned her about. And she was intrigued.

"Oh, damn it! I'm going to have one anyway." Venetia pulled a cigarette from her evening bag and lit it. "Gosh, that's better," she said, after exhaling ostentatiously.

Olivia stood next to her nervously, noticing the heads of the nearby girls turn in the direction of the smoke.

Venetia shrugged dramatically. "What will they do? Arrest me and throw me in the Tower? The king himself smokes like a trooper. Want one?" She offered the case to Olivia.

"No, thank you. I don't."

"Don't approve or don't smoke? So," Venetia drawled, "didn't see you at any of the pre-Season tea dances or the lunches. Where do you hail from?"

"India."

"Really, how very . . . exotic." Venetia looked Olivia up and down. "You're awfully pretty, you know. Should catch a good fish this Season, if that's what you want. I'd say you're in the top five."

"I'm not sure that *is* what I want," said Olivia boldly.

Venetia looked at her with new respect. "Really? Then what are you doing here?"

"The same as you, I should think. Doing what our mothers did before us and keeping up the tradition."

"Quite so, quite so." Venetia nodded approvingly. "But I intend to have a lot more fun than my mother was allowed. And, like you, I'm not frantic to get hitched. So my motto is, if one has to go through the process, one might as well enjoy it as much as one can. Don't you agree?"

At that moment, a beautiful dark-haired girl with sparkling eyes and a dress that reeked of Paris couture, rather than the private English dressmakers most of the girls had used, came to join them.

"Honey." The girl wrapped her arms round Venetia. "Please, I'm gasping, be a sweetheart and give me a drag."

"All yours, Kick, why don't you finish it for me?"

Olivia watched as the beautiful American girl grinned. "Thanks. Listen, you going on to the Ritz? There's a party of us leaving in twenty minutes. Daddy said he'd come down later too."

"Perhaps, Kick," said Venetia casually. "I'll see what else is happening."

"Okay, sugar, see you at the next one." Kick raised an eyebrow, turned, and swept a glance over Olivia. "Who's this?" she questioned, sounding more royal than the king and queen.

"Olivia Drew-Norris. And I think," whispered Venetia conspiratorially, "*she* might be one of 'us.' "

"Good-oh." The very English phrase sounded strange coming out of an American mouth. "See you around, Olivia." And she swept off.

Venetia's eyes followed Kick as she crossed the room. All other eyes seemed to follow her too.

"You know who that is, don't you?" Venetia eyed Olivia.

"Yes, I recognize her from the newspapers," said Olivia. "It's Kathleen Kennedy."

"And the uncrowned queen of the Season, darling. Everybody loves her."

"I can understand why," sighed Olivia. "She's terribly beautiful."

"She's like a breath of fresh air, and if she likes you"—Venetia squeezed Olivia's arm—"she'll make sure the Season's fun for you. You must come and meet Mup. That's what I call my mother, I think you'll like her. Are you attending Tip Chandler's dance tomorrow at the Savoy?"

"Yes, I am."

"That should be fun, at least. Geraldo's playing there with his marvelous orchestra. We'll make plans then." Venetia winked as another girl waved to her across the room. "Must fly, darling, got to do the rounds. See you tomorrow."

Olivia arrived home that night feeling, for the first time, a tingle of excitement about the Season to come.

13

Elsie woke up, glad to see the May sun streaming through the thin cotton curtains over her window. It had been such a miserable winter, with the sea frets descending and refusing to budge for most of the day until it was dark again, and the bitterly cold weather. Elsie had been feeling a bit blue recently, what with her being put back to work as a downstairs maid. There had been no house parties at Wharton Park and therefore no ladies to look after. Her "upstairs" wage of £1/1/6 had returned to £1, which was a pound of butter lost for her family every week.

The house was quiet because of his Lordship's spending most of his time in London for meetings about the coming war. And her Ladyship had endured a particularly bad winter, suffering from a series of conditions, including influenza, when the entire household was worried for her life. Her Ladyship had always been a delicate flower, and when she wasn't well, nothing was right in the house.

Elsie sprang out of bed, her ungraceful exit eliciting a moan of displeasure from her younger sister, who shared it with her, and flung back the curtains. This provoked a further groan from the bed as her sister rolled over and put a pillow over her head.

Elsie studied the sun and saw it was probably only just past five. She had an hour before she started work, and she wanted to lay out and prepare her best clothes for later. It was her half day, and this afternoon Bill was taking her to the Regal in Cromer. They were going to see *Goodbye, Mr. Chips* with Robert Donat, and she was to meet him at one thirty in the Quad, where Bill had said he would have a surprise for her.

Elsie couldn't help wondering whether it might be a ring. She had just turned eighteen and they had been courting for over a year now. It was time, she thought. Especially as Bill had recently joined the Territorial Army and was going to the drill hall in Dereham two nights a week to practice, with brooms and spades as his weapons. What if he got called up and sent abroad to fight? Elsie had lost two uncles at the Somme and she knew what war could mean.

If it was down to her, she would marry him as soon as possible, which would mean that they wouldn't have any more arguments if Bill tried to go too far when they were having a kiss and a cuddle in the woods. She just wasn't one of those girls. Bill knew he had to wait until they were married.

She had already eyed the comfortable gardener's cottage, which Bill would inherit from his parents in a few years' time. It was set back from the Quad, in its very own garden, and was twice the size of the one her own family inhabited, with eight of them packed in tight.

She knew her ma would be happy to be rid of her, as long as she still contributed to the family finances, but Bill earned double what she did. And her Ladyship seemed to have a real soft spot for him because Bill had the gift of making all her beautiful flowers grow. Whenever she visited the hothouse and Bill presented her with a new specimen he had grown, her Ladyship would slip him a shilling or two. Over the years, those shillings had mounted up, and Elsie knew that Bill had quite a stash hidden under the floorboards in his bedroom. When they got wed, they could almost certainly afford a proper sit-down "do" in the village hall. She wanted it to be the best wedding the Quad had ever seen.

Realizing she was wasting precious time daydreaming, Elsie pulled open the drawer and laid out her hat, skirt, and blouse on the chair. She had made the skirt herself, out of the navy tablecloth Mrs. Combe, the housekeeper, had thrown out. It was in the new short style—only just skimming her knees, tightly fitted at the waist, and falling in folds over her hips. She was pleased with her handiwork and hoped it would encourage Bill to do the "right" thing.

She flung on her uniform, ran down the stairs, and said good morning to her ma, who was stirring some porridge at the range.

"Want some?" asked her ma.

Elsie shook her head. "I'll be back at lunchtime, but don't forget, I'm gone for the rest of the day." Before her mother could ask for her help with the little ones or to run an errand while she was in Cromer, Elsie opened the door. "Bye, Ma!" She waved gaily and closed it behind her.

As she walked through the orchard, Elsie glanced toward the hothouse to see if Bill had yet arrived—she liked watching him when he didn't know she was there—and saw him through the window, bent over a plant, his face a picture of concentration. She could hardly believe her luck that she had found someone as handsome and as bright as he was.

Her family sometimes accused Elsie of having ideas above her station, but that wasn't the case at all. Both she and Bill were young, fit, and hardworking, and she wanted them to make the most of any opportunities that came their way. She also knew they were the lucky ones, with a safe roof over their heads and a job for life, when she had seen on the Pathé newsreel so many others in the cities were starving on the streets. When they were married and the little ones started to come along, Elsie knew that she would be grateful for the security Wharton Park gave her.

Besides, she worshipped her Ladyship, just as the rest of the household did. Elsie knew her employer was different from many of the grand ladies who ran their estates. Lady Crawford did not rule with fear, as many visiting maids confided . . . no, she ruled with kindness and understanding. Rarely did a member of her household ever let her down or come below her expectations. She would issue instructions in her low, gentle voice and make everyone feel as though they were doing her a favor. If on the rare occasion something was not absolutely as she had instructed it to be, a raise of an eyebrow or a small moue of displeasure on her Ladyship's lips was enough to send the perpetrator into a deep funk for days. Her Ladyship genuinely seemed to care for her staff. Elsie remembered one occasion when she was a little girl, sitting at the table in the big kitchen while her ma helped bake for the annual Wharton Park garden party. Elsie had been struggling with her letters, and her Ladyship had walked into the kitchen, passed a careful eye over the racks of scones and sponges, then, on spying Elsie sitting at the table, crossed toward her.

"It's Elsie, *n'est ce pas?*"

Elsie didn't understand the funny words her Ladyship sometimes used, but she had nodded anyway. "Yes, your Ladyship."

"What are you doing?" Her Ladyship had looked down at the clumsily formed words in Elsie's book.

"I'm copying, your Ladyship, from this, but I don't understand some of the words," Elsie had said truthfully.

"Ah, the English language! It is so complicated. Let me see . . ." And she had sat down next to Elsie and spent the next twenty minutes helping her.

The talk belowstairs was that her Ladyship had wanted more children, but it was not to be. Giving birth to Harry had placed a strain on her health, and there had been no more babies. Elsie knew that she would die if she and Bill couldn't produce a healthy brood of children. Big families were what life was all about, weren't they?

Wharton Park stood straight ahead of her, its many windows glinting in the morning sun. Elsie loved the house; its solidness, and the security that seemed to emanate from its sturdily built walls. Other things would change, she knew that, but the Big House had stood there for almost three centuries and would almost certainly be there for another three.

Walking around the side of Wharton Park to the servants' entrance, Elsie took off her boots to change into her house slippers and entered the kitchen.

"You're early for once, miss," commented Mrs. Combe, who was sitting at the table studying the menu lists. "The kettle's boiling. Sit yourself down with a cup of tea and then it's into the dining room to polish the silver. Her Ladyship wants to see you at ten. Should think it's about this big dance they're holding for Miss Penelope, her Ladyship's niece, next month."

Elsie felt a tingle of excitement. "A dance? I haven't heard about it."

"And why would you, miss?" Mrs. Combe retorted. "Does her Ladyship have to ask permission from you before she makes a plan?"

Elsie knew the housekeeper was teasing her. She was a hard worker and Mrs. Combe had few grounds for complaint. Besides, she was almost family, being second cousin to Elsie's mother.

"Will it be a big do, Mrs. Combe? How many will attend?" asked Elsie eagerly.

"It's Miss Penelope's coming-out dance, so I'm sure her Ladyship will pull out all the stops, seeing as she has no daughter of her own to present. I'll be hearing the details later on this week, but mark my words, young miss, June will be a very busy month at Wharton Park.

And I, for one, will be glad of it." Mrs. Combe sighed in pleasure. "The whole place could do with a party and some cheer."

"You mean the other debutantes will be coming from London for the dance?"

Mrs. Combe nodded. "They'll be staying at houses around the county, but we'll be full to bursting here too."

Elsie's eyes shone as she clasped her hands together in delight. "Oh, Mrs. Combe, can you imagine? All them beautiful young things, right here in this house! I saw them being presented at the palace on the Pathé newsreel when Bill took me to Cromer last month."

"Now don't you be getting carried away with yourself, young miss. You've got work to do, and as you haven't made that cup of tea, I can only assume you didn't want it. So get yourself upstairs to the dining room and them silver spoons, and make sure you're clean and tidy before you go to see her Ladyship in the library at ten sharp."

"Yes, Mrs. Combe," replied Elsie obediently.

At ten o clock, Elsie duly presented herself outside the library door. She knocked and a voice said, *"Entrez."* Elsie did so.

"Please, Elsie," Adrienne indicated the chair opposite her, "sit down. So"—she smiled—"I have been hearing from Mrs. Combe that you have a talent for styling the hair."

Elsie blushed. "Oh, no, your Ladyship, not really. I like the modern styles and I just enjoy copying them."

"C'est parfait!" Adrienne clasped her hands together. "You have heard, no doubt, about the dance we will host for my niece next month?"

"I have, your Ladyship, yes." Elsie nodded.

"There will be many young ladies here, sophisticated girls who will be used to having the best in London, where everything is on their doorstep, including hairdressers. Some will be bringing their own maids, others will not. Would you be willing to offer your services as a hairstylist that night?"

"Oh, your Ladyship!" Elsie was overwhelmed. "As you said, they're used to the best, I'm just an amateur. But I'll try my hardest."

"*Voilà!* Then that is settled. I will say we have a young lady in our employ who is able to help the debutantes with their hair before the dance."

"Oh, yes, your Ladyship, thank you. I'll do my best not to let you down."

"I know you will, Elsie." Adrienne smiled. She stood up slowly and walked to the window, then let out a sigh. "I want this party to be very special." She turned back to Elsie. "It may be the last one this house sees for a very long time, if war comes." She nodded at her. "You may go."

"Thank you, your Ladyship."

Adrienne watched Elsie as she left the room. Elsie was a good girl and she was fond of her. And she approved of her relationship with Bill, the gardener's son. She also wondered if either of them, at the start of their young lives, had any idea of the severity of the storm clouds gathering over them. Christopher said it wouldn't be long now. Hitler's power and support were growing daily. It was only a matter of time, and then . . .

Adrienne had lost her brother in the Great War. She had been lucky to keep her husband. Now, she was looking at the possibility of losing her son. She couldn't bear the thought. She knew how rank and privilege meant nothing on the battlefield in the lottery of who lived and who died. Both her son and the gardener's boy, Bill, would sooner or later be sent off to fight. Then God alone would choose.

It was the British way not to show emotion. Adrienne had tried hard, and sadly failed, to perfect the technique. She was French and had been taught that emotions were better displayed than kept inside. But perhaps, at times such as these, it was easier to distance oneself from what one truly felt. The wish to protect her son was currently overwhelming. She knew Harry was not a natural soldier and was forced to lead a life unsuited to his personality and ability. Now he might die for it.

Adrienne checked herself, knowing she must force maudlin thoughts from her mind before they consumed her. Harry must not see her fear. Her energy must be directed at making her niece's coming-out dance the event of the Season. She decided to take a walk through the park, down to the hothouse, and discuss with Jack and Bill the flowers they would need for the many floral arrangements she had planned.

14

Back in London, Olivia eyed the invitation to Penelope Crawford's coming-out dance with far less excitement than she would have felt a few weeks earlier. In the beginning, she had thought of Harry Crawford nonstop, but recently, as the Season went into full swing, Olivia had been swept along on the wave of the hectic social circuit, or "circus" as Venetia and her other chums aptly termed it.

Olivia wandered, bleary-eyed, through to the dining room to join her grandmother for breakfast, the invitation to Wharton Park clutched in her hand. Lady Vare was on her habitual postfood cup of coffee, wearing her *cache-misère* turban and reading the *Telegraph*. She eyed Olivia's entrance with displeasure.

"Olivia, I do realize your schedule is busy, but it is not acceptable to be late for meals. When I was in your shoes, any tardiness with timekeeping would render me hungry until luncheon."

"Sorry, Grandmother," Olivia said as the maid set some dried-up eggs and bacon in front of her. "I was out last night at the Henderson dance. We went on for late-night supper at Quaglino's." Olivia eyed the food on the plate in front of her and wished she had not had that last Gin and It. Small hammers were knocking nails into her temples, and she looked away from the congealing, cold bacon.

"It was three o'clock when I heard you come in," Lady Vare reprimanded sternly. "I hope, Olivia, you are heeding what I said to you at the beginning of the Season, and not being tempted to join the wrong crowd."

"Oh, no, Grandmother," Olivia lied. "I'm sure you'd approve of the people I was with last night. John Cavendish, Marquess of Hartington, was there, with his younger brother, Andrew." Olivia knew this would impress her grandmother, as John Cavendish was the heir to the Devonshire estate, which included Chatsworth House. She did not, however, add how they had been so raucous that the maître d' had asked them to leave, or how, walking away from the restaurant giggling like naughty schoolchildren, they had continued the party at someone's house in Mayfair.

"And is there any young beau so far who has shown particular interest in you?" Lady Vare asked.

In truth, a succession of what her grandmother would term "eligible" squires had been eager to dance with Olivia, to invite her to dine in their party, and ask her to accompany them to whichever nightclub everyone was going to that evening after the dance. Yet, as her grandmother had suggested, things were different now. Her newfound circle included many young men, but she knew them as friends, not prospective husbands. With the specter of war looming, many of them recognized that if and when the day came, their lives as they knew them would be over. Before they were packed off to possible death, they wanted to live every day as if it were their last.

This was not, however, the answer to give to her grandmother.

"Yes, there are a couple of young men who seem to be . . . interested," Olivia said as she waved away her untouched plate. The maid cleared it and provided her with some much-needed coffee.

"And may I inquire who?"

"Oh," replied Olivia airily, "Angus MacGeorge—he owns half of Scotland and is awfully good fun—and Richard Ingatestone, whose father is something huge in the navy and—"

"Well," Lady Vare interjected, "perhaps it would be nice if you brought one of these young men to tea here, Olivia, so that I could meet them."

"I'll ask them, Grandmother, but everything is so busy just now, and people are literally booked up weeks in advance." Olivia raised her invitation. "There's a dance next month at Wharton Park for Penelope Crawford. They have offered me a room for the night at the house."

"I used to find country dances such a bore, myself. Are you sure it's worth the trouble, Olivia, dear? Penelope Crawford is, after all, only borrowing her uncle's house for the occasion. Her own family doesn't have tuppence to rub together. Charles, her father, was killed in a trench during the Great War. I doubt it will be well attended."

Olivia sipped her coffee. "As a matter of fact, Grandmother, I went with Mummy and Daddy to Wharton Park just after Christmas. I rather liked it, so may I say yes?"

"As long as it interferes with nothing in town and you provide the guest list for me to peruse, then, yes, you may go." Lady Vare stood up from the table, unhooked her walking stick from the edge of it, then asked, "Are you in for luncheon?"

"No, I have an engagement at the Berkeley, and then I must stop off afterward to collect the gown I tore last week. The dressmaker hopes to have it mended by this afternoon, and I'd like to wear it to-night."

Her grandmother nodded, pacified. "Then I will see you at break-fast tomorrow morning," she said as she left the room. "On time, if you please."

"Yes, Grandmother, of course," Olivia called after her. Relieved, she sank her head into her hands and massaged her temples, trying to stem her headache.

At first she had thought that not having her mother with her to take her through the Season was a disadvantage. But her grandmoth-er's being too old and too tired to chaperone her had turned out to be an absolute blessing. It meant she'd had complete freedom to do as she wished, and with whom she wished. Although the set she was mixing with would have been seen as unsuitable by her grandmother, Olivia was having the time of her life.

Venetia had taken Olivia under her wing. They had become firm friends, and Venetia had introduced her to the more interesting el-ement of that year's Season. Despite having a reputation for being "fast," the girls and young men Olivia knew were cultured, intelligent, and politically aware. Most of them, like her, were making their way through the Season because they had to. But, rather than spending their luncheons and late-night suppers discussing the colors of their gowns for the following night's dance, the girls often mused on what they wanted to do with their lives. Which didn't necessarily involve immediate marriage or children, but perhaps university or, if the war interfered, playing an active role in that.

Olivia's favorite place in London was Venetia's town house in Chester Square. It was always full of unusual people, culled from the bohemian intelligentsia set to which Venetia's parents belonged.

Ferdinand Burroughs, Venetia's father, was a well-known avant-garde painter, with whom Venetia's mother, Christina, a "lady" by birth and from one of the grandest families in the land, had fallen in love and subsequently married under a cloud. Christina Burroughs was everything Olivia would have liked her *own* mother to be: she had jet black hair to her waist—though Olivia thought it was almost certainly dyed—wore dramatic eye makeup, and smoked cigarettes through a jade holder.

Venetia had told Olivia how, when her mother had told her family she was going to marry the penniless young artist, they had refused even to countenance it. So Christina had run away to London to be with Ferdinand and they had lived virtually penniless for years, until Ferdinand's paintings started to sell. The town house in Chester Square had been left to Christina by a great-aunt, the one member of her family who seemed to have some sympathy for her plight. So at least, eventually, the young couple had gained a roof over their heads. But there had been no money to spend on the interior, so the curtains were moldering, the furniture gleaned from thrift shops, and due to the absence of staff, the whole place needed a jolly good clean with a vatful of disinfectant.

"Pup's awfully rich now, you know. His paintings sell for hundreds and they could afford to buy whatever they wanted," Venetia had told Olivia. "But they like the house just as it is. And so do I," she had added defensively.

Venetia was doing the Season specifically to upset her mother's family, who were aghast that the daughter of a common painter could be presented at court.

"But because *I* was presented, there's nothing they can do to stop me, darling," Christina had tittered one day over a martini with the girls before they went out to a dance. "Letty, my sister, is horrified—of course, her daughter, the ghastly Deborah, is coming out this Season too. I shall never forget the look on Letty's face when she saw me at Queen Charlotte's ball. I thought she might faint in horror." Christina giggled, ruffling Venetia's hair affectionately. "And, of course, to make matters worse, my daughter is beautiful, whereas hers is spotty, overweight, and downright stupid."

Olivia had often thought that Venetia was more mother to Christina than Christina was to her. Perhaps, coming from such an eccentric background, Venetia had been forced to develop a degree of wisdom and practicality that belied her years. She was an intriguing mix of bohemianism and common sense, and Olivia adored her.

Venetia would casually drop in the names of luminaries such as Virginia Woolf, who—accompanied by Vita Sackville-West, her lover—had often come by for tea when Venetia had been a child. The glamour of the Bloomsbury set and the Burroughses' attachment to it fascinated Olivia. Even though it had mainly dispersed now, radical thoughts still held fast in the household, and Venetia was passionate about women's rights and the struggle for equality. She had already determined that she would not be taking her husband's name when and if she married.

For Olivia, the Season had so far encompassed the best of both worlds: terrific fun, yet with a set of like-minded new friends. Olivia's inquiring mind had been stimulated and opened, and ironically, she was now dreading the Season coming to an end, for then she had to make some decisions about her future.

Returning to her parents' house in Surrey, then sitting and waiting to be plucked from the shelf by a suitable husband, was just not an option. She would start to receive a small income on her twenty-first birthday, but for the next two and a half years she was financially reliant on her parents.

Unless she found herself a job . . .

Olivia stood up from the dining-room table and made her way upstairs to her rooms. She needed to get dressed as she was going to Venetia's house for lunch.

Ferdinand Burroughs, Venetia's father, had returned home only yesterday from Germany, where he had been sketching images of the mounting power of the Third Reich for a series of paintings he wanted to complete. Having only heard about Ferdinand through the eyes of his adoring daughter, Olivia was eager to meet the man himself. And perhaps hear firsthand his experience of the threat posed by the Nazis. Pinning on her hat and donning her gloves, she gathered up her handbag and set off for Chester Square.

When Venetia greeted her, her face was pale and her brow furrowed with anxiety.

"What's up?" asked Olivia as she followed Venetia through the hall and into the kitchen, which was the room the family used to entertain in the summer as it fed out onto the delightful walled garden at the rear of the house.

"Gin?" asked Venetia.

Olivia looked at her watch; it was only eleven thirty. She shook her head. "Not for me, thank you, darling, not after last night, anyway."

"I wouldn't usually, but Pup came home last night and he's so awfully distressed." Venetia poured herself a healthy measure of gin and took a large slug. "He was talking to Mup mostly, but from what I heard, he says that all the ghastly things that are happening in Germany are not being reported properly in any of the newspapers here. And they are beastly, just beastly!" Venetia's eyes filled with tears. "Pup actually witnessed a synagogue just outside Munich being set on fire by a group of Nazi youths. Oh, Olivia, it seems Herr Hitler wants to wipe the Jews off the face of the earth!"

"Surely, that can't be true?" Olivia moved across to Venetia and put her arms round her.

"It is!" Venetia sobbed on Olivia's shoulder. "Mup's upstairs with him now. He looks . . . broken. And he was in such terrible danger. And we didn't realize it!"

"Well, darling, at least he's home now and safe."

"Thank goodness," agreed Venetia, wiping her eyes. "The things he's seen . . . he said he could never bring himself to paint them. It was so awfully violent, so full of hatred. Did you know that it's illegal for an Aryan and a Jew to make love, let alone get married? And that thousands of synagogues have been burnt to the ground in the past eighteen months? They can't own a radio and their children are forbidden to attend schools where there are Aryan children."

Olivia listened in shocked silence. Eventually she said, "But why doesn't the world know of this?"

Venetia shook her head. "I have no idea and neither does Pup. He said he's going to do what he can to spread the word among his influential political friends." She grasped Olivia's arm. "Oh, I know we keep trying to forget, but this is real and it's going to happen."

15

Harry Crawford woke up, enormously grateful to be home. At least, unlike many of his fellow officers, who had no idea what their fate might hold in the next few months, his was assured. He was to take charge of training a group of local new recruits to the Fifth Royal Norfolks. This would mean that, for the next few weeks at least, he could enjoy high summer in his own home and in his own bed.

He had been ribbed for what was considered a jammy number by his fellow officers, some of whom were being posted to far less salubrious locations—many asked whether his father had had a proverbial word in the right ear, but Harry doubted it. With Germany marching into Czechoslovakia, his father's thoughts were hardly likely to be focused on his son's creature comforts.

Harry heaved up the sash window, leaned out, and breathed in the fresh, sweet smell of the jasmine his mother had planted in great swathes along the terrace, enjoying a rare moment of peace. He would have preferred his cousin Penelope's dance not to fall on his first day home—he would have to do his bit and squire horse-faced girls around the dance floor later—but it was good to see the old place being brought to life again. And he knew how much the event meant to his mother.

When Harry arrived downstairs, the house was a flurry of activity. Extra staff had been brought up from the village to help with the preparation. Furniture was being carted across the hall, and chairs and tables were being moved into the ballroom to accommodate 150 guests for dinner. After the meal, the guests would be herded into the drawing room or onto the terrace if the night was warm, while the tables and chairs were removed from the ballroom and the band set up, so that the dancing could begin.

Harry picked his way through the chaos and walked toward the ballroom, glad that, in answer to his mother's prayers, the unpredictable English weather seemed set fair for the rest of the day. Jack and his son, Bill, appeared on the terrace, wheeling wheelbarrows piled high with colorful flowers.

"Need some help, chaps?"

"Thanks, Master Harry, but we can manage. I knows you only came home yesterday—you take it easy, young sir," said Jack, doffing his cap.

Harry ignored him and began unloading the flowers onto the terrace. "Hear you're signed up for the Fifth Norfolks, Bill?"

"Yes, Master Harry, I am, sir."

"Well, it looks as if we might be getting to know each other a lot better. I've been put in charge of bringing you all up to scratch. I will be seeing you at the Drill Hall in Dereham on Monday. It will be good to know a familiar face, and you can introduce me to all the other fellows."

Bill gave him a broad smile. "And we'll all be glad to have you, sir."

Jack turned his wheelbarrow around. "Bill, you go and tell her Ladyship the flowers are here and I'm off to collect the rest. She'll want to work out where they'll all look best. You know how her Ladyship is particular about her flowers." Jack winked at Harry. "Thanks for your help, sir. I'll be seeing you later, I'm sure."

Olivia and Venetia had left London at ten o'clock that morning. Venetia had borrowed her parents' Ford, promising Olivia she was a competent driver. This had not proved to be the case. Olivia had spent the past five hours in fear for her life, as Venetia veered to the other side of the road, stalled, then put the car into the wrong gear, narrowly missing a fatal collision on endless occasions.

Olivia's skills as a map reader had been little better than Venetia's driving. They had taken numerous wrong turns, which had engendered more bad maneuvers by Venetia. Instead of the four-and-a-half-hour journey they had imagined, they were still at least an hour from Wharton Park and would not be there in time for afternoon tea.

At least the countryside had recently become far prettier, and Olivia was fairly certain they were on the right road.

"Are you sure we're not going to simply plunge off the side of this island into the North Sea?" questioned Venetia. "I can't get over how long this journey's taken, and I'm absolutely famished. Pup always says he's allergic to fresh air. I don't think he's left the city since the day I was born. I think I might follow in his footsteps," she added petulantly.

Olivia raised her eyebrows and ignored the comment. Venetia was in a bait, but Olivia was sure that, once she saw Wharton Park, her friend would feel that the journey had been worthwhile.

One and a half hours later, they turned into the long drive that led to Wharton Park. The sun was hanging soft in the sky, casting a glow over the park.

Venetia was still complaining next to her about her empty stomach, her stiff back, and her sore foot from so much gear-changing. Olivia wound down the window and breathed in the smell of the warm, balmy evening to come.

"There's the house," she said as it came into view. "Don't you think it's absolutely beautiful?" she added dreamily.

Venetia, past making pleasantries and just to be obtuse, said, "Has the lightbulb made it here yet?"

"Don't be facetious, Venetia, of course it has! Besides, it's the twenty-first of June, the longest day of the year. So we'd hardly need light even if it hadn't. Anyway," Olivia said as Venetia brought the car to a bumpy halt in front of the house, "if you want to spend the weekend in a funk, go ahead. I think it's a heavenly place. And I'm all set to enjoy it, even if you're not."

At that moment, the front door opened and a young man she vaguely recognized came running down the steps toward them.

"Hello, Miss Drew-Norris," the young man said, as she stepped out of the car and smoothed down her creased dress. "Good to see you back at Wharton Park again."

Olivia recognized him as Bill, the gardener's son, whom she had met briefly in the hothouse in January.

"How are the flowers?" she asked, smiling at him. "My frangipani is looking awfully pretty on my windowsill in London."

"They're doing well, Miss Drew-Norris. Thank you for asking."

"I can't wait to see the gardens," Olivia breathed. "Harry said they were magnificent in high summer."

"That they are, and you've picked exactly the right moment to see them; everything's still fresh and budded. By the time mid-July is here, it all starts to look tired and parched. Miss Drew-Norris, do you have anything to be taken into the house from the car? I'll carry it in for you, then if I may have the keys to your car, I'll take it off and park it for you."

"It's my car, actually." Venetia sidled around it and dangled the keys in front of Bill. She smiled at him seductively. "Take care with it, won't you?"

"Course I will, miss," said Bill, opening the trunk and removing the two small suitcases.

As he carried them up the steps and inside the house, Venetia said, "Now that's what I call scenery. He's heavenly, who is he?"

"Will you please behave yourself?" admonished Olivia, but she was smiling. "He's the gardener's boy. You've been reading too much *Lady Chatterley*. Now come on, I'm gasping for a cup of tea."

At seven o'clock, Adrienne was standing on the terrace, a glass of champagne in her hand. The night was as perfect as she could possibly have hoped. Only on nights like this did Wharton Park rival the beauty of her childhood home in Provence. The softness of an English country evening, when land and sky seemed to melt into each other, the smell of freshly mown grass, mingling with the scent of roses, had its own special magic.

Inside the house, everything was ready. The ballroom behind her looked exquisite, the fifteen tables laid with crisp white linen, antique crystal glassware, and, in the center of each, a vase containing fresh blooms from the hothouse.

Adrienne loved moments such as this. Everything was finished, yet nothing had begun, and one was filled with optimism that it would live up to expectation.

"Mother, you look ravishing." Harry was behind her, looking hopelessly handsome in evening dress.

"*Merci, mon chéri.* I am taking just a few seconds to enjoy this perfect evening."

Harry lit a cigarette and gazed across the magnificent gardens. "It's so very still, calm . . . the lull before the storm." He smiled.

Adrienne turned to him, putting her hand gently on his shoulder. "I have hardly seen you since you arrived home. How are you, my darling?"

Harry nodded. "I'm well, Mother."

"And happy?" she asked, although she knew the answer.

"I am . . . accepting that I'm a mere cog in the wheel and don't control the universe. What will be, will be," he sighed, "and one must simply get on with it."

"My Harry," Adrienne sighed. "If only the world could be a different place, but it cannot. *Mon Dieu!*" Adrienne clapped a hand to her mouth. "I am becoming maudlin and I must stop this instant. I am so very fortunate to have you here, and we will enjoy the time we have together."

"No fear!" He smiled down at her, thinking how much he loved her.

"Now, your cousin Hugo was unable to attend tonight. He too is training with his battalion, in Wales. So, rather than your father leading poor Penelope in her first dance, it must be you, Harry. I went up to see her in her gown a few minutes ago." Adrienne shrugged elegantly. "Even though it is difficult to turn a sow's ear into a silk purse, between my choice of the dress and Elsie styling her hair, we have at least made her presentable."

"Then you must really be a miracle worker, Mother," he replied, thinking of his plain, dumpy cousin.

"Perhaps she will be a late bloomer." Adrienne reached for his hand and squeezed it. "I must go, *chéri*, and search out your father. Last time I saw him he was upstairs, deciding on his choice of dress shirts. He can hardly believe his luck that all the young debutantes have come to his house. He is very excited." Adrienne raised an eyebrow. "We will let him have his little game, *n'est ce pas*?"

Harry watched her cross the terrace. She looked radiant tonight, in a saffron-colored silk gown that accentuated her perfect, petite physique. Her dark hair was styled into a chignon, and large diamond-drop earrings emphasized her swanlike neck. Harry thought back to their conversation and wondered whether it was a hindrance to have such a beautiful mother. It was difficult to imagine any girl matching up to her. He pondered sometimes whether that accounted for his lack of interest in women. The magical feeling that other men would describe as "love," or some of his fellow officers described on a more base, physical level, had not happened to him yet.

Olivia Drew-Norris, the girl from India he'd met a few months ago, had been the nearest to his idea of an attractive woman. She was here tonight, he knew, and perhaps he'd make an effort to dance with her.

He heard the faint sound of tires crunching on gravel at the front of the house, indicating the first guest had arrived. His moment of contemplation at an end, Harry walked back inside the house to do his duty.

16

"Golly, Olivia! You look rather marvelous tonight!" Venetia had walked into Olivia's bedroom to see if she was ready to go downstairs. "Why, you're positively glowing! Is that a new gown? The pink suits your complexion perfectly. And I absolutely adore the rosebuds in your hair. Who did it for you?"

"Elsie, the maid. She's a complete sweetheart. And awfully good, to boot. Would you like her to style yours?"

Venetia flicked her thick mane of unbound black hair over her shoulder and shook her head. "No fear, darling, the Pretty Princess look just isn't me. How do you like *my* dress?"

Intent on flouting convention again, Venetia was dressed in a figure-hugging sheath of gold that accentuated her ample cleavage. She looked arresting, but rather out of place in the setting of an English country house.

"Breathtaking," said Olivia. "It's so very . . . *you*."

"I found it in Mup's wardrobe. And I'm going to wear it for the rest of the Season." Venetia giggled. "You know me, darling, forever tripping over acres of net and tulle while I'm dancing and stepping on the poor chaps' toes." She indicated the door. "Shall we?"

"Rather!" Olivia smiled.

The two girls linked arms, walked companionably across the wide landing and down the grand main staircase, which led directly into the entrance hall, now buzzing with voices.

Venetia surveyed the crowd beneath her. "Golly! Must have been a fearfully dull night in London. Everyone's here."

Adrienne spotted them and glided toward them. "Olivia, why, *ma chérie*, you look truly beautiful! You are surely *la belle de la soirée*!"

"Thank you, Adrienne." Olivia blushed in embarrassment. As Venetia was standing by her side, Olivia quickly introduced her. "This is my friend, Venetia Burroughs."

Adrienne took in the gold sheath dress and Venetia's unstyled hair. She smiled widely. "And you, you are a beauty too. I admire people who wish to shock, and that is what you wish to do, *n'est ce pas*?" She kissed Venetia on both cheeks. "*Bienvenu, chérie*, and enjoy the evening."

"Gosh!" murmured Venetia as they made their way out onto the terrace, where everyone was gathering in the warm evening air. "She rather got me in one, didn't she? As she would say, *elle est formidable*!"

"Adrienne has an unerring habit of knowing instantly exactly who one is," said Olivia, taking two glasses of champagne from a passing tray. "Personally, I think she's utterly sweet and very beautiful."

"She's that, for certain," agreed Venetia, as a young man in a red waistcoat wound his arms round her. "Teddy, you've dug yourself out of the bar at the Ritz to come here? I'm overwhelmed!"

"My dear Venetia," the young man replied, as his hands wandered freely over her body, "may I say you look absolutely ravishing in that dress. Hello, Olivia," he offered, "you're looking rather topping yourself."

"Thank you." Olivia nodded as Teddy turned away to talk to Venetia and steal covert glances at her cleavage.

Olivia walked across the terrace and stood by the balustrade overlooking the park. As Harry had promised her, the gardens in high summer were magnificent.

"Miss Drew-Norris! Olivia." A familiar voice beside her made her turn round. "May I say, you look like a dream."

"Hello, Harry." Olivia could feel the heat rising in her cheeks. Although she had been convinced the mental image of him she had carried with her for the past few months was accurate, he was actually far more handsome in the flesh.

"So, how has the Season been?"

"Actually, it's been far more fun than I thought it would be. And I've made some heavenly new chums."

"Good-oh. And have you settled down in England now? You certainly look happier than the last time I saw you."

"Yes, I rather think I have. And on nights like this"—she indicated the park in front of her—"it would be hard to refute its charms."

"Agreed." Harry nodded. "And have you any notion of what happens next for you, once the Season's finished?"

"No. Not yet. Anyway, let's not think about that tonight. I want to enjoy being back at Wharton Park and this simply divine evening. How are you, Harry?"

"At present, I have the whole summer at home and I intend to make the most of it." He smiled at her. "It's awfully good to see you, Olivia, it really is."

"Olivia, darling, how are you?"

A man Harry did not know appeared beside them. He took the cue to leave. "If you'll excuse me, Olivia, I must do my duty and circulate. I can see there are certain young ladies, including my cousin, who seem to be doing an accurate impression of a wallflower." Harry indicated a plump girl standing alone farther along the terrace. "I shall no doubt see you later."

He ambled off to save Penelope from wilting, but before he reached her, he was struck on the shoulder by a familiar figure.

"Harry! My dear chap! How are you?"

"Sebastian!" Harry shook his old friend's hand heartily. "Long time, no see. Fourth of June at Eton a couple of years back, wasn't it?"

"I rather think it was!" Sebastian removed his thick-lensed, round glasses and wiped them. "Rather gathered you might be here tonight. How's tricks? Sandhurst as ghastly as you thought it would be?"

"Worse!" joked Harry, enjoying that Sebastian was one of the only chaps he could make that comment to. They had met at Eton, and the bookish, asthmatic, and chronically shortsighted Sebastian had clung to the musical and painfully shy young man Harry had been. They had both suffered their share of bullying and, though they had little in common, had found mutual ground through their positions as outsiders. "Over, thank heavens. Now there's simply the war and getting my leg shot off to look forward to," Harry added grimly.

"Well, that at least is one fate from which I've been saved." Sebastian returned his glasses to his nose. "No one in their right mind would put me in charge of a shooter! Couldn't see where the bally thing was pointing to begin with!"

"I wouldn't want you in my battalion, old chap, but then I'm not sure that I'd want me either, to be honest." Harry smiled, removing a couple of glasses of champagne from a tray and handing one to Sebastian. "So, what are you doing with yourself these days?"

"Working for my pater in his trading company. I've been learning the ropes in the London office, and I'm about to be shipped off to run things in the head office in Bangkok. Papa is rather eager to come home after twenty years of being an expat. Even if he is arriving to face the uncertainty that gathers daily on these shores."

"I'll say," muttered Harry grimly.

"The most contact I'll have with the war, *if* it heads that way, is organizing some of our ships to carry troops and supplies out to the Far East. Rather looking forward to it, actually—they say the Siamese girls are just the ticket!"

"Sounds as if you're leaving at the perfect time," Harry commented enviously. "Getting out of the bloody great mess that is Europe. Can't see it spreading to where you're heading."

"No, but one never knows, does one? One feels rather guilty, not being able to make a tangible contribution to one's country, but perhaps it's a small compensation for being given such a duff pair of eyeballs and a dicky chest."

Harry touched Sebastian's shoulder briefly, noticing Penelope still standing alone. "Must dash, old chap, drop me a line with your forwarding address."

"Will do. Awfully good to see you, Harry," said Sebastian fondly. "Try and stay alive if the worst happens, won't you? I'll have some of those Siamese girls lined up for you!"

Over dinner, Olivia enjoyed the company of her high-spirited table, mostly containing people she knew from London. To her left sat Angus, the Scottish laird who seemed to be keen on her, and to her right was Archie, Viscount Manners. Talk among some friends in London was that Archie "batted for the other side." Olivia was not experienced enough to tell.

After dinner, they were ushered out while the room was cleared of tables. Olivia stood on the terrace with Archie, smoking a rare Abdulla cigarette with him companionably.

Archie looked over the park, which was bathed in the half glow of night, and sighed. "I can hardly stand its beauty. As Blake so aptly describes, one knows it's leaving as soon as it arrives."

The band struck up and people made their way back into the ballroom.

"I hope you won't mind awfully if I don't ask you to dance. I have two quite ghastly left feet and don't wish to maim you, Olivia," confessed Archie. "Please, feel free to find an alternative squire."

"I'm perfectly happy standing here, really."

"Well, it shan't be the case for long. I can see a beau approaching us already."

Sure enough, Harry was crossing the terrace toward them. He stopped short of them, suddenly uncomfortable. "I'm not disturbing you two, am I?"

"Not at all," said Olivia a little too eagerly. "Please, come and meet Archie. Archie, this is Harry Crawford, son of the house."

The two men stared at each other for a while, before Harry extended his hand toward him. "Archie, a pleasure to meet you."

"And you, Harry." Archie smiled suddenly for the first time that evening.

Eventually, Olivia broke the silence that had descended. "Archie and I had such a jolly time at dinner, discussing the great romantic poets. And, of course, Archie is a poet himself."

"You write poetry?" Harry asked.

"I do. For myself, of course. I wouldn't wish to subject any other poor soul to it. It's rather maudlin, I fear."

"Sounds right up my street." Harry grinned. "I'm a fan of Rupert Brooke, myself."

Archie's face brightened. "What a coincidence! So am I. I've been boring poor Olivia half to death with him over dinner." Archie closed his eyes and began to quote:

Tenderly, day that I have loved, I close your eyes,
And smooth your quiet brow, and fold your thin dead hands.
The grey veils of the half-light deepen; colour dies.
I bear you, a light burden, to the shrouded sands . . .

Harry took up the words:

Where lies your waiting boat, by wreaths of the sea's making
Mist-garlanded, with all grey weeds of the water crowned.

They smiled at each other, acknowledging the pleasure of a passion shared.

"One day, I mean to go to Skyros to see his grave for myself," offered Archie.

"I was lucky enough to visit the Old Vicarage at Grantchester. Marvelous to see the very house where Brooke spent his boyhood," replied Harry.

Olivia listened as they talked animatedly, feeling like a spare part. Luckily, Venetia arrived by her side. Olivia could see she was a little the worse for wear.

"Hello, my darling," she said, looking Harry up and down with a glint in her eye. "Who's this?"

Harry was still deep in conversation with Archie, so Olivia whispered, "Harry, the chap I told you about."

Venetia nodded approvingly. "He's . . . dreamy! And if you don't want him," she giggled, "then I'll have him. Harry"—she broke into the conversation—"I'm Venetia Burroughs, Olivia's closest chum, and I've heard all about you." She reached up and kissed him on both cheeks. "I feel as if I know you already."

Olivia could have died on the spot from embarrassment.

Harry looked rather taken aback by the exuberant greeting, but recovered his manners to say, "Venetia, it's my pleasure to meet you."

"You too, Harry. I shall be expecting a dance later. And talking of dancing, I vote we all pile in. It's getting chilly out here."

"Good idea." Harry smiled down fondly at Olivia. "I came over to ask you to dance. May I have the pleasure?" He extended his arm to Olivia, who took it, blushing with pleasure.

He looked at Archie. "We must talk some more another time."

"Perhaps, before I leave."

"I do hope so," replied Harry.

Then, with Olivia on his arm, he turned and walked into the ballroom.

As Olivia partnered Harry on the dance floor again and again, she thought back to London and how many times she had dreamed of being held in his arms. And here she was with him at Wharton Park, the place she had decided she loved best in the whole of England, on a beautiful midsummer's night.

Later, Harry led her outside for some fresh air.

"Well," he said, lighting his cigarette, "I think one could say that the evening has been an unqualified success, don't you?"

Olivia was gazing up at the stars in the clear night sky. "Perfect," she murmured contentedly.

"And Mother looks happier than I've seen her for a long time," added Harry. "Listen, the band is playing my favorite Cole Porter song, 'Begin the Beguine.' " Harry started to hum it under his breath. "One last dance, Miss Drew-Norris?" he asked, as he put his arm round her waist.

"If you insist, Captain Crawford."

They swayed to the music together, Olivia resting her head against Harry's chest and giving herself up to the moment.

"Olivia, I've loved dancing with you this evening. Thank you." Then Harry reached down and kissed her on the lips.

Adrienne, who had herself stepped outside farther along the terrace to gaze at the night sky, watched them and allowed herself a smile.

17

Olivia headed back to London the following day, wrapped in a gossamer shroud of happiness. Finally she understood what the "magic" was all about. She had confided in Venetia on the journey back to London. Venetia had snorted derisorily when Olivia had indicated that Harry was "the one."

"Darling, really! How can you possibly know that? He's the first boy you've even kissed. You are absolutely mad!"

Olivia shook her head defiantly. "No. I'm not. I know how I feel, and sometimes it just happens that way. Look at your mother and father, they were eighteen and nineteen when they met and fell in love."

"Touché, but that was then and this is now. And besides, Olivia, you've always promised me you didn't want to marry until you were a lot older. You haven't even done the 'thing' yet," added Venetia. "How can you 'know' without doing that?"

Olivia knew Venetia *had* done the "thing." And not just with one chap either. And hadn't seemed to give it a second thought. This was one area where their thoughts differed and could not be reconciled. Venetia's pronouncement that it was "her" body and she could use it as she wished without guilt was not an attitude Olivia shared. Whether it was upbringing or her nature, she felt strongly that her virgin state should remain intact until she married the man she found to love.

"It doesn't matter to me," Olivia answered feebly. "That's secondary."

"Golly, Olivia! I thought in the last few months I'd managed to instill some feminism into you. And here you are, imagining the wedding already. And don't tell me you're not"—Venetia wagged her finger as the car veered dangerously into the center of the road—"because I jolly well know you are."

• • •

After two weeks of floating on air, and being detached from the final round of parties and other events that saw the Season coming to a close, before everyone left London like a swarm of flies to head for the warmer climes of the Riviera, Olivia had still heard nothing from Harry.

After the euphoria came the uncertainty and the pain. Olivia sank into a black mood as she contemplated that Venetia may have been correct in her assessment and, for Harry, the kiss had meant nothing more than a pleasant end to the evening.

She had been invited, along with Venetia, to spend a month at a villa in Saint-Raphaël, owned by the parents of Angus, the Scottish laird. She knew Angus was awfully fond of her and he had made his intentions clear. Joining him at his family home would mean, on some level, an acceptance of his affection.

"Well, I'm going along, whether or not you come," Venetia had declared. "The atmosphere here is quite dreadful. Pup's locked away in his studio, and Mup is sulking because Pup has refused to let anyone come to the house. And that's before I've stepped out of the back door and tripped over the beastly air-raid shelter spoiling our beautiful garden."

The two of them were walking toward the Ritz, having just left Dudley House in Park Lane after Kick Kennedy's dance.

"It's hardly fair though, is it, Venetia?" insisted Olivia. "Angus is delightful, but I don't want him to think that I like him in *that* way."

"Darling, all's fair in love and war"—Venetia eyed her—"and presently, anything goes. Besides, beautiful girls were born to break some hearts along the way. Angus's villa is said to be utterly fabulous. And what will you do if you don't come? Spend the entire summer mooning in a funk over lover boy and waiting for the Germans to drop their bombs?" They turned off the main road to walk down to the side door of the Ritz. "For goodness' sake, do pull yourself together and have some fun while you can."

As Venetia began to climb the steps into the Ritz, Olivia glanced to her left and saw a familiar figure emerging from a doorway and walking swiftly down the street away from her. She grasped Venetia's shoulder, her heart pounding.

"I think I've just seen him."

"Seen who?"

"Harry, of course."

Venetia stopped at the top of the stairs and sighed heavily. "Olivia, my dear, I do believe you are going queer in the head. What would Harry be doing in London?"

"I'm sure it was him," she said determinedly.

Venetia grabbed her by the arm. "Obviously too many martinis at Kick's dance. Now come on, darling, buck up. You're starting to become a bore."

Three further days of agony later, Olivia awoke from a restless sleep and realized that Venetia was almost certainly right about Harry. Today she would accept Angus's invitation, go to France, and nurse her broken heart. At least the weather would be warm, it would be good to get out of London, and as the alternative was returning to Surrey, she supposed it was the best thing to do. She would telephone Angus today and tell him that she would join his house party in Saint-Raphaël.

Just as she was on her way out to visit Venetia and make arrangements for the journey to France, the telephone rang.

"Operator here, you have a call from Cromer 6521, may I put you through?"

"Yes, thank you," she replied. "Hello, Olivia Drew-Norris speaking."

"Olivia! It is Adrienne Crawford here, from Wharton Park."

"Adrienne, how delightful to hear from you. Is everything all right?"

"Of course, everything is perfect. Except for the fact I am a little lonely and I was wondering if you were busy for the month of August. If you are not, I thought that perhaps you could come and spend some of it here with me. We could walk in the gardens together and enjoy this glorious summer weather we have. I know Harry would love to see you. He is working so hard, poor boy, training his unrehearsed battalion for the opening night."

Olivia sat down abruptly in the chair next to the telephone.

"I . . ." She knew she had to make a quick decision. The truth was, there was no decision to be made. "I would love to join you, Adrienne. It's awfully kind of you to ask me."

"*C'est parfait!* Then that is settled. How soon can you come?"

"I have arranged to visit my parents in Surrey, but I could be with you by the beginning of next week. Does that suit?"

"Perfectly. I will send our chauffeur to fetch you from Surrey if that would be helpful. The train is so tiresome."

"Thank you."

"Well, I look forward so much to seeing you next week, Olivia. And it is very kind of you to agree to keep me company."

"Not at all. Wharton Park is my favorite place on earth," Olivia answered truthfully. "Good-bye."

"À bientôt, chérie."

Olivia put the receiver down and held her hands up to her cheeks to cool them. She could feel the adrenaline coursing round her body and upping her heart rate.

A whole month at Wharton Park . . . with Harry.

She closed the front door behind her and virtually skipped all the way to Venetia's house.

Venetia did not seem as excited about the news as Olivia hoped she might be. Olivia put this down to Venetia's own selfishness; and that she would now be journeying to France alone.

"You say it was his mother who telephoned you?" sniffed Venetia. "Do you think he's a mummy's boy? Sounds pretty queer to me."

Olivia was not to be brought down. "Surely it would be the lady of the house who'd invite me, in terms of protocol? And besides, I love Adrienne and I love Wharton Park." She hugged herself inwardly at the thought of it.

"You're mad, giving up the Riviera for some drafty mausoleum in the middle of nowhere," sighed Venetia. "But I'll think of you as I'm taking dips in the Med and drinking cocktails in the sunshine."

And I won't be jealous at all, thought Olivia happily.

The following day, Olivia packed up all her belongings, thanked her grandmother, and left for her parents' house in Surrey.

The two nights she spent there were difficult and uncomfortable. Her parents were still the same as they had always been, yet Olivia was so different. It was almost as if she had grown out of them in the past few months. Long silences lingered over the dinner table as Olivia struggled to find subjects they had in common. Even if she managed it, they seemed to disagree with her opinion on everything.

On the night before she left for Wharton Park, she sat with her mother in the drawing room, drinking coffee after dinner.

"So"—her mother concentrated on her knitting as she spoke—"am I to presume there is an affection between you and Harry Crawford?"

"He's an awfully nice chap, yes. But he's busy training his battalion, so I doubt I'll see much of him when I'm there."

"You haven't answered my question, Olivia." Her mother looked up from her knitting.

Olivia spoke guardedly. "We get on very well, Mother."

Her mother smiled. "When I met him in January, he seemed like a good chap. I just want to say that your father and I would approve."

"Mother!" Olivia blushed at the way things were being assumed, partly out of embarrassment, but also from hearing her own wish being voiced by another. "It's very early days."

"Yet, I can see that you're more than fond of him. Every time you say his name, your face lights up."

Olivia surrendered. "Yes, I think I probably am."

"My goodness, what a lot of money we could have saved on your Season if we'd realized the right chap was sitting right under our noses in January! Lady Crawford has kindly asked myself and your father to Wharton Park for a weekend visit. I've suggested we come at the end of August. By then, there might be good news. The world is so uncertain at present, Olivia." Her mother sighed. "Enjoy any happiness while you can, won't you, dear?"

Olivia wandered upstairs to bed later, taken aback by her mother's emotional honesty. Perhaps the impending war had brought out in everyone the need to say what they felt.

The following morning, Olivia was awake by six; dressed, packed, and ready by eight. Fredericks, the Crawfords' chauffeur, arrived on the dot of nine.

Her mother stood with her on the doorstep. "Do write, darling, to let me know how you're getting on." She kissed her daughter on both cheeks. "And have a marvelous time."

"I will, Mother." Olivia wrapped her arms round her mother's shoulders and gave her a spontaneous hug. "You and Daddy take care too."

Adrienne greeted Olivia on the doorstep of Wharton Park. "*Ma chérie*, you must be exhausted! Come inside. Sable will sort out your luggage and show you to your room. It is the same one as you stayed in before. Take a rest before dinner. There is no rush. Christopher is in London, and Harry does not arrive back until ten, or sometimes later."

Having been escorted to her bedroom by Sable, the butler, Olivia was amazed she had once thought it cold and ugly. With the late-afternoon sun casting a restful glow across the pretty, floral wallpaper, Olivia climbed onto the bed, thinking how much she liked it, and, exhausted from the tension and buildup of the trip, promptly fell asleep.

She was awoken by a knock on the door. Elsie, the maid, peered round it.

"Hello again, Miss Olivia. How lovely to see you back here! I'm going to be looking after you during your stay. Her Ladyship told me to come and wake you, as it's past seven. You won't get no sleep tonight unless you get up now. May I come in?"

"Of course. Gosh!" Olivia smiled, happy to see Elsie's bright, familiar face. "I had no idea I'd been asleep for so long."

"I've drawn you a bath, Miss Olivia, so if you hop in, I'll unpack while you do. Dinner is at eight, and her Ladyship says it's informal, so may I pick out something pretty for you to wear?"

"Yes, of course. Thank you, Elsie." Olivia drew back the covers and climbed out of bed. "So, tell me, have you and Bill named the day yet?"

"Yes. In just over four weeks, I'll be Mrs. William Stafford," Elsie said proudly. "You might still be here, Miss Olivia. I'd love you to come to the church and watch me get wed if you were. Her Ladyship has kindly given me a bolt of lace, and my auntie's making my dress. Oh, miss, I'm so excited!"

Elsie's happiness was infectious and Olivia could not help but feel a small tinge of envy.

At five to eight, Olivia wandered downstairs and found Sable waiting for her in the entrance hall.

"Her Ladyship is outside on the terrace, Miss Drew-Norris. Follow me."

She did so and, when she stepped outside, saw a small table had been set for two in the corner of the terrace. Large candles, shielded from the wind in glass containers, cast their soft glow in the fading light.

"Olivia, do come and sit down." Adrienne indicated the other chair. "I hope it is warm enough for you out here. I've brought you a wrap in case you get cold, but I like to eat out here while I can. In France, we barely ate inside at all between May and September. Now, I have some rosé, a pink wine we produce in the vineyards of our château in Provence. I have twelve cases shipped over every year. Would you like to try a glass?"

Olivia sat down. "I'd love to. Thank you."

Adrienne indicated that Sable should pour the wine. "We will eat in fifteen minutes, Sable. *Merci.*"

"Very good, your Ladyship." The butler nodded and disappeared inside the house.

"Santé." Adrienne reached her glass to Olivia's, then they both took a sip.

Olivia tasted the wine and found she liked it. White wine was too acidic and red wine too heavy for her; this seemed to be the perfect combination.

"It is good, *non*?" Adrienne asked.

"Very good indeed."

"My family used to drink it out of large jugs, fresh from our *cave*." Adrienne sighed. "*Eh bien!* It is just one more thing that I miss."

"But you are happy here in England, aren't you?"

"Yes, of course, but this year I am a little sad. Always in August, we spend a month at my family château. This year, with Christopher so busy at Whitehall and Harry training his recruits, I felt I could not go without them. Christopher believes war is imminent."

"In London, it's impossible to ignore the preparations. I was watching the air-raid sirens being erected along the Embankment on the day I left," said Olivia.

"I am sure." Adrienne skillfully steered the subject to more palatable subjects. "You must tell me all about your Season. Was it all you imagined it would be?"

"Actually, it was better. I met some marvelous people who were not at all as dull as I thought they would be."

"Like your friend, Venetia Burroughs? She is unusual, like you. So," said Adrienne as Sable wheeled a large trolley, replete with silver salvers, out onto the terrace, "tell me of the dances that you attended. Were they indeed as beautiful as I remember them?"

Over a dinner of fresh watercress soup and a salad made up of crisp, fresh ingredients from the kitchen garden, Olivia regaled Adrienne with as many interesting anecdotes of her experiences as she could think of.

"Voilà!" Adrienne clapped her hands together in pleasure. "It all sounds very much the same as when I came out. And, of course, I am sure there were many young men who were charmed by you. The question is, were you charmed by any of them?"

"I . . . no. At least, no one I thought was special."

"Well, I am sure it will not be long before you are." Adrienne had read her discomfort. "Olivia, I would like you to feel as if this house were your own while you are here. You may have Fredericks, our chauffeur, to drive you anywhere, anytime you wish. And perhaps we will go to the beaches together, of which there are many nearby, and you will see what a beautiful county Norfolk is. And Harry will be home for the weekends, to keep you company. He's so tired, poor boy, but he was very happy when I told him you were coming here. It will be good for him too, to have some younger company. Now, I think it is time for bed, *non*?" Adrienne rose, walked over to Olivia, and kissed her on both cheeks. "*Bonne nuit, ma chérie,* sleep well."

"And you, Adrienne." Olivia stood up too. "I've enjoyed tonight very much indeed."

The two women moved inside and walked through the series of rooms that led to the entrance hall.

"Elsie will bring you a breakfast tray in your room tomorrow morning, at an hour that suits you. And we will meet at one o'clock tomorrow for luncheon, after which I will take you round the gardens and show you the hothouse. You must take whatever you wish to read from the shelves in the library. There is a summerhouse tucked away behind the rose arbor, in the left-hand corner of the walled garden, where I often sit to read."

"Thank you, Adrienne. You are very kind."

Together they walked up the staircase.

"And you are most kind to be my guest. *À bientôt*, Olivia. Sleep well."

18

In the following few days, Olivia fell into a regular and relaxed routine, spending the mornings reading in the summerhouse, then, after lunch, taking a stroll with Adrienne before an afternoon rest. They would enjoy dinner together on the terrace, talking of art, literature, and France, whose culture Adrienne was so passionate about.

Olivia found the beauty of her surroundings and the slow pace of life at Wharton Park were lulling her mind into almost catatonic peace. The impending war, and what exactly she was going to do with her life if there was one, slipped from her mind as easily as the spiderwebs on the many roses in the garden dissolved through her fingertips.

One afternoon, Adrienne drove them out to the coast. Olivia gasped when she saw the beauty of Holkham beach spread in front of her like a vast, golden apron. They picnicked in the dunes, Adrienne dozing off after lunch, her straw hat over her face to protect her ivory skin from the sun's rays.

Olivia walked down to the shore to dip her toes tentatively in the biting, salty water. It was not as cold as she had expected it to be, and—with the wind whipping through her hair, the sun shining, and the magnificence of the deserted beach around her—Olivia imagined that she could indeed live in this part of England.

When they arrived back at Wharton Park, Olivia crossed the hall to escape to her bedroom and climb out of her wet and creased dress. But a familiar, much-imagined face was coming down the stairs toward her.

"Olivia, how absolutely marvelous to see you."

Harry kissed her warmly on both cheeks, and she immediately regretted her disheveled state. He was still in his officer's uniform and looked imposingly handsome.

"Hello, Harry, how are you?"

He rolled his eyes. "Oh, fair to middling, I'd say, but you look awfully well."

Olivia blushed. "Do I? Your mother and I have just been to the beach and I fear I look rather bedraggled."

"Well, I think you look perfect. I love blowing the cobwebs away with some sea air. What say you we go tomorrow, if you can bear to go again? I have the weekend off duty and I mean to enjoy it."

There was a lightness, almost a euphoria, about Harry that Olivia hadn't witnessed before.

"That sounds fun. And now, if you'll excuse me, I really must get out of this damp dress."

"Of course. See you at dinner, Olivia."

"Yes," she said as she tripped up the stairs. "I'll see you later."

That evening, Olivia asked Elsie to style her hair, with the front of it taken up in a roll, the rest hanging in ebullient golden curls around her shoulders. She donned her favorite blue gown, then checked her reflection in the mirror.

"You look a picture," said Elsie admiringly. "Master Harry is joining you this evening, isn't he?"

"I believe so." Olivia was too nervous to indulge in gossip. She walked downstairs and onto the terrace and saw Adrienne and Harry were already there.

"Harry was just telling me that you have arranged to go to the beach together tomorrow." Adrienne smiled approvingly. "Olivia, *chérie*, the fresh air must suit you. You look beautiful tonight." She handed Olivia a glass of rosé from the silver tray on the table. "And tomorrow, Christopher is home too. So, on Sunday, we shall have a luncheon party for some of our neighbors, so that you can meet them. Shall we sit down?"

The evening passed pleasantly enough. Harry was attentive to Olivia, asking questions about the Season and London. Adrienne retired early, feigning tiredness, and the two of them were left alone together on the terrace. Olivia did her utmost to quell her shiver of anticipation and keep her composure.

"I'm rather glad you're here, Olivia. It's marvelous for my mother to have a companion with her at Wharton Park while she can't be in France with her family, especially with my father away so much. She is so very fond of you."

"As I am of her."

"And is the beauty of this part of the world appealing to you more than before?" Harry smiled at her, and they both shared the memory of their first conversation.

"Oh, yes! I adore it. Your mother has turned me into a complete convert."

"She's awfully good at being persuasive." Harry raised his eyebrows. "But I am glad you like it here. It's a jolly special place."

"And it must be a bonus for you to be able to spend this time at home."

"It is." Harry nodded. "It makes the whole damned thing rather more bearable. Anyway"—he stubbed out his cigarette—"bed for me, I'm bushed. You too?" He offered her his hand and she took it and stood up. He dropped it again as soon as they started walking through the house and made their way up the stairs. "Good night, Olivia." He kissed her politely on both cheeks, said, "Sleep well," and ambled off in the direction of his bedroom.

Olivia climbed into bed, feeling confused as to why Harry had not tried to kiss her again. However, she comforted herself, it was only the start of her holiday here and Harry's first day off in weeks. She must give him time.

The following morning, Harry seemed to be in high spirits as he drove her up toward the coast.

"I won't bore you with Holkham again. I thought we'd take a trip into Cromer. Take in some lunch and have a stroll along the front," he suggested.

Olivia's vision of lying in Harry's arms in the sand dunes immediately evaporated. She tried not to allow her disappointment to spoil the precious time she had with him.

They passed a pleasant day together, if not quite the one Olivia had envisaged. Over lunch in the restaurant of a hotel, Harry entertained her with tales of the raw recruits in his battalion, some of whom hailed from the Wharton Park estate.

"I'm particularly impressed with Bill Stafford, Elsie's chap." Harry lit a cigarette. "There's no doubt he's officer material. He has that air of calm authority that makes the other men listen to him. He'll make a far better soldier than I ever will, in a month of Sundays."

"I am sure that's not true, Harry."

"I fear it is, my darling girl." He sighed, stubbing his cigarette out morosely in the ashtray. "Well now, shall we head back?"

Dinner that evening was held in the dining room, in tribute to Lord Crawford's being home from London. Adrienne was sparkling with happiness at having both her men at the table with her, and the atmosphere was infectious. Afterward, Olivia made up a four for bridge. She and Christopher won, courtesy of Mr. Christian and his careful tutelage.

At the end of the evening, Harry escorted her up the stairs, and again she was fizzing with excitement when the time for a good-night kiss came. But, again, he only offered her a chaste kiss on the cheek before retiring to his bedroom.

There were twenty for luncheon the next day, the party made up of Lord and Lady Crawford's friends and neighbors. Olivia enjoyed the lunch, used as she was to the company of older people, but had the queerest feeling she was being paraded for approval. She hoped she had acquitted herself well. Harry had behaved as he had over the last couple of days: attentive but distant.

That night in bed, Olivia decided stoically, but sadly, that it was time to think of plans for the future that did not include him.

As the dying summer sped on toward September, the fields were shorn bare of their bounty and the smell of burning stubble pervaded the estate. Olivia, in soporific mood, read voraciously, took long walks through the park, and often went to visit Jack in the hothouse. She had not seen Harry since the Sunday luncheon party—he had spent the past weekend in London—and at the very least, his obvious ambivalence made her more determined to focus on what exactly she was going to do when she left Wharton Park in a few days' time. She would have departed sooner, but Elsie, with whom she had become firm friends, had begged her to stay on for her wedding, and Olivia had agreed.

Three days before Elsie's wedding, Christopher arrived home unexpectedly from London. He and Adrienne were cloistered in his study for much of the afternoon. Olivia was reading in the library when a white-faced Adrienne came to find her.

"Oh, my dear"—Adrienne put her hands to her cheeks—"it looks as if the war is upon us. Christopher has told me the British government has received intelligence telling them that the *Kriegsmarine* has ordered all German-flagged merchant ships to head to German ports immediately, in anticipation of the invasion of Poland. They are not going to honor the German-Soviet nonaggression pact." She sat down abruptly in a chair, her head in her hands. "It is here, Olivia, it is here."

Olivia immediately stood up and went to comfort her. "Surely Herr Hitler will not do this? He knows what it will mean?"

"He knows what it will mean and it is what he wants, what he has always wanted. Christopher believes that, by tomorrow morning, the German invasion of Poland will have begun. And then, of course, Britain must declare war." Adrienne grabbed Olivia's hand. "We must not let Elsie hear of this any sooner than she needs to. Let her enjoy a few more hours of her preparations. You must say nothing to anyone until this is common knowledge, do you understand?"

"Of course I do, Adrienne. I won't say a thing, I promise."

"I only hope they can enjoy their wedding day like any other couple. They must feel they have a future, even if they have not." Adrienne's eyes were full of tears. She pulled out a lace hankie and wiped them. "*Mon Dieu!* That is enough! I must compose myself. I apologize, *ma petite.* Sometimes it is a bad thing to know too much. Christopher must leave to go back to London immediately. But he wished to impart the news to me himself."

• • •

That night, Adrienne stayed up to wait for Harry to return. When he did, she took him into the library and poured them both an Armagnac.

"Mother, I've heard," Harry said, seeing the distress on her beautiful face. "Please try not to panic, nothing is for certain yet, and we're all unclear as to how this will play out and what implications it may have. It's hardly a shock; to us in the know, anyway. The die was cast when Hitler walked into Czechoslovakia. We've all been preparing for months, and I think all my chaps will be glad once they know where they are and can put into action what they've learned."

Adrienne raised her hand to her brow. "I can't believe I must live through another war. The last one claimed so many people I loved and now"—she looked at him—"my Harry . . ." She shrugged helplessly and he went to comfort her.

"*Maman*, please try not to upset yourself," he begged, as she sobbed in his arms. It was one of the few occasions in his life when he wished he had a British-born, stiff-upper-lip sort for a mother. Seeing her in so much distress pained him terribly.

"But what will I do here, Harry? When you are gone to war, and your father is in London? And most of the young men on the estate missing? How will I manage Wharton Park alone?"

"You have Olivia here," Harry offered.

"Pouf!" Adrienne gesticulated with her delicate hand. "She will not stay here when war begins, why should she?" Her heightened emotions made her speak the truth. "I've watched you together, Harry, and I can see how she loves you, but you . . . I do not think that you care for her in the same way. Yes, and I admit I invited her here because I could see there was an attraction between the two of you. Now I can see I was wrong. And, as she is only here for you, she will go and I will be alone."

Harry was completely taken aback, shocked by what she was telling him.

"You think Olivia is in love with me?" he said in amazement.

This statement made Adrienne angry. "Of course! It is written all over her, can you not see? And she is such a lovely girl, so bright, so intelligent, so unusual for an Englishwoman. Yes, I had plans for you . . . because, of course, you are the sole heir and—oh!" She put her hands to her burning cheeks. "I can hardly say it, but if you do not survive the war, there will be no heir for Wharton Park. It will pass to your father's nephew, Hugo, and our line will be ended after three hundred years."

"Good God!" Harry took his arms from her shoulders and paced around the library, nursing his Armagnac. "You are absolutely right. If I don't come back, then . . ." His voice trailed off.

"Harry, my deepest apologies, really. I am not myself tonight. Please forgive me and forget what I've said to you."

He turned to face her. "What you say is merely the truth. And Olivia is a lovely girl and I am extremely fond of her. And you like her too. She would be company for you, if—"

"No, Harry! Do not listen to me!" Adrienne said, agonized. "I assumed too much. I thought—"

"Perhaps you thought right." Harry nodded in agreement. "But I'm a man and too insensitive to see the signs."

"Maybe, but remember that love cannot be manufactured. If it does not exist, then one cannot make it so." Adrienne watched him for a while, then stood up. "I have such a headache, I must go to bed."

"Of course you must, *Maman*, it has been a difficult day for all of us."

Adrienne walked toward the door, then stopped and turned around to look at Harry. "Please believe I do not wish you to do anything that does not suit your heart. It is not the French way, and neither is it mine. Good night, my darling. Let us hope for a brighter day tomorrow."

When she had gone, Harry poured himself another Armagnac and sat down in the comfortable leather chair to think.

19

The following morning, on September 1, 1939, it was announced on the wireless that Hitler's troops had marched into Poland. Two days later, on the eve of Elsie's wedding to Bill, Chamberlain spoke to his nation to confirm that a state of war now existed between Great Britain and Germany.

Perhaps because of the impending disaster and the knowledge that war was now under way, an air of expectation seemed to pervade the entire estate. The following morning, as Olivia was packing up her belongings into her suitcase, there was a knock on her door.

"Come in," she said.

Harry was standing there. "Sorry to disturb you, Olivia, but you've been invited along to Elsie's wedding, haven't you?"

"Yes, I have," she agreed coldly. The confirmation of the war and Harry's continued ambivalence had numbed any romantic thoughts she had been harboring. She simply wanted to get on with her life.

"Would you mind awfully if I accompanied you? I could do with a bit of cheering up. I'm awfully fond of Elsie, and Bill in particular, and a celebration like that seems just the ticket."

Olivia eyed him in surprise. Realizing she could hardly refuse, she said, "Of course, if that's what you would like. The ceremony's at two this afternoon."

"Then I shall meet you downstairs in the hall at half past one, and we can take a stroll together across the park to the church." He eyed the suitcase on the bed behind her. "Packing?"

Olivia nodded. "Yes, I'm going home tomorrow to my parents' house in Surrey. Then it's straight off to London to sign up. I'm going to join the Wrens, if they'll have me."

"That's wonderful, Olivia. But we shall all miss you here."

"I doubt it," Olivia said, feeling contrary and hardly caring.

"I assure you, we will *all* be sad to see you go. Half past one, then?"

"Yes." She nodded and turned back to her packing. Really, Harry's behavior was most confusing.

Harry and Olivia sat at the back of the church and watched Elsie glow with pride and happiness in her pretty lace dress, as she walked down the aisle to meet her future husband. There was not a dry eye in the congregation as they said their vows; every person present knew that their life together as a couple would soon be curtailed. It was a sobering moment, and as Olivia glanced in Harry's direction, she could see that he too was moved.

At the reception, Olivia watched in admiration as Harry sat at a trestle table in the village hall, surrounded by those who worked for him, joking and joshing as if he were one of them. She could plainly see how much they respected and liked the young man who would one day be their master; it showed a side to him she had not witnessed before, and her heart softened somewhat toward him.

After the wedding breakfast, the speeches took place, and Jack, Bill's father, asked whether Master Harry would be prepared to come up and propose a toast to the happy couple. To cheers, Harry pushed his way through to the front and up onto the dais.

"Ladies and gentlemen, I've had the honor to know Bill and Elsie for all of my life," he began. "Who was to know that these two naughty children, whom I was always catching scrumpying apples in the orchard, would one day marry? *And* they never offered an apple to me!"

Peals of laughter came from the audience.

"Due to the less than pleasant circumstances we all find ourselves facing presently, I've got to know Bill rather better in recent weeks. I'd like to assure his dear wife that his sweeping-brush skills are coming along a treat." Harry smiled at Elsie. "And I can also tell her that when it's replaced with a real gun, I can think of no one I'd prefer to be hiding behind! Elsie, you've got a good and brave man there. Treat him well and enjoy him while you can."

Elsie's eyes filled with tears and she gripped her new husband's hand. "I will, Master Harry, I swear."

Harry raised his glass. "To Bill and Elsie."

"Bill and Elsie!" chorused the guests as Harry stepped down off the dais to loud cheers.

Jack clapped his hands for silence. "And may we also give three cheers for Master Harry, whom one day we will be proud and happy to call his Lordship, and to young Miss Olivia, who's been so kind to our Elsie. Thank you both for coming. And perhaps we should all be asking"—Jack grinned wickedly—"when you two are going to name the day?" Further cheers greeted Jack's speech as Harry arrived back by Olivia's side.

"Ladies and gentlemen, grab your partners and let the dancing begin," announced Bill.

Harry sat down next to Olivia. He glanced at her, a twinkle in his eye. "I say! I think they like you."

"And I think they like you too, Harry. You were absolutely marvelous up there," Olivia said generously, trying to break the tension that had been engendered by Jack's pointed remark.

Harry held out his hand to her. "Dance?"

She smiled. "Why not?"

An hour later, Harry and Olivia emerged from the stuffy hall into the bliss of the fast-cooling night air.

Olivia had been asked to dance by everyone and had partnered Jack, Bill, and even Sable, the butler, around the floor.

Harry reached for her hand as they set off in the direction of the house. Olivia's heart skipped a beat as he did so, but she decided she would simply enjoy the moment and think little of it.

"You know, you're very good with the servants, Olivia. It's a gift my mother has too."

"Thank you." Olivia glanced around her and tried to take in the beauty of the estate for the last time. "I'll be sad to go. I've grown to love it here."

The sun was just setting as they walked across newly shaven cornfields and into the park itself.

"You know, Olivia," Harry said quietly, "sometimes a chap doesn't see what's right under his nose."

Olivia looked up at him in surprise. "What exactly do you mean?"

"Well, this morning, when I saw you packing your suitcase, it suddenly hit me how I've enjoyed having you here. And how much I'll miss you when you go."

Olivia raised an eyebrow disparagingly. "Thanks awfully for saying so, Harry, but you've hardly seen me."

"No, but I've known you've *been* here."

Olivia did not reply. She had no idea how to. They entered the formal gardens and walked toward the fountain. Suddenly, Harry turned to her and took her into his arms. He kissed her full on the mouth, this time with passion.

Olivia was stunned. It was the last thing she had been expecting, yet she couldn't help but enjoy the touch of his lips on hers.

Eventually, he stopped kissing her and held her by the shoulders as he looked at her. "Olivia, I don't want you to go, I want you to stay here with me at Wharton Park."

"I—Harry, I—can't," she stammered.

"Why not?"

"What would I do? I must go back to London and sign up."

"Darling Olivia, there will be a war effort here in Norfolk, you know," he chuckled.

"Harry, that really isn't the point. I—"

"Marry me."

She stared at him as if he had gone utterly mad. She could not think of a single thing to say in reply.

Then Harry went down on one knee and took her hands in his. "Olivia, I have no idea what your feelings are for me, but if you could bear to have me, I would like it awfully if you were prepared to spend the rest of your life here at Wharton Park."

Olivia finally managed to budge some words from her throat. "I'm sorry, Harry, I'm just shocked. I didn't think that you"—she swallowed—"felt that way for me at all. Why suddenly now?"

"Perhaps I didn't realize how I felt until I had a chat with my mother last night and then saw you packing to leave this morning. Darling girl, please say yes. I promise to cherish you as best I can. And, between the two of us, I'm sure we can safeguard Wharton Park into the next generation."

She looked down at him, at his handsome face, which she had truly believed would never be hers to gaze at. All the love she had felt and tried so desperately to squash reignited.

"Please say yes before my kneecap cracks on this gravel," he joked, grinning boyishly. "Darling, please?"

Olivia searched her soul, but realized it was pointless to find reasons not to. She loved him. No other reason mattered.

"Yes, Harry, I'll marry you."

He stood up, took her into his arms, and pulled her to him. Then he kissed her again. "Oh, my darling, I'm so very happy. Come on, let's go inside and find my mother. I can't wait to tell her."

Only later that evening—after she had climbed into bed, exhausted from the extraordinary turn of events, and the celebrations over champagne that had ensued with Adrienne—did Olivia realize Harry had not once said he loved her.

20

The wedding of the Honorable Harry Crawford to Miss Olivia Drew-Norris was set for early December. Harry was away with his battalion, who had been charged with securing the vulnerable beaches around the Norfolk coast, building lookout posts, barbed-wire barricades, and laying mines. This would take him through until at least January, before new orders were issued as to their battalion's future whereabouts. Other battalions had already been mobilized overseas, so Harry and everyone at Wharton Park, many of whom had relatives in the Fifth Royal Norfolks, were thanking their lucky stars at the stay of execution.

Adrienne had suggested that Olivia wait until after the wedding to sign up for the Wrens. "There will be plenty of time afterward, *ma chérie*, but not for now. You are to be a bride and the future Lady Crawford! You must relish the preparation with me."

The forthcoming nuptials had prevented any dramatic spiral downward in Adrienne, as the festivities had given her something to focus on. She was determined, even as the news from overseas became more serious with each passing day, to celebrate as best she could.

Olivia felt a little as though she had gone back to the beginning of the Season: her life seemed to be another round of dressmakers—a trip to London with Adrienne had secured her a couture dress by Norman Hartnell himself. Guest lists had to be composed for both the engagement party and the wedding, and the invitations sent out. A society wedding such as this was usually a year in the planning, but between them, Olivia and Adrienne had most things under control.

Olivia's parents were, of course, over the moon. They had come to Wharton Park to celebrate for the weekend. Both her father and Christopher had made after-dinner speeches, declaring their approval and happiness for the young couple.

Olivia felt rather sorry for her mother, who, yet again, seemed to have had her nose pushed out on organizing arrangements for her daughter. She had taken it with her usual good grace, commenting to Olivia that Lord and Lady Crawford were paying for the entire event, which was a jolly good job, as Daddy's army pension wouldn't have run to the bridesmaids' dresses, let alone anything else.

The night before the wedding, a dinner was thrown at the house for friends and close relations of both families. Venetia had arrived with a group of Olivia's other friends from London. She sat on Olivia's bed as the bride-to-be put her makeup on at her dressing table.

"I can't help feeling rather miffed that you've let me down, Olivia, darling. I thought we made a 'no-marriage' pact, and here you are, waltzing up the aisle a few months later! Are you completely sure Harry is the 'one'?"

"I absolutely adore him, and Wharton Park," said Olivia staunchly.

"You do realize you'll be chained to this house for the rest of your life, don't you? And jolly well have to produce an heir, and at least one spare?"

"I like children," Olivia protested. "I want them."

"And are you absolutely sure that Harry loves you?"

"Of course he does," Olivia said abruptly, Venetia's comment touching a raw nerve. "Why on earth would he be marrying me if he didn't?"

After the dinner, Olivia walked along the landing toward her bedroom, exhausted. She jumped as a pair of hands caught her waist from behind. "Hello, my darling girl, how are you feeling?" Harry nuzzled into her neck. Olivia could smell drink on his breath.

"I'm a little nervous," she admitted. "You?"

"I think I'll be glad now when it's all over, and we can get on with being Mr. and Mrs. Crawford. Won't you?"

"Yes."

He kissed her gently on the forehead. "Enjoy your last night of freedom, darling. I'll see you in church tomorrow."

A few minutes later, as Olivia climbed into bed, her stomach butterflies unnetted themselves and circulated around her body. It wasn't the wedding ceremony that she was nervous about—it was this time tomorrow night, when she and Harry would enter the large master suite overlooking the park, and the door would close behind them.

She knew, of course, what to expect—Venetia had delighted in enlightening her as to the physical scenario. But, try as she might, she found it difficult to imagine that degree of intimacy with Harry. She'd no idea if he was as innocent as she was; she rather hoped he wasn't, and then at least one of them would know what they were doing. She comforted herself that it was a rite of passage, which all married women had been through. And also, Olivia thought as she drifted off, the only way in which babies could be brought into the world.

The following morning dawned bright and crisp.

Brimming over with excitement, Elsie arrived in Olivia's bedroom with a breakfast tray at eight o'clock.

"Now, there's no rush, miss, I've got everything under control. See"—Elsie indicated a piece of paper—"I've written us out a timetable for the morning, so we'll both know what we're doing."

Olivia felt comforted by Elsie's calm presence. "You are a wonder, you really are. Thank you," she said as Elsie placed the tray across her knees.

"Ooh, I can't wait to see you in that dress." Elsie indicated the exquisite oyster satin creation placed on a dummy in the corner of Olivia's bedroom. "Her Ladyship says she'll be up to see you after breakfast. Then I'll run you a bath and we'll sort out your hair."

At nine o'clock, there was a tap at Olivia's door.

"Come in."

Adrienne appeared, holding a large leather box. She came over to kiss Olivia on both cheeks. "*Chérie*, truly, this is the happiest day of my life. Seeing my son marry a woman whom I love like my own daughter . . . what more could a mother want? Come here and let me show you what I have for you."

Adrienne walked over to the stool, sat down, and patted the space next to her for Olivia to sit too. Adrienne opened the box to reveal an exquisite diamond necklace and a matching pair of large teardrop earrings.

"These are for you, Olivia, to wear today. Every Crawford bride has worn them for the past two hundred years. You will keep them, then hand them on to your son's bride on the day that he marries."

"They are beautiful," breathed Olivia. "Thank you, Adrienne."

"Do not thank me, *chérie.*" She stood up. "I ask for nothing more than that we remain the dear friends we already are. Now, I must go and oversee the arrangements, and I look forward to welcoming you formally into our family later today."

At eleven thirty, Olivia was dressed and ready. Elsie stared at her with a look of awe.

"Oh, Miss Olivia, you do look that beautiful I think *I* could marry you," she giggled as she handed Olivia the long, white satin gloves.

"Thank you. I am so dreadfully nervous." Olivia opened her arms to Elsie. "Come and give me a hug. I think I need one."

"Of course, miss." Tentatively, so as not to spoil Olivia's dress, Elsie put her arms round her mistress.

"Thank you for looking after me so beautifully over these past few weeks," said Olivia. "I've asked Adrienne if this could be a permanent arrangement in the future."

"You mean, I'm to be your lady's maid? Forever, like?" Elsie's eyes were wide with wonder.

"Yes. Who else could do better? As long as you are happy with the idea too. There'll be a few extra shillings for you as well."

"Oh, miss, I'd love it! Thank you so much," said Elsie, her voice breaking. "Now, you'd better be getting yourself downstairs; they're waiting for you."

"Yes." Olivia took a few seconds to compose herself. "Wish me luck, Elsie."

Elsie watched as Olivia walked toward the door. "Good luck, miss," she breathed as Olivia left the room.

Whenever Olivia looked back on her wedding day, she struggled to remember much of it. She could see Harry in her mind's eye, resplendent in full military uniform, standing waiting for her at the front of the church. And the guard of honor his battalion had arranged as they walked from the church a newly married couple. At the reception, which took place in the ballroom, Olivia could remember a sea of faces, some of which she knew from London and many she had never before seen. She had no memory of what she'd eaten—probably little, given her corset—or much about the speeches.

She remembered the first dance with Harry, as everyone clapped, then partnering Lord Crawford, her father, Angus, and Archie.

At ten o'clock, the guests gathered in the hall to wave the happy couple upstairs to bed. Due to Harry's immediate return to his battalion, plans for a honeymoon had been shelved. Harry took Olivia's arm and kissed her on the cheek as she threw her bouquet from the top of the stairs. Everyone cheered when Adrienne's five-year-old niece caught it.

"All right, darling?" Harry asked as he led her along the corridor in the opposite direction from her old bedroom.

"I think so, yes," she answered nervously.

He opened the door to their new quarters and they walked inside.

He shut the door behind them and threw himself onto the large bed, where the sheets were already pulled back.

"Well, I don't know about you," he said as he rested his hands behind his head, "but I don't fancy going through that ever again. I'm absolutely bushed!"

Olivia was exhausted too, but felt uncomfortable about joining him on the bed. In the end, she sank into a chair by the newly lit fire.

He surveyed her from his elevated position. "Do you need Elsie's help to get all that stuff off? I don't know whether I'm much of an expert."

"Perhaps you could learn," she suggested timidly, unnerved by the utilitarian approach he was taking to this moment.

He sprang off the bed and came to her. "Stand up and let's have a look, then," he commanded.

She did so and turned her back to him so he could survey the seed-pearl buttons that had taken Elsie twenty minutes to fasten that morning.

He shook his head. "Beats me, I'm afraid. Tell you what, darling,

I'll go and find Elsie, and then come back when she's finished releasing you." He smiled at her, then promptly left the room.

Olivia didn't know whether to laugh or cry at his insensitivity. A few minutes later, Elsie was at the door.

"Master Harry said you needed my help and I'm not surprised. Those buttons are a nightmare for the nimblest of fingers."

Elsie began unbuttoning the dress as Olivia stood silently.

"You all right, miss? You're very quiet."

"I . . . oh, Elsie . . ." To Olivia's embarrassment, tears began to flow down her cheeks.

"Oh, miss, don't you be crying now, please. You're just tired, that's all, and emotional. I cried on my wedding night too, if you must know." Elsie reached for a handkerchief in her pocket and handed it to Olivia. "Don't you be spoiling your pretty face for Master Harry with them tears. I'll be as quick as I can, and then you'll be back in his arms."

"Thank you, Elsie, you're probably right." Olivia blew her nose. "I'm just being silly."

"We're all nervous on our wedding night, miss." Elsie undid the last button, and Olivia stepped out of the dress. "But Master Harry will look after you, I know he will." She handed Olivia her nightgown. "There now, you climb into that and I'll take the dress and hang it in your old room. And I'll tell Master Harry that you're ready for him on my way down. All right, miss?"

"Yes." Olivia nodded. "Thank you, Elsie."

Elsie picked up the wedding dress, put it over her arm, and walked toward the door. She opened it, then, as an afterthought, turned back and smiled shyly. "And I promise you, it's not as bad as you think it's going to be. See you tomorrow, Miss Olivia, good night."

Calmer now, Olivia sat back down in the chair, waiting for Harry to reappear. Ten minutes later, yawning, she decided to climb into bed, wondering where he could have gone. The tension of waiting was killing her, but she could hardly leave the room and search for him. Surely he must be on his way?

Half an hour later, with still no sign of him, the exhaustion of the day catching up with her, Olivia closed her eyes and fell asleep.

Sometime during the night, she heard a door open and felt a bend of the mattress as Harry climbed in next to her. She waited in an agony of suspense to see if he would lean over and touch her. He did not. A few minutes later, she heard him snoring gently.

Olivia woke up early the next morning, a feeling of dread lodged in the pit of her stomach. She knew, beyond a doubt, that last night was not how it should have been.

Harry was still asleep beside her, so she climbed out of bed and tiptoed across the carpet and into the room next door. Their private quarters comprised the bedroom, a sitting room, a bathroom, and a dressing room each. Hers contained a wardrobe, whereas Harry's contained a narrow bed.

Olivia was aware it was considered normal for man and wife to have separate sleeping quarters, although her own parents had never had that luxury in Poona, their house being too compact. She looked at the bed and sat down on it, wondering miserably if this was where Harry would have preferred to spend the night.

She dressed swiftly, uncomfortable with the thought of Harry bursting in and seeing her half-naked. When she walked quietly back into the bedroom, she saw that Harry was still fast asleep. She hovered by the door, unsure of what to do. If she went downstairs, eyebrows would be raised as to why she was up so early on her first morning of married life. But if she stayed . . . she'd have to face an uncomfortable scenario with Harry.

The decision was taken out of her hands as Harry stirred and saw her standing by the door.

He smiled at her, rubbing his eyes. "Hello, darling. Sleep well?"

She shrugged silently, despair written on her face.

He opened his arms to her. "Come here and give me a hug."

Olivia didn't move.

"Come on, darling, please. I won't bite, you know."

She walked toward him tentatively and sat right on the edge of the bed.

"I suppose you're wondering where I went last night?"

"Yes."

"Well, some of the chaps caught me as I was coming back along the corridor to you and asked me to join them for a swift brandy to celebrate. I knew you were exhausted, so I thought I'd let you sleep." He reached for her hand and squeezed it. "Darling, you're upset, aren't you?"

"Of course I am, Harry! It was our wedding night, for pity's sake!" she shouted, unable to contain her frustration.

"Of course. I'm sorry." He sat up and stroked her back. "You know, darling, we have the whole of our life together to get to know each other. There's no rush, is there?"

"I suppose not," she said without conviction. "I just . . . don't want anyone else to know."

"Well, they won't hear it from me, I swear. Let's just take it slowly, shall we?"

Somehow, Olivia got through the day, keeping busy, dodging questions from Venetia and Adrienne, and trying to look as content and replete as a new bride should.

That evening, when all the guests had left and Olivia had retired for the night, Harry entered the room. He came to sit on the bed and took her hand.

"Darling, I think it's better if I sleep in my dressing room tonight. I have to be up at the crack of dawn tomorrow morning and I don't want to wake you." He leaned toward her and gave her a kiss on the cheek. "Good night, sleep well." Then he stood and left the room.

Olivia lay wide-awake into the small hours, her stomach churning, knowing that something was dreadfully, horribly wrong.

21

In the two weeks leading up to Christmas, Harry did not try to initiate anything intimate in the bedroom. In fact, Olivia hardly saw her new husband. He would arrive home, sometimes after midnight, grab a few hours' sleep in his dressing room, and be off the following morning by six. At weekends too he was working.

Olivia felt she could hardly complain, knowing that the war was ratcheting up. Already a German U-boat had sunk the British battleship HMS *Royal Oak*, and young men were disappearing every week from the estate to train full time with their battalions.

Olivia could only hope that when Harry had two days off at Christmas, they would be able to spend some time together. And, at the very least, discuss their relationship and its obvious problems.

Thankfully, there was much to keep her occupied on the estate, due to the diminishing manpower. With Bill no longer able to help Jack, Olivia spent time helping to tend the kitchen garden and watering the flowers in the hothouse. Working outside in the bitter cold numbed her brain and stopped her from brooding. But sometimes, she found it difficult to keep cheerful. She felt she could not turn to anyone for advice, even though she was desperate to.

Adrienne, sensing her new daughter-in-law's misery, and putting it down to having her husband so unavailable to her in the first few weeks of their married life, suggested that Olivia invite a house party of her friends from London, just before Christmas.

Even Harry brightened at the thought. "I think it's a splendid idea, darling. I'm sure you'll be inviting Venetia; now there's a game girl who'll light up any party. And . . . how about that poet chap, Archie? And Angus, your Scottish chum?"

Olivia's friends duly arrived, full of horror stories about London and impending rationing. Venetia tipped up in her smart Wrens uniform, telling Olivia she was undergoing training of the top-secret variety, and that she couldn't really talk about it.

After dinner, the two of them sat by the fire in the library to enjoy what had become a traditional catch-up session. Venetia eyed Olivia critically.

"Darling, for someone who's living in the country, you're looking awfully peaky these days. You're not pregnant already, are you?" she chuckled.

Venetia's glib comment brought tears to Olivia's eyes.

"Gosh! I'm sorry, have I said the wrong thing?"

"No—yes—oh, Venetia, it's just *too* awful for words!"

Venetia went to Olivia and put her arms round her shoulders. "I'm sure it can't be that bad, whatever it is. You're not ill, are you, darling?"

"No, I'm not ill . . . I—" Olivia didn't know where to start. "The thing is, Venetia, I—I'm still a . . . virgin!"

Venetia looked at her in amazement. "How can you be? Oh, darling, please tell. I might be able to help," she soothed.

So, haltingly, between tears, Olivia told her the whole sorry story.

"I must say, I can't understand at all," Venetia said bluntly. "It strikes me that most men seem to spend their lives trying to extract what Harry has on offer from his wife every night."

"I know. The question is, why?"

"Have you asked him?"

"No. I keep telling myself I must, but then—I can't bring myself to say the words."

"Well, you absolutely must, darling, because it isn't normal," Venetia implored. "And besides, you're so utterly lovely, it's hard to imagine that any man could resist you."

Olivia gave her a wan smile. "Thank you, Venetia, but really, I'm at my wit's end. My mother-in-law keeps making pointed comments about when the next heir to Wharton Park is going to come along, and, of course, I know there's no possibility of that happening. Perhaps," she sighed, "I'm just not his sort."

"Now you *are* being silly," Venetia comforted, "you're every man's 'sort.' You must try to remember that this is most certainly Harry's problem, not yours." Venetia paced the library, thinking. Finally she stopped and turned to Olivia. "Perhaps it's simply that he's desperately shy. What you are going to have to do is pounce on him."

"No! I absolutely couldn't."

Venetia yawned. "Oh, well, darling, if all else fails, you can comfort yourself with the fact that he probably won't be here for much longer. They're mobilizing like billy-oh, and there's every chance that Harry will be shipped off soon to France. Then, of course"—she grinned—"you can take a lover. You are a married woman after all, and it's de rigueur. Now, my darling Olivia, I must go and get some shut-eye. I had a particularly raucous night in London with my new amour and I'm bushed. We'll talk some more in the morning. This has nothing to do with you, promise. Night, night, darling, sweet dreams."

Having mulled over what her friend had said, Olivia thought she might be right and Harry could simply be desperately shy. She decided there was nothing to it, but to do as Venetia had suggested and "pounce" on her husband.

That night, dressed in her prettiest peignoir, and before her courage failed her, Olivia wandered through the sitting room toward Harry's dressing room. But, on opening the door, found the bed was empty. Looking at the clock beside his bed, she saw that it was past midnight. Intrigued as to where he'd been since they'd left the dinner table earlier, she let herself out of the room and crossed the landing, tiptoeing down the stairs.

All the lights were off, and Sable had closed up for the night, which normally indicated that everyone in the household had retired. Walking across the entrance hall, she stopped as she saw a shaft of light coming from under the library door.

Creeping toward it, she turned the handle silently and pushed the door open.

Olivia let out a gasp of horror. Harry was standing by the fireplace, with his back toward her. She could see Archie's eyes were closed as he continued to kiss her husband, unaware of Olivia's presence. She stood there for a few seconds longer, looking at the way Archie was clasping Harry to him, as his lips moved against her husband's mouth. . . .

Feeling the bile come to her throat, she gagged, then fled down the corridor in the direction of the nearest lavatory and was violently sick.

• • •

After a nearly sleepless night, a devastated Olivia woke to Christmas Eve. She was glad to have the distraction of helping Adrienne decorate the traditional Christmas tree—culled from the grounds of Wharton Park and placed in the entrance hall. Carols were playing from a wireless somewhere in the background, and everyone, apart from Olivia, seemed to be full of Christmas cheer. She dug deep inside her soul to garner strength, biting her lip hard again and again to prevent herself from crying out loud in sheer misery.

Venetia, Archie, and Angus were ready to depart for London at lunchtime. Olivia hid upstairs in her bedroom, unable to face the thought of seeing Archie and having to be polite. Venetia came to find her.

"Darling, I'm awfully worried about you. You look quite ghastly today. If you ever need me, you know where I am," Venetia said, as she kissed Olivia good-bye.

"Thank you," Olivia gulped. She couldn't bring herself to tell Venetia what she'd seen the night before.

Somehow she got through the day, and the traditional present-opening that took place after dinner. As soon as she could, Olivia took herself off to bed and lay miserably, huddled up under the blankets against the cold, which tonight seemed to be eating into her bones.

An hour later, Harry came into the bedroom.

"Darling, are you awake?"

When she did not reply, he walked around the side of the bed. She felt his face lean down toward hers.

She sat bolt upright and screamed, "*No!* Don't touch me!"

Harry stepped backward, shocked by her reaction. "Whatever is it?"

She jumped out of bed, desperate to be away from him. "I know I can't do anything about the fact I've married you, fool that I am! But I beg you, promise me now you will never try and touch me again. You . . . *repulse* me!"

Harry turned and followed her as she walked over to the fireplace, shivering from cold and anger. "Darling, please calm down. What on earth are you talking about?"

She looked straight at him, disgust in her eyes. "I saw you—with *him*," she spat. "Last night, in the library."

Harry looked away from her into the distance, then nodded. "I see."

"For all these weeks, I've been wondering why you didn't want your wife as any husband should, why you never tried to touch me. I've been utterly desperate, thinking it was me, that I was doing something wrong. And, of course"—Olivia laughed harshly—"you were never going to want me, were you?"

She watched him without sympathy as he sank down into a chair by the fire and put his head in his hands.

"Olivia, I'm so dreadfully sorry. You shouldn't have seen what you saw last night—"

"And you shouldn't have been *doing* what I saw last night! How could you, Harry? In this house! Anyone could have walked in and caught you!"

"I swear to you, it has never happened before and it'll never happen again. I—we—were drunk . . . got carried away—"

"Please, spare me the excuses, Harry." Olivia wrung her hands in despair. She checked herself, knowing that she was in danger of becoming hysterical.

"Darling—"

"Don't call me 'darling'! I am not your 'darling,' *he* is!" Then she started to sob helplessly. She walked over to the bed and sank onto the end of it. "Harry, how could you be so cruel? How could you marry me?"

"I didn't—I don't know—Olivia, maybe you don't understand, but at school—"

"I don't care what happened at school!" She looked at him in disgust. "You are married now, with a wife! How could you allow me to waste my life with you, knowing that you could never really love me? I know you are shy, Harry, but I didn't think you were cruel."

"Please, I promise you, Olivia, I do have feelings for you. And after last night, I know that—what you saw—it's not for me, really."

"Oh, how jolly convenient for you to say so, now you've been discovered. You do realize you could be thrown out of the army in disgrace for this? And your parents, your poor parents." She shook her head. "Your mother keeps asking me when I'm going to produce the next heir. Harry," she said, as the last of her reserve crumbled, "how can I bear this?"

"Darling, please don't cry." He meant to come over to her, but she put her arms out in front of her.

"I said, *don't touch me*!"

Harry walked back to the chair and sank down into it. They sat in silence for a while.

"You know," said Harry eventually, "it's not completely unusual for men to struggle with—who they *are*, Olivia. And I promise you, my darling, after last night, I know who I am now. And please, if you'd let me, I wish to make it up to you, make our marriage work. I accept last night was very wrong, but I honestly did it with the best of intentions, if you'd only let me explain how—"

"Please"—Olivia shuddered—"spare me the details. Forgive me for not wanting to enter your grubby little world." She gave a long sigh. "I think, when we have both calmed down, we must discuss what we must do. I have to decide whether I can live with this." She looked up at him. "If I can't, Harry, will you grant me a divorce?"

Harry looked horrified. "There's never been a divorce in our family."

"Maybe there's never been a homosexual in your family!" She spoke the word bluntly, saw Harry flinch, and enjoyed it.

"Please stop saying that, Olivia!" he begged. "Truly, it's not what I am. Yes, I did think for a time it was a possibility, which was why I needed to find out. But really, darling girl, believe me, I'm not. So many things have become clearer in my mind today. And that's the very reason why I came to you tonight. I wanted to finally consummate our marriage."

"That's awfully noble of you, Harry"—Olivia was suddenly exhausted—"but I'm afraid I don't believe you. I don't think you love me and I wish I'd never fallen in love with you. Now, please, we have another long day tomorrow and I must try to get some sleep." She looked up at him. "And I want you to promise me one thing."

"Anything, Olivia, darling, really."

"I want you to promise me that you won't come near me or touch me while I think what to do."

"Of course," he agreed sadly, "I understand."

22

In the weeks that followed, Olivia needn't have worried about Harry's touching her. Harry was barely home. He was out with his men, working round the clock manning the North Norfolk coastal defenses. Food rationing had begun in earnest, and the Ministry of Agriculture had visited Wharton Park to discuss the fallow fields that should be turned over to growing further crops and vegetables.

Olivia had visited the local recruiting station to sign up as a Wren. But when they heard she lived at Wharton Park, the woman in charge had suggested to her that she might meet with the local head of the Women's Land Army to see if that would suit her better.

"There's going to be a number of girls billeted at estates around the county, including yours. You might find, given your credentials, you're just what the WLA needs."

Olivia duly met with the woman concerned, who was thrilled at the prospect of having someone who'd be of a similar age to the girls and already living on an estate. Olivia took on the role of organizing secretary for the area, in charge of liaising with the local farms to discuss how many girls would be needed and where to billet them.

Between that and trying to help Adrienne keep the house going on with what was fast becoming a skeleton staff, Olivia was extremely busy. Not having a moment to think helped her to bury the pain of what had happened, and the hole it had torn in her heart. This wasn't a time to think of herself or the future. The situation had an ironic comfort, and she managed to take each day as it came. Besides, at least now she knew the reason "why," and that helped enormously.

Harry had done all he could, in the rare time he had, to convince her of his love. He copied out, in his exquisite writing, her favorite romantic poems and left them for her under her bedroom door, had flowers from the hothouse delivered to her daily, so that their suite of rooms basked permanently in a fragrant smell, ordered packages of books he knew she particularly liked and had them sent from London.

She had wanted exactly this kind of behavior from him when they were courting. But now . . . it meant nothing.

Her heart was numb.

The Land Girls assigned to Wharton Park arrived by bus at the beginning of March. Olivia had been warned by the WLA representative that many of the girls were from industrial towns, with no idea of the job ahead of them. She had commandeered three workers' cottages in the Quadrangle to house them. The cottages had been unoccupied for a number of years, pending renovation. They were damp and dark, but Olivia had set to, with the help of Elsie and others, scrub and brighten the cottages and make them habitable.

On the night the Land Girls arrived, they filed into the kitchen, all of them overawed at the size of the house. Olivia ate with them, hearing about where they'd come from and how ghastly the uniform was that they had to wear.

"You should try them Aertex shirts, Mrs. Crawford," said a girl with a strong Birmingham accent. "They scratch like no one's business."

"And they're too big for us," commented another girl. "I think the breeches were made for men, not women. We're all going to look a sight tomorrow morning, aren't we, girls!"

Everyone giggled and Olivia was glad to see they seemed like a good bunch. She'd had warnings from the WLA representative about the problems of girls who were complete strangers being billeted together, and the catfighting that could ensue.

After supper, Olivia stood up and clapped her hands for silence. "Now, girls, first of all, I want to say welcome to Wharton Park. It's a beautiful estate in a lovely part of the country, and you should all count yourselves lucky to have ended up here. Mr. Combe will talk you through how you will be organized on the land, but I wanted to brief you about the domestic arrangements while you're all staying here. Bread, milk, and eggs will be provided for you in the cottages at breakfast time. Work will commence at eight o'clock, and you are to assemble in the Quadrangle, where Mr. Combe and his staff will give you your allotted tasks for the day. There's to be one morning break of fifteen minutes, then, at noon, a sandwich lunch will be sent down from the house to wherever you are working. The afternoon resumes at one o'clock, finishing at five, and supper will be provided here in this kitchen at six. We'd appreciate it if, between five and six, you would wash and change and not arrive up here in your muddy uniforms." Olivia smiled.

"I'm going to wear me ball gown and tiara to eat me tea here, missus, never you fear," chirped one girl, to resounding laughter.

"You will all have one day off a week," Olivia continued, "and that will be on a rotation basis. There's a bus to Cromer that leaves from the front drive at eleven a.m., if you wish to go into town for supplies. It returns at four thirty. There's a copy of all these details in each of your cottages. Many of you will be unused to living in the country. There are no picture houses or bright lights on your doorstep. I suggest you arrange among yourselves the evenings' entertainment—quiz nights, board games, and such."

Olivia saw the lack of enthusiasm at her suggestion, so she swiftly carried on, "We've also decided to hold a Wharton Park knitting competition. My mother-in-law, Lady Crawford, is organizing socks, hats, and scarves to be sent from Norfolk to our boys overseas. If you don't know how to knit, you'll be taught. And the girl who produces the most items within a one-month period will get a pair of"—she opened a paper bag that was on the table and pulled out its contents—"these."

The girls oohed and aahed at the pair of nylon stockings Olivia was holding up. She was relieved to see that her carrot-and-stick technique had been the right approach.

As Olivia left the kitchen, Adrienne, who had been out of sorts all week, barely leaving her bedroom, was standing in the entrance hall. "Will you join me for a drink in the library, Olivia? I certainly feel I need one."

"Of course," agreed Olivia, although she was exhausted after her long day and it was the last thing she felt like.

With Sable second to driving a tractor, Adrienne had to pour her own drinks. "Gin?" she asked Olivia.

"That would be absolutely marvelous." Olivia flopped into a chair.

"How did it go with the girls? What are they like?" Adrienne asked nervously, passing Olivia her drink and sitting down opposite her.

"They seem like a nice sort, but I suppose one can never tell. They don't have one jot of experience between them, but they'll learn. And any port in a storm . . ."

"Yes. And whatever hardships we must face here, it is nothing compared to what our boys will face. And it will not be long, Olivia," Adrienne sighed. "But at least you and Harry have had more time than most."

"We have, yes," Olivia answered mechanically.

Adrienne stared at her daughter-in-law. "*Chérie*, I do not mean to interfere, but is all as it should be between you and Harry?"

"Yes." Olivia nodded, a shiver of apprehension running through her at Adrienne's gift for perception. "We enjoy what time we have."

Adrienne looked at Olivia, searching her face. "Yes, perhaps it is because you see each other so little, as you say. But I have felt, when I have seen the two of you together, that there is some . . . distance between you."

"I'm sure you're right, Adrienne." Olivia continued the train of thought that her mother-in-law had begun. "We've barely had more than a few hours together for the past few weeks."

"Well, perhaps if Harry has some leave, you two could go away together. After all, you did not have a honeymoon."

The thought of being cloistered alone somewhere with Harry made Olivia feel physically sick. "Adrienne, I think we both realize our priorities are to the war effort. We have a lifetime together ahead of us."

"That is noble of both of you, Olivia, and"—Adrienne shuddered—"let us pray that is right."

Germany invaded Denmark and Norway in April, and the British campaign was commenced simultaneously. Yet, despite the dire backdrop of war, and the tension that existed as to when Germany would invade British shores, Olivia found she enjoyed her new life. The WLA kept her busy, and she'd become rather an expert at doing the "welcome" meetings for the girls who arrived in the county, and sorting out their subsequent problems.

The Wharton Land Girls were, in the main, a jolly bunch, and when she ferried their sandwiches down at lunchtime, she would often sit with them in the fields, enjoying their lighthearted banter. When she wasn't looking after her girls, or dealing with a broken tractor, or returning a runaway pig to its pen, she was up at the house with Adrienne. The ballroom had become a collecting station for the hundreds of balaclavas, scarves, and socks that the women of Norfolk were knitting to send to their boys. Ironically, Wharton Park was more alive than it had been before the war, with the girls popping in and out, and the women in the ballroom packing boxes of woolens.

Olivia had come to realize that Adrienne was extremely delicate. She would plead a headache at the slightest sign of a problem and retire to her room, sometimes for days. Olivia dreaded to think what would have happened to Wharton Park if she had not been there. More and more, the household staff were turning to her for instructions.

As winter turned to spring, the "Phoney War" gave way to the real thing in earnest when Germany invaded France. The Germans continued their domination of Europe in the Netherlands, then advanced westward through Belgium.

Harry moved, with the rest of his battalion, into the local boarding school in Holt. Due to the now very real threat of invasion, as Germany drew nearer to the English Channel, security along the Norfolk coast was on full alert.

At the end of May, the Battle of Dunkirk began. Olivia spent the evenings huddled over the wireless in the Land Girls' cottages, listening to the news. Two of the girls, Bridge and Mary, both had young men involved in the battle. Two days later, the broadcaster announced that Dunkirk was being evacuated and the British troops were being pulled out. There was no more joking and chatter, as everyone on the estate waited with bated breath to hear whether it would be successful.

When Winston Churchill, their new prime minister, broadcast his nightly address to the nation and informed them that 338,000 men had been rescued from the beaches and harbors of Dunkirk, there was cheering and tears. Even though they all realized it was a dreadful defeat.

"Please let Charlie be one of them," cried Mary on Olivia's shoulder. "I'd give anything, just as long as he's safe and sound."

Olivia decided a treat was in order for the girls to keep their spirits up and procured two jugs of cider for them to celebrate with. Elsie, without Bill around, had become fast friends with Mary and joined the Land Girls as unofficial guide on their expeditions into Cromer.

Olivia saw Elsie was sitting quietly in the corner. She went over to her.

"Elsie, you look awfully glum. Are you all right?"

"To be truthful, no, Miss Olivia. I'm sitting here, listening to this broadcast, and thinking that soon it'll be my Bill and your Harry. How I'll cope without him when he's gone, I really don't know." Elsie wiped a tear from her eye.

Olivia gave her a hug. "Try not to worry, Elsie," she comforted, feeling rather guilty that the thought of her own husband's leaving produced little emotional response. "Harry says Bill's just about the best soldier in his battalion, and a little bird tells me he's about to be promoted to sergeant, but"—Olivia put her finger to her lips—"don't tell anyone I said so."

Elsie's face brightened. "Ooh! Really, Miss Olivia? If he was, it'd be the proudest day of my life," she announced happily.

23

In the middle of June, as Olivia woke to the beauty of Wharton Park in full, dewy bloom, she heard on the wireless that France had surrendered to Germany.

Hitler was now in Paris, surveying his latest trophy, and she wondered how long it would be before the Battle for Britain, as Mr. Churchill had termed it on the radio this morning, would begin.

As she walked into the kitchen garden to collect the daily ration of fruit and vegetables to feed the estate, she thought how difficult it was to imagine actually arriving here in England, the kind of mass-scale death and destruction she'd seen with the girls on the newsreel two nights before. When she entered the kitchen with her two heavy baskets of fresh produce, she found Harry, looking gaunt and exhausted, sitting at the table drinking a cup of tea.

"Hello, darling." He smiled wearily. "Guess what? I've been given a day off."

"Gosh!" Olivia continued unpacking her basket of vegetables. The prospect of Harry's being home didn't excite her at all; rather the opposite in fact. "I'm sure you just want to go to bed and sleep."

"Actually, I thought we might use it to go out somewhere together. How do you fancy a picnic on the beach?"

Mrs. Jenks, the cook, hands in the sink, smiled and said, "Yes, Master Harry, take your wife out. She's been running this place single-handedly for the past few weeks, as far as I can see. She needs a break as much as you do." Mrs. Jenks looked at Olivia admiringly. "You've picked a good one there. She's just wonderful, she is. And we all think so," she added, so there could be no mistake.

Olivia blushed at the compliments and frantically began to cast around for excuses. "But I've got to take the girls' sandwiches down and—"

"Hush now! You leave it to me, Mrs. Crawford, and go and have a day out with your husband," said Mrs. Jenks.

Realizing that she was beaten, Olivia surrendered. "I'll run upstairs and get out of these trousers."

"I'll meet you by the car in ten minutes, darling," Harry called after her.

"My goodness, I'm glad to be out of it for a few hours," Harry breathed as they drove away from the house. "It's a beautiful day and I have a picnic from Mrs. Jenks in the trunk. I thought we might go to Holkham. It's perhaps the only beach I can think of that hasn't been completely spoilt by barbed wire and barrage balloons." He looked at her questioningly.

Olivia nodded silently.

They parked a few minutes' walk away from the beach and headed up to the dunes, Harry carrying their picnic basket. The beach was completely deserted, not a soul in sight. Harry threw himself down full length in the sand, rolled over, and closed his eyes against the sun.

"What a treat!" he said. "This is the life! Here, it's actually possible to imagine that the war is a nightmare I dreamt up in my sleep last night."

Olivia sat down on the sand a few feet away from him. She did not reply. She stared out to sea, willing this day to be over as quickly as possible. When she turned, she saw he was watching her.

"Fancy a stroll down to the waves?" he asked.

"If that's what you would like."

They stood up and walked together toward the sea.

"I just wanted to say, Olivia, that you've done the most marvelous job at home. I really don't know what would have happened if mother had been there alone. She has such delicate health and is so easily upset. I know you've been doing the lion's share of running the place."

"I've enjoyed it. It's been good to be busy."

"You're obviously a natural and everyone at Wharton Park adores you." He smiled down at her fondly. "As do I."

"Oh, Harry." Olivia was suddenly irritated. "Really, there's no need to pretend any longer."

They walked on in silence. Just before they reached the sea, Harry stopped and turned to her. "Olivia, I . . . I've been thinking a lot about when we first met. Before any of . . . *it* happened. I remember thinking to myself you were the brightest girl I'd ever had the pleasure to meet. Not silly and stupid and vain, like so many of the women I'd come across before, but a girl with real intelligence and integrity. I think you liked me then too."

"Of course I did, Harry," Olivia agreed quietly.

"Do you remember how we used to tease each other, laugh together?"

"Yes—"

"And perhaps," he said urgently, "I should have told you then and there that I thought you the most beautiful girl I'd ever seen."

Olivia shook her head in frustration. "Harry, do please stop! I understand what you're trying to do. But it's just too late!"

"Darling, please, with things as they stand, I'll be lucky if we ever have this chance again to be together, for me to be able to explain! I beg you, Olivia, I must at least tell you what happened to me. Please, can we sit down?"

Olivia looked at the desperation in his eyes and relented. "Well, I can't see how it can make any difference, but, yes, if that's what you'd like to do, I promise I'll listen." They both sat down on the sand.

"I'm going to tell you from the beginning. I accept, as you say, it probably won't make any difference, but at the very least, you deserve to know."

"Please, Harry, just talk."

"Very well. And, I swear, I expect no sympathy from you. It is merely an honest explanation. Right." Harry was visibly gathering his thoughts. "I tried to tell you that night, that when boys are together at boarding school—which I have to tell you are jolly cruel places to spend one's formative years—sometimes, out of sheer loneliness and desperation, they develop crushes on each other."

Olivia could not help but shudder at the thought.

Harry continued, "I was particularly desperate and dreadfully homesick for my mother. There was a boy in my year who I got on well with, and we became close. Not on any physical level, may I add. But it was the nearest thing to an intimate relationship I had. He showed me affection, Olivia, he seemed to care about me. And I wondered at the time, to be perfectly honest about it, whether I might well have been in love with him. Which then led me to wonder for the rest of my teenage years whether I was indeed, as you once put it so bluntly, a homosexual."

He looked at her for a response. Olivia lowered her eyes. She had none to give. Harry forged on.

"This feeling was, of course, exacerbated at Sandhurst. As you know, I'm hardly a natural soldier, and I really began to believe my lack of eagerness to fight and to be aggressive, combined with my fondness for the piano, was due to my lack of masculinity. When I first met you, I admit I was very confused. I'd had few dealings with women and certainly no intimacy. To be brutally honest, they scared me half to death. I didn't understand what they wanted and I didn't know how to please them. Then . . ." Harry sighed. "I met Archie that night at Penelope's dance. And he seemed so very like me in so many ways: his sensitivity, his love of the arts . . . and, of course, I realized immediately that he was homosexual. He was very encouraging, and I traveled to London a couple of times to meet him."

"I *knew* I saw you once in London," Olivia butted in, "when I was going into the Ritz late one night. You were walking up the steps of a club, further down the street."

Harry nodded. "Yes, I was there. Archie had introduced me to some of his—friends. He'd taken it for granted, right from the start, that I was 'one of them.' He put a lot of effort into trying to persuade me." Harry hung his head. "When he came up for our wedding, he tried to talk me out of marrying you, said that it was all a terrible mistake. And, to be frank, Olivia, I was so confused that day, I really didn't know what to think. Archie had filled my head with horror stories, about how I'd be unable to perform as a husband with you on my wedding night." Harry looked into Olivia's eyes. "I was so damned scared he'd be proved right. Oh, God, Olivia! Believe me when I tell you I'm so dreadfully sorry for what happened that night. I was, quite simply, terrified out of my wits."

Despite her determined efforts not to believe a word Harry said, when Olivia looked into his haunted, sad eyes, she could not help but feel they were filled with some kind of basic honesty. If he wasn't telling her the truth, then he was a talented storyteller.

"That night," Harry continued, now on a mission to finish, "when I left you in the bedroom with Elsie, while I waited, I went into the library to pour myself a brandy for courage. Archie found me and told me he loved me then and there. I asked him to leave me be—I was very angry and terribly confused." Harry sighed. "While you were waiting for me in the bedroom, wondering what the hell had happened to me, I was taking a long walk through the park with a bottle of brandy for company. And that, my darling, on my mother's life, is the truth."

"I see." Unable to look at him, Olivia concentrated on sieving the soft sand through her fingers.

"As you know, three weeks later, at Christmas, Archie reappeared. I was at the height of my confusion, couldn't see a way out. I looked at you, at your grace, your gentleness, your beauty; yet, at the same time you were so confused and hurt, because of what I'd done to you."

"So you knew what you'd done was wrong? Or at least, what you hadn't?"

"Of *course* I did, darling! I just didn't know how to put it right. And that night you caught me, I'd just told Archie I didn't ever want to see him again, that I was convinced now I loved you and wanted to be a proper husband to you. He became very angry, then grabbed me and kissed me."

"From what I saw, you were hardly struggling to get away from him."

"If you'd waited for just a few more seconds, you would have seen me trying to get out of his grasp—he was literally smothering me." Tears were in Harry's eyes. "I *hated* it! It felt wrong and unnatural and, whether you believe me or not, I am a *man*!"

Olivia watched him as he sat next to her in genuine despair. She thought it best to stay quiet until she knew what she wanted to say.

Harry recovered his composure. He grabbed her hand and held it fast, twisting himself to look into her eyes. "And finally, darling, I just wanted to say this: not only has my admiration and respect for you grown apace in the past few months, but with it, my love. And, because I'm no longer confused about who I am, and I don't have Archie whispering in my ear, my natural physical urges have surfaced. Olivia, I understand you may find me repulsive, but I must tell you now that I want you. Just as any normal man would want his beautiful wife."

He reached out his other hand to stroke her cheek gently. And she didn't flinch. "And you are so very beautiful," he said softly. "And I am so dreadfully sorry."

"Oh, Harry, I . . ." She gave a huge sigh of confusion as he continued to stroke her cheek. She felt alarmingly comfortable and comforted by it. "It's almost destroyed me," she whispered. Harry moved closer to her and put an arm round her shoulder.

"I know, my darling, darling girl. I understand how much I've hurt you, and that I may never be able to mend it. But, Olivia, if you can forgive me, find it in your heart to give me one last chance, I'd really like to try. I swear to you on everything that's precious, I will not let you down."

Her tears fell then, unstoppable, and she buried her head in Harry's chest. He put both arms round her and held her tight. "Olivia, you are strong and brave and beautiful. What more could a man ask for in a wife? I know how jolly lucky I am, and I'll do anything not to lose you."

"Oh, Harry, I've loved you so much. The problem is, how can I ever believe you truly love me? That you're not saying all this to save your own skin? How can I trust you?"

"Because, my darling," he said as he stroked her hair, "you've already seen how I find it impossible to hide the truth."

She managed a chuckle at that. "You're right. It was so very obvious to me that something was terribly wrong, even before we were married."

"There then! I wear my heart on my sleeve, and I always will. Olivia, I don't know how much time I have left before I'm shipped overseas. At best, it may be a couple of months, at worst a few days. I didn't want to pressurize you, but neither did I want to leave you like this. I couldn't bear to think that I'd ruined your life, that, even if I don't come back, you would find it hard ever to trust another man because of what I'd done to you."

Olivia let his words sink in, and she understood what they meant and what he was saying.

"So, even if you tell me now, or in the next few days, that you can never forgive me, at least I'll feel when I have to leave you that I did the right thing by telling you the truth. And, whatever you may have thought or still think, I love you, my darling. I really do."

It was Harry's turn to cry then, and Olivia laid his head on her knee as he wept and blurted out how he felt about his imminent transfer overseas.

"Even though I have to buoy up my men with stories of the camaraderie and jokes that we'll have when we leave to fight, I know what war is really like. And it's not the dying I'm frightened of, it's the fear of knowing it might happen at any second. At best, you might be blown into oblivion. At worst, you might take days to die an agonizing death. Either way, you're snuffed out, just another name on a memorial stone. I'm frightened, Olivia. And I am so bloody tired of being brave for everyone else."

When his tears had stopped, Olivia suggested they go back to the dunes and eat some of the picnic they'd brought with them. Mrs. Jenks had also packed a bottle of wine from Adrienne's French vineyards. Harry opened it and handed her a glass.

"Please don't drink to my health. At present, I'd give anything to have poor eyesight, flat feet, or asthma." He smiled. "Perhaps I am a coward."

"Of course you're not, Harry, you're just voicing what every other man in your position feels, but never says."

"I love you, Olivia." The words felt natural on his tongue. "The question is—can you believe me?"

She took a long time before she answered, searching his eyes for the truth.

"Yes, Harry, I do."

24

Southwold

I stare at the snowflakes dancing down like fat, falling angels on the other side of the window, every now and then the snow sets off Elsie's security lights, illuminating the thick, white flakes and presenting a surreal backdrop to the story Elsie has just told.

Even though the story so far seems to have little to do with me, and at present, I cannot see the significance, it has somehow comforted me. Hearing how others—including my grandmother—dealt with the fear of losing their loved ones, and the complexity of their lives inside the walls of Wharton Park, shows me I am not the only one to have suffered.

Perhaps the difference is that I had no forewarning, no moment on a windswept beach where I could right any wrongs, make my peace, tell them of my love, and say good-bye. . . .

There was no expectation and no preparation. And, unlike all the women who watched their husbands leave for war and took solace from one another in their mutual understanding, I feel I have had no one to turn to.

I have felt alone.

The world has continued around me as if nothing has changed. Two lives, snuffed out, with no Remembrance Day for them. Just a wife and mother in solitary mourning.

And yet . . . I did not live through the hardships of war, and at least, for my boys, there was no gut-wrenching fear of walking into death, unlike poor Harry Crawford or Grandfather Bill. And if my precious boys suffered at the end, I can only pray it would have been mercifully quick.

Someone once told me that death is as natural as birth, all part of the endless cycle of human joy and pain. It will come to all of us, and our inability to accept our own mortality and that of those we love is part of the human condition too.

Whichever way death comes, the loss is unacceptable to those left behind.

Julia roused herself from her thoughts. "So what happened next, Granny?"

"Well, Olivia came back from Holkham beach a changed girl. She began to laugh again, smile . . . it was like the sun had come out," Elsie remembered. "You could see the happiness shining from both of them. When he was home, Harry no longer slept in his dressing room. And I used to watch them, walking through the park, hand in hand. They looked like any other young couple in love. Of course, it didn't last long for either of them, but at least they had a few weeks together. And by the time Harry left with Bill for overseas, Olivia was in the family way."

Julia raised an eyebrow. "So, he wasn't gay?"

Elsie sighed. "No, he wasn't, Julia, I can vouch for that. In some ways, for Olivia's sake, it might have been better if he had been, and the whole tragic business could've been stopped then and there."

"What do you mean?" asked Julia. "Surely they got their happy ending?"

"Oh, Julia"—Elsie looked at her fondly—"not everyone in life gets that, as you know so well. The best we can hope for is moments of happiness and learn to enjoy them while we can. At least Olivia and Harry had theirs, albeit short." Elsie yawned. "Excuse me. After all that talking, I need to go and put my head down."

"Of course, can I make you a drink?" Julia suggested, as Elsie heaved herself from the sofa and turned off the gas fire.

"That'd be lovely. There's some cocoa in the cupboard." Elsie indicated the kitchen as she walked along the small corridor and into her bedroom.

"I'll bring it in to you," said Julia, following her out of the sitting room. She made the cocoa and took it through to the bedroom, where Elsie lay, resplendent under a pink satin coverlet.

"Thank you, my love," said Elsie, as Julia put the cocoa down on the bedside table. "It's not often these days that someone brings me a hot drink before bed."

Julia leaned down to kiss Elsie's forehead. "Night, Granny, and thank you for sharing your story with me."

"Well, sad to say, that's really only the start of it. But we can talk more tomorrow. The bed's all ready for you next door. Sleep tight, my love, and don't let them bedbugs bite."

Julia left Elsie's bedroom and wandered next door. She undressed and climbed beneath the flower-sprigged duvet, leaving the curtains open so she could watch the snow continue to fall. She loved watching it, loved the silence and calm it engendered.

Xavier had grown up in Moscow, and snow for him had been like rain in Norfolk; ordinary and an irritation. He'd taken her there once. . . . Julia shifted positions and forced her mind onto other thoughts.

She wasn't ready to go back yet.

Julia woke to the smell of bacon sizzling in the pan. She reached across to the bedside table for her mobile and looked at the time. It was almost ten o'clock. She lay back on her pillows with a sigh, hardly believing she'd slept in so late. *And* slept through the night.

There was a knock on her door.

"Come in."

Elsie peered round it. "Morning, my love. There's a full English on its way for you, ready in ten minutes. Come and get it when you've had a shower and got dressed."

Julia duly did so, still feeling inexplicably tired, then went into the kitchen to sit down and tuck into the kind of breakfast that, these days, she wouldn't normally have the appetite for. Yet, five minutes later, her plate was empty, and Elsie was giving her a second helping of bacon.

"You always did like your breakfasts, my love, didn't you?" Elsie smiled.

"It must have been the fresh air at Wharton Park. I remember I never stopped eating when I was there."

"Looks to me as though you could try doing that again." Elsie indicated Julia's thin arms.

"Really, Granny, I am getting much better, I promise you." Julia looked beyond Elsie to the outside and saw the snow had already started to melt. "Perhaps I should make a move while the going's good."

"Yes." Elsie was busy with the washing up.

"Are you too tired to tell me any more?"

Elsie's hands in the soapsuds paused for a second, as she thought. "Well, it drained me a bit, that's for sure. Perhaps you could come back another time and I can tell you the rest of the story?"

"Of course I can. Just one question, Granny—what happened to the baby you said Olivia was having after Harry left for the war?"

The hands in the soapsuds stopped moving altogether. "She had a miscarriage at five months, bless her. Just enough time to feel the baby starting to kick. It broke her heart, it did. I was always nagging at her to take it slowly, not to run around working them long hours like she did. Adrienne, her Ladyship, went to pieces once Harry had left, and Olivia took on the lion's share of running the estate. I know there's some women who can pick turnips right up to the moment the baby lands between their legs, but Olivia, for all she liked to appear strong, was born a lady. That baby meant everything to her. It was the heir to Wharton Park they needed."

"But, surely, when Harry returned from the war, Olivia could only have been in her midtwenties still, which gave her plenty of time to have another baby?"

Elsie turned away from the washing up to face her granddaughter. She shook her head. "Sorry, my love, these are all questions for another time."

"Of course," Julia agreed, guilty for wanting to know more.

"I'd like to keep the diary if I may. I never did read it," murmured Elsie.

"It's yours more than anyone else's, so you must keep it."

"That's not quite true, my love. . . ." Elsie's voice tailed off, then Julia watched as she visibly pulled herself together. "Anyways, let's save it for next time, shall we? Right, my girl, you'd better be on your way. I'll get your coat for you."

Elsie stood on the doorstep and watched Julia reverse the car out of the drive. She waved gaily as the car began to pick up speed and eventually disappeared. Elsie closed the door and went into the sitting room. She picked up the diary from the coffee table. She held it between both hands and looked up, as if in prayer.

"Oh, Bill," she whispered. "I wish you was here to tell me what to do. I don't know what's right to tell her, I really don't."

She sat down heavily, the diary on her lap, then opened the cover and started reading.

On the journey back, Julia began to feel decidedly unwell. As she neared home, she started to ache all over and developed a thumping headache. Having parked the car and walked wearily up to her front door, she let herself in and collapsed onto the sofa. She was aware the cottage was bitterly cold, and that she should switch the storage heaters on to full power and make a fire. She had the energy to do neither. Eventually, garnering the strength to climb the stairs, thinking that perhaps a short rest might restore her, she found some paracetamol in the bathroom cupboard. She washed them down with an old glass of water on her bedside table and fell into bed.

That night, Julia suffered the disturbed hallucinatory dreams that accompanied a severe fever. When she woke, she could hardly remember where she was—in France, Moscow, at Wharton Park, in the hothouses with Grandfather Bill . . .

She was too weak to do more than stagger to the bathroom and gulp back some water to quench her raging thirst. The trip rendered her so faint that she had to crawl back along the floor to reach the bed.

Somewhere in her mind, she knew she should call Alicia or her father to come to help her, but in her dreams the mobile was always just out of reach. Or, if she did manage to grasp it, it would fall from her hands into a deep ravine. And Xavier was here, surely it was him! Yes . . .

"Julia! Julia! Wake up!"

She felt a gentle arm shaking her and opened her eyes. Her vision was blurred and the face above her swam before her eyes, although she was sure she knew the voice.

"Julia, what's wrong? Please, can you speak to me!" The voice was urgent now.

Julia concentrated on focusing and saw a man standing over her. With huge effort she mouthed the word "Kit."

"Thank God!" His voice was full of relief. "At least you recognize me. Julia, have you taken something? Tell me what they were, it's very important you do."

Julia closed her eyes, feeling she might faint again if she didn't, and managed to shake her head. "No, no, taken nothing . . . just . . . feel terrible . . . and so hot."

A cool hand went to her forehead. "My God, you're burning up. When did this start?"

"Last night," Julia managed, "suddenly . . . felt awful."

"Are you aching?"

"All over . . . dreadful . . . dizzy . . . head hurts . . ."

"Right." Kit pulled his mobile out of his pocket. "I'm pretty sure it's the flu, but I'm calling the doctor now to come and double-check."

"Really, don't worry . . . be fine . . . I . . ." Julia stopped. She felt too weak to argue.

Half an hour later, an elderly doctor had finished examining Julia.

"Well, my dear, as Lord Crawford so rightly suggested, you have a nasty bout of the flu. I'll pop down and speak to him," said the doctor, stowing his thermometer in his bag. "He looked rather worried when he met me at the door."

Kit was pacing the sitting room like an anxious mother.

"Nothing too serious, Lord Crawford. As you suspected, it's flu, but the young lady does have a very high temperature. Does she have someone to come here and nurse her? She really can't stay here alone until that fever is under control."

"She has a sister. I'll get in touch with her. I presume it's the usual treatment: paracetamol every four hours and, if her temperature doesn't come down, revert to the old-fashioned but reliable method of sponging her with tepid water," Kit said. "And as many fluids as we can get down her."

"Spot on." The doctor eyed him. "You have some medical training, Lord Crawford?"

"Yes, some. Thank you for coming so swiftly."

"Always a pleasure, Lord Crawford. I was fond of the late Lady

Crawford. So sad she is no longer with us, but perhaps it was for the best. Her quality of life wasn't much toward the end."

"No," acknowledged Kit, feeling uncomfortable he hadn't bothered to come home for the funeral.

"Well now, I'll leave her in your capable hands. Good day to you, Lord Crawford."

When Julia eventually woke up properly, she had no sense of how much time had passed. All she knew was that she felt slightly better, that her eyes were focusing and the aches that had been attacking the muscles in her body had lessened. Needing to use the bathroom, she drew back the covers with a shaking hand and put her feet on the floor. She hauled herself up onto them and just made it to the bedroom door before sinking onto the carpet, feeling horribly faint.

She heard footsteps on the stairs and a knock on the door.

"Julia? Are you all right?"

The door opened onto Julia's kneecap and she struggled to move her weak limbs so that Kit could enter the room.

"What on earth are you doing down there?" he asked, as his hand swept over her forehead at the same time.

"Trying to get to the bathroom," she murmured, embarrassed.

"Mmnn. Well, at least you don't seem to have a temperature any longer. Come on, let's get you upright."

Julia had no choice but to let Kit heave her to standing and walk her like an invalid across the small landing to the bathroom. He opened the door, and when it looked as though he was going to accompany her inside, she said, "Really, I'll be okay."

"I'll wait here so I can help you when you come out. And don't lock the door in case you faint and I can't get to you."

"Yes, thank you," Julia muttered as she shut the bathroom door behind her.

When she reappeared, Kit, having respectfully withdrawn to the bedroom, came immediately to her side and helped her walk back to the bed.

Once she was in and settled, he sat on the edge of the bed and looked down at her, studying her face. "Dr. Crawford deduces that his patient may finally be over the worst." He smiled and reached for a glass beside her bed and put it to her mouth. "Drink this please, Miss Forrester. It's full of glucose and it'll help bring back your strength."

Julia almost gagged on the sugary taste. "Yuck," she muttered. "It's disgusting."

"But far better than Lucozade. So the doctor tells me, anyway."

Julia laid her head back gratefully onto the pillow. "What day is it?"

"Thursday I believe, as yesterday was Wednesday."

Julia gave a halfhearted gasp. "You mean I've been in bed for three days?"

"Yes, Miss Forrester, you have. Ranting and raving and thrashing about like a lunatic. One night you were making so much noise, I almost had you sectioned."

Julia blushed. "Oh, God, Kit, I'm so sorry. You've not been here the whole time, have you?"

"Not all the time, no," he replied gallantly. "Alicia couldn't stay, what with her brood. I could have put you into the cottage hospital with all the geriatrics, but I thought that would've been rather cruel."

"Oh, Kit," Julia moaned. "Playing nurse to me, with everything else you've got on, was the last thing you needed."

"As a matter of fact, it's given me a great excuse to get out of Wharton Park for a few days. Besides, I completed the first part of my medical degree in Edinburgh before I dropped out. You'll be comforted to know that you haven't been in the hands of a complete amateur."

"Thank you . . ." Julia could feel her eyelids were drooping. She closed them and began to drift off to sleep.

Kit smiled down at her, removed a stray piece of hair from her forehead, then tiptoed to the door and closed it softly behind him.

25

By the evening, Julia had managed to sit up in bed and sip a little soup from the bowl Kit proffered.

"It is rather good, isn't it? Alicia dropped it round earlier when you were asleep. She said she'd pop back to see you tonight when Max arrives home, so he can babysit the children while she's out. She's been very concerned about you. We all have."

"Well, please feel free to go home now," Julia answered guiltily. "I really am feeling a lot better."

"What? And miss out on the first lucid conversation I've had in the past four days? No." He shook his head. "I'm afraid you're stuck with me until you're up and about."

There was a knock on the front door downstairs. "That will be Alicia," said Kit. "You up to seeing her?"

"Yes! I told you, I'm feeling better."

"Right." Kit walked to the door, his long legs covering the space in two strides. "Seems to me we've moved on to the grumpy stage of our illness." He raised an eyebrow. "I'll just go and get your sister."

Alicia appeared at the bedroom door a few seconds later, her pretty face creased into a worried frown.

"Julia, thank God you're okay! We've all been so worried about you." Alicia walked over to the bed, bent over, and gave her sister a hug. "How are you?"

"Better"—Julia nodded—"definitely better."

Alicia sat down on the edge of the bed and took Julia's hand in hers. "I'm so glad. You've been really ill, poor old thing. And I suppose your immune system has been weakened from, well—all the trauma."

"Probably," agreed Julia, not inclined to use up precious energy arguing. "And thank you for your soup. It was very sweet of you to bring it over for me."

Alicia raised her eyebrows. "Goodness me, it was nothing. The person you need to thank is Kit. He's been amazing. When he realized I couldn't come because of the kids, he offered to stay here with you. I've only been a support worker in this whole drama."

"I'm feeling very guilty I've been so much trouble." Julia sighed. "It seems to be my middle name at the moment, doesn't it?"

"Come on now, Julia, none of that self-indulgence, thank you," Alicia chided. "Nobody can help getting sick. We all love you and want to look after you. And when you're better, I'm hoping you can tell me what Granny said about the diary."

Julia nodded, thinking it seemed ages ago since she'd been in Southwold with Elsie and traveled back to the Wharton Park of 1939. "Of course I will. It was absolutely fascinating."

"I can't wait to hear all about it. Is there anything I can bring you over tomorrow? What do you fancy food-wise?"

"Not much." Julia shook her head. "I'm just about managing some of your soup. Perhaps I might move on to bread at some point."

"I'll bake you a fresh loaf," agreed Alicia. "Kit needs feeding as well. I'll pop in with it tomorrow." She leaned forward and kissed Julia. "So good to see you looking better, darling. Keep up the good work."

"I'll try," she said, waving feebly as Alicia left the room.

Alicia went downstairs and found Kit laying a fire.

"She seems a lot better, thank goodness, and thanks to you. You really have been a brick, Kit," Alicia added gratefully.

"No problem. Fancy a quick glass of wine before you leave? I could do with some coherent conversation." He grinned.

Alicia briefly checked her watch. "I should be getting back, but I'm sure Max can manage for a while longer."

"Great." Kit stood up as the fire began to burn. "I'll get a couple of glasses."

Alicia sat down in the armchair next to the fire as Kit brought in a bottle, uncorked it, and handed her a glass.

"Cheers," he said, filling his own, "here's to Julia's continued recovery."

"Absolutely. Poor thing, she's really been through the mill recently, to put it mildly."

"Yes, so I gather. Can I ask what exactly did happen?"

Alicia took a sip of wine. "Julia's husband and son were killed in a car crash in the South of France last summer. The worst thing was"—Alicia shuddered involuntarily—"that the car veered off the road, exploded on the hillside, and started a forest fire. Their remains weren't able to be formally identified. Which means there's been no closure for her. No bodies, therefore no funeral."

"Christ," Kit breathed. "Poor Julia. How old was her son?"

"Almost three. He was called Gabriel. And he was"—Alicia's words caught in her throat as her eyes filled with tears—"an angel." She took another gulp of wine. "To lose a husband is dreadful, but to lose a child at the same time . . . How Julia's coped, I just don't know. I mean, she hasn't, but . . . no one has known how to reach her. She's been locked away in her grief. I've felt so—useless. I don't know what to say or do, and most of what I try seems so inadequate. Sorry." Alicia swiftly wiped her eyes. "Not me that should be crying. It's Julia's tragedy. I just feel for her so much and don't know how to help or comfort."

"The answer is, you can't." Kit reached forward and topped off Alicia's glass. "Everyone around her wants to do *something*, but, actually, no one can. The kindness you offer, as someone who loves the person suffering, makes the sufferer feel guilty that they can't respond, which puts further pressure on them to recover. Which, of course, they can't cope with, so they retreat even further into themselves." Kit looked into the fire and sighed. "Alicia, believe me: yes, be there for her, but understand the only one who can help Julia is Julia."

"You sound as if you know what it feels like."

"I do," Kit agreed shortly, "and you just have to give her time. Personally, from what little I've seen of her, I'd say she's getting there. Julia's a survivor, Alicia. She'll pull through this, I know she will."

"The problem is," Alicia sighed, "Julia worshipped Xavier, her husband. I've never seen a woman adore a man as she did. Actually, I found him conceited and arrogant. He was a pianist too, but a real prima donna, and Julia was happy to pander to him. Yet he wasn't nearly as talented as she is. I suppose there's no accounting for taste, is there?"

"No. And it sounds like he made Julia happy."

"He seemed to, yes. And I was glad that at least she was able to open up to someone emotionally. I always worried she wouldn't be able to, after we both lost our mother. Julia changed, Kit. She really changed. She withdrew. From me, from Dad, from everything, except her beloved piano. This time, well, she's even withdrawn from that."

"Have you asked her why?"

"I think I know," Alicia said grimly. "She had just given a recital in Paris of Rachmaninov's Concerto No. 2 when she got the call to tell her they were dead." Alicia shrugged. "I can only assume it's that—the association with the piano, and pain."

"And guilt, of course. She probably felt she should have been with them when they died."

"I'm sure you're right. I know Julia hated leaving Gabriel behind when she had a recital. She was, as many working mothers are, torn between her child and her career."

"Why did she return to Norfolk afterward?" Kit asked.

"I flew to Paris the following day. When I arrived, I didn't know what to do. I couldn't leave her alone in France, but neither could I stay there with her because of my kids. Julia was in too much shock to make any rational decisions, so I brought her home with me to my house. She then insisted on coming here to the cottage, even though I begged her to stay with us."

"She needed solitude. I understand that. People react in different ways to tragedy. And no way is wrong. I lost someone once . . . and, to say the least, the aftermath wasn't very pretty. What was it John Lennon said?" Kit looked to the ceiling for inspiration. "Yes—'Life happens while you're busy making other plans.' And no truer words were spoken. None of us are in control, and even though it usually takes pain to realize this, the sooner one does, the sooner one can try to take each day as it comes and make the most of life."

"You're very wise, Kit," Alicia said admiringly. "Personally, being out of control scares me to death. Anyway, I'd better be off to *take control*." She smiled, standing up. "Left to Max, the kids run wild."

Kit stood too. "I appreciate you filling me in on my patient. I'll do my best to restore her physically, but the mental has to be up to her."

"I know." Alicia walked to the door. "Thanks, Kit, for all your help."

"Believe me, it's been a pleasure."

• • •

An hour later, after Julia had used the bathroom and found her legs were no longer the puddles of unset jelly they had been, she gingerly attempted the stairs.

Kit was reading a book in front of a roaring fire. He'd closed the curtains against the evening chill, and the sitting room looked far more welcoming and cozy than it normally did.

"Hello," she said from the stairs, not wanting to startle him.

He turned round and stood up immediately. "Julia, what are you doing out of bed? You'll catch your death."

He moved to steer her back up the stairs, but she shook her head. "How will I catch my death? It's absolutely boiling in here. Besides, I'm bored upstairs. I wanted a change of scene." She felt like a defiant child as she stood there, waiting for Kit to agree.

"All right, but not for long." He put his hand under her elbow and led her to the sofa. You lie down on there and I'll run upstairs and get you some blankets."

"Really, Kit, it's lovely and warm in here, and I've had enough of being wrapped up." She sighed as she lay back on the cushions he had provided for her head.

"Feeling hungry or thirsty? Can I get you anything?"

"No, really, please, sit down. I'm fine."

"What you mean to say is, will you please stop fussing over me," Kit acknowledged as he sat down in the armchair by the fire. "Sorry."

"Oh, Kit, please don't apologize!" Julia said, contrite. "You've been wonderful and I'm very grateful. I just feel guilty, that's all. And I'm sorry if I've been grumpy." She grinned at him. "I don't mean to be, really."

"Apology accepted." Kit nodded. "Personally, I prefer grumpy to sweaty and incoherent, so it's fine by me."

"As you can see, I am getting better. You really are free to leave tomorrow, Dr. Crawford."

"Yes, I must anyway, actually. Things are starting to pile up back at Wharton Park. But, listen, while I've got you with your marbles more in place, tell me what your grandmother had to say about the Changi diary."

"Yes . . ." Julia's mind strayed back to what felt like a lifetime ago. "I don't know how much you already know about the Wharton Crawfords . . ."

"More these days than I used to. And, remember, my great-grandfather Charles was Lord Christopher Crawford's younger brother, so he grew up at Wharton Park. Unfortunately, he got blown up in a trench in 1918, leaving his wife, Leonora, with two young babies, one of whom was my grandfather Hugo."

"That would have been before Elsie's time, but how fascinating," mused Julia. "I certainly heard a lot about Lord Christopher—"

"My namesake. Sorry, I'll try not to interrupt. Please, begin." He settled back in his chair to listen.

Julia began to tell him, conjuring up as best she could the world that Elsie had so vividly described to her.

Kit sat quietly until Julia reached the end of her tale. "What a story," he breathed. "Of course, Penelope, the girl who had the dance at Wharton Park, was my great-aunt, sister to my grandfather Hugo, who also died in action, in the Second World War. His wife, Christiana, my grandmother, gave birth in 1943 to my father, Charles, who became the heir to Wharton Park on Harry Crawford's death, just before I was born. We didn't move into the house, though. For some reason. My father loathed the place and certainly didn't have the wherewithal to restore it. Besides, Aunt Crawford was still alive and very much the chatelaine. Thanks for telling me, Julia. It's interesting, tying the family history together."

"It must be, and to be honest, from what Elsie's told me so far, it all seems far more relevant to the Crawfords, and therefore to you, than it does to my family's past."

"Well, I'm sure there'll be a link in there somewhere, though I can't quite see how, unless it's to do with Harry and Bill being in the same battalion during the war. Yes"—Kit nodded—"I'll bet that's it. Perhaps there's some dark Crawford secret lurking somewhere in the pages of Bill's diary." He smiled, his eyes twinkling.

"Maybe, but I won't speculate until I've heard the full story. It's also odd for me to think that my grandmother was in service to your family, and my grandfather still working for them when I was a child. So much can change within two generations, can't it?"

"You mean that a mere gardener's granddaughter can achieve the kind of fame and riches Elsie could never have dreamt of?" Kit teased.

"I suppose I do." Julia blushed again. "I think what really struck me was the fact that Wharton Park was a throwback to a completely different era, even though it was only seventy years ago."

"That's certainly what I felt when I stayed there during the summer. And of course, Olivia, who was technically not related by blood to me, but was always known as 'Aunt' to our family, never left it until the day she died. I'm sure her continued presence held Wharton Park in a time warp."

"Oh my goodness, I've just realized . . ."

"What?" Kit asked.

"That the scary old lady with those cold blue eyes, who came and ordered me to stop playing the piano on the day I first met you, was Olivia Crawford!"

"Yes"—Kit raised his eyebrows—"and what a bundle of laughs she was, poor thing. Lord knows what had happened to her during her life, but it must have been pretty awful to change the lovely young girl you describe into the sour old boot I knew."

"Don't mince your words, Kit." Julia grinned.

"Well, she was. And I used to dread going to stay with her."

"To be fair, it must have been pretty awful to discover your husband kissing another man."

"But then, from what you said, Olivia and Harry did manage to sort out their problems before he went off to war."

"Yes, it seems they did."

Kit saw Julia yawn. "Right, bed for you, young lady. I don't want you exhausting yourself. Come on, I'll help you up the stairs." He stood up and came over to her. Julia was grateful for his arm.

As he settled her under the sheets, she smiled up at him.

"Pity you didn't continue your medical career. You seem awfully good at all this."

"Seems like life had other plans for me." He shrugged as he handed Julia her paracetamol and a glass of water. "Drink up."

"Why did you stay away abroad for so long?" she asked, handing him the glass back.

"It's a long story," Kit replied shortly. "Sleep for you now."

"Okay." Julia snuggled under the covers and watched as he moved toward the door. He stopped just in front of it and paused.

"I do understand, you know."

"Understand what?"

"Some of your pain. Night, Julia."

"Night, Kit."

26

The following day, Julia took a bath and got dressed. As she lay on her bed, exhausted from putting on her jeans and a sweater, she glanced out the window and saw that since she had been sick, spring had arrived. She could hear birds singing and smelled a hint of the freshness that indicated nature coming back to life.

She felt it was a metaphor for her own existence, as there was no doubt that, although physically weakened, she felt mentally stronger. Just because she no longer thought of them for every second of the day—occasionally, whole minutes—did not mean she loved them or missed them any less. Just like the spring appearing, it was nature's way of helping her heal and regrow.

She heard Kit climb the stairs and shut the bathroom door behind him. He was sleeping on one of the narrow bunk beds meant for children, not for six-foot-plus adults. She smiled as she thought of his kindness. He was a true-life Good Samaritan, who'd helped her in her hour of need. She realized how much she had enjoyed being looked after.

Even though Julia didn't doubt that Xavier had loved her, *she* had been the carer in the relationship. He had been far too wrapped up in his music to think of Julia's domestic and practical needs. Like the adorable child he was, he looked to her for constant reassurance and praise.

Julia pushed down the ember of guilt that told her she must remember her husband as she had for the past eight months: perfect.

There was a soft tap on her bedroom door. "Come in," she called.

Kit's head, with its mop of curly hair, appeared round it. He smiled when he saw she was dressed.

"I don't think I need to ask if you're feeling better, do I?"

"And I'm sure you'll be relieved," retorted Julia quickly. She indicated the window. "I was thinking how much I'd like to go and have a breath of fresh air. I've been in this house almost a week now—Oh, God!" she uttered as a thought struck her. "Is it Friday today?"

"Last time I looked it was, yes."

"Oh, no!" she cried, sinking back into her pillows. "I was meant to see my agent for lunch yesterday at Claridge's. No one stands up Olav Stein. I'll have to call him immediately and explain."

"No, you won't, he knows already," replied Kit calmly.

Julia looked at him, puzzled. "How?"

"With your sister's permission, I listened to your voice mail. This Olav chap had left you a message on Wednesday reconfirming that you were coming to meet him. So I called him back and explained you were at death's door. He was very understanding. He sent you his best wishes and said to ring him as soon as you were back in the land of the living. Oh, and there were some other messages as well."

"Tell me later." Julia wasn't sure she could cope with more from the outside world just yet. "But, thank you, Kit, I really appreciate it."

"I confess I felt uncomfortable listening to your private messages, but under the circumstances, there was nothing else to be done." He shrugged. "Now, I'm going to go and make some breakfast for both of us, then I suggest a short walk down to the harbor and back, to give you some fresh air and test your sea legs. See you downstairs in a few minutes."

After a breakfast of porridge, laced with double cream and brown sugar, Kit and Julia took a slow walk through the harbor and headed along the spit of land beyond it. Julia remembered somberly the last time she had walked along here and the despair she'd felt. Now, being with Kit, on a sunny, springlike day, the world seemed a far brighter place.

"I have to leave fairly soon, I'm afraid." Kit sighed. "Among other things, I have to see the estate solicitor. There's a problem with the sale of Wharton Park. The buyer's trying to screw an even better deal out of me than the one he's already got."

"Christ, I'm sorry. I hope you can sort it out."

"I'm sure I will, one way or the other. Odd, really, isn't it? The way life turns out. Last thing I thought I'd be doing was dealing with the sale of Wharton Park," Kit said as they turned back for home.

"You must have known you'd inherit it one day, surely?"

"Yes, but it was something far in the future and a responsibility

I preferred to forget. Especially given that it's only mine by default, as the true Wharton Park branch of the Crawfords didn't manage to produce an heir."

"I really get the feeling you can't wait to get rid of it."

"No, that's wrong. I—" Kit's mobile rang in his pocket. "Excuse me, Julia. Hello? . . . Oh, hi, Annie. Everything okay?"

Julia walked discreetly ahead as Kit talked. He caught up with her at the door of the cottage. "Sorry about that. Looks like I've got to make a move," he said, as she opened the door and they stepped inside. "Now, are you sure you're going to be okay here alone?"

"Of course I will. I've been here for seven months by myself and no harm's come to me so far. I'll be fine, really."

"Can I get you some lunch?"

"I think I might just be able to stagger to the kitchen and get a sandwich. You get off, really."

"Okay. You've got my numbers, both mobile and landline, and Alicia said she'll call later and check you're okay."

"Oh, good." Julia rolled her eyes and sank onto the sofa.

"Alicia is only trying to help. She loves you."

"I know." Julia felt suitably admonished. "She just makes me feel useless. She's so terribly organized."

"That's her way of surviving life. We all have one, you know, even you." Kit smiled down at her and kissed her on top of her head. "Keep in touch, won't you? Let me know how you're getting on."

"I will," she said, feeling suddenly vulnerable and close to tears. She stood up again and then, unsure of what to do, shrugged and said, "Thank you. For everything."

"Don't mention it. See you around then." He opened the front door.

Julia nodded. "Yes. See you around."

She watched as the door shut behind him.

After Kit left, Julia went upstairs for a nap, but struggled to fall asleep. She tried reading a book that had been sitting on her bedside table for ages, but she couldn't concentrate on the story. Eventually, she must have drifted off, for when she woke it was almost six o'clock.

She was hungry, and with no Kit to make her supper, she wandered downstairs to prepare it herself. The spring day had disappeared like a memory and the evening had turned chilly. She lit the fire, using what she was sure were Kit's exact techniques, but as usual, it refused to ignite with the same verve.

After a supper of cheese on toast, the evening hours stretched out before her. Julia resolved she would buy a television—anything to dull the heavy silence that had fallen across the cottage since Kit had left.

Later, she took herself upstairs to bed. As she heard the clock from the church strike midnight, Julia admitted to herself that she missed him.

The next morning, Julia sat on the bench in front of her cottage, enjoying the warm, springlike air, and pondered her future. That she believed she even had one was a revelation to her.

The only certainty in her mind was that she no longer wanted to stay here at the cottage. Since Kit had left, the hours had dragged interminably. She knew she had too much time to think. Although it galled her to admit it, she was probably emotionally vulnerable. She was sure she missed Kit simply because he had shown her kindness.

If nothing else, the feelings engendered by his departure had given her the prod she needed to make some decisions at last. Frustrated by her lack of inspiration, she slammed her palm down on the wooden bench, making two nearby ducks ruffle their feathers and turn tail in disgust.

"Enough," she muttered to herself. She would make arrangements to go back to France as soon as possible. There might be difficult memories, but at least it was home. And far away from here.

Her mobile rang and she picked it up, glad of the distraction.

"Hello?"

"Hi, Julia, it's Kit."

"Hi." She felt her cheeks flush involuntarily.

"I was just calling to find out how my patient is."

"Better, definitely better, thank you."

"Good. Then do you think you might be able to stagger over to Wharton Park for supper with me tonight?"

"I think I might, yes." Julia smiled.

"About eightish?"

"Okay. Do you need me to bring anything?"

"Just you will do fine."

Julia felt her cheeks redden further. "See you then."

"Look forward to it. Bye, Julia."

"Bye."

Julia put her mobile down on the bench and stared into space, horrified by how happy she suddenly felt. Surely, *surely* it was impossible for her to be, well, interested in a man? Only months after her husband had died?

Of course it was.

Julia stood up, as if the physical motion would clear the thoughts from her mind, wipe away the tingling feeling that had surged up her spine when she'd heard his voice, stem the sudden excitement at the thought of seeing him again tonight. . . .

It didn't. She sauntered inside, feeling guilty and confused, but also, in spite of herself, experiencing something she vaguely recognized as expectation.

After lunch, she drove to Holt and bought a silk shirt, jeans, two soft cashmere sweaters, and a pair of boots. She'd wear the shirt and jeans tonight, she thought, as she walked down the High Street to stow her bags in the car, then chided herself for even thinking about it. It was hardly a date . . . was it?

Just as she was turning into the car park, she heard someone calling her name. She turned round and saw Alicia waving at her.

"Hi, Julia!" Alicia caught up with her and smiled. "You've saved me a wasted journey. I was just on my way to see you." Alicia eyed the carrier bags. "Been shopping?"

"Yes."

"You're feeling better, then?"

"Yes, thanks, lots."

"Good." Alicia nodded. "Good. Actually, Julia, if you're up for it, I was wondering whether you'd like to come to supper tonight? We have some friends joining us. It might be nice for you to meet some people locally."

"I can't, but thanks for the invite."

Alicia looked at her sister suspiciously. "Can't or won't?"

"Can't." Julia was reluctant to say more.

"Why?"

Julia sighed in frustration. "Because I've already accepted another invitation, that's why."

"Really?" The surprise showed on Alicia's face. As far as she was aware, Julia knew no one and had not been out of the cottage socially since she had arrived. "Where to?"

"Honestly, Alicia!" Julia snapped, her irritation getting the better of her. "Kit's invited me to Wharton Park for supper, okay?"

"Okay, okay. Sorry. I—" Alicia grinned and indicated the bag. "Planning on wearing something new?"

"Probably." Julia mentally begged her cheeks not to color. "Look, Alicia, I really have to go and buy a television before the shop closes at five. I'll call you."

"Promise?" Alicia asked Julia's back as she walked away hastily toward the car park.

"Yes. Bye."

"Have a good time tonight."

As Julia disappeared from view, Alicia allowed herself a smile, then set off for the dry cleaners to pick up Max's shirts.

27

Julia pulled her car to a stop in front of the crumbling stone steps that led up to the main entrance of Wharton Park. The house was dark, with the magnificent oak front door ominously closed. She realized she hadn't asked Kit which entrance she should use. It didn't seem this was the one. Stepping out of the car, clutching her bottle of wine, Julia locked it and walked round the corner of the house toward the more familiar servants' entrance.

As she walked, she noticed adrenaline pumping through her system; why she felt nervous, she couldn't fathom. This was simply a relaxed supper with a friend, after all. A man she knew almost nothing about, who might well be married with kids. Kit had never said and she hadn't asked.

Julia stood in front of the servants' door, glad to see a light on inside. She took a deep breath and knocked.

A few seconds later, Kit appeared and unlocked the door.

"Hi, Julia." He kissed her on both cheeks. "Come in."

"Thanks." Julia duly followed him through the boot room and into the kitchen. "I brought you some wine." She indicated the bottle as she set it down on the same pine table she had once sat at as a child.

"Thanks." Kit stared at her. "Blimey, you look better. And that color you're wearing really suits you," he said admiringly, indicating her new shirt. "Seems Dr. Crawford's care has worked wonders. White or red?" he asked, hovering by the pantry door.

"Either," said Julia, wishing her tongue could untie itself and she could relax. She gazed at Kit as he walked to the fridge, his long legs clad in jeans, his torso in a freshly ironed pink shirt.

"We'll start with white, then." He took a bottle from the fridge door and came back into the kitchen. "I'm afraid it's a voyage of discovery in terms of what this will taste like. The cellar's full of French wine, some of it dating back years. Some have aged better than others, as you can imagine. This will be nectar or vinegar." He pulled out the cork and sniffed it. "Neither, actually, but definitely drinkable."

"Perhaps you should get an expert in to take a look. There might be some valuable bottles down there. Xavier, my . . . husband, once bought a bottle for two thousand euros at an auction."

"And did it taste like two thousand euros when you drank it?" asked Kit, handing her a glass.

"It tasted nice, but not exceptional. I always said he must have been drunk when he bought it." Julia grinned.

"Emperor's New Clothes and all that, in my opinion." Kit took a tentative sip of his wine. "Bit like caviar and truffles; call me a Philistine but I don't understand the appeal of a few fish eggs or a simple mushroom. But, then, I eat to live, not vice versa. Or perhaps I'm simply jealous of the money it takes to indulge these whims. In the hierarchy of my needs, they currently feature somewhere down in Australia. Anyway, cheers, Julia. Welcome back to Wharton Park."

"Thank you for inviting me," Julia replied stiffly, taking a gulp of wine and hoping it would loosen her up. "How did the meeting with the solicitor go?"

"Actually, that's why I asked you here tonight. I need another opinion on the situation. And who better than someone who's always loved this old place?" He moved toward the ancient black range. "While I concoct the pasta sauce, I shall pour out my troubles to you."

"Fire away, it'll make a change listening to someone else's woes."

"The sale of Wharton Park has fallen through."

"Oh, Kit! No! Why?"

"Just another story of our times," he answered evenly. "We were meant to close yesterday, but when it got to the table, the buyer's solicitor announced he wanted the price reduced by a million, to take into account the drop in house prices since this deal was first negotiated. Apparently, Mr. Hedge-Fund has taken a bit of a lashing on the markets and can't afford to pay any more."

"Do you believe him?" ventured Julia.

"Who knows? At present, I can't decide whether he's an evil, conniving bastard, or an evil, conniving bastard," Kit muttered, poking the boiling pasta with a fork. "The point is, he realizes that in a market like this, I'm going to struggle to find another buyer."

"I see. What an evil, conniving bastard," Julia sympathized, trying to concentrate on what he was saying. "Can you afford to sell it for less?"

"Not with the debt the estate is currently in, plus the death duties on the small amount that's left over. But, to cap it all, Mr. Hedge-Fund has also demanded I throw in the Quadrangle. He's decided he doesn't want neighbors at such close quarters and, to be frank, that has really pissed me off."

"I can imagine. Especially as he's waited till the last minute to make these demands."

"Well"—Kit raised his eyebrows—"that's how the rich get richer, isn't it? The fact I'd negotiated the Quad out of the deal and decided to make my home there, somehow managed to make the idea of selling the estate more palatable. And . . . I admit it"—Kit held up his hands—"this place is getting to me. Which has surprised me, given that I never formed an attachment to it when I was here as a child."

"So, what are you going to do?"

Kit poured the pasta into a strainer and served it with the sauce into two bowls. "Well now, that's the million-dollar question. Right, dinner is served." He refilled their wineglasses and sat down at the table opposite her.

"Thanks for this, Kit. It smells yummy."

"Good. I like cooking. Or, at least, experimenting. Dig in before it gets cold."

"I'm afraid I'm not much of an expert in the cooking department." She took a mouthful.

"Merely a matter of practice, and I can't imagine you've had much of that, given your lifestyle. Besides, pretty disastrous if you managed to chop off a finger while peeling the veg." Kit's eyes twinkled. "Might engender a few missing notes in Mr. Chopin's Études."

"So, what are you going to do about Wharton Park?"

"I honestly don't know. What would you do?"

"Oh, Kit." Julia shook her head. "I'm probably not the person to ask. You know how I love Wharton Park. And I also know my sense of fair play would get the better of me. So, I'd almost certainly tell him to bugger off." She smiled. "But that's just me and doesn't take into account the financial ramifications. I mean, if you don't sell it to Mr.

Hedge-Fund, what will you do? Can you afford to keep the place going until someone else comes along?"

"Well, last night I looked through the books, and this morning I paid a visit to the estate accountant. It seems that, with the income from the farm and the tenants in the cottages on the estate, it currently runs at a small loss. But that's because any profit is servicing the interest on the debt." Kit poured himself some more wine. "The accountant pointed out that the estate could easily be turned round with a little attention to detail. The debts could be consolidated into a single mortgage on a lower interest rate, to free up funds to plow back into buying some modern equipment, and finding a good estate manager who knows what he's doing."

"That all sounds very positive."

"Yes, but there still isn't a bean to spare to sort out the house itself." Kit sighed. "The surveyor who came round when I was first thinking of selling reckoned it would cost a couple of million at least to prevent the building from crumbling. And that doesn't take into account any interior refurbishment, like a new kitchen or perhaps baths one can use without becoming dirtier than before one climbed in. There are sixteen bathrooms in the house, and, of course, I just don't have that kind of money."

"So, might it be possible to hold out for a few months until another buyer comes along?"

Kit nodded. "Yes, if I take on the job of managing the estate myself, which would mean putting other plans I had on hold. The thing is, the longer I'm here, the less I'm going to want to part with it. And, of course, *you* haven't helped."

Julia looked at him in surprise. "Thanks. What do you mean?"

"Hearing the story of my family has given Wharton Park some sort of meaning and value it didn't have before. And, I might add, it's part of our shared history too. If it hadn't been for Wharton Park, I'd never have met you all those years ago."

Kit's expression had changed. He stared at her, and abruptly Julia felt awkward under his gaze.

"Well then," she said, sounding more brisk than she meant to, "you've got a hard decision to make."

Kit nodded. "I have indeed. And not long to make it. And, to be honest, it wasn't *just* that I wanted to check up on you tonight, it was for the state of my own mental health too. I rather missed watching you slurp your soup and mopping your fevered brow."

"God knows why," said Julia, still stubbornly deflecting the change of atmosphere. "I was hardly a good conversationalist, given I was catatonic for most of the time."

Kit placed his fork in his empty bowl and stared at her thoughtfully across the table. "Yes, you were. But your catatonia had a quirky eloquence to it. Far better silence from one whose company you enjoy, than constant chatter from someone who irritates the hell out of you."

In the pause that followed, Julia finished her pasta, put down her fork and studied her bowl.

"Anyway," Kit continued, "it's been lovely getting to know you again. I never forgot that day, hearing you play. . . . Are you thinking of staying here in Norfolk?"

"I just don't know, Kit," she replied honestly. "I've only just begun to contemplate my future."

"I understand." He nodded. "I really do. I went through something similar a long time ago. It changes your life—and *you*—irrevocably. The upshot was, I found it almost impossible to form any kind of long-term relationship. In fact, I've been a nightmare until a couple of years ago." He grinned at her. "There's honesty for you."

"Yes," Julia muttered, not knowing how else to respond.

"Having said that, I hope I'm a better man now. And it could also be the fact that I've not come across the right person since then." He paused and stared at her across the table. "You don't meet many soul mates in life, do you?"

"No." Julia could feel her eyes filling with tears. She glanced at her watch. "Listen, Kit, I really must be getting home. I'm . . . tired."

"Of course. You must be." Kit stretched his hand across the table and laid it on hers. "Could we do this again another time, when you're feeling better? I'd really like to see you again, Julia."

"Yes." Julia pulled her hand away abruptly, stood up, and headed toward the door.

Kit followed her. "How about Monday night?"

"I don't know." Julia simply wanted to leave, unsure what was causing the strong emotions washing over her.

Kit put his hand on the latch before she could escape, blocking her way out. Then he bent down to kiss her. His lips touched hers and a sharp bolt of electricity ran through her. She pulled her lips away, but he enfolded her tightly in his arms.

"Julia, please, I'm sorry if I've said the wrong thing, if it's all too soon." He sighed. "We can take it slowly, I promise. I understand, really I do."

"I . . ." Julia extricated herself, confused. "Good night, Kit."

"I'll call you in the next couple of days. Perhaps on Monday we—"

But she had the door open now and was off, haring away from the house and toward the sanctuary of her car.

28

Over the next two days, Julia moped about the cottage, unable to relax in front of the brand-new flat-screen television that had been delivered and set up in the corner of her sitting room. She went out for long walks across the marshes, trying to understand exactly why she was feeling so unsettled.

It was all so confusing. *Kit* was confusing. One minute trying to warn her what a "nightmare" he was, the next saying he wanted to see her again and kissing her. And besides, what was she doing even *caring*? She was a recently widowed woman, still in mourning for her late husband; only two weeks earlier she had been unable to face the world. The next thing she knew, she was lying in bed, remembering how it had been when Kit had kissed her and imagining—well, more.

She simply couldn't fathom the effect he had on her.

The worst of it was that she had an impulse to check her mobile for messages every few minutes. Because of the weak signal, even in the bathroom, she had to keep walking up the High Street to make sure.

And, four days later, the mobile had remained steadfastly message-free.

When a week had passed with no word from him, Julia woke from a restless sleep, knowing she had to forget Kit and move on. That he'd said he would call, then failed to do so, was unassailable proof of a man who was not to be trusted.

As she took a shower, her mobile rang from the edge of the bath and she grabbed it, still dripping.

"Hello?"

"It's me, Alicia. How are you?"

Julia's heart sank. "Fine, thanks. You?" She balanced the mobile under her chin while she toweled herself dry.

"Yes, fine. Sorry I haven't been in touch. I've had a very busy week. How was your dinner with Kit?"

"Fine, yes, fine," Julia barked.

"Good. Seen him since?"

"No."

"Okay. So, there's no . . . romance then?"

"God, no! We're just friends, that's all."

"Good, I'm glad."

"Are you? Why? I thought you really liked him?" Julia was indignant, despite herself.

"Oh, I do like him. At least, I did, but—it's nothing, really. I just think . . ."

"Think what? Come on, Alicia, what are you trying to say?"

"Calm down, Julia. Besides, it really doesn't matter if you're not involved with him. I just wanted to warn you that perhaps Lord Crawford's world isn't quite as straightforward as I believed. Anyway, look, none of my business."

"No, it isn't," Julia snapped, and changed the subject. "How are the kids?"

"In fighting form, with an emphasis on the fighting." Alicia sighed. "Max and I wondered if you wanted to come for Sunday lunch tomorrow?"

"Thanks, Alicia, but, no. I'm"—Julia searched desperately for an excuse—"walking."

"Walking?!"

"Yes." Julia moved through to her bedroom, aware the signal would drop. "Call you soon. Bye."

She threw the mobile onto the bed in frustration, hating Alicia and Kit for having the capacity to upset her; but hating herself most for reacting.

In desperation, Julia drove to Holt to try to while away an hour or two. She bought food she had no appetite for and a scented candle she'd almost certainly forget to light. She walked listlessly up the High Street to the small boutique where she had bought her clothes a week ago and browsed through the racks. Nothing appealed, and the place only reminded her of the excitement she had felt when she'd been in there last. She spotted a toddler, about the same age as Gabriel, also with a head of curls and big blue eyes, but not as beautiful—no, never as beautiful—trotting round the boutique as his mother paid for her clothes.

Julia left, tears pricking the backs of her eyes, and wandered along the street toward her car. And then, she saw them: *him*, climbing out of his car and walking round to the passenger door to open it, and *her*, radiant, smiling at him in thanks as he moved to the rear door of the car and carefully extricated a tiny newborn from its seat. He kissed the baby tenderly on its head, then handed it to its mother as he opened the boot to remove the stroller. With the baby settled inside it, the three of them set off toward Julia, he with his arm draped protectively around the mother's shoulder.

Julia instinctively ducked behind the nearest car as they passed her, close enough for her to hear Annie's American accent and Kit's distinctive laugh.

"Oh, God." Julia breathed deeply as soon as they'd disappeared from view, ran to her car, and climbed in. "Jesus Christ! How *could* he?" she screamed, thumping the steering wheel as hard as her heart was hammering in her chest. She started the engine and hurtled out of the car park.

That night, she drank a bottle of wine, becoming more outraged with each glass. Kit had played with her, it was as simple as that. All that "I understand how you feel" talk he'd spouted was obviously a front for a man who had a heart as hard as a highly polished diamond. Perhaps, thought Julia, draining the dregs of the bottle, that was how he got his kicks. He was nothing more than your average lothario, with a better pedigree.

"Poor baby, poor Annie," she whispered as she walked unsteadily up the stairs and sank, fully dressed, onto the bed.

And yet he'd been so kind when she was sick, so caring . . .

A tear ran down her face. Being angry wasn't working anymore.

She missed him.

"Oh, no," she moaned, the alcohol making her honest enough to see and feel the truth. And the truth was, somehow, though God only knew how, she had fallen for Kit Crawford.

• • •

On Monday morning, Julia visited the travel agent to book a flight to France. Sunday had passed in a hungover, solitary blur, and after hours of afternoon television, Julia had made herself supper and given herself a good talking to. She could not let the Kit episode ruin her path back to life. She must use the experience, acknowledge how vulnerable she was to any form of affection right now, and make sure she did not become involved until she was "whole" and ready.

With her flight details in her handbag, Julia drove home feeling much more optimistic. She was flying on Wednesday, which gave her a couple of days to say good-bye to her family, pack, and prepare herself.

As she turned into Blakeney village, her mobile rang. A few moments later, it rang again. Glancing at the screen, she saw it was a voice message. Probably Alicia checking up on her, she thought, as she popped into Spar for a pint of milk and put the mobile to her ear.

"Hi, Julia, it's Kit. Many apologies for not calling. It turned out to be an unexpectedly hectic week. Wondered if you can make lunch tomorrow? Hope you're feeling better, anyway. Give me a call back at some point. Bye."

"Hah!" Julia startled a pensioner taking some butter out of the cold cabinet next to her. "Sorry," she said, taking her milk to the counter, paying, and scuttling out of the shop. As she drove around the corner to park near her cottage, Julia threw back her head and laughed out loud.

"Hectic week, eh, Kit? Well, it would be, wouldn't it, when your girlfriend, or maybe even your *wife*—who knows?!—was giving birth to your baby! Hah! Hah! Hah!"

Feeling ridiculously better that Kit had proved himself to be just what she'd thought he was—maybe worse—Julia continued laughing manically as she entered the cottage. The adrenaline inspired a frenzied session, as she packed the few clothes and odds and ends she wanted to take back to France.

Fifteen minutes later, she was done. She flopped down on the sofa, exhausted, occasionally shaking her head in disbelief at Kit's message.

To think at one point she'd even measured him up against Xavier, her poor dead husband, who might have had his faults, but had always adored her.

"Jesus," she muttered, then stood up and left the cottage to drive to Alicia's house and say good-bye.

"I'll miss you, darling," said Alicia, "but I'm glad you feel you can face going back. I know how hard it'll be for the first few weeks. If you ever want to talk, I'm always here, you know," she added pointedly.

"I promise I'll try and keep in contact," said Julia. "I know I wasn't great at it before. I was always so busy, traveling, playing, Xavier and Gabriel . . ."

Julia's voice trailed off, but she persevered, knowing she had to, *had* to be able to talk about them openly, if she was to survive in a place where everyone had known and loved them. "I think the thing I'm dreading most is walking into the house, knowing they won't be there." Julia bit her lip hard to stem the tears. "But, as you say, it will get easier eventually. I just have to find the courage to go through the pain."

"You will, Julia, and you can." Alicia sat down next to her and took her hand. "I just want to say, well, how much I admire you."

Julia raised an eyebrow. "Admire me? Hardly, Alicia. I'm always such a mess and you're always so together, sorting me out."

"That's simply our different personalities. And let me tell you, I honestly don't think I'd have survived what you've been through. Yes, I'm very organized, so I can run a house and a family and life. But put me in your current shoes and I'd be completely broken."

"Would you?"

"Yes, I would." Alicia nodded vehemently.

It was rare to see Alicia vulnerable and it made Julia feel churlish for her resentment. "You've been wonderful too Alicia. Thank you for everything. If you ever fancy a quick trip to France, you know you're always welcome."

"I'd love it, but I can't see it happening, can you?" Alicia waved her hand around her immaculate kitchen. "Mum going away? Their little worlds would fall apart." She smiled.

"Well, the offer's there, anyway."

"Thanks. So, all packed?"

"Yup. Took me all of ten minutes. Is Dad still here in Norfolk? I should go and say good-bye."

"He was in London, preparing for his trip to the Galápagos, when I last spoke to him, but give him a call," advised Alicia. "What about Elsie, and the other half of the story?"

"Actually, I thought I'd leave that to you. Why not take a trip down to see her sometime? She'd love it." The last thing Julia wanted just now was to hear further Crawford intrigue.

"I will. Are you going to say good-bye to Kit?"

Julia's eyes blazed. "No. I think he's rather busy at the moment, don't you?"

"I . . . don't know," Alicia replied weakly. "Well, bon voyage, little sis." Julia allowed herself to be enveloped in a hug. "Please, please, keep in touch this time."

"I will, and thanks for everything, really."

"You know I'm always here for you, Julia."

"Yes. Bye, Alicia. Give my love to the kids."

On her way home, Julia listened to half of a new message from Kit, wondering whether she'd received his last. She gave another loud "Hah!" and deleted it and switched off her mobile.

The next day, Julia sat out in the weak sunshine of the local pub garden and called Elsie and her father, to tell them she had decided to return home. Elsie, recovering from a lesser version of Julia's flu, could hardly speak, and George's mind seemed to be already in the Galápagos Islands.

"Going home, darling? To the cottage? Good, good. Lovely to hear from you."

"No, to France, Dad," Julia explained patiently, used to him being distracted when he was preparing for a trip.

"Oh, I see. That's the spirit! Got to get back into the swing at some point. And back to that piano too."

"One step at a time, Dad."

"Yes, of course. Well, I'm off this weekend. If you're back on e-mail, I'll keep in contact as usual. Though what communications are like out there, I've no idea."

"Keep safe, Dad."

"And you, darling. Just remember, I'm proud of you."

"Thanks, Dad. Bye."

"Good-bye, darling."

As Julia ended the call, she saw a text from Kit had come through. She pressed delete without reading it and finished her glass of wine and sandwich, thinking about tomorrow and the next difficult step of her journey. Now that it was imminent, she was dreading it. As she strolled back to her cottage, Julia pondered whether she *was* ready to leave. However irritating she found Alicia's clucking attention, it had provided a sense of security.

Back in France, she'd be on her own with the memories.

But what choice did she have? There was nothing for her here, nothing.

29

By eight that evening, the rental car she'd used for the past few months had been returned. The cottage was clean and tidy, and the airport taxi booked for seven thirty the following morning. Her traveling case was waiting by the door; she was ready to leave.

She looked around the sitting room, suddenly fond of the four walls that had witnessed her distress and provided stoic, if basic, sanctuary when she had needed it most. She stood up, went to the front door, and opened it. She breathed in the cool, clean smell of the North Sea and looked one last time at the boats bobbing in the harbor below.

"Hello, Julia."

A voice came out of the darkness and her heart jumped into her mouth.

"It's me, Kit," the voice said, as a figure moved into the pool of dim light emanating from the inside of the house.

Julia froze. She urged her body to take just three steps backward, shut and bolt the door, and hide behind the sofa until he'd gone. It didn't respond.

"Look, I know you're leaving tomorrow—"

"How?" she barked, pleased that at least her voice worked.

"I called your sister. When I didn't hear from you, I was worried."

"Hah!" Julia couldn't help herself.

"Julia . . ." Kit took another couple of steps forward, and Julia's arms reached out instinctively to bar the door.

"Look, I really do think there's been a misunderstanding. Could I come in and explain?"

"I don't think that's necessary, actually. I understand the misunderstanding, Kit, all too well. Now, if you'll excuse me, I have an early start tomorrow and I want to go to bed. Good night."

Julia took two steps inside and made to close the door.

"Please, Julia." Kit reached out the flat of his hand to keep the door open. "Just let me explain, even if only so we don't part on bad terms. I'd hate that, I really would."

Julia sighed, shrugged her shoulders, and relented. "If you insist. Five minutes, then." She turned and walked to the sofa.

Kit followed her inside and hovered by the fireplace.

"The reason I didn't call you last week was because Annie had her baby."

"Yes, I know. Congratulations." Julia forced a smile.

"Thank you. I'll pass that on to her when I next speak to her."

Julia arched an eyebrow in disgust. "Please don't bullshit me, Kit. I saw the three of you in Holt, looking very cozy. It's fine, it really is."

"Yes, it is fine, Julia, at least now, anyway. Look"—Kit scratched his head in agitation—"do you want to hear the reality or would you prefer to stick to the script that the whole of North Norfolk has conjured up for me in the past few weeks? Really, it's up to you."

"Sure." Julia shrugged noncommittally. "If you want."

"Whether you're interested in hearing it or not, I feel I owe you the truth. So," Kit sighed, "in brief, Annie is a very old and dear friend of mine. Twelve years ago, she helped me through a difficult time in my life. Anyway, she subsequently moved to the States and I visited her quite often. Then last year, she told me she'd finally met the love of her life. I'd never heard her sound so happy. The only problem, as she put it, was that he was a commitment-phobe. She was sure he loved her, but he couldn't quite take the next step of joining forces domestically, let alone marriage. Then, bingo! Annie finds herself pregnant. She's thirty-four, carrying the child of the man she loves, and there was no way she was going to terminate the pregnancy."

"No. I wouldn't have either." Julia agreed.

"Of course, Jed, the boyfriend, freaks and breaks off the relationship. Annie is heartbroken and decides the best thing she can do is get away from the memories and concentrate on the pregnancy. So she calls me and asks if it's okay to come and stay with me until the baby's born. I say, yes, of course. At the time, I was just moving to Wharton Park and it's not exactly lacking in space. To be honest, I was glad of her company. So, last week, Annie goes into labor two weeks early, and there I am, trying to play the supportive-partner role."

"That was very kind of you," said Julia grudgingly.

"It was the least I could do for someone who'd been there for me when I'd needed them. Although I felt like a total fraud. One of the nurses even commented the baby looked like me!" he chuckled. "After Charlie was born, I e-mailed Jed in the States to let him know he had a beautiful son. And sent a photo I'd taken just after the birth."

"Did Annie know you were doing this?"

"No, she didn't. But I knew she wanted Jed to be told. And I took a bet that seeing one's tiny, perfect progeny might stir the emotions of the most impenetrable heart. And, voilà! It did." Kit smiled. "Two days ago, he turned up at Wharton Park, fell instantly in love with his son, and is whisking mother and child off to the States to a future of domestic bliss."

"Wow!" Julia breathed. "Quite a story."

"With a spectacularly happy ending, which is a change. For now, anyway," Kit added cynically.

"I don't know whether I could have forgiven being abandoned like that. How can Annie ever trust him again?"

"She has to. She loves him, Julia. And if anything will change him, a small baby has to be the very best weapon. Add to that a very large diamond ring and a wedding as soon as Annie's up to it, not to mention a list of appointments scheduled with realtors in Greenwich, and at least you have as positive a new beginning as one could hope for. She's been brave and taken the leap of faith. I just hope it works out for her. Christ, Annie deserves it. She's been through hell in the past few months. I did my best, but I was only a poor stand-in for the real thing."

"She was lucky to have you, Kit."

"Even if it meant putting you through unnecessary pain and letting you down. I had to be there for her, Julia, I really did."

"Yes." Julia stared into the fire for a while. Then she looked up at him. "Kit, why didn't you tell me where you were? At the very least, I thought we were friends."

"Julia, Julia"—Kit shook his head in despair—"can't you see why I didn't?"

"No. Sorry, I can't."

"Okay then, I'll spell it out for you. I vividly remember the pain on your face when you met Annie in the Quad a few weeks ago. Seeing that pain, and understanding it was because you had recently lost your own young son, I thought the last thing you needed was a blow-by-blow account of a woman about to give birth, then bulletins from the hospital telling you how it was all progressing. Or, being confronted with a tiny newborn baby if you showed up to see me at Wharton Park. I didn't want to upset you when you were making such good progress."

"Oh." Julia's eyes filled with tears.

Kit stood up and moved to sit on the sofa next to her. He took one of her hands and placed it in his own. "I completely admit to being naïve and making a mess of things. I'd underestimated this small community, how word spreads, and the fact everyone seems interested in my 'goings-on,' as my cleaner referred to it the other day. I'm used to being invisible, you see. I've never lived anywhere for long, always been a visitor. It's going to take quite some getting used to. Half the country are raising their eyebrows at me at present, wondering where my 'wife' and newborn child have gone to."

"I can imagine. You did look very 'together' when I saw you in Holt. I'm afraid I assumed the same."

"As did your sister, who spoke to me earlier as if there was a particularly nasty smell under her nose. Anyway, I accept it was my fault entirely. Perhaps I should have told you, but please believe that I didn't out of the best of intentions, really. I wasn't prepared to lie and say I was somewhere else, so silence was the best option. I'm so sorry, Julia, I really am. In retrospect, I handled it badly. You must have thought me a complete bastard, kissing you and arranging dates one minute, parading a newborn baby around Holt the next!"

"That's what I thought." Julia could feel she was losing ground, being drawn back into wanting to trust him, believe him. Yet if his story *was* true, it actually made him a good person on all sorts of levels. And the contrast to her recent negative thoughts was a huge emotional leap to make. "Were you and Annie ever . . . involved?" she asked quietly.

"Absolutely not. We really do have that rare close male/female friendship without a hint of sexual chemistry. Annie's like my sister—or should I say, like the sister I'd have wanted if I hadn't got Bella. No, I'm afraid I wasn't Annie's type at all. She's always liked the rippling muscles and bulging chests." Kit glanced down at his slim torso and grinned. "Not me, really, is it? And she wasn't mine either; far too ballsy. I watched her eat men up and spit them out. Until, of course, she met the love of her life. Now she's a pussycat."

"Where did you meet her?"

"University. We shared a house when I was at med school in Edinburgh. Until I dropped out, anyway."

"Why did you drop out?"

Kit sighed. "Look, it's not something I talk about very often. Do you really want to hear? It's not a pretty story."

"Yes." She nodded, knowing intuitively that this was the missing link to who he was. "Actually, I do. But only if you are up to telling it."

"Okay," Kit breathed. "Is there any wine left in this house? I could do with a glass."

"There's half a bottle in the fridge, but it's a couple of days old."

"Any port in a storm," Kit quipped. "I'll restoke this pathetic apology of a fire while you get the wine and the glasses."

Julia padded off to the kitchen, feeling shell-shocked. Having struggled to find the strength to place Kit firmly in the past, she was now trying to accept what seemed a plausible story. When he'd held her hand, that same irritating bolt of electricity had ignited and slid up her spine.

"Here you are. Probably disgusting by now," she said, as she poured the remnants into the glasses and handed one to him. "So, fire away."

"It is," said Kit, after taking a gulp, "disgusting, but never mind. Right . . . if you don't mind, I'll rattle through it, tell you the bare bones; it makes it easier, somehow." He sighed. "As I mentioned, I shared a house at uni with Annie, who was studying architecture, and a couple of other students. Annie's best friend, Milla, came up from London to stay with her one weekend. I was twenty-two at the time, and from the first moment I set eyes on Milla, I fell in love. She was the most vivacious, beautiful, charismatic human being I'd ever met. The room came alive when she walked in. She was at drama college, training to be an actress." Kit shook his head. "I know she would have been a huge success if . . ."

"If what?"

"I'll get to that soon. Anyway, even though Annie warned me not to become involved, that Milla was a flighty butterfly with all sorts of hidden issues, I jumped in headlong. And Milla seemed to like me too, even though we were so different, and we became a couple. In the following few months, I spent more time on the motorways between Edinburgh and London than I did working. She was like a drug. I just couldn't be without her."

"First love," whispered Julia, thinking of Xavier and the moment she had met him.

"Yes. Completely. And, of course, I decided to fall in love with the most complex, needy woman of the lot. But I know now that was partly what appealed. It was the excitement of the roller coaster, never knowing where I was with her; whether she was really mine. She'd tell me she adored me, that she loved me more than anything, and then I wouldn't hear from her for a week or so. Suffice to say, my work suffered and I was living on borrowed time as far as my studies were concerned, but I didn't care." Kit gave a strangled chuckle. "Julia, I was a basket case."

"So, what happened next?"

"I staggered on, up and down to London, and after a while even I realized Milla was beginning to behave oddly. She'd always had lots of energy, able to stay up all night dancing and partying, but the energy began to take on a manic quality. Sometimes I'd spend an entire weekend with her and she wouldn't sleep at all. She seemed to be mixing in some pretty seedy groups in London and was starting to lose weight. Then, one weekend, I caught her in the bathroom, injecting herself. She was using heroin."

"Oh, God," Julia muttered.

"I knew Milla sometimes used coke, but this was a whole new level. She swore she could come off it, but said she needed me there to help her."

"And you agreed?"

"Like a lamb to the slaughter. I dropped out of med school and hotfooted it down to London to save her."

"Oh, Kit! After all that hard work. You must have been about to get your degree."

"Yes." Kit sighed. "Told you I was a basket case."

"So did you save Milla?"

"No. If only I'd known then that the one person who can save an addict is the addict themselves. Yes, Milla tried, I know she did, going cold turkey for a couple of weeks, or maybe a month, but then it would start over again. And, naturally, I became the 'enemy,' the beast who took money away from her, refused to let her walk down the street without me, listened to her calls in case she was contacting her dealer. She hated me. Hated me." Kit ran a hand through his unruly hair. "This went on for months, until I came back to the flat after a trip to the supermarket and found her gone. She was picked up by the police the following day, lying in a gutter, unconscious. She'd overdosed. The hospital booked her into a rehab center, and she promised me she'd stick with it. She was desperate I didn't leave her. I agreed not to, on the condition she stayed there and received the help she needed. I also told her if she went back on it, I would leave for good."

"You had no choice, Kit, surely? For Milla's sake and yours."

"That was certainly what the professionals told me, yes. And that was the last good moment, really, when she came out of the rehab center. We had three glorious months when I got my Milla back. She even talked of returning to drama school, and I looked into restarting my medical studies in London." Kit shrugged. "It was normal, and wonderful because of it."

"But it didn't last?"

"No." Kit shook his head wistfully. "By then I knew the signs: the mania, the purple shadows under her eyes, the weight loss . . . I may have given up my studies, but by this time I had a PhD in Milla and addiction. Milla denied it, but I knew she was using again. So, I carried out my threat, hoping it might jolt her into realization. God, Julia, it was dreadful. She screamed and cried, begged me not to go, said she'd kill herself if I left . . ." Kit put his head in his hands. "It was the worst thing I've ever had to do. I loved her so very much, but I knew nothing would change if I didn't leave her, and by this point, I knew I was being dragged down with her."

Julia instinctively reached out a hand to comfort him. "Kit, I can't imagine . . ." she whispered. "Did it help?"

"No! Of course it didn't." He gave a short, despairing laugh. "I stayed away for a week, literally having to stop myself going to her twenty times a day, then went back to find the flat deserted. I alerted the police, of course. And, eventually, two weeks later, they found her in the squat of a dealer. She was dead."

"I'm so sorry, Kit," Julia whispered, finding the words as useless as when the phrase had repeatedly been said to her.

"Yup, well . . . so was I." He raised his head from his hands. "She'd said she'd kill herself if I left her, and in essence, that's what she did. The autopsy showed she died of a massive overdose, but there was worse: it also showed she'd been raped repeatedly before she died. She'd obviously turned to prostitution to get her fix. I'd seen bruises in strange places on her body before, which I'd tried to ignore, but I had to accept she'd probably slept with men for money when she was with me."

As Kit paused and stared into the fire, she could see in his eyes he was reliving the pain.

"I—oh, Kit, I don't know what to say," she whispered.

"As you know so well, Julia, it's always best to say nothing, because there's nothing to say. I felt so bloody guilty for leaving her, so angry she'd wasted her life, and, actually, most of all, bitter she had chosen heroin and death over me. I simply lost my faith in human nature. All that stuff about 'doing the right thing,' that 'love will prevail' . . . well, it hadn't worked. There was no 'happy ending,' just the dead, broken body of a young woman and the wreck of a man still alive." Kit smiled bitterly.

"You mean, you had to accept you had no control? That sometimes it doesn't matter what you do, how much effort and love you pour into life, it makes no difference to the outcome? That's what I've learned in the past few months, anyway," Julia said quietly.

"Yes, that's it. And it's taken me years to learn the flip side; that sometimes it *does* make a difference and one mustn't lose belief. Of course, in the long run, these tragedies do make you wiser, more accepting of the frailty of human nature. But, my God, it took me a long time. I suppose I had a breakdown of sorts, afterward."

"Is that where Annie came in?"

"Yes. She was amazing. When she heard, she zoomed down to London and carted me back to Edinburgh, where she proceeded to give me the kind of TLC one reads about in books. She explained over and over again that Milla had always been fragile mentally, that there was nothing more I could have done, how I'd loved her and cared for her, and that I mustn't feel responsible for what had happened to her. I, of course, ignored her," Kit chuckled, "and carried on down the road to destruction and self-inflicted isolation. Let me promise you, Julia"—he looked her straight in the eye—"you have nothing on me. I wallowed in self-indulgence. For years, actually. I was so angry!"

"Hardly self-indulgence, Kit. You'd been through hell. How did the anger stop?"

"I had what I suppose one would call an epiphany a couple of years ago. On my travels, I did a three-month stint teaching English to a camp of orphaned Burmese children on the Thai border. Even though I'd seen some pretty horrific things before, this really got to me. Most of the kids had simply the clothes they stood up in. Their parents were gone, shot in Burma or escaped into the Thai countryside, desperate to find work. These kids were stranded in no-man's-land. They weren't in a place of safety—the Thai government refused to let them in, but they'd face death if they went home. There was literally no future for them. And yet"—for the first time, Kit's eyes glinted with tears—"they were all so grateful for the smallest thing you gave them. A new football was like handing over World Cup Final tickets. Each one of them had hopes and dreams for the future, even if they had none. They didn't give up on life, even if life had given up on them." He wiped his eyes harshly. "It's a cliché, I know, but seeing those kids, who'd suffered the kind of pain in their short lives that I couldn't even begin to imagine, yet still arriving each morning with smiles on their faces and anticipation for the day ahead . . . it gave me the kick up the backside I needed. To put it bluntly, I realized I was a self-indulgent shit, who'd wasted the past ten years feeling sorry for myself. If these kids could look to the future *and*, more important, still trust in the goodness of human nature, then surely, with the advantages I'd been given, so could I?"

They sat in silence, deep in their own thoughts.

"When I was little," Julia eventually cleared her throat and spoke, "my mother told me about the Glad Game in a book called *Pollyanna*. You have to think of what you have, not what you don't. It's trite and simplistic, I know, but it's true."

"Yes, it is. That's exactly how those Burmese kids looked at life." Kit smiled suddenly. "We're quite a pair, aren't we? Although you've had such"—Kit searched for the words—"dignity throughout. Yes, dignity. And I'm sorry if my recent actions have added to your distrust of human nature. I swear I'm not what you thought I was. Believe me, I was trying to protect you."

"It's okay, Kit. I do believe you, really," said Julia, surprised to find that she did, but still feeling an element of uncertainty.

"You see?" Kit shrugged. "There's the difference between you and me; in the old days, I wouldn't have been generous enough to even listen to an explanation. I was looking for an excuse to push them away. I promise, I'm different now. Especially with you, Julia."

"Don't be so hard on yourself. You cared for Annie too, when she needed you."

"I think I'm improving, yes. At least . . ." Kit paused and looked at her. "This is the first time I've actually wanted to race round to a woman and explain my actions, before she sailed off into the French sunset."

"I appreciate it, Kit."

"Are you really leaving, Julia? I don't want you to. I really don't," he blurted out suddenly.

There was a pause as Julia digested what Kit had just said. She felt suddenly hot and uncomfortable.

"Don't, Kit, please don't," she whispered. "I . . . can't cope."

"Mistrust has crept in, hasn't it? Because of Annie and the baby?"

"Sorry," Julia muttered.

"Christ!" Kit stood up and paced about the small room. "Of course, the first time since Milla that I actually *feel* for a woman, and look how I've managed to mess it up. Sorry"—he waved an arm at Julia—"what did I tell you about my tendency to self-indulgence? Look, Julia, I have to tell you this . . ." Kit was still pacing, faster now, his words tumbling out. "I have to tell you I think I'm in love with you. I knew it when I was looking after you and not resenting it at all. I loved the fact you needed me, after all these years of running in the opposite direction from any woman that did."

Kit smiled at her then, such an open smile of genuine joy that Julia wanted to react spontaneously and throw herself into his arms. But she stopped herself. Neither of them was a teenager, embarking on their first taste of romance. They were both at least a third of the way through their life's journey and damaged irreparably by it.

She opened her mouth to speak, but Kit spoke first.

"Of course, it was Annie who spotted it, saw the signs, grinned when I talked about you constantly"—Kit was pacing again—"made herself scarce that night you came to supper at Wharton Park. Which, of course, subsequently added to your suspicions, I'm sure . . . and begged me to come clean to you about how I felt. I said you weren't ready, she said you'd cope."

"I'm not ready, Kit."

The words were out of Julia's mouth before she could stop them. "It's been such a short time since . . . I thought I was . . ." Julia bit her lip. "But I'm not."

Kit looked as if he was physically diminishing in front of her. "Right," he said eventually. "Okay. Well then"—he cleared his throat—"serves me right, I suppose. And that *isn't* self-indulgence, it's a fact. I'll leave you be."

"I'm sorry. I . . . just . . . can't."

"No. I understand. Really, I do." Kit dug his hands in his pockets, walked toward the door, then turned back and took a deep breath. "What I want to say is that, if—*if* you ever feel in a position to, well, make the leap of faith and take a chance on me again, I promise I'll be there for you. I really am very good at it. Or, at least, I was once. I'd never hurt you, not intentionally, anyway."

"Thank you, Kit."

"And the weird thing is"—Kit stopped at the door—"*you* were always there."

Julia could not look up at him as tears were flooding her eyes.

"You know where I am," said Kit. "Try and take care of yourself for me, won't you? Good-bye, sweetheart."

The door closed behind him.

30

The following morning, wan and exhausted from a sleepless night, Julia came down the stairs to wait for her taxi. Cradling a mug of coffee, she stared into the now dead, ash-filled fireplace. Her brain was numb, unable to compute what Kit had said to her last night.

No. Julia stopped herself. Perhaps, when she was back in France, she could take the time to work it out and come to terms with her feelings for him, but not now.

She simply could not allow herself to love again.

Hearing footsteps coming up to the front door, Julia rose and walked toward it, picking up her traveling case in anticipation of her taxi waiting outside. In fact it was the postman. Putting down her traveling case, she said, "Glad I caught you. I'm leaving for France. I've redirected the post, what there is of it, mainly bills, usually . . ." Her voice trailed off. She didn't have the energy to make small talk.

"Right-ho, Miss Forrester, I'll take any post back to the sorting office and see it gets on its way to France for you." He handed her one obvious bill and one cream vellum envelope, addressed to her in a hand Julia didn't recognize.

"Thank you." She smiled at him weakly.

"Bon voyage, Miss Forrester."

Julia closed the door and sat down on the sofa while she opened the cream envelope.

Heathrow Airport

Dear Julia,

In haste!

My name is Annie. We met once a few weeks ago. I've heard from Kit what pain you've been through. He's been through pain too. He understands and he will do all he can to mend you, because, for the first time in years, he's fallen in love. Once he has (and, trust me, it's rare!) you never need doubt him. I promise, he's yours!

I'm now off to a new life, mostly because of Kit. He's been wonderful—there for me when no one else was. He's a truly good person. Before I left, I wanted to do something for him in return. As you know so well, life is short. We all think too much these days and analyze everything. Forget thoughts, just go with your heart—I have, God help me, and I've never felt happier than I do at this moment!

Pain can only be cured by love. I get the feeling you both need that.

Everyone deserves a second chance.

With very best wishes,

Annie

x

Julia heard the knock at the door. She stood up to open it.

"Hi," she said numbly to the taxi driver, "be out in a second."

"Okay, madam. I'm up the hill to the left. Bit of a walk, I'm afraid. Parking's terrible around here."

"Thanks."

Julia did a swift double check to make sure everything electrical was turned off, before taking her traveling case and locking up the cottage. She trudged slowly up the hill toward the taxi that would carry her away from Norfolk . . . and from Kit.

"There you go, madam. Let me take that from you." The taxi driver held the door open as she climbed inside, then stowed her traveling case in the trunk. "All set?"

"Yes."

"Should do the journey to the airport in a couple of hours, if we're lucky." The driver set off back down the hill, along the narrow road toward the harbor. Julia gazed out of the window, watching the bobbing boats for the last time. The place was deserted, apart from a figure sitting on a bench, staring out to sea.

"Stop! Sorry, can you just pull over for a second? I—wait here."

Julia opened the door and walked back toward the figure. As she drew closer, she saw she hadn't been mistaken. She stopped just short of the bench, knowing he hadn't seen her.

"Kit. What are you doing here?"

He turned in surprise and stared at her.

"Oh. Thought you'd gone. I went up there just now—the cottage was deserted."

"I had to walk right up the hill to the taxi. We obviously just missed each other."

"Right." Kit nodded. "So you're off?"

"Yes."

"Okay. Just thought I'd come and say good-bye." He shrugged. "Apologize again for my insensitive behavior."

Julia perched on the bench next to him. "Kit, please, I understand, I really do."

"Do you?"

"Yes."

Kit studied his fingers. "Good. Actually, Julia, I didn't really come to say good-bye."

"No?"

"No." He looked up at her and smiled wanly. "In fact, my intention was to prostrate myself at your feet and beg you to stay."

"Oh."

"Yes. I had the whole speech planned out. I was going to plead with you to give me a chance. To tell you I love you, and that I understand we would need to go slowly, for your sake. That I'd do anything to at least give us a try because, certainly for me, I know this feeling only comes once or twice in a lifetime. And it's killing me to have to let it go. Selfish, I know. I decided in the early hours of this morning, I wouldn't give up without a fight. So here I am. I was just bemoaning my normal bad luck that I'd obviously missed you. And, in fact, I haven't."

"No. Looks like you've been given a second chance, Kit," she whispered, almost to herself.

"So"—Kit knelt down in front of her and took her hands in his—"here goes. Julia, please don't go back to France. I want you to stay here, with me. I love you, I really do." He chuckled sadly. "Give me another chance, please, and I'll never let you down again, I promise."

"Oh, God, Kit—I—" She looked at him, trying to think rationally. Then, remembering Annie's words about not analyzing, she asked her heart what it wanted. Finally she said:

"Okay."

"Okay?"

"Yes, okay."

"You mean you'll stay?"

"Yes, for now, anyway. Maybe we should give us a try? What do we have to lose?"

Kit stood up, at the same time pulling Julia into his arms. "I promise, sweetheart, I will look after you for as long as you want me to."

"And I'll look after you too."

"Really?" He tipped her chin up to look at her.

"Yes. Especially as we seem to suffer from the same . . . afflictions."

"Two basket cases together, you mean?"

"Something like that," she murmured as he covered her face in kisses. She pulled away, spying the taxi driver leaning against the back of his car, arms folded, surveying them. "Better go and retrieve my traveling case and tell Bob he can go home."

"Yes. And then, my darling Julia, I'm taking *you* home."

"Where's 'home'?" Julia asked, confused.

"To Wharton Park, of course. Where you belong."

PART TWO

Summer

31

Wharton Park

Sometimes, when I wake to see the early-morning sun streaming in through the unshuttered windows of Wharton Park, I find it difficult to believe I feel the peace and contentment I believed would never be mine again.

Yet here I am, basking like a cat as the warmth hits my face, turning to see Kit's face on the pillow beside me. His hair, which I insisted he should cut so I could see his eyes, has defied the hairdresser's scissors, and a lock of it is falling over one closed lid. An arm is thrown back above his head, indicating total abandonment and trust in his surroundings.

I love watching him sleep in the morning and have the opportunity often, given that I usually wake first. It is my secret time, when I can cast away my fear and simply enjoy him. He knows nothing of these moments—he is an innocent victim of sleep—and does not realize I am studying every detail of his face and logging it in my memory.

I've learned recently how important these things are. I can no longer picture my husband's face—only a vague outline, a shape in which the finer details have become blurred and undefined.

When I have finished my study, I lie back and gaze at the room in which so many generations of Crawfords have slept. I doubt it's changed since the day Olivia Crawford walked into it on her wedding night, seventy years ago. The once-magnificent hand-painted Chinese wallpaper has faded from a warm, buttery yellow to a blanched and dreary shade of rice pudding. The butterflies and flowers adorning it are now shadowy images of their former selves.

The heavy, mahogany dressing table, with its three-sided mirror, sits along one wall. It is so ugly that no one wanted it in the contents sale, so I reinstated it where it belongs. I sometimes imagine Olivia sitting at it, putting on all the makeup a girl had to wear in those days, with Elsie patiently styling her hair.

I creep out of bed so as not to disturb Kit, and the carpet beneath my feet is threadbare, though around the edges of the bedroom one can see the thickness of the original weave.

I make my way to the bathroom, the floor covered in cracked linoleum, the bathtub with its snail trails of green lime-scale behind the tarnished tap.

As I dress, I smile to myself, simply because I am at Wharton Park. Clumsy, dysfunctional, and irritating in its unpredictability, it reminds me of a toddler who has not received enough attention from its mother, and yet is so endearing, one cannot fail to be won over by its charm.

As I tiptoe back through the bedroom to go downstairs and put the kettle on, I think how much I love it here, with Kit. And how I feel I have come home.

Julia sat on the terrace of Wharton Park in the warm, early-morning air and looked down onto the garden below her. June had always been her favorite month. It was the moment when flowers revealed their beauty hour by hour, blossoming into their short, perfect life span. The trees across the park hung heavy with leaves—so many different hues of green—set against the clear, soft, blue skies of an English summer.

She took her coffee and walked toward the crumbling steps into the garden—Adrienne Crawford's creation—and smelled the almost sickly scent of the jasmine planted along the terrace. They, like the rest of the garden, had been neglected for years; only the lawns were granted a cursory cut by the lone gardener, who had far too many acres to maintain to worry about individual pruning and clipping. The roses, set in their beds around the fountain, were now a sprawling, overgrown mass. But apparently unperturbed by this neglect, they still bloomed untidily into obscenely large, bulbous pink flowers.

Gabriel had loved flowers. . . .

Julia smiled sadly as she remembered how he'd appear in her study, his chubby hand clutching a motley collection of wilting wild orchids and lavender, which he and Agnes had found on a walk into the surrounding French countryside.

"Pour toi, Maman." He'd hand them to her so proudly, and Julia would make a big fuss of putting them in a glass, their stems uneven lengths where he had torn them clumsily from the plants.

She thought how much Gabriel would have loved it here at Wharton Park. He'd always been an outdoor child, just like his mother, and sometimes she'd tell him stories of the beautiful house in England she'd visited as a child. And how, one day, she would take him there and show him.

Julia sighed heavily. That was never to be.

Walking on, her fingers itched to set to work and restore this wonderful haven to its former beauty before it was too late.

"Grandfather Bill would be turning in his grave," she told the cherub, still perching listlessly atop the fountain that played no more.

Walking slowly back to the house, Julia felt as though she had stepped through a looking glass. There was still the pain of losing her husband and her precious little boy, and guilt, and fear, for daring to be happy. Yet Kit's love for her felt as undemanding as Xavier's had demanded.

"Sweetheart," Kit had murmured as they lay entwined on the bed after they'd first made love. "I understand it's still early days for you, and what a leap of faith you've taken to be here with me. I know you need time to heal. If you feel like some space, or I crowd you, I won't be offended if you want to retreat."

Three months later, and Julia had not yet felt the need. Besides, the house was vast enough to allow her as much space as she could want. As Kit had refused Mr. Hedge-Fund's offer and was out on the estate most days, she was often alone here.

But never lonely, she thought, as she climbed up the steps and passed through the door that would lead her eventually into the kitchen. It was strange how, even though she had rarely set foot inside the house and never been upstairs, it all felt familiar and wonderfully comforting. Perhaps it had to do with hearing Elsie's vividly told story, and because the house had changed so little since the days she'd described. Julia loved the atmosphere and had spent hours wandering along corridors, becoming familiar with every nook and cranny, each faded quilt cover and dusty ornament that evoked the history she'd heard so much about.

It was midsummer too, and many of the things that needed fixing in the house were far less noticeable than they would be in winter: the leaking roofs, for example, and the archaic heating, which sent a mere trickle of warmth through the cast-iron radiators, doing little to heat the bathwater too.

That she had all but moved in to Wharton Park with Kit had never "officially" been discussed. It had just happened naturally, out of mutual consent. Since the drama of their initial courtship, everything between them had been breathtakingly easy. They had slipped into a relaxed and comfortable routine: Kit would arrive in the kitchen for their six o'clock sundowner, and they would chat about their day as they shared the preparation of supper. Julia was determined to learn to cook and was enjoying her newfound skills. Afterward, they'd often retire early to bed to make love. They rarely went out, neither of them needing the stimulation of other company, preferring instead to spend time alone together.

Kit did really seem to understand that the sadness of what she had lost would sometimes creep in, often unexpectedly. A memory, perhaps prompted by an indirect comment, would render her quiet and thoughtful. He was remarkably unthreatened by her past, acknowledging and respecting it, and never forcing her to talk about it unless she indicated she wished to.

Their relationship was completely unlike the one she'd shared with Xavier: none of the grand statements her husband had so loved making, no volatile arguments, and little of the emotional insecurity or mood swings that had made Xavier so exhausting, but exciting to live with.

They had a stability, Julia thought, as she walked upstairs to make the bed, a quiet contentment that didn't have the drama of her former relationship but engendered tranquillity, which she knew was healing her more as each day passed. She hoped her presence in Kit's life was having the same effect on him.

She had discovered recently that, rather than wasting his life being "self-indulgent"—as he'd initially described the past ten years—Kit had spent his time abroad working tirelessly for charities around the globe. He had used both his academic and medical skills to help those most in need of them.

"The fact I didn't value my own existence enabled me to go into places most wouldn't venture," Kit had added, when Julia had listened in wonder and admiration to stories of his adventures in the most dangerous hot spots on earth. "Don't praise me, Julia, I was simply running away."

Whatever Kit's reasons, his experiences had made him a far wiser and braver man than he gave himself credit for. Julia, occasionally irritated by his continual self-deprecation, told him so. Slowly, Kit began to open up about a possible path he'd envisaged for his future, counseling and treating children damaged by events beyond their control.

"I've seen so much innocent suffering," he'd sighed one night over supper. "If I'm honest, I think caring for all the kids I met on my travels was a substitute for not daring to commit myself on a personal level again. They needed me, but I could always leave and move on. There was nothing altruistic about it."

"I understand, Kit," Julia had answered, "but I'm sure they benefited from having you, even for a short time."

"Well, I learned that kids are the building blocks of the human race. If they're wrong, the next generation will be wrong too. And, in retrospect, out of all that pain I witnessed, I admit I've found something I'm passionate about."

So Julia had encouraged him to apply for the appropriate course to convert his time at medical school into what he needed, to allow him to practice child psychology professionally.

"When this house is sorted out, I just might," he'd agreed. Then he had turned to her. "Long time since I let myself be nagged by a female."

"Kit! I—"

He had rolled over in bed and tickled her mercilessly. Then he'd looked down at her, his eyes serious. "Thanks, Julia, for caring enough to do it."

"We are sharing a moment in time," Kit had announced one night, as they lay together outside in the park, staring up at the full moon. "Like the universe, there is no beginning or end. We just *are*."

Julia loved that thought. And held on to it when her mind turned to another problem haunting her. The serenity of Wharton Park and Kit's undemanding love had gone a long way toward rehabilitating her, but every time she approached the drawing room, wrapped her fingers around the tarnished brass handle to open the door and walk toward the grand piano, her courage failed her.

Two weeks ago, she'd taken the train to London to have lunch with Olav, her agent.

"Well now, I have a variety of concert halls still offering you dates, including"—Olav had paused dramatically—"the Carnegie Hall."

"Really?" Julia had been excited despite herself. It was the one venue that she had never been invited to before. And had always longed to play.

"Yes, sir." Olav had nodded. "Your story went big in the papers across the pond—the Yanks love a drama. So, the deal with them is that the Carnegie will be your comeback performance. Being blunt, honey, it's less to do with your talent and more to do with the fact that the PR machines can go into overdrive."

"When is the recital?"

"Ten months' time, at the end of next April. Which gives you enough time to get your fingers back on those keys and build up your confidence. Whaddya say, Julia? It's one hell of an offer and I can guarantee it will never come again."

Clutching a pillow, Julia walked over to the bedroom window and stared down at the garden beneath her. She had less than a week to give Olav her decision. Could she do it? she asked herself for the umpteenth time. Find a way somehow to climb over the mental void? Julia shut her eyes and imagined playing. As usual, adrenaline started to pump through her veins and she broke out in a cold sweat.

She had not, up to now, broached the subject with Kit. How could she explain that the instrument she used to love held such fear for her now? He might think she was being silly, force her, pressure her to start playing, and she couldn't cope with that.

On the other hand, she thought, as she walked away from the window and laid the pillow with its delicious smell of Kit onto the bed, he might be able to help her. She had to trust that he would understand: she was desperate.

• • •

That night, she mentioned the Carnegie offer casually over supper.

"Wow!" he said. "Julia, that's amazing! What an honor. Will you take me with you so that I can sit in the front row, catch your eye, and stick my tongue out at you during a particularly tense crescendo?"

She smiled tightly, then shook her head. "I just don't know whether I can do it, Kit. It might be too much, too soon. I can't really explain why I'm so frightened, why my body reacts the way it does every time I go near a piano."

His expression became serious and he reached his hand across to hers. "I know, sweetheart. How long have you got to think about it?"

"A few days."

"I wish I could help, wave a magic wand, and make it all right for you." Kit sighed. "But I know I can't. It has to be up to you."

"Yes." Julia nodded slowly and withdrew her hand. "If you don't mind, I'm going to take a walk around the park and try and think."

"Good idea." Kit watched her leave the kitchen, then cleared the empty plates and washed and dried them, deep in thought.

A couple of days later, before Kit left for an early meeting with the farm manager in the estate office, he brought Julia a cup of tea and sat on the bed beside her.

"Better be on my way." He leaned over and kissed her. He studied her. "You look tired, sweetheart. You okay?"

"Yes," she lied, "have a good meeting."

"Thanks." Kit stood up from the bed. "By the way, I've got a mate who I've allowed to fish in our stream. He said he'd probably have a couple of trout for our supper tonight. He'll drop them off this afternoon."

"I've never cooked trout. What do I do?" Julia asked.

"I'll show you how to gut them later." He walked toward the door. "Oh, I nearly forgot—in case I'm not back, there's a piano tuner coming in at eleven this morning. I doubt that beautiful old instrument gathering dust in the drawing room has been played since you last played on it. And as it's rather valuable, I thought I'd better get it serviced. See you later, sweetheart." He blew her a kiss and disappeared out the door.

• • •

Promptly at eleven, the rusty front doorbell tinkled, and Julia went to let the piano tuner into the house.

"Thank you, madam," the old man said respectfully. "Could I trouble you to show me where the piano is? Last time I came here was over fifty-five years ago, when Lady Olivia asked my father to tune it, before Lord Harry came back from the war."

Julia looked at him in amazement. "It's this way." She led him through the series of rooms, put her hands to the brass knob of the drawing room, and immediately felt them start to shake.

"Here, madam, let me."

"Thank you. It's rather . . . stiff," she replied, embarrassed, as the piano tuner turned the handle easily. She had no choice but to follow him into the room. She hovered by the door and watched him walk toward the piano, then lift the dust sheets.

"Beautiful instrument this," he commented admiringly. "My father always said it had the purest sound of any piano he'd heard. And he'd heard a few," he chuckled. "Now then." He opened the lid, studied the yellowing keys, and lovingly put his fingers to them. He played a fast arpeggio, sighed, and shook his head. "Dearie me, we do sound in a bad way." He turned to Julia. "It'll take me a good while, but I'll sort it, don't you worry, madam."

"Thank you," Julia replied weakly.

"Yes"—the piano tuner bent down to open his tool case—"the sad thing is, my father told me Lord Harry never played again when he came home."

"Really? I've heard he was a wonderful pianist."

"He was, but for some reason"—the piano tuner sighed and began to play the first few bars of Liszt's Sonata in B Minor—"he never did. Perhaps it was something that had happened to him in the war. Such a shame he wasted his talent, isn't it?"

Julia could take no more. "I'll leave you to it then," she answered abruptly. "And send the invoice to Lord Crawford, please." She turned tail and hurried away from the drawing room.

Later, she went to pick patiently through the remnants of vegetables in the kitchen garden to cook with the trout that evening. She would have liked to sort the area out, to clear it and reseed it, but as there was no guarantee they would be here longer than it took to find a new buyer, Julia supposed it was pointless.

Suddenly, her ears pricked up. She could hear Rachmaninov's Concerto No. 2 floating out of the drawing room on the breeze toward her.

Kneeling among the weeds, she put her hands to her ears.

"Stop it! *Stop it!*"

She could still hear the music through her fingers, the notes she could not bear to play assaulting her senses. She gave up trying to block the sound, and as her hands fell to her sides, she began to sob.

"Why do you have to play *that*? Anything else . . . anything else." She shook her head and wiped her streaming nose on the back of her hand.

It was the signature tune to her grief.

That terrible night, as she had played for her enraptured audience, wrapped up in her beautiful music, lost in her own world, then enjoyed the applause and the cheers and the bouquets and felt the selfish exhilaration of her achievement, her little boy and her husband had been dying in agony.

Julia had tortured herself over and over, agonizing about just *when* it would have been during the concerto that they had drawn their last breaths. Would Gabriel have screamed out for her as he lay suffering intolerable pain and fear, wondering why his *maman* wasn't there to help him, to comfort him, to protect him?

She'd let him down at the moment he'd needed her so very much.

The thought was unbearable.

Julia knew the worst part was that the piano—an inanimate instrument, with no heart or soul—had stolen her love and attention. It had come before the needs of her child and her husband and now represented all that was selfish and inadequate about her. She slumped in despair, only comforted by the thought that the skinny carrots and the one lettuce she'd found were self-sown descendants of those planted by her beloved grandfather.

"Oh, Grandfather Bill!" she entreated the heavens. "What would *you* have said to me right now, if we'd been sitting together in the hothouse?"

She knew he would have been calm and rational, the way he always was when she had gone to him with a problem. He'd have looked at the facts, not the emotions surrounding them. He was a great believer in fate, and God, she knew that. When her mother had died, Grandfather Bill had taken Julia into his arms after the funeral. She had wept on his shoulder, inconsolable, the thought of her mother alone in the cold, hard ground unbearable.

"Your mum's safe now and at peace, up there. I know she is," he had soothed. "It's us lot left behind that are suffering without her."

"Why couldn't the doctors make her better?" she'd asked pitifully.

"It was her time to go, my love. And if it *is* that time, then there's nothing to be done."

"But I wanted to save her . . ."

"Don't punish yourself, Julia. There was nothing more any of us could have done for her. Us humans think we are in control, but we're not, you know. I've seen enough of life to realize that's a fact and there isn't no changing it."

Julia sat quietly, thinking about what Grandfather Bill had said that day. Was this also true of Xavier and Gabriel? Had it been their "time"? Could she have made the difference if she'd been with them?

It was an unanswerable question.

And as for the fact she'd been playing the piano . . . Julia wiped her streaming nose and knew she could in reality, just as easily have been at home, waiting for the two of them to come back from the local beach along the same treacherous road.

Was she, as Grandfather Bill had said all those years ago, punishing herself? Depriving herself of the one thing in her life she knew could provide comfort for her troubled soul?

More of Grandfather Bill's words came back to her as the piano tuner played the last few notes. *You have a God-given gift. Don't waste it, will you, Julia . . .*

As silence descended from the drawing room, a thought came into Julia's mind: she'd lost so many people she'd loved, but the one thing she still had that was *hers* and could never be taken away from her was her talent.

Eventually, as the piano tuner's car drove away, Julia stood up and walked slowly back toward the house. She stood on the terrace, a sudden ray of hope and understanding lighting up her face. Her gift was the one thing she could count on, it would be there for her until the day she died. It couldn't desert her because it was part of who she was.

And she mustn't desert *it.*

Would Xavier and Gabriel thank her for never touching the keys again? Would they wish that, out of their deaths, came the death of her "God-given" gift?

No.

Julia put an instinctive hand to her mouth as she realized clearly for the first time how her grieving, guilt-ridden mind had played tricks on her. She had allowed the demons in when she was so vulnerable and let them take root.

They had to be banished.

She strode purposefully toward the drawing room, her head full of all those who had loved her and did still love her, and sat down at the piano. Ignoring her body's reaction, she placed her shaking hands on the keys.

She would play for them all.

And for herself.

When Kit arrived home from his meeting an hour later and heard Chopin's Études coming from the drawing room, his eyes filled with tears. He sat down abruptly on the staircase in the entrance hall, in the spot where he'd first set eyes on Julia. And listened in awe, humbled by her magnificent talent.

"I'm so proud of you, my darling," he murmured to himself. "You not only have a rare gift but you are brave and beautiful and strong. And, God help me"—Kit wiped his eyes on his forearm—"I only hope I can be worthy of you, and keep you with me forever."

32

From then on, the silence that had held dominion for so many years over Wharton Park was broken. Instead, the house was filled with the sound of beautiful music, as Julia banished her demons and played on the exquisite piano in the drawing room for hour after hour, relishing her return to the instrument that was simply part of her soul.

"Thank you for helping to lead me back," she had whispered to Kit as they lay in bed on the night that her fingers had first retouched the keys.

"Don't thank me, sweetheart. It's you that's managed to be brave enough to break the spell," he had generously answered. "Besides, the piano *did* need tuning."

But Julia knew that, without Kit's thoughtfully executed prod in the right direction, she would not have got there alone.

"I spoke to Elsie today," said Julia over supper a couple of weeks later, "and she announced that now I'm living at Wharton Park, she'd like very much to visit us. She suggested this coming weekend. Would you mind if she stayed for a couple of nights?"

"Of course not," Kit was quick to reply, "you don't need to ask. This is your home too. Actually, I've been asked to play cricket for the village team this weekend, so that'll keep me out of your hair on Saturday, at least."

Julia could see Kit was pleased about the cricket invitation. "I'd also like to ask Alicia and her family over for Sunday lunch. They haven't seen Elsie for years."

"Good idea. And, actually, if Elsie's up to divulging the rest of her tale from the past, it'll be evocative listening to it here. Living in the house makes it even more fascinating to find out what my relatives were up to in days gone by."

After supper, they went to sit outside on the terrace, in Julia's favorite corner spot. The old metal furniture set was rusty but proved that someone before her had also decided this was the best and most sheltered vantage point from which to view the park.

"What a glorious evening." Kit breathed, enjoying the warm night air. "I've spent most of my adult life trying to find new vistas to enjoy. Yet here I am, sitting on a terrace that's part of my roots, thinking there really can't be a more beautiful spot in the world."

Julia took a sip of the vintage Armagnac Kit had found on a dusty rack in the cellar. "Actually, I wanted to . . . discuss something with you."

He frowned and looked at her. "Sounds serious. Is it?"

"I need to go back to France," Julia replied quietly.

There was a silence as Kit digested this information. "Right. I knew you'd have to go at some point."

"I don't want to," she sighed, "but I have things I need to do there. And, if I'm going to resolve the past and finally put it where it belongs, I must go back."

"Yes. Do you want me to come with you?"

"No. I think it's something I have to do alone. Besides, I know how busy you're going to be here in the next few weeks, what with the harvest."

"Yes, I will be." Kit raised his eyebrows. "Never thought for a second I'd be learning to drive a combine, but it's all hands to the pump, we're so short-staffed. How long will you be away?"

Julia shrugged. "I really don't know. For as long as it takes to do what I need to and make some decisions."

"Yes." Kit was quiet for a while as he stared out into the blackness, then he reached for her hand. "Julia, you know that no matter how long it takes you to return, I'll be here waiting for you."

In the darkness Julia held on to his hand like a lifeline. "Thank you."

Later that night they made love with heightened passion and urgency. Long after Julia had fallen asleep, Kit lay watching her, unable to shake off the feeling of unease that had lodged in his gut from the moment Julia had said she had to go away.

• • •

Julia spent Saturday morning freshening up one of the bedrooms in preparation for Elsie's arrival. She realized it would be the first time Elsie had come to Wharton Park as a guest, rather than a servant. Julia wanted to make sure her grandmother felt comfortable.

Next, she drove into Holt to buy supplies. It was a warm, sunny day, and the pretty town was bustling with the influx of tourists and second-home owners who swarmed into the region during the summer months.

As she piled her purchases into the trunk of the car, she resolved that—even though she was now confident she'd be ready for the Carnegie Hall recital—she would not return to the punishing schedules of the past. If the last few months had taught her anything, it was that there was beauty and pleasure in the simple things of life.

The thought of going back to France terrified her. She didn't want to lose her newfound sense of tranquillity. She knew too that Kit had helped her find it, and she would be leaving his strength behind. But she could only undertake the odyssey alone if she was to be completely free to love him the way he deserved.

At half past three that afternoon, Julia heard a car coming up the drive. Watching the driver help her grandmother out of the car, Julia ran to the front door and hurried down the steps toward her.

"Julia, sweetheart, come and give your old granny a hug." Julia did so, then Elsie stepped back to look at her. "My goodness me! I always said the Wharton Park air did something magic to you. Look at you! You're beautiful!"

Julia was still in her apron, covered in a dusting of flour. "I'm sure I'm not, Granny, but, yes, I'm certainly feeling a lot better than when I last saw you."

Julia paid the driver, then picked up Elsie's small overnight case and walked with her to the front steps of the house.

Elsie stopped just before the steps and looked up. "It's exactly the same. Strange, isn't it? When all our lives have changed so much, these bricks and mortar never alter."

"I wish that was true." Julia sighed as she helped her grandmother slowly up the steps. "It may look the same, but unfortunately, large parts of it are suffering from old age and need to be rebuilt before the whole lot falls down."

"Bit like me then, my love, isn't it?" Elsie chuckled. "Do you know, in all my years at Wharton Park, it's the first time I've ever entered it by the front door."

"I was thinking this morning that it might be strange for you coming here. Why don't I take you up to your room so you can freshen up, and then we can have a nice cup of tea?"

By the time they'd climbed the stairs and reached the bedroom, Elsie was panting.

"Gracious! My legs aren't what they used to be," she gasped. "I used to trip up and down them forty times a day and not even notice."

"I've put you in here, Granny." Julia opened the door to the bedroom. "It's so pretty, and not too big."

Elsie stepped over the threshold and sighed with surprise and pleasure. "My goodness me! Of all the rooms you could have chosen, you picked the very room that Lady Olivia stayed in when she first came to Wharton Park. It was in here that I first set eyes on her. And," Elsie added as she looked around the room, "I don't think anything has changed since." She walked across to the fraying tapestry stool at the end of the bed and sat down, trying to get her breath back. "Sorry, Julia, that bout of flu really did for me and I haven't recovered my strength proper since."

Julia watched her with concern. "Would you like to have a rest now? I'll bring your cup of tea up here?"

"That's what *I* used to say to Lady Olivia," Elsie chuckled. "I do feel a bit weary, but it's probably the shock of seeing this place again."

"You take your time, Granny, there's no rush. Have a rest and come down when you're ready. We've plenty of time to chat—Kit's out playing cricket for the village team and won't be back until after seven."

"Young Christopher . . . ," Elsie mused. "Fancy you ending up with him! I remember when he used to come and stay. Cook and I used to joke that he looked like a lollipop; all skin and bone, topped off with a big head and that great pile of curly hair."

"He hasn't changed"—Julia grinned—"and he's really looking forward to seeing you again."

"And me him." Elsie moved toward the bed and heaved herself onto it. "Strange the way life works out, isn't it? All of us back at the old place again. Right, my love, you take yourself off, and don't bother bringing me a cup of tea. I'll come down when I've had a little nap."

"I'll see you later," Julia whispered, leaning over to kiss Elsie's forehead. Her eyes were already closing.

An hour and a half later, Elsie arrived in the kitchen, looking refreshed.

"That's better," she said. "Now, where's that cup of tea you promised me? I want to hear all about how you and Kit got together."

The two of them sat at the kitchen table, and Julia told Elsie how Kit had come to her rescue when she was so ill, and the subsequent move to Wharton Park.

"Julia, I'm over the moon for you, my love. I can see in your eyes how happy you are. After the terrible time you've been through"—Elsie shook her head, tears in her eyes—"it's wonderful the two of you have found happiness together." She took a sip of her tea. "And I'll be honest, that's what has really brought me here today. What with you and Kit getting together, it's like everything has come full circle. And I've decided you should know the whole story. And maybe"—Elsie glanced around the kitchen—"telling it here in the place it all happened will help me remember."

Twenty minutes later, Kit walked through the kitchen door, looking tanned and healthy in his cricket whites.

"Elsie, how wonderful to see you again, after all these years." Kit walked over to her and kissed her warmly. "You've hardly changed."

"Flatterer." Elsie grinned. "Well, let me tell you, *you* have, Master Kit. You've filled out good and proper, and grown into a fine-looking young man."

"So, you no longer think I'm a lollipop?" Kit eyed her sternly, then, as Elsie blushed, broke into a wide smile. "I heard you and Cook talking about me one day, when you didn't know I was lurking outside. I didn't mind. I was grateful to you two for always filling me up."

"Well," said Elsie defensively, "you were always far too skinny. In fact, you both were."

"Well, look at the two of us now," said Kit, putting an arm round Julia's shoulder affectionately. "Glass of wine, Elsie? I'm going to have one to celebrate a win. I bowled two overs and thoroughly enjoyed being proclaimed man of the match."

Elsie caught Julia's eye as Kit opened the wine and nodded appreciatively. "Grown into quite a looker that one, hasn't he? Who'd have thought it?"

As Kit sat with Elsie at the table, chatting companionably about her years at Wharton Park, Julia worked in the kitchen preparing supper. She could see that Elsie was completely at ease, as Kit's warmth and gentle teasing relaxed her. Julia put a chicken casserole and fresh Jersey new potatoes on the table and sat down with them to eat.

Elsie swallowed and said appreciatively, "My, my, Julia, never thought you'd be one for the cooking, but this is really tasty."

"Julia has lots of hidden talents, Elsie," added Kit, sneaking a sly wink at Julia.

After supper, Julia made coffee and suggested they go through to the library. Having settled Elsie in the comfortable chair by the fireplace, Julia joined Kit on the sofa opposite her.

The air was suddenly tense with expectation.

"Now," said Elsie, after taking a sip of her coffee, then placing it down on the table, "as I said to Julia earlier, I've thought long and hard about whether I should tell you this. But under the circumstances . . ."

"What 'circumstances'?" queried Kit.

"Be patient, young man, and by the end of it, you'll understand. Right." Elsie took a deep breath. "Last time, Julia, we had got to the part about Lord Harry and Lady Olivia making up their differences, just before Harry went off to the war?"

"Yes," Julia confirmed.

"Well now, I'm going to tell you Harry's story, and though it happened a long, long way from here, I can promise you that what I'm going to tell you is the truth, even if the ending isn't in the diary he wrote."

"*Harry* wrote?" questioned Julia.

"Yes, it was Harry's diary. Always had beautiful writing, he did. It could never have been written by my Bill," she chuckled, "he could barely sign his name, bless him. Now, my love, please don't interrupt my train of thought. What I was trying to say is that Bill, your grandfather, was out in Malaya with him during the war. Then, when Harry finally returned home, Bill and me were drawn into his story in a way we could never have thought possible. This part really begins after the war had ended, when your grandfather and Harry were liberated from Changi jail, after three and a half long years in captivity. . . ."

33

Bangkok

1945

When Harry regained consciousness, he was confused by the unfamiliar feeling of having slept for a long time without being disturbed. He was used to changing positions constantly as the pain in one hip bone, resting on the rudimentary bed he had managed to gather for himself, woke him to insist the other hip take the strain. Nor did he remember waking to swat the endless mosquitoes or to rub away the sharp, sudden sting of a red ant.

And there was none of the sticky sweat that normally drenched his thin torso on waking. In fact, he felt positively cool, but perhaps he was imagining the light breeze that seemed to brush gently against his face.

In short, he felt comfortable. A sensation he barely remembered.

He wondered whether he was hallucinating. During the long three and a half years of his captivity, he had often dreamed of Wharton Park, and of the queerest things, such as his father handing him a tin of sardines, of jumping into the cool, clean water of the fountain in the center of his mother's garden, and of Olivia, holding out his son to him. . . .

But mostly his dreams had been of food. He and the other fellows had spent many a long, humid night discussing their mothers' best recipes. It had kept them sane, if *sane* was a word that could be used for the inmates of Changi jail.

There wasn't much left of any of them, physically or mentally, and Harry awoke every morning simply amazed he was still alive. And sometimes, rather wishing he weren't.

He decided to keep his eyes closed and enjoy the comfort, while pondering how miraculous it was that his body had withstood starvation, and the kind of physical exercise that would tax a healthy man in a moderate climate, let alone in this kind of brutal heat. Many of the fellows hadn't made it: over a thousand were buried in Changi cemetery, and on occasions he had envied them their eternal rest. During his recurring bouts of dengue fever, nicknamed breakbone fever for the excruciating pain it caused in every limb, Harry had expected to join them at any moment. But Lady Luck, if one could suggest that spending another day here alive *was* luck, had been on his side. And so far, he had survived.

Harry understood now that life and death depended on a throw of the dice: many of the fellows he had come into the camp with had been physically stronger than he was, yet he had seen malaria and dysentery strike them down like newly hatched chicks. The diet of rice and raw tea, supplemented occasionally by a couple of ounces of rice polishings, complete with maggots for protein, required an inner engine of the strongest stuff. It seemed that Harry—although not a natural soldier and so afraid he was not a "man"—had been genetically issued with the main necessity for surviving such a place.

Given that he had been awake for some time now—or it felt as if he had—and was still comfortable, Harry tried to collect his thoughts and coordinate the events of the past few days.

He had some memory of lying in Changi hospital with a high fever. Then he thought he remembered a familiar face staring down at him, Sebastian Ainsley, his old friend from Eton, who was now working for his father's shipping company in the Far East. Harry had some vague recollection of being stretchered onto the back of a truck.

The continuing silence, physical comfort, and clean smell indicated that something was definitely up. Perhaps this was heaven. Harry decided to open his eyes to check.

The glare of white walls, hazy through the mosquito net, was a stark contrast to the dark, squalidly filthy wooden huts, with their fetid stench of unwashed human bodies hanging heavy in the humid air.

He then saw a woman . . . *a woman*! Again in white, approaching his bed.

"Well now, Captain Crawford, we've decided to wake up, have we? About time too. Open wide, please."

Before Harry could say anything, a thermometer was popped

under his tongue. The woman took his thin wrist in her soft hands and checked his pulse.

"Much better." She nodded approvingly, then added with a smile, "I suppose you have no idea where you are?"

He shook his head, the thermometer preventing him from speaking.

"You're in Bangkok, in a private nursing home. They didn't want you at the public hospital. The last thing they need there is more dengue fever. So your kind friend Mr. Ainsley brought you to us. He will be in to visit you shortly, I'm sure. He's checked on you every day so far."

The thermometer was removed from his mouth. Harry licked his lips and tried to swallow, but his throat was dry.

"May I have a glass of water?" he croaked.

"Of course. First, let's sit you up." The woman took Harry by the armpits and raised him into a sitting position. He tried to help, but could feel the exertion making the sweat pour from his brow.

"There's a good chap."

The woman, whom Harry now realized was a nurse, held a glass of water with a straw in it under his mouth. "Drink it slowly. Your stomach's had nothing in it for the past few days. We had to feed you intravenously for a while. That fever of yours just wouldn't abate." The nurse was glancing at her thermometer. "The good news is, it has now. Thought we might lose you for a while, but you're obviously made of stronger stuff, eh?"

As Harry struggled to get the muscles in his throat to swallow, he thought he had never felt less strong.

"You should be proud of yourself, young man." The nurse smiled. "You've made it through. Not only the war, but that hellhole of a camp in Singapore we're hearing so much about. Get yourself better and you'll be on your way home to Blighty. How about that?"

Harry sank back onto his pillows, feeling faint and dizzy. It was all too much to take in. Now that he thought about it, he did remember being told the Nips had surrendered and the camp was to be liberated. But after years of hearing rumors, to be frank, he and the other fellows hardly dared believe it.

"We won? It's true? It's all over?" The short, staccato sentences were all he could put together.

"Yes, Captain Crawford. It's all over. You are a free man. Now, I suggest a rest for an hour, then I'll bring you some chicken broth for lunch."

Chicken broth . . . in Changi, chicken had been the meat everyone yearned for—if a fellow managed to get hold of a live chicken to lay eggs for him, it lasted no more than twenty-four hours before it was part of someone's stew. Harry sighed. After years dreaming of such a dish, he felt sad to have so little appetite.

"Thank you," he answered huskily, his voice still not his own.

The nurse walked toward the door. "I'll see you in a while."

Harry watched her leave, then lay there pondering the extraordinary fact that, if he had the legs for it, he could climb out of bed and follow her through the door, walk down the corridor and out of the hospital. He could stand outside for as long as he wished and nobody would point a gun at him. Then he could walk down the street, whistling if he fancied it, and no one would take the slightest bit of notice of him. It was a thought that beggared belief.

Five minutes later, there was a knock on his door. A familiar bald pate and thick, pebble glasses appeared round it.

"Harry, old boy, how utterly marvelous to see you conscious! We were all getting frightfully concerned that you might fall at the final fence, so to speak, and that really would have been the most terrible shame."

"Bad luck, Sebastian," Harry croaked, "as you can see, I'm still alive and kicking."

"And it's wonderful to see that you are. Changi seemed to be a bad show all round, from what I saw that day on my mission of mercy."

"How did you know I was there?"

"Your mother wrote, telling me you'd been imprisoned there. And when I heard Changi was being liberated, I thought the least I could do was come and welcome you out and perhaps offer some help, as a relative local. Of course, I wasn't expecting to find you in such a state. Had to bribe some Malayan to drive you to the Thai border, where my car and driver were waiting."

"It was awfully good of you to come."

"Think nothing of it. It's what old chums are for, isn't it?" Sebastian said, reddening. "Besides, it gave me my only proper glimpse of what had been going on. Had some rather hairy moments on the way down. Singapore was in chaos. Did think about stopping off there, as you were so ill, but the hospitals were overflowing. I had to pray you would make it up to Bangkok, where I knew I could find you some proper medical help."

"Thank you," Harry rasped, panting.

"Been bally awful here in Thailand too, let me tell you. The Nips took over the country. Pretty impressive show they put on too, arriving in their hordes in their civvy clothes at first, masquerading as workers for the new factories they were building here. They were all over the place, taking photographs, pretending to be tourists. Then, the day they made their move, their wives and children were put out of harm's way on boats around the coast, while the Nips donned their army uniforms and emerged from their houses in every city in the land. The photographs had obviously been sent back to HQ in Tokyo to strategically plan where they should place their troops to hold the country under control."

"My God," breathed Harry, "did they really?"

"They did. Got to hand it to them, their organization was impeccable. And, of course, with the element of surprise, unstoppable. They wanted Thailand as their unrestricted path from Burma down to Malaya. And the Siamese, or Thais, as we must now call them, were forced to declare war on Great Britain and America."

"I hadn't heard," replied Harry weakly.

"Well, didn't come to much, mind you, but we've had to put up with nasty people running the show around here for the past two years. I, for one, will be glad to see the back of them. They're currently leaving Bangkok in droves, their heads either lowered or bobbing in the Chao Phraya River. At least sixty have been washed up so far," Sebastian chortled. "Good riddance to the little buggers, that's what I say!"

Harry nodded in heartfelt agreement.

Sebastian pulled up a chair and sat down beside him. "I know you've had one hell of a time in there, old boy. As soon as you're fit enough, we can put you on a ship home, first class, of course." Sebastian grinned. "And you'll stand once more on the green grass of England. Or what's left of it, after the Krauts dropped their bombs."

"I've heard so little of what's happened there," Harry managed to whisper.

"All you need to know now is we won, that your parents and Olivia are all fit as fleas and can't wait to welcome you home."

"Good news," Harry muttered, as Sebastian strained forward to hear him. "I only received letters from my mother while I was in Changi, not my wife."

Sebastian raised an eyebrow. "I'm sure Olivia was writing to you. But the censors have been very tough."

"Did she? Am I . . . ? " Harry sighed. "My mother didn't say anything about the baby. Olivia was pregnant when I left home. Have you heard?" he wheezed.

There was an embarrassed pause as Sebastian gauged how best to tell Harry the news.

"Sorry, old boy," he said gruffly. "Just one of those things, I believe. A miscarriage, apparently. Still, no reason why you can't return home now and produce a brood of children. *And* have the pleasure of being there to watch them grow up."

Harry closed his eyes for a moment, allowing the news to sink in. The whole idea of returning to Wharton Park was so alien to him, so far removed from where he had been, he couldn't contemplate it.

"Anyway, my dear chap, having come back from the dead, this is not the time to be dwelling on what might have been," Sebastian comforted. "As soon as you're in the clear, I'm taking you out of here. I should think you've had enough of institutions for the rest of your life. So buck up and get better as soon as possible. Then I can start reminding you that life can be quite jolly, especially here in Bangkok."

"I'll do my best, Sebastian, I promise."

"That's the spirit, old boy." Sebastian got to his feet. "I'll pop in to see you tomorrow, around eleven o'clock. And I'll send a telegram to Wharton Park, letting them know that you're on the mend."

"Thank you."

Sebastian nodded, as he strode toward the door. "Get better now, won't you?"

Harry returned the nod and offered Sebastian a wan smile before the door closed. He lay back, disappointed not to feel euphoric that he was free at last. He imagined he was simply tired and still recovering from his illness. That was why his newfound freedom felt like rather a letdown.

No one in Changi had ever contemplated how it would actually *feel* to be free. All the talk had been of home, of family and food. The mere thought of these things had kept them all going, given them hope. Harry had witnessed a couple of chaps who had given up: they'd been found hanging by whatever the poor blighters could put together—socks, remnants of bootlaces, scraps of shirt.

For a second, Harry longed for the familiarity of Changi; for the routine, the shared suffering and objectives, and the understanding of each other's plight.

Would the experience mark him forever? Was it possible he could ever go back to a normal life?

Harry drifted off to sleep, hoping his mood would be more positive when he woke.

Three weeks later, Harry was deemed well enough to leave the hospital. Sebastian came to collect him in his Rolls-Royce, a car Sebastian's father had shipped over to Bangkok twenty years before.

As they walked out of the hospital, Harry briefly enjoyed the feeling of leaving somewhere. It was the first time in three and a half years he had done so of his own will. Sebastian's Thai chauffeur opened the door for Harry respectfully and settled him on the backseat. Sebastian sat beside him. They drove through the bustling streets, their chauffeur tooting his horn as bicycle taxis, oxen, and a couple of elephants caused jams.

For the first time since marching his battalion off the *Duchess of Atholl*, the ship that had carried the Fifth Royal Norfolks to Singapore, Harry could take in the exotic atmosphere with interest rather than fear.

"Best way to see the city is by boat, along the narrow canals they call klongs," continued Sebastian. "The people live in houses built out onto the river on stilts. Awfully quaint. Perhaps, before you go back to Blighty, we might take a boat and I can show you. There are also some rather magnificent temples. Ah, here we are, just pull up in front, driver, Giselle's expecting us." Sebastian turned to Harry. "Harry, my dear chap, welcome to the Oriental Hotel."

Harry noticed little as he was ushered through the lobby and Sebastian spoke to the woman called Giselle, who obviously ran or owned the hotel. Harry felt exhausted and overloaded and had found the car journey through the busy streets claustrophobic. As he was led along the corridor by a Thai porter, who had no bags to carry because Harry had no possessions, he wondered whether he would suffer from claustrophobia for the rest of his life.

Still etched in his mind was the time spent in Selarang Barracks, when the Nips moved out the entire camp because the British officers had refused to sign a "no escape" pact. Selarang had been built to house a thousand men, and eighteen thousand Changi prisoners had arrived there. This had engendered two days of standing in the burning sun for hours, packed so tightly in the compound one couldn't lift a hand to scratch one's nose. And then, at night, sleeping nose to tail on a concrete floor—sardines in a tin had known more comfort and space.

To save the men from what would quickly become an epidemic of dysentery and death by the thousands, given the appalling conditions, the "no escape" pact had been signed under duress by Colonel Holmes, commander of the troops in Changi.

Harry had suffered continual nightmares ever since, and knew the experience had given him the most fearful problem with crowds.

The porter unlocked the door to his room, and Harry was pleased to see that it was deliciously cool, with shuttered windows, a mosquito net draped over the bed, and basic but comfortable furniture. He tipped the porter the last few cents he had in his possession, closed the door behind him, walked to the bed, and lay down on it, relieved to be in peace and have some space.

When Harry woke a couple of hours later, he imagined it was night, but when he checked the clock by the bed he saw it was barely teatime. The shutters had shrouded his room in darkness. He got up and went to open them and gasped in delight at the view. Before him was a large green lawn dotted with easy chairs and parasols. Beyond that, a vast expanse of river, perhaps a hundred feet wide, with wooden craft bobbing along it. The beauty and openness of the vista brought tears to Harry's eyes.

The tap above the small basin in the corner of the room managed a trickle of water for him, but it was nectar after years of bathing only when the rains fell. Harry dressed in the shirt and trousers Sebastian had kindly provided until he could acquire some clothes of his own. He struggled to do up the trousers over his "rice belly," something all the fellows had—they'd joked they all looked six months pregnant. Then he set off to find his way to the terrace overlooking the river.

Once there, he planted himself in a chair under a parasol.

Immediately, a young Thai boy was at his side. "May I serve you tea, sir?"

Harry wanted to laugh out loud. Where he had been, the thought of being served tea would have been absurd, especially sitting in a comfortable chair shaded by a parasol.

"Thank you. That would be just the ticket," he answered, and the boy walked away to arrange it.

Perhaps, Harry thought, he had to get used to how anything normal would seem abnormal to him until he settled into freedom. And maybe he also had to accept that no one, other than those who had been there with him, would ever understand what he had been through.

"Sir, your tea, with milk and sugar." The boy placed the tray on the small table next to Harry.

He restrained himself from diving for the sugar bowl and tipping the lot into his mouth. It was the first time he had seen sugar in three and a half years.

Sebastian joined him half an hour later, as the sun began to set over the river. He ordered a gin and tonic for himself and one for Harry, although, after taking a whiff of it, Harry abstained. Alcohol was something else he hadn't tasted since he'd left England. In his current state, it would knock him out completely.

"By the way, before I forget, I believe this is yours." Sebastian placed a small, leatherbound diary on the table. "When they removed what was left of your clothes at the hospital in Bangkok, the nurse found it in your long johns." Sebastian raised an eyebrow. "She handed it to me for safekeeping."

Harry had assiduously kept the diary from the moment his ship had left the English coast. If the Nips had found it in Changi, he could have been shot. So he had kept it hidden by sewing a makeshift pocket inside his underwear. Writing down his thoughts and feelings every night had been one of the ways he'd managed to survive.

"Thank you, Sebastian, I'm grateful, although I doubt I'll be turning the pages for a trip down memory lane in the near future."

"No. So, dear boy, there's a boat sailing in three weeks' time that will take you rather comfortably to Felixstowe and home. You'd better send a telegram to your family letting them know you'll be on it. I'm sure they would all love to be there to greet you when it docks." Sebastian smiled.

"That sounds great, and thank you for organizing it, but would you mind if we talked of future plans another time? It's my first proper night of freedom and I simply want to enjoy the moment."

"Of course, of course, old chap! No rush and all that. I just rather thought you'd like to be on your way as soon as you can."

"We'll talk of it tomorrow. Now, tell me all about this beautiful city."

"Rather surprised you're not more interested in what's been going on in Blighty," commented Sebastian over dinner later on, as he tucked into a large Australian steak. Harry looked down at his similar steak, watched the blood trickle out of it, and knew he couldn't stomach it. Embarrassed, he changed his order to a bowl of soupy rice.

"I am interested, Sebastian, of course," said Harry. "But I feel I've only been out, so to speak, for the past few hours. And talk of the war is a little beyond me tonight."

Sebastian looked at him through his thick lenses and nodded sympathetically. "Early days, old chap, early days. Tomorrow, I have my tailor coming to visit you, to outfit you with an entire wardrobe. They're skilled with the old needle and thread out here. Anything you want, dear boy, he'll make it for you."

"That's awfully kind of you. Although I'm hardly aware of what's in vogue at present."

"Wouldn't think it's altered that much. Doubt the chaps back home are wearing skirts, as they do out here," chuckled Sebastian.

"I suppose, until I'm demobbed, I should technically be wearing my uniform," Harry said flatly. "But all I had left of it in Changi was a pair of shorts patched with tent canvas and one sock."

"Well, need I say, you don't have to worry about that. The authorities have enough to do getting the thousands of POWs back home. And if I were you, I'd view this as a bit of a holiday. Sounds as though you deserve it, dear boy. And when you're up to it, I can show you a few sights, eh what? The girls here are . . . how shall I put it? A little more relaxed than the fillies at home." Sebastian's eyebrows appeared over the top of his glasses. "You must still be exhausted from your ordeal. Was it . . . bloody?"

"Beyond imagining," Harry replied bluntly. "And I was one of the lucky ones. I was an officer and was treated a little better than the men. Plus, I could play the piano, which the Nips rather admired. They used to have me go to their quarters and play for them." Harry sighed. "If anything, the piano saved my life."

Sebastian's face lit up. "Of course! I'd forgotten your talent in the midst of everything else that's been going on. I must have a word with Giselle. She's rather intent on setting up a little bar here for all the expats, and she's looking for band members. Perhaps, in the next few days, she could get a crowd together and you could play for us all."

"Perhaps," Harry muttered noncommittally. "I wonder what happened to Bill?"

Sebastian frowned at the sudden change of thought. "Who on earth's Bill?"

"He was my sergeant in the battalion. He came from Wharton Park and was with me throughout my captivity. He saved my life during the fall of Singapore and always came to visit me in Changi hospital when I was ill with dengue fever. I'd like to know that he's safe home. I'll send a telegram to ask." Harry was fading. "Sorry, Sebastian, but I'm bushed, and I must get some sleep."

"Of course. You take yourself off to your room, dear boy, get a good night's shut-eye, and my tailor will be with you at ten."

Harry stood up, his legs feeling dreadfully shaky. "I really am most terribly grateful for everything you've done, Sebastian. You must let me know what I owe you for all your trouble. I'll have the money wired through to you from England."

"Just call it my contribution to the war effort." Sebastian brushed talk of finances away with a dismissive hand. "Think nothing of it, glad to be of help."

Harry bade him good night, then walked slowly back to his room. He was still relishing the thought of resting his aching bones on cool, clean white sheets, under the breeze from the ceiling fan. As he climbed into bed, all that concerned him before he drifted off was the whereabouts of his friend Bill.

34

In the following weeks, Harry had plenty of rest and began to build up his strength, as his beleaguered stomach started coping with the kind of nourishing food he had only been able to dream about in Changi.

At night, he was still plagued by nightmares. He would wake, drenched in sweat, and reach for the light, which often didn't work, due to the continued blackouts in Bangkok. His heart racing, he would struggle to light a candle, see the sanctuary of his room, and convince himself that it was truly over.

In the mornings, he would make his way down to breakfast on the veranda, then take a newspaper into the shade of the large palms in the garden. The river hummed with life, the wooden boats with their diesel engines providing a background noise that lulled him. He watched the activities of other guests from behind his newspaper; some had been POWs on the Burma railway, but he did not indulge in conversation.

Sebastian often visited from his office nearby, and they would lunch together before Harry took himself off for his afternoon nap. He did not venture outside the hotel. The serenity of this spot, and the gentle, courteous Thai staff, who floated gracefully about their business, made him feel safe.

Sebastian asked him every day if he wanted to send a telegram to Wharton Park letting them know when he would return, but Harry was reticent. The thought of the journey home—coupled with the responsibilities he would face on arrival—was too much to cope with. Here, within the tranquillity of the hotel, Harry was healing.

One searingly hot afternoon, on his way across the lobby after lunch, Harry saw Giselle directing her Thai workers as they carried an old upright piano precariously along the corridor and into a room.

After his nap, Harry ambled back downstairs and took a look inside. Bamboo fans had recently been fixed to the ceiling, and tables and chairs arranged around the room. A wooden service area was still under construction in one corner, with the piano and a drum kit in another. Harry walked over and pulled up the lid. He brought over a chair, sat down, and put his fingers to the keys.

Although he had played in Changi, the Nips had, ironically, only wanted popular American tunes. His fingers felt rusty as he played the opening bars of Chopin's "Grande Polonaise." He persevered, willing his hands to move across the keys as they used to. Eventually, they seemed to remember, and the familiar notes flowed in a torrent of unexpressed pain. For the first time since the war had begun, Harry found peace in his music.

When he finished, he sat sweating with exertion and emotion and heard clapping from the doorway. A young Thai maid was standing shyly by the door, floor-sweeper in hand, a look of wonderment on her face.

Harry smiled at her, thinking how beautiful she was, even in her drab maid's uniform.

"I sorry, sir, to disturb you. I hear music when I sweep terrace and I come in to listen."

"Of course." Harry looked more closely, taking in her tiny, childlike body, perfectly proportioned, and then her lovely face. "You like music?"

"Very much." She nodded. "Before war, I train too."

"You were at music school?"

The girl shook her head. "No. Only lesson, once a week. But I love, I love Chopin very much," she said with passion.

"You want to play?" Harry offered as he stood up.

"No, Madame would not like. Besides, I am"—she searched for the right English word and smiled as she found it—"amateur. I think you are professional."

"Hardly," muttered Harry. "But I too enjoy playing."

"You play for new bar, yes?" The girl smiled again, showing Harry a perfect set of pearl white teeth, underneath full pink lips.

"Maybe if Giselle asks me"—Harry shrugged—"but it won't be Chopin. You are a maid here?" he asked, rather superfluously, loath to end the conversation.

The girl nodded. "Yes."

"I'd say it was unusual to find a maid who speaks good English and plays the piano."

The girl shrugged. "Many things change for many during war."

"Yes," Harry agreed with feeling, "yes, they do. But you are educated. Why are you working here?"

Her eyes filled with sadness. "My father in Free Thai movement, get taken away by Japanese army. And disappear a year ago."

"I see."

"Before, he is editor of newspaper here. We have good life. I am educated at British school here in Bangkok. But my mother, she have three young children and cannot leave them alone to earn money. So I work to feed my family." She spoke in a matter-of-fact manner, not asking for his sympathy, merely explaining her circumstances.

"And Madame Giselle, she was once a journalist too, I believe?" recalled Harry.

"Yes. She was French war correspondent. She help me by giving me job because she know and respect my father."

Harry nodded. "I understand. Perhaps, when the chaos of the war is over, you can use your education once more."

"But you, sir, have many worse than me. Madame say you are prisoner in Changi. I hear it very bad place to be."

The sympathy in the girl's eyes brought tears to his own. She understood the cruelty war could inflict. They both stood for a moment, staring at each other, as an inexplicable feeling passed between them.

She broke the silence. "I must go now."

"Yes."

As if in prayer, she drew her fingers together beneath the tip of her nose and bowed her head toward them, a traditional Thai gesture Harry had come to recognize.

"*Kop khun ka*, sir. I enjoy your playing very much." She began to walk out.

"My name is Harry," he called.

"Haree," she repeated, and he loved the way she said it.

"And what is yours?"

"My name, it is Lidia."

"Lidia." Harry mouthed the name, as she had his.

"Good-bye, Harry, I see you soon."

"Good-bye, Lidia."

• • •

After this meeting, Harry watched Lidia every day for the next two weeks, enjoying her graceful movements as she went about her tasks. He sat in his favorite spot on the terrace, with Somerset Maugham's *The Gentleman in the Parlour*—written in this very hotel some years back—on his lap. Instead of reading, though, he studied Lidia, fascinated by her for reasons he could not explain. Everything about her was delicate, fragile, and so terribly feminine. Against Lidia, Olivia would seem like a cart horse, even though she was considered slim.

He chuckled to himself that he had found his own, real-life Cinderella. Of course, Lidia had no idea he was a prince—or as near as, dammit. She smiled up at him occasionally, but never approached him. He did not feel it fitting to approach her.

Harry had no idea how old she was. From careful observation he could tell that, under her uniform, she had the shape of a woman; but she could have been anything from fourteen to twenty-four. He worried he was becoming obsessed with her, working out when she swept the veranda and the terrace, and making sure he was there so he could watch her. The more he saw her, the more beautiful she became. He spent hours lying on his bed in his room pondering how he could restart their conversation and get to know her better.

One morning, as he passed through the lobby, he saw Lidia sitting behind the reception desk. She was no longer in her maid's uniform, but instead wore a Western-style blouse and skirt.

Encouraged by a smile from her, he walked over and said, "Hello there. Have you been promoted?"

"Yes." Her huge amber eyes sparkled with pleasure. "I am now helping Madame with paperwork and reception. Also, I have new position as guest relations."

"Good for you!" Harry felt the kind of pleasure one would associate with something good happening to oneself. "I'm glad Madame has recognized your abilities and put them to good use."

"It is because I speak English and Thai, and Madame speak French. We are good team." Lidia's eyes twinkled. "I get pay rise too, so my family very happy. And new bar open tomorrow night. I hope it is okay with you, but I tell Madame we have guest who play piano very well. I think she speak to you about it later."

"Of course. You will be there?"

"Of course," mimicked Lidia. "I see you soon, Harry." She nodded and went back to her paperwork.

As he took breakfast on the veranda, Harry smiled in secret delight at this unexpected contact with Lidia. If she was to be there in the bar tomorrow night, he would play.

He realized he felt better physically this morning—better than he had felt in years. Besides that, an energy vaguely remembered from before the horror of Changi surged through him. Harry thought it might be expectation for the future, a future he had not dared dream he would have.

The beauty of his tropical surroundings seemed to be more vivid today. Everything he saw and touched had a shine, a luster to it. He was obviously on the mend. Which meant he must start thinking about returning home.

Harry lit a cigarette and sipped his coffee. When he'd left Wharton Park over four years ago, he had at least felt comfortable knowing he had righted the wrongs he had committed against Olivia. He believed she fully understood what had happened to him with Archie, and that, in the few weeks he and Olivia had together afterward, they had managed to put that in the past.

That he had left her with their child in her belly was further comfort and physical proof theirs was a normal marriage. That the child had not made it into the world was a sadness for him but, he acknowledged, far more of a sadness for his wife.

Harry had suffered a surfeit of uncomfortable, humid nights during which to ponder his feelings for Olivia. Some of the other fellows would weep with the pain of missing their wives, talking of them endlessly to anyone who would listen, and keep battered, fading photographs next to their hearts. They would discuss their deep feelings of love, and how much they had enjoyed and now missed the physical side of their relationship. Harry would listen patiently, feeling guilty that he seemed to feel none of these poetically expressed emotions for his own wife.

He was awfully fond of Olivia. He always had been. He respected her intelligence, her strength, and her beauty, and the way she had organized Wharton Park when Adrienne had needed her to. She was the perfect mistress of the estate and a suitable replacement for his mother.

But . . .

Did he love her? And why wasn't he desperate to return home immediately?

Harry took another sip of his coffee, still piping hot in the blistering heat, and lit another cigarette. He took a little comfort in that the fellows he had listened to pouring out their hearts had been able to choose for themselves whom they married. He had not. Without his mother suggesting marriage and pointing out its advantages, Harry would have left for war a single man. The thought of marrying Olivia, or any woman for that matter, would simply not have crossed his mind.

He knew his situation was far from unusual. Arranged marriages had taken place across the globe for centuries. As always, his own feelings were secondary to his heritage. For some, that was simply the way it was.

Harry stubbed out his cigarette. Perhaps he was asking too much. Perhaps he did love her . . . how was he to know what love really was between a man and a woman? He had been a late developer emotionally and sexually unsure of himself. Olivia was the first woman he had ever known. Once they had got the hang of it, things in that department had gone quite well, he thought.

The good news was that any fear he had held about latent tendencies toward his own sexuality had been proved unfounded in the past three and a half years. He had seen other men in the camp take comfort in each other. Everyone had turned a blind eye to this; whatever got you through hell and kept you alive was acceptable. But not once had he felt the need to turn to another man's arms, even during his darkest moments.

Well, Harry thought, there was no fighting it any longer. He had to return home and face the music. Over lunch with Sebastian, he confirmed he felt fit enough to contemplate the journey back to England.

"Jolly good, dear boy. I know there's a ship leaving in a week. Let me see what strings I can pull and try and get you on board. Sooner the better now, I should think."

Unable to join in Sebastian's enthusiasm for stepping back onto the green, green grass of England, Harry drowned his sorrows and drank far more than he normally would. After lunch, as he headed rather unsteadily back to his room, he resolved he should enjoy the short time he had left in Bangkok. To that end, and with alcohol fueling his courage, he took a deep breath and walked across to the reception desk. Lidia smiled up at him.

"Yes, please, how can I help you?"

"Well . . ." Harry cleared his throat. "I was thinking, Lidia, that I should be seeing a little of the city before I leave for England. As you are now in charge of guest relations, I was wondering whether accompanying me on a river tour might be included in your remit?"

"I'm sorry, Harry"—Lidia looked confused—"what is the word *remit*?"

"What I am asking, Lidia, is whether you would be my guide for the day?" Harry explained, his heart pounding.

Lidia looked doubtful. "I would have to ask Madame."

"Madame is right behind you. What would you like to ask her?" said a heavily accented voice as Giselle appeared from the office.

Harry repeated his request to her. "I'd appreciate awfully someone with local knowledge and, of course, good English," he added, feeling rather a heel, but determined to get his way.

Giselle thought about it for a while, then said, "Well, Captain Crawford, I think we might be able to reach a mutually convenient agreement, *n'est-ce pas*? Lidia and Monsieur Ainsley have both told me you play the piano very well. You might have heard that tomorrow night is the opening of my bar here at the hotel? I am in need of a pianist. If you will play for me, I will allow Lidia to take you out on the river and show you Bangkok."

Harry put out his hand, delighted. "Deal."

"*C'est parfait*, Captain Crawford," Giselle said, shaking his hand. "I have a saxophonist and a drummer. They will be in the bar at six tomorrow evening. Perhaps you can make yourself available at that time for a rehearsal with them. I will leave the arrangements for you to make for your tour with the young lady."

"Of course. *Merci*, Madame," he replied.

When she had disappeared into her office, Harry leaned contentedly over the desk, stared into Lidia's beautiful amber eyes, and said, "Right, that is settled. Now, where do you suggest you take me?"

35

The opening of the newly named Bamboo Bar was well attended by the expat community, who, after years of suffering under Japanese rule, were glad to have something to celebrate. They arrived in droves, knocking back the local Mekong whiskey and making *sanuk*, the Thai word for "fun."

With less than an hour's rehearsal, Harry was glad of his skills as a pianist and the practice he'd had playing jazz to the Nips in Changi. He was teamed with a Dutch drummer—an ex-POW like himself—and a Russian saxophonist, who was in Bangkok for reasons unknown. They'd made a list of tunes all three of them knew.

The atmosphere was vibrant, smoky, and sweaty. Having never played with other musicians, Harry enjoyed the camaraderie enormously. The enthusiastic applause as his fingers flew across the keys in a virtuoso solo gave Harry a thrill he had seldom felt. He glanced at Lidia, looking wonderful in a silk sarong and gliding about the room with a tray of drinks.

When all three musicians declared there could be no more encores, as they were dripping with sweat and exhausted, Harry walked out of the bar and across the terrace to the lawn, which led directly down to the river below. Due to a blackout, the last part of the evening had been conducted by candlelight, and the only light on the river was the full moon above him.

Harry lit a cigarette and sighed heavily. Tonight, just for those few hours, he'd felt he belonged. Never mind that he was a stray among strays, a disparate ragbag of people collected together from the four corners of the earth, through unknown tragedy. He had not been a captain in the army or a hereditary peer of the British realm with a vast estate to inherit. He had been nothing more than a pianist, and his talent had entertained and brought pleasure to others.

He had loved it because he had simply been himself.

• • •

The following day, as arranged, Lidia met him in the lobby of the hotel.

Madame had acquired a wooden boat for them, complete with a boatman who would take them wherever Lidia suggested. As Harry stepped in, his legs felt more jellylike than they had in the past few days, thanks to the late night and four whiskeys.

"Captain Crawford, I think we go upriver and pass Grand Temple first," said Lidia, sitting on the wooden bench opposite him. "Then we go on to floating market, okay?"

It seemed odd to hear the American expression coming from her oriental lips.

"Okay," he agreed, finding the word strange on his own lips too. "And for goodness' sake, call me Harry."

"Okay, Harry." She smiled.

They set off from the hotel pier and joined the traffic. The Chao Phraya River acted as a thoroughfare for the entire city, and Harry was amazed there weren't more collisions, as drivers expertly steered away from oncoming boats with inches to spare. Huge black barges, sometimes four or five in a row, held together with bits of rope, and pulled by tiny craft at the front, would appear on the horizon like menacing whales. After a couple of near misses, Harry found his hands were shaking.

Lidia read his tension. "Do not worry, Harry. Our driver, Sing-tu, he been steering this boat for thirty years. And he never have accident, okay?"

She leaned forward and patted Harry's hand.

The gentle gesture, he was sure, meant nothing to Lidia, but for a man starved of affection for years, it was a moment to treasure.

"Harry, look."

He followed her delicate outstretched hand and saw a building he could truly say warranted the word *palace*. With its Thai-style inverted-*V* roofs, clad in gold and covered with what resembled huge emeralds and rubies glinting in the sunlight, it was like a picture from one of the storybooks his mother had read to him as a child.

"This is home of our king and queen. They are gods to us. You want to go in and see Emerald Buddha in *wat*? He is very beautiful and very famous. He is looked after by many monk."

"Why not? What, may I ask, is a *wat*?" Harry chuckled as the driver steered the boat and hooked a rope over a wooden post by the pier.

"You would say a *temple*," Lidia clarified, stepping out expertly and hauling Harry after her.

The gardens surrounding the palace and the Temple of the Emerald Buddha were spectacularly beautiful, full of vibrant colors, the smell of jasmine pervading everything.

Harry stopped in front of an exquisite flowering plant with delicate blooms of soft pink and white. "Orchids," he murmured. "They grew in the foliage around Changi, and I've seen them everywhere since I arrived in Bangkok. They are rare in England."

"They are like weeds here," said Lidia.

"Golly! I wish we had weeds at home like this," Harry said, thinking he must take some back to his mother.

He followed Lidia up the steps to the temple and removed his shoes as she did. Inside it was dark and airy, the monks in their saffron robes kneeling in prayer in front of the exquisite and surprisingly small Emerald Buddha. Lidia knelt too, with her hands in the prayer position, head bowed. Harry did the same.

After a few moments, he lifted his head and stayed there for a while, enjoying the peace and tranquillity of the temple. During his time in Changi, for want of anything better to do, he had attended a couple of lectures on religion. One of them had been on Buddhism, and he remembered thinking that its ethos came closer than others to his own feelings and thoughts on the world.

Eventually, they left the temple and went back into the bright sunshine.

"You want to go to floating market now?" Lidia asked as they stepped back onto the boat. "It is long boat journey, but I think you will enjoy."

"Whatever you suggest."

"Okay, I suggest this." Lidia spoke to the driver in fast Thai, and they took off at top speed along the river. Harry lay back in the stern and watched as Bangkok floated past him. The day was hot, despite the cool river breeze, and he wished he had bought a hat to protect his head.

After a while, the driver turned off into a narrow klong and navigated his way along the crowded waterway. As they reached the floating market, they came to a halt, for they were surrounded by wooden boats filled with merchandise and people shouting prices at their customers, who shouted back from their own boats.

The scene was delightful; colorful silks, ground spices tumbling out of burlap sacks, the smell of chicken roasting on spits, mingling with the scent of freshly cut flowers, all added to the exotic atmosphere of the place.

"You want to eat, Harry?" Lidia asked.

"Yes," Harry managed, although he was feeling peculiar. Perhaps it was the sun, but he was dizzy and rather nauseous. Lidia stood up and shouted to a boatman selling chicken on sticks, and they struck a deal. Harry closed his eyes, sweat breaking out on his forehead as the noise in his ears became overwhelming. The clamoring, high-pitched voices, the strong smells, and the heat . . . good God, the heat! He needed some water urgently. . . .

"Harry, Harry, wake up."

He opened his eyes and saw Lidia looking down at him; she was holding a cool cloth to his forehead. They were in a darkened room and he was lying on a narrow pallet on the floor. "Where am I? What . . . happened?"

"You faint in boat and you fall back and hit your head on wood. Are you okay?" Lidia's huge eyes were full of concern.

"I see. Sorry about that." He struggled to sit up. "Could I have a drink of water?" His parched throat and desperation for fluids brought back dark memories of Changi.

Lidia passed him a flask and he drank from it thirstily.

"We take you to hospital, yes?" Lidia suggested. "You not well."

"No, really, I'll be fine now I've had a drink. I think I may have had too much sun and got dehydrated, that's all."

"You sure?" Lidia did not look convinced. "You have been sick with dengue fever. Maybe it back."

"I am sure, Lidia, really."

"Then we return to hotel now. Can you stand?"

"Of course." Harry persuaded his legs to support him, and with Lidia's and the driver's help, he left the small shack in which Lidia had sheltered him from the sun and climbed back into their boat. As they set off, Harry could not help a wry smile at the irony of fainting in a floating market when he had never once fainted in Changi, even under the most appalling conditions.

"You wear this. I get brown and ugly on my face just for you." Lidia removed her coolie-style hat and put it on Harry's head. "Drink some more water." She handed him the flask.

"What do you mean, brown and ugly?" Harry asked as he lay back, grateful for the shade the hat provided.

"It is a mark of class in Thailand. If you have pale skin, you are of good class; dark and you are peasant!"

"I see." Harry smiled as the driver navigated his way out of the floating market and they headed for the Chao Phraya River. Lidia sat watching him, never taking her eyes away from his face. He closed his eyes, feeling far less faint now, but knowing that something was wrong.

Back at the hotel, Lidia helped him out of the boat and up to the veranda.

"You go to your room now and get some rest, Harry," she told him. "I tell Madame you sick."

Harry spent the afternoon sleeping and was woken later by a bell-boy knocking on his door to inform him that Mr. Ainsley wanted to pop in and see him.

"Send him in." Harry nodded, inwardly groaning at the familiar ache in his bones.

"Dear boy, heard from Giselle you had a bit of an incident at the floating market this afternoon," Sebastian said as he came in. "Feeling rough again, are we?"

"I'm afraid so, thought it might be the crowds, but it feels now as though it's almost certainly not."

"Blast it!" Sebastian sat down in a wicker chair. "I suppose that means you'll be unable to travel home in a couple of days' time. I came to tell you I'm booked on the ship too and was going to make the journey back to Blighty with you."

"I am sorry, old fellow, but just now, I doubt I will be fit enough to join you."

"I'll get the doctor in to see you as soon as possible," said Sebastian morosely. "Bally shame and all that, though. Looking forward to sharing the high seas with you. Being stuck here for the past four years, I thought I would take the opportunity to go home and see the parents. The mater's getting on rather, you know, dear old thing. Well now"—Sebastian levered himself out of his chair—"I shall get the bellboy and tell him to send for the doctor forthwith. Will you be all right in Bangkok without me here?"

"Of course I will."

"Strange it's me returning home rather than you, but there we are. I shall leave you some funds, of course, and have them reimbursed in Blighty. I'll pop in to see your folks and reassure them you will be returning at some point. Don't want them to think you've gone AWOL."

"No," muttered Harry, feeling ghastly.

"Just one thing." Sebastian paused as he reached the door. "This country tends to be rather seductive, and the longer you stay, the more attractive it becomes. Don't fall in love with it, dear boy, will you? Otherwise you may never return home."

The doctor arrived and confirmed that Harry was suffering another bout of dengue fever.

"You have been doing too much, too soon, my boy," he said, giving Harry a hefty dose of quinine to bring down his temperature. "I heard you playing in the bar the other night." The doctor smiled. "And jolly good you were too. That's off the agenda for now, along with alcohol. You know the ropes: rest, fluids, quinine when you need it, and let us hope we can keep you out of the hospital this time."

"Yes, Doctor."

"I'm also going to prescribe you some vitamins. I shall get one of the boys to run down the road for them. And I shall be in to see you tomorrow. I will inform Madame, and I am sure she will send someone to keep an eye on you."

"What do I owe you for your trouble, Doctor?"

The doctor turned round and gave a short smile. "It is I who owe you, my boy. It's brave soldiers like you who won this damned war for us. Good day, Captain Crawford."

Harry drifted in and out of a fitful, feverish sleep, and sometime during the evening, there was a soft tap on his door.

"Come," he said. The door opened and there was Lidia, her eyes full of concern.

"Madame tell me you still feel unwell. That you have dengue fever back again. It is my fault. I should not have taken you to such a hot, busy place when you are not strong."

"Lidia, really, I asked you to take me."

Despite feeling so dreadful, Harry couldn't help but stare at her. In the soft glow of the lamp, she looked so perfect; everything about her was exquisite to his feverish eyes. He felt a sudden unexpected and inappropriate surge of desire.

"May I see your forehead?" she asked, walking toward him.

"*Feel* my forehead? Of course." He nodded and enjoyed the sensation of her cool palm on his brow, not to mention the heavenly scent of her in such proximity.

"Yes, you are too warm." She produced a small bag of herbs from her skirt pocket. "At home, we use Chinese medicine always. This one especially for fever and aching bones. You want to try? I can make up as tea for you."

"Lidia, I will try anything," Harry said with fervor. "I am so damned sick of being sick."

"Then I will bring it to you and you will feel better by the morning. I promise." She smiled. "It contain magic."

"I do hope so." Harry managed a smile in return.

"I go and make it now."

"Thank you."

Harry watched her leave and lay back. As he gazed up at the ceiling fan, he realized this seemingly rotten bad luck could have benefits.

Lidia was back ten minutes later, holding a glass. "I warn you, Harry, it taste very bad." She helped him sit up.

"Then it will work. Or, at least, that's what my mother used to say when I was a little boy and she was feeding me some foul medicine," joked Harry weakly.

"Very bad," she reiterated as she put the glass to his mouth.

Harry almost gagged on the first mouthful but, remembering the live maggots he had eaten in Changi, told himself to stop being a coward and drank it all down.

"Gosh," he spluttered, "you were right."

Lidia passed him some water to take away the taste.

"Now, Harry, you rest. If you need anything, you ring bell. Madame has asked me to sleep in room across from you tonight. I check you in one hour. You will feel very, very hot soon, but is only herbs helping break fever and it will stop."

"I look forward to that," he gulped as she walked to the door. He wondered whether he had been foolish to trust her.

"Do not worry, Harry. I will be here."

Lidia's prediction proved right: within an hour, Harry was on fire. Lidia arrived with cool cloths for his forehead, as he tossed and turned with a raging fever. A couple of hours later it abated. Exhausted, Harry fell into sleep.

36

Late the following morning, Harry woke feeling far better than he had expected. Although his bones still ached, the intensity had diminished, and when the doctor arrived, he confirmed with surprise that his patient's temperature was indeed only one degree above normal.

"Remarkable," the doctor surmised. "I thought you were in for another bad bout, but it seems not. Well done and keep up the good work."

Lidia popped her head round the door after the doctor had left. She was holding another glass of evil-smelling herbs.

"How are you, Harry?"

"Better, thank you." He eyed the glass suspiciously. "You've not come to set me on fire again, have you?"

Lidia giggled, showing her perfect teeth. "Of course not," she answered, proud of the new words she had learned from him. "This is for big strength, to build up body and stop bad dengue fever coming back. It give you energy and appetite. No fire, I promise."

"Does it taste as bad as the last one?" Harry sat up, bracing himself.

"Worse, so even better for you."

Harry drank the foul-tasting mixture, then lay back panting, trying not to gag. "Are you a witch? The doctor couldn't believe how much I'd improved."

"Perhaps"—she smiled—"but a good one. Now I must leave you, as I have new guests arriving very soon. I will come back later to see how strong you have grown."

Harry chuckled as she left the room, thinking how delightful it was to watch her personality emerge as her confidence with him grew. Whatever these brews of hers were, they certainly worked.

By suppertime, Harry felt hungry and ordered some noodles to be brought to his room. As he sat up in bed to eat them, he decided he was happy to continue having occasional bouts of the dreaded dengue fever if Lidia could be his nurse and his savior.

Over the next couple of weeks, Harry slept far more than he felt he should and ate whatever was put in front of him. When he wasn't sleeping, he thought about Lidia. She looked in to see him whenever she could, her eyes alight with pleasure that he was recovering.

And every day she looked more beautiful.

Harry began to live for her visits, fantasized afterward about beckoning her over to the bed, enfolding her tiny body in his arms, kissing the perfectly formed arcs of her lips, feeling her small, sharp, pearl white teeth with his tongue . . . In his rational moments, Harry tried to reason that his enforced separation from females accounted for the effect she was having on him. On the other hand, he could not remember, in all his adult life, feeling like this about a woman.

He hardly knew her, or anything about her life beyond the little she had told him. But he *did* know her . . . she was kind, with a sense of humor, and bright. Her grasp of English, the way she could make herself understood, despite her lack of vocabulary, was impressive. Used to the riddles of English girls with their full command of the language, he found it refreshing that Lidia said what she meant in so few words. And then there was her beauty. Harry had never been easily aroused physically, certainly not by thoughts alone, but with Lidia he was. He supposed it was reassuring that all parts of him were still in full working order, after the physical and emotional beatings he had taken in Changi. And that, after all his doubting, a woman could finally induce such a strong physical reaction.

It was something he had never felt for Olivia.

His wife.

Harry thought back to all the times the fellows in Changi had discussed their feelings of lust and love. Was this what he felt for Lidia? *Love?*

On the fourth day of his incarceration, and when, unusually, Lidia had not popped her head round the door to see how he was, Harry ventured out of his room at sunset. He strolled across the lobby to the Bamboo Bar, for want of something better to do, glancing at the reception desk on his way.

"You are better?" Giselle appeared behind him.

"Yes, much, thank you. I was just wondering where Lidia had gone to."

"She has taken a day off," Giselle said distractedly. "Family problems, I believe."

Harry's heart started to pound. "She's all right, isn't she?"

"I do not know, Captain Crawford. I'm her employer, not her mother, although I am very fond of Lidia. She has a difficult life."

Rattled, Harry headed to the Bamboo Bar, which was not due to open for an hour and was currently deserted. He sat down at the piano, lifted the lid, and began to play.

Soon, the other musicians and the bartender started to drift through the door.

"We've missed you. You good for tonight?" asked Yogi, the Dutch drummer.

"I'm good for tonight." Harry nodded, thinking it might help take his mind off Lidia.

Harry played until midnight, drinking pints of water while the clientele succumbed to the effects of whiskey. He was propositioned by a couple of tipsy middle-aged women, who offered to show him the sights of Bangkok if he would play naked for them. Harry thought the whole thing was a marvelous joke: his body was still skeletal, with a lumpy rice belly and flaky, vitamin-deprived skin.

On waking the following morning, his first thought was of Lidia, and whether she would be back today. He got out of bed and went down to the veranda for breakfast, having checked whether she was behind the desk. She was not.

The day wore on, punctuated only by the tailor who came to fit his new clothes, muttering under his breath at having to alter the waistbands of Harry's trousers now that his rice belly was diminishing.

Harry kept passing through the lobby to check whether Lidia had arrived. After the third time, Giselle came over to him and shook her head. "She's not in today either. I can only hope she's not going to do what so many of these natives do here and just disappear."

The thought made Harry's stomach churn. He walked back to his room for his afternoon nap, lay on his bed, and tried to sleep. He eventually gave up and started pacing around the room instead, wondering whether Giselle had Lidia's address. If she didn't show up again tomorrow, perhaps he should go and hunt her down.

"Don't be so ridiculous," he chided himself out loud. "For pity's sake; you're just another guest at the hotel. You can hardly go chasing round Bangkok after a random girl you hardly know!" But, despite giving himself a jolly good talking to, Harry could think of nothing else. The rest of the day passed in an agony of suspense as he imagined the dreadful things that might have happened to her. He lay on his back at three in the morning, head resting on his hands, and realized this had to be more than simply a crush.

He was in love with her.

His relief when he walked into the lobby the next morning and Lidia was sitting behind the reception desk as usual was palpable. He had to restrain himself from running over and putting his arms round her.

"Lidia, you're back! Are you . . . all right?"

"Yes, Harry." Her eyes seemed darker than usual, her demeanor somehow dimmed, but she added, "I am all right."

He studied her. "Are you sure?"

"Of course."

"Good. I'm glad." Not wanting to leave her, but unsure what else to say, he wandered off.

Harry paced his room, unable to settle. He had felt fine before Lidia had gone AWOL. But the intensity of the panic he had suffered when she wasn't there had frightened him. How could he love a woman he hardly knew?

Unable to stay in his room, he walked across the veranda and strolled down toward the river. He lit a cigarette and thought of

Sebastian, now probably well on his way across the sea; he wished he had been well enough to travel with him. Even if he had "fallen in love," the turmoil he was feeling about Lidia was pointless. He was a captain in the British army, a hereditary peer of the British realm, heir to a vast country estate . . .

And married.

Harry threw the remainder of his cigarette viciously into the river. It caught in the detritus of tangled weeds that constantly floated past. Maybe the dengue fever had affected his brain—or perhaps the time in Changi. The first woman to come along and give him any form of comfort, and he was lost.

He went back up to the hotel and marched determinedly into the lobby. He would book a passage on the next boat home. He caught sight of Lidia at the reception desk and tried to ignore her. But out of the corner of his eye, he saw her take a handkerchief from her small basket and dab her eyes. Immediately, he weakened and turned back toward her.

As he reached her, he leaned forward and said quietly, "Lidia, what is wrong?"

She shook her head, too choked to speak.

"What is it? What's happened?"

"Please, Harry," she said with a note of panic. "Leave me. I do not want to draw attention. Madame would not be happy to see me behind reception like this."

"I understand. I will go away, but only if you promise to meet me outside the hotel on your lunch break. I'll be at the end of the road, by the small food stall on the corner."

She looked up at him. "Oh, Harry, Madame—"

"I'll make sure we're not seen. Say yes and I'll leave you be."

"If it mean you go away now, I meet you by the stall at noon."

"Deal." He smiled and walked away, completely forgetting the reason he had come into the lobby in the first place.

Lidia was waiting for him on the corner as arranged, glancing nervously from side to side.

"I know place we can go." She beckoned him to follow her and walked smartly away along the busy road. After a couple of minutes, she turned into a narrow alley, packed with barrows selling all manner of food. She walked halfway along it, then indicated a rough wooden bench, sheltered from the sun by a ragged parasol.

"You want something to eat?" asked Lidia.

The smell of drains mingling with sizzling, indeterminate meat in the airless alley made Harry feel nauseous. "I think I'll just take a beer if there is one, thank you."

"Of course." Lidia spoke in fast Thai to the vendor and a beer and a glass of water appeared in front of them.

Harry tried to concentrate on Lidia, rather than the stifling, claustrophobic atmosphere. He felt sweat breaking out on his forehead, opened his beer, and took a hefty swig from it.

"So, Lidia, can you tell me why you were crying this morning?"

Lidia looked at him, her eyes full of sadness. "Oh, Harry, I have very difficult problem at home."

"Lidia, having seen countless men die right in front of me, I really can handle most things."

"Okay, Harry, I will tell you," Lidia sighed. "My mother, she is getting married."

"And this is a bad thing?"

Lidia's eyes filled with tears. "Yes. Because . . . he is Japanese general."

"I see." Harry now understood just how bad this was.

"They met during occupation here. But she did not tell me because she understand how I will feel. Now he is back in Japan. And wishes her to go there—with *all* of us."

Harry was silent for a moment. Then he nodded. "You are right. This is a really big problem."

"How could she do this?" Lidia whispered. "She is traitor!" She spat the words. "How can she think of this when my father, he die trying to free Thailand from Japanese?"

"He died?"

"They put him in prison one year ago, when they found he was publishing underground newspaper. Just before end of war, six months ago, we hear they shoot him."

Harry instinctively reached a hand across the wooden table and rested it on Lidia's. It felt so tiny, so fragile under his grasp. "Lidia, I am so terribly sorry."

She wiped the tears roughly from her cheeks. "Thank you. Now worst thing is, I cannot believe my mother ever love my father. How can she?"

"I am sure she did, Lidia," Harry tried to rationalize, "but there are a lot of reasons why people do what they do, when they need to. You have many brothers and sisters and, from what you tell me, little money. Is this general rich?"

"Oh, yes, very. He is powerful too and live in big house in Japan. My mother is very beautiful. Every man fall in love with her." Lidia sighed. "But you are right. She want her children to have new life, good life, better than she can have here as a widow. This is how she explain it to me. She tell me she does not love him, but must do right thing for future."

"And what will you do?" he asked, hardly able to bear the answer.

"She want me to go with her. She say Japan not enemy, that occupation peaceful and only political agreement." Lidia shook her head. "But they *shoot* my father because they worry he cause trouble and unrest. How can I go to this place?"

"I don't know, Lidia, I really don't. May I ask how old you are?"

"I am seventeen, eighteen in six weeks."

"Then you can make your own decisions. Must you go?"

"Harry, if I do not, I may never see my mother or my brothers and sisters again." Lidia fiddled with her glass, distraught. "I have lost my father. How can I lose them too?"

Harry shook his head. "You are in an impossible situation." He took a swig of his beer. "But you are almost an adult now, not a child. You must think of *your* life and what you want."

"But my mother, she is saying I must go to Japan. I cannot disobey her."

"Lidia, everything is not just about family."

Her amber eyes burnt with passion. "Harry, you are wrong. Here in Thailand, *everything* is about family. You must obey your parents."

"Even when you are an adult?"

Lidia was crying freely now. "Yes."

"I really am awfully sorry. Seems I'm upsetting you more." Harry rooted in his trouser pocket for a handkerchief and passed it to her.

"No, you are not. It is good to talk." She blew her nose loudly. "Madame say too I should not go. That I have good job at hotel and will progress."

Harry thanked God for Giselle. "Remember, this war has changed all the rules, for everyone, and things are not what they were. You must try to forgive your mother, she is only doing what she thinks is best. But what she wants for herself and your younger brothers and sisters may not be appropriate for you. Do you have any other relatives here in Thailand?"

"Yes. My father's family, they come from an island, many miles away." The cloud suddenly lifted from Lidia's face and she smiled. "It is very beautiful; I went there many times as a child. It is known as Elephant Island and it floats in the sea like a jewel."

"So you would not be alone in this country?"

"No."

"And you have a way of earning money here."

"Yes." She looked up at him. "You think I should stay behind?"

"Only you can make that decision, Lidia. But there is no reason, if you decided to stay here, why you can't visit your mother and brothers and sisters often."

"But it is so far away, Harry, many thousands of miles, and cold." Lidia shuddered. "I hate the cold."

Harry wondered what Lidia would make of Norfolk in midwinter. "It is simple," he said, then drained his beer bottle. "You must decide what *you* want."

Lidia looked into the distance and gave a sigh. "I want"—then she crumpled—"not to make this decision."

"No. But you must. When does your mother leave for Japan?"

"In ten days. The general has booked passage for her and my brothers and sisters. And me," she added, frowning.

"Well then, why don't you let the dust settle for a few days, as we say in England? Which means, get over the shock and take your time to think?"

Lidia offered him a wan smile. "You are right. Thank you, Harry. What is the time?"

"I am afraid my watch was blown up in my kit bag four years ago and I haven't got round to replacing it."

Lidia stood up. "Well, I'm sure it time for me to go back to work. *Kop khun ka*, Harry."

"What does that mean?"

"It means 'thank you,' for everything. You help me, really." She gave him a smile and hurried away toward the hotel.

The next time Harry saw Lidia was in the lobby that afternoon. She looked more composed as she handed him a telegram. It was from Olivia, telling him all was well at Wharton Park, and they hoped he would soon be fit enough to make the journey home.

"It is from your family in England?" Lidia asked.

"Yes." He nodded.

"Your mother?"

"Yes."

Harry returned to his room, telegram in hand, and berated himself for lying to her.

The doctor came to see him the following morning and pronounced him well enough to travel. Harry knew it would be best to leave as soon as possible; return to reality and cease fantasizing about a life and a woman that could never be his.

He telexed Sebastian's office and asked them to book him the next available passage home.

When he was trying to settle for his afternoon nap, there was a soft tap on his door.

It was Lidia. His face lit up at the sight of her.

"So sorry to disturb you, Harry, but I come to tell you I go away for this weekend. And I do not want you to worry for me. It is *Songkran*, special New Year Thai celebration. In your country, you would call it water festival."

Harry's heart sank. "How long are you going for?"

"Three days. I think about what you say to me and I decide I will spend *Songkran* with my father's parents in Koh Chang."

"When do you leave?" Harry felt agitated. His time here was running out.

"Early tomorrow morning. It is long journey and will take me whole day to get there."

"Can I come with you?"

She looked at him, surprised.

"Sorry, Lidia." Harry was embarrassed by his forward behavior. "I'm sure the last thing you want is me tagging along beside you. It's just I've seen so little of the Thai countryside. Please, forget I even said it. It would be too much of an imposition."

Her amber eyes were thoughtful. "Ah, Harry, you are lonely without your family, yes?" She did not give him time to reply before adding, "*Songkran* is all about family and welcoming people into it." She gave a sudden, wide smile of decision. "I think my grandparents very happy to welcome brave British soldier who help fight Japanese. Yes"—she nodded—"you come with me."

"Really?" Harry was overwhelmed.

"Yes." Lidia nodded. "Then I can show you the beautiful island of my father's birth. It will be present from me to say thank you for helping me decide what to do."

"You have decided?"

"As you say, I am adult. And I cannot go to Japan and live with people who murder my father and many others. I stay here. In country I love."

Harry's own lips broke into a wide smile. "I am glad you've made your decision, Lidia. And, personally, I think it's the right one."

"I will miss my brothers and sisters, but even for them, I cannot do this. One day, when I make great life and money here in Bangkok, I can bring them back, if they wish to come. So, we meet on corner by food stall tomorrow at six o'clock in morning? Then we will take tuk-tuk to the station."

"Six o'clock tomorrow morning," Harry agreed.

"Oh, and I must tell you, Koh Chang not like this." Lidia swept her arms around the room. "No electricity, no tap, but good sea."

"That is not a problem for me, Lidia." After Changi, Harry could cope with most conditions.

"I must go now," said Lidia. "I see you tomorrow at six."

• • •

Harry went to let Giselle know he would not be playing in the bar for the following three nights.

"May I inquire where you are going?"

"Yes, I thought I should see a little of the country before I leave."

"Of course," she agreed, "and I have heard Koh Chang is rather beautiful, although I have never been there myself."

Harry's expression told Giselle everything she needed to know.

"I will return on Monday."

"Captain Crawford? Harry?" She stopped him.

"Yes?"

"Lidia is a lovely girl. And she has a very difficult time. I am very fond of her and hope she will be with me here for many years to come. Do not hurt her, will you?"

"Of course not." Harry was indignant.

"*D'accord.* Enjoy getting wet." Giselle smiled and walked back into her office.

37

Lidia was waiting for him at the appointed meeting place. She hailed a tuk-tuk and they set off. The sun was still rising and Bangkok was quiet, which meant Harry was able to enjoy the city, with its miscellany of colonial architecture, wooden shacks, and Thai-style houses. He only wished he'd had the physical stamina to explore more of it.

They arrived at the railway station, which was a hive of activity. Ancient trains stood in sidings, covered in rust produced by many years of unrelenting rain in the monsoon season. Lidia bought their tickets, refusing to take money from Harry, and walked down the platforms until she found the right train. They climbed into an already packed carriage, and chattering locals stared at Harry in fascination as he and Lidia made their way down the narrow aisle to a free bench.

Harry had looked at the map in Giselle's office and knew they were traveling east down the coast, to a region called Trat. Koh Chang, a tiny dot suspended in the sea, was presumably reached by boat.

"How long is the journey?" Harry asked.

"It take four hours to Chanthaburi, then we change. And another three hours to Trat," Lidia replied, while expertly slicing a fresh mango from her basket and handing it to him. "Then my uncle come on his fishing boat and take us across to Koh Chang."

"Are your family expecting me?"

"I cannot get word to them as no telephone on the island. But they will not mind. I promise, Harry. But at Chanthaburi"—she waved her knife at him and smiled—"we buy you some clothes."

"I have clothes, Lidia." Harry indicated the small case on the rack above his head.

Lidia giggled. "No, no, Harry, your clothes no good to wear for *Songkran* festival. You will see what I mean." She smiled mysteriously.

The train, belching a plume of smoke, left the straggling outskirts of the city and made its way along a track lined with hundreds of huge banana plants. Children waved to them as they passed, smiling eagerly. Lidia dozed next to him; how she could sleep on the hard wooden bench, Harry could not imagine. But with her head dropping onto his shoulder and the sweet smell of the oil she used on her hair filling his nostrils, Harry felt at peace. He was with her, close to her, for an entire three days, and just now could think of anywhere he would rather be.

He must have dozed off too, for the next thing he knew the train was coming to a halt and Lidia was shaking him gently. He roused himself, collected his case, and followed Lidia onto the platform. They were immediately surrounded by hawkers, plying them with food, drink, jasmine garlands, and roughly carved wooden animals. Lidia led Harry away and sat him down on a bench under a bamboo canopy.

"You stay here. I go to get lunch."

A small Thai child approached him, smiling shyly, fascinated by him. Harry mopped his brow and took a sip of water, as Lidia returned with lunch and put a pile of thin cotton sheets in front of him. "Try these on."

"For me to wear?" He held up a red tablecloth and discovered it was a pair of trousers with what seemed to be a small apron attached to the front. There was also a loose white cotton shirt.

She pointed to a bamboo cabin nearby. "Try on in there."

He stripped as fast as he could, relieved to be out of his heavy twill trousers and finest-quality cotton shirt, and put on the items Lidia had given him. He struggled to navigate the workings of the unusual three-quarter-length trousers, but eventually managed to secure the apron across his front as the locals did, making him look as though he were wearing a skirt.

The Thai child was standing waiting outside with Lidia and let out peals of laughter when she saw him.

"I'm sure I do look awfully silly," he said, embarrassed.

"No, Harry," said Lidia softly. "You look like Thai man now. Better for island and *Songkran.* Now, I go to change." Lidia left, and Harry amused himself teaching the child English words. He was rewarded with a beautiful smile and a rough pronunciation of the words he spoke to her.

Harry couldn't help a gasp when Lidia reappeared. Instead of her Western uniform, she was wearing a pair of trousers similar to his and a simple Chinese-style cotton blouse in pink. But the most noticeable change was in her hair: she had freed it from the tight knot at the back of her head. It now cascaded in a shining, ebony mass over her shoulders and down to her waist.

Harry reached out his fingers involuntarily, longing to run them through the utterly luxuriant femininity of it. He looked down and saw her tiny, delicate feet were bare. The perfect toes transfixed him. He wasn't used to seeing women's feet in England. The sight seemed so intimate, so naked, that Harry experienced a surge of attraction.

"Now, we must get on new train," said Lidia.

Harry said good-bye to the little girl and stood up to follow Lidia.

A voice behind them shouted, "You two in love! You get marry!"

They traveled for three exhausting hours. Harry felt terribly relieved when the train finally stopped. A short bus ride took them to a pier, and when Harry stepped off, he was greeted by an idyllic expanse of turquoise sea and a cloud-covered, mountainous landmass in the distance.

"That is Koh Chang." Lidia pointed out. "See, there is my uncle, waiting for us!"

Harry followed Lidia to one of the numerous wooden fishing boats that bobbed gently by the pier. He hung back as Lidia greeted her uncle affectionately. After a conversation in fast Thai and some pointing at Harry, Lidia beckoned him over.

"Harry, this is Tong, my uncle, but he speak no English."

Uncle Tong bowed to Harry in the traditional Thai greeting and rose with a big, toothless grin and a hearty handshake. He spoke to Harry, and Lidia translated for him that he was pleased to welcome him into the family for the tradition of *Songkran*.

"Please tell your uncle I am honored to be here," Harry replied as Tong helped him down into the boat, and they set off toward Koh Chang.

As they crossed the calm ocean, the sinking sun made its sudden dive into the sea and the light began to fade. Within fifteen minutes, they were pulling into the shore and darkness had fallen. Tong reached beneath him and pulled out two oil lamps, which he lit. Lidia glanced at Harry excitedly as her uncle helped him onto terra firma, and he felt the touch of soft sand beneath his feet.

"Welcome, Harry, to my father's island home." Lidia smiled.

It was difficult for Harry to have any reaction to his surroundings as it was now pitch black, but they were walking along a beach. Nestled among high palm trees were wooden huts, lit by the soft glow of oil lamps. As they drew nearer, a group of children and an elderly woman came across the sand to them. They shouted greetings to Lidia and she ran toward them. Harry watched as she was encircled in the old woman's arms and presumed this was Lidia's grandmother. When Lidia turned back to him, the oil lamp reflected the glistening in her eyes.

"Come, Harry, come and meet my family. They are pleased that you are here to celebrate *Songkran* with us."

Harry met the extended family: Lidia's grandmother and grandfather, her uncle and aunt with their four children, and another aunt and her husband, with their three children.

After being handed a bottle of beer by Tong, Harry sat down on one of the mats on the sand and was immediately surrounded by small nieces and nephews. They all spoke a little English and fired questions at Harry about his fighting in the war and whether he had killed any Japs. He answered them as best he could, not sure they understood much of what he was saying, but becoming adept as a mime. When he pointed his pretend gun at a pretend Japanese soldier, the children veered off round the beach, aiming their own imaginary guns and shouting, "Bang! Bang!"

Lidia came out of the darkness and sat down gracefully next to him. "Tonight you sleep here in hut on beach. My aunt, she prepare it for you now."

"Thank you," Harry answered. "Where will you stay?"

"At my grandmother's house, in village behind beach."

"So who lives here?"

"My Uncle Tong, Aunt Kitima, and their children. He is fisherman, so he like to be near work. They are building big house in village now, and one day they go to live there."

"I would stay right here," he murmured as he glanced up at the moon. He had studied its cycle for want of anything better to do on those long nights in Changi. From the size and shape of it now, Harry knew it would be full this time tomorrow. He could hear the waves breaking gently on the sand, only fifty yards from him. "It's so marvelously soothing."

"I am glad you like. You are ready for food now?" Lidia indicated the smoky fire and the grill of fat, fresh fish suspended over it.

Harry nodded and heaved himself upright.

They all sat together at a long wooden table, the children sitting on mats around the adults, eating the best fish Harry had ever tasted in his life. The children had big coconuts and drank the milk inside with relish. Much of the talk around him he couldn't understand; yet the language of a happy, warm, comfortable family gathering was universal. Lidia was sitting between her grandparents, and she often glanced over to him, her eyes asking him if he was all right.

He always smiled back: he was.

An hour or so later, Harry felt the exertions of the day catching up with him. He yawned, but tried to disguise it.

Lidia noticed immediately, then whispered across the table to her aunt, who clapped her hands together. The children around her fell silent. She spoke to them and they nodded sadly, knowing that their time cavorting around the beach was coming to a close and they must go to bed.

Lidia walked over to Harry. "My aunt show you where you sleep. I come and get you tomorrow, okay?"

"There is absolutely no rush, Lidia. Please enjoy your family. I am very content just to be here. And your family has been very welcoming. Please say thank you to them for me."

"Now, Harry, you can say that for yourself."

"Yes, of course. *Kop khun krup*," he said, and bowed rather stiffly. The smiles he received were affectionate and appreciative, not derisive. He followed Lidia's aunt along the beach and she indicated the last hut.

"Mr. Harry, we pleased . . . have you," she returned his effort with halting English.

"Thank you," he said, turning the wooden handle of the hut. "Good night." He stepped inside, closed the door, and turned to see that the hut was bare, bar a mattress on the floor, a freshly laundered sheet, and a mosquito net. Too exhausted to remove his clothes, he lay down on the mattress and fell asleep immediately.

38

When Harry woke to a slight ache in his hip bone from the thin mattress, he had a moment of panic. Then he realized where he was and opened his eyes. The room was still in shadow, the only light coming from a small mesh window facing the palm trees at the back of the hut. Harry stretched, stood upright, and went to open the door.

He gasped at the sight that met his eyes.

He was standing on a magnificent beach, its powdery, white sand stretching in a curve and ending in a hilly, wooded peninsula. The sand shelved gently toward a calm, deep green sea. He looked to his left, then to his right, and could not see another living soul.

Harry stripped to his long johns and raced across the burning-hot sand to jump into the sea. He swam hard for a while, then turned over and lay on his back, looking first at the perfect azure sky, then back toward land, where coconut palms drooped and swayed idyllically, framing the beach. Behind the beach and stretching, cloud-topped, into the distance were jungle-covered mountains, providing what must be an impassable hinterland.

He floated there for a long time, hardly believing that this paradise was his, and his alone to enjoy. Finally, he came out of the sea and flopped onto the hot white sand, feeling euphoric at the sheer beauty of this magical place.

He saw a small figure holding a parasol walking toward him and sat up. It was Lidia, wearing a concerned frown. "You okay, Harry?" she called. "We think you gone away, but then we see your clothes." She smiled at him shyly.

Embarrassed that she had caught him in his soggy long johns, Harry stood up and walked swiftly back toward the hut.

"I decided to go for a swim. Lidia, this beach is the most glorious spot I have ever seen in my life."

Her face lit up. "I glad you like it, Harry. It is good for peace, yes?"

"Gosh, yes." He wagged his finger at her. "I am warning you, I may never want to leave."

"Then you must become fisherman." She handed him his clothes.

"I can learn"—Harry nodded—"if it means I can stay here forever."

"You want to go for wash? There is water pipe behind my uncle and aunt's hut, and cloth for you to dry yourself. I wait here." Lidia sat down on the doorstep of his hut.

Harry returned five minutes later, feeling refreshed after a blast of clean, cold water.

"Now, we walk to village and I take you to my grandmother house, okay?" She reached for his hand and squeezed it. "And happy *Songkran*, *Khun* Harry."

He loved the touch of her fingers on his. "And the same to you," Harry replied.

They made their way along a narrow, sandy path for ten minutes to reach the village. As they turned into the dusty main street, they were both drenched by a pail of water thrown by a couple of children, who screamed in glee at their accuracy.

"What the heck!" exclaimed Harry, the cold water taking him by surprise.

Lidia was doing her best to shake herself dry. She giggled. "*Songkran*, it is about cleansing, taking away all dirt from past, and making new and fresh for the future. Look . . ."

Harry followed where she was pointing. Everywhere along the street, people of assorted ages, holding a miscellany of implements, were throwing water onto any hapless passerby.

"Today is one day you will never get too hot"—Lidia laughed—"and you will not be dry either!"

She was climbing up the steps to a wooden house built on stilts. On the veranda was a collection of pails and buckets, filled with water.

"This is my grandparents' house, and now you must throw some water like this. See?" Lidia took one of the pails and chucked it into the street; Harry did the same, hitting a small boy, who shrieked and giggled as he shook the water out of his eyes.

"Sorry," called Harry guiltily.

"No!" Lidia shook her head. "You must not say sorry! The more people you hit, the luckier for New Year."

"I see."

Lidia led Harry inside the house and into the kitchen at the back, where three or four women were busy preparing vegetables, fish, noodles, and soup for later in the day.

"Harry is here," she called to her grandmother, who turned round and gave him a wide, toothless grin. "You see, we make special feast for our lunch. It is tradition."

"Thank you. Can I do anything to help?" Harry asked.

"No, you are guest. And we Thais never ask men to do woman's work. You stay here, you relax, okay?"

Lidia headed back into the kitchen and Harry sat on the veranda, watching the water rituals in the street below him. The sound of laughter and the sense of joy that pervaded the village were uplifting. Even though this tiny community, adrift in the middle of the sea, had little in the way of material possessions, he felt the warmth. Having only seen the brutal side of humanity for four long years, the sight brought a tear to his eye.

When Lidia reappeared from the kitchen, she was holding a large basket of fruit and vegetables.

"We go visiting, Harry, to bring *Songkran* gift to the old and sick of the village. You come with me?"

Harry stood up. "Of course. Here, let me take that." He hooked the heavy basket over his arm and followed Lidia down the steps.

They spent the next hour in and out of the houses all over the village. Lidia encouraged Harry to put his hands together in the *wai* and pronounce the traditional greeting: *Sawadee krup.* She explained that they offered gifts to the elderly, who, in return, offered to cleanse their souls and forgive their wrongdoings of the past year.

Harry felt this tradition was so much more jolly and all-encompassing than Communion, or the lonely Catholic confessional box. He watched Lidia kneel down beside a frail old man and talk animatedly to him. She took his hand in hers and stroked it gently.

While they walked back toward her grandparents' house, long tables were being set up in the middle of the street in preparation for the feast. The familiar faces of the extended family he had met last night gathered at a table. Two monks from the local temple joined them, resplendent in their saffron robes. Harry looked at the tables of families winding in a long line down the street. It seemed every single resident was present.

He tasted every dish he was offered, then, under duress, played football with any number of small children along the street and got drenched by countless dousings.

When the night drew in, Lidia's grandfather stood up and made a speech. The atmosphere changed swiftly as the old man spoke and let the tears run freely down his cheeks. Harry looked around at Lidia's other relatives and saw they too had tears in their eyes. Then one of the monks stood up and chanted in a melodic, high-pitched voice.

The somber air lasted no longer than fifteen minutes, and when the villagers began to drift away to recover from the day's festivities, Lidia left her place at the table and came over to Harry.

"*Khun* Harry, you are tired now, yes? I walk you home."

After a round of thank-you's and much bowing and pressing of fingers to their noses, Lidia and Harry left the village and began to walk back toward the hut on the beach.

"Why was your grandfather crying?" he asked gently.

"He talked of my father," Lidia replied sadly. "We were remembering him on this special day and wishing his soul well. The monk said it will be well, for he has learned the lesson of suffering in this life. When he come back for next life, maybe his lesson will not be so hard. That is what we Buddhists believe."

"It must be comforting to believe suffering has a purpose beyond our lives," mused Harry. "If it's true, then many of the poor buggers who suffered so badly and died in Changi will be very happy next time around."

She looked up at him. "You believe in your God?"

"Well, religion was never explained to me very well as a child. It was just something I *did.* Every Sunday at home and every day at school, I went to chapel. I didn't think beyond the fact that it was tedious having to sit still for a long time, sing dull tunes, and listen to some old chap boring the pants off me. And all for someone I couldn't even see, or feel, and seemed to do nothing, but still had to be worshipped."

"What is 'boring the pants'?"

This made Harry smile. "An English expression. When I was in Changi, many of the men began to believe in God. Perhaps they had to believe in something. But I . . ." Harry shook his head and sighed. "I suppose I found it hard to believe that any *good* God could make innocent men suffer the way we did."

Lidia nodded. "I also, when my father die, do not take comfort through belief. I think to myself, 'Perhaps he go to a better place, but what about me?' I lose my father before I am ready. But now," she added quietly, "I accept."

"Does your family know your mother is leaving for Japan?" asked Harry, as they arrived on the beach.

"No. It is better this way. It would cause too much pain, and they have enough. They lose their son. They are from different world, here on Koh Chang. They would not understand." Lidia sighed and managed a weak smile. "Sometimes, Harry, life seems very hard."

"I know." He looked up at the moon, full tonight and shining directly above the sea, giving the ripples a silvery gleam. "But I learned in Changi that when I lose my faith in human nature, I put my faith in nature." He indicated the scene in front of him, sweeping his arms wide open. "Someone must have made and designed this beauty, in all its extraordinary intricacy."

"Then you are Buddhist already. Nature nourish the soul," Lidia agreed as they gazed at the moon together.

They walked along the sand, past the empty hut that belonged to Lidia's aunt and uncle, and arrived outside his.

Lidia smiled at him. "I hope tonight you will sleep peacefully and well, Harry. I see you tomorrow."

As she turned to walk away from him, he grabbed her arm and pulled her back toward him.

"Oh, Lidia, Lidia . . ." She did not resist as he took her into his arms, but rested her head on his shoulder while he stroked her magnificent hair. "My darling Lidia, I have to tell you, because if I don't, I will burst." He laughed. "So please forgive me. I think I fell in love with you the moment I saw you at the Oriental, holding a broom! I love you, Lidia, I love you so very, very much." He continued stroking her hair as all the words he had longed to say poured out of him. "I don't know why, or how this has happened, and I know we come from different worlds, but please forgive me, I must tell you, because I feel I am being driven half-mad."

Lidia stood silently, not moving from his shoulder.

Suddenly the relief of telling her, coupled with her silence—which might indicate nonreciprocation—were too much for him.

"I am sorry, Lidia—I—"

"Harry, Harry, it is okay. . . . Come." She took his hand, led him to the step outside the hut, and sat him down on it. She sat slightly behind him, put her arms round his shoulders, and he rested his head against her chest.

"Harry, Harry," Lidia murmured.

She whispered something in Thai. "I didn't understand what you said."

She had tears in her eyes. She hung her head shyly. "I say—I love you too."

He looked at her in amazement, eventually managing to whisper, "You do?"

Lidia nodded. Then she looked him in the eye and smiled sadly. "It is same for me. When I first see you . . . I"—she shook her head, frustrated—"do not have words to explain."

"Oh, my darling girl," Harry choked out as he wrapped her in his arms and kissed her, his passion overwhelming. He had to control himself, not wishing to hurt her fragile body. With all the willpower he possessed, he made his lips leave hers and sat with her, wrapped in his arms.

He had little idea of how much time passed as he managed to content himself with finally holding Lidia in his arms.

"Harry, I must go," she said eventually.

"I know." He kissed her lips once more.

When she stood up, she gazed down at him thoughtfully. "I never believe this happen to me."

"What?"

"To fall in love. To get this feeling . . . here." She indicated her heart. "My grandmother, she say truly loving another person is to find heaven on earth."

"Or hell," Harry muttered under his breath as he stood up to take her in his arms one last time. "I can hardly bear to let you go."

She pulled away from him and reached her small hand out to his; he folded it in his own, then kissed the delicate skin of her palm.

"I come back tomorrow," she said, her hands leaving his. "Good night, Harry."

"Good night, my love," he murmured, as he watched her walk away in the moonlight.

Harry was awake at sunrise, filled with excitement about seeing Lidia. To pass the time until she arrived, he took himself off along the beach for a stroll and went for a long dip in the calm, turquoise sea. Eventually, when each minute had begun to seem like an hour, Lidia arrived. Her eyes warned him not to take her in his arms—her nieces and nephews were playing on the beach in front of their parents' hut—so he nodded at her politely.

"Good morning, Lidia, did you sleep well?"

"Yes, Harry, I did." Her eyes sparkled in delight at the shared games they were playing. "I think this morning, maybe you like to see waterfall in mountains in center of island? It is very beautiful and you can swim in fresh water. Yes?"

"Yes," he agreed immediately. Any chance to be alone with her, he would willingly take.

Lidia put together a basket with water, beer, and some fresh fruit from her aunt's hut, and they set off past the village along a rough, uphill track.

When they were alone, surrounded by jungle, and Lidia was comfortable there could be no prying eyes, she reached up and gave him a delicate kiss on the cheek as a signal. Harry's arms immediately encircled her as he kissed her.

"Come," she said, extricating herself, "it is not far now and we can be comfortable."

Twenty minutes later, with scratched feet and bites from insects that lurked in the undergrowth, Harry entered the clearing around the waterfall to the sound of crashing water, cascading down from the mountain. He looked down into a cool, clean lagoon surrounded by lush vegetation. Lidia pulled a bamboo mat out of her basket and Harry sank down onto it and reached for some water.

He was puffing and panting. "I am sorry, I'm afraid I'm yet to get back to full physical strength."

Lidia knelt like a small, delicate Buddha next to him and handed him some fruit. "Eat this. I understand. Your poor body, it need rest and peace to recover. But"—she indicated the magnificent setting—"I think it is worth it, yes?"

A shack in a shantytown would have sufficed Harry, as long as Lidia was by his side, but he nodded. "It is indeed wonderful. Now, my darling, come here."

She lay her head on his knee and they talked like lovers, eager to discover how and when their mutual feeling had begun and then developed. After a while, he lay down and she lay next to him and nestled into his body. He kissed her lips, her eyes, her cheeks, her hair, and unable to resist, his hand began to travel downward.

When he unbuttoned her blouse, she did not stop him—if anything, she seemed eager. He took his time exploring every part of her soft, honey-colored skin. He undid the three buttons that kept his own torso from her and pulled off his shirt so that their naked skins touched for the first time. A timid hand searched to find the ties of his trousers.

Finally, unable to contain himself any longer, Harry rose above her and looked down into her eyes. "Lidia, please, tell me if you don't want—"

She raised one finger to his lips to silence him. "Harry, I do want, I love you. And I trust you."

He understood that she was telling him this was new to her, that he would be the first.

Gently, he eased himself inside her. He bent toward her face, kissing her gently and asking her to tell him if it hurt and he would stop. When he penetrated her more deeply, she stared into his eyes, and they rose and fell together as the gentleness turned to urgency, she meeting him with the same passionate need, until the moment came and Harry drowned in the pain and pleasure of ecstasy.

39

They began the return journey to Bangkok the following morning, Harry sitting in Tong's boat, staring back at the island that had restored his belief in the beauty and sanctity of life. He only prayed he would see it again one day.

On the train, Harry kept his arms round Lidia. She felt so small, her weight so light against him. He dozed intermittently, but woke with a jump, not wanting to miss the last precious moments of her being his completely.

They parted near the hotel, behaving like strangers because Lidia was afraid someone might see her with him.

"Tomorrow, my love," he whispered into her hair.

"Tomorrow," she answered, climbing back into the tuk-tuk to head home.

That evening, Harry was grateful for the distraction provided by his piano and the lively atmosphere in the bar. But, afterward, although it was past midnight and he was exhausted from the long journey, he didn't feel like sleeping. He wandered down to the river, smoked a cigarette, and replayed in his mind every moment of the past three days.

He paced for some time, wanting so much to stay in the cocoon of what had been, but knowing the future was already upon him. The fact was, he had ten days before his ship sailed for home. And everything here was at an end.

It was an untenable thought.

Harry walked slowly back to his room, lay down on his bed, and tried to sleep. But when dawn rose beyond his shuttered windows, he had still found no rest.

He kept telling himself to buck up and remember he was a married man with responsibilities, not only to his family but to the estate workers and their families, people who would one day depend on him. Yet he could not dismiss the incredible changes to himself since he'd been shipped overseas four years ago. He had survived deprivation and brutality, the like of which was impossible for any civilian to imagine. And then he had fallen in love for the first time, not only with Lidia but with a country and its people.

How could he leave it behind? Or her?

Guiltily, Harry turned over and forced himself to face that he had lied to Lidia. If he had told her he was married, she almost certainly would not have given herself to him as she had.

I trust you, Harry . . .

He groaned, feeling like the bounder he was.

As the new day began, Harry finally drifted into sleep, his turmoil unresolved.

In the following three days, Lidia and Harry met whenever they could. She refused to come to his room, driving Harry into a miasma of frustration. He had to make do instead with snatched kisses across the wooden table where they spent her lunch hour, and some hand-holding as she took him along the river after she had finished for the day. She was distracted by her family's imminent move to Japan, and Harry was at a loss to know how to begin to tell her what he should. Instead, he held her as often as their circumstances allowed, left her little notes of love at reception, and made himself available to her whenever she had the time to see him.

One afternoon, less than a week before Harry was to leave, Giselle stopped him in the lobby and handed him a telegram.

"Thank you," he murmured, and made to walk away.

"Captain Crawford, a word in my office, *oui*?"

"Of course." As he followed her, Harry felt like a naughty schoolboy about to be reprimanded by his teacher.

Giselle shut the door and smiled at him. "It seems Thailand has worked its charms with you, *n'est-ce pas*? And one *jeune femme* in particular." She picked up one of the notes he had sent to Lidia and flapped it in front of him.

Harry reddened and nodded. "Yes. And," he added defensively, "I am in love with her."

"So I gather." Giselle handed the note back to him. "Take it, it is yours after all. Captain Crawford—"

"Call me Harry, please." He took the note and stowed it in his trouser pocket.

"Harry," Giselle corrected herself, "it would not be my usual way to interfere in affairs of the heart. But do you realize you are running the risk of Lidia losing her employment here? It is strictly forbidden for members of staff to fraternize with the guests."

"I'm so sorry, Giselle. I had no idea. Please don't dismiss her. She needs the work. Her mother is—"

Giselle held up her hand to silence him. "I know all about Lidia's family. Which is why I must come up with a solution. I am aware it is quite pointless and cruel to stop two young adults from being together. Lidia is in love with you, Harry. I see it in her eyes every moment of the day. Forgive me, but I am concerned for her. You are leaving for England soon, are you not?"

Harry sank into a chair. He shook his head in despair. "I just don't know."

"I see. I presume Lidia does not know you have a wife?"

He blushed. "Sebastian told you?"

"Eh, oui," Giselle confirmed ruefully.

"No, she doesn't, but believe me, my marriage is only in name. Because of"—Harry shrugged—"who I am, I had to marry before I went to war, to try and secure the future of our family estate with an heir. Unfortunately, the child my wife was carrying when I left was lost."

"I understand this." Giselle nodded. "It is similar in France for aristocratic families to plan for the future. And Lidia knows nothing of your . . . heritage?"

"No."

Giselle sighed. "I ask this now as someone who cares for Lidia: for you, is she an amusement, a distraction before you return home?"

Harry looked Giselle squarely in the eye. "No. If I could, I would stay here with her for the rest of my life. But what can I do?"

"Harry, it is not for me to say," she sighed. "Perhaps you must tell Lidia the truth."

"How can I?" he muttered. "She has trusted me. And I have lied to her."

Giselle studied him in silence. "Well, maybe, if you can explain to her the responsibilities you have, she will love you enough to understand. Here in Thailand too, and all over the world, these things happen."

"I don't see how I can return to England. I doubt I can live without her," Harry replied helplessly.

Giselle reached out and patted his shoulder gently. "*C'est un coup de coeur.* Well, I cannot tell you what to do, for only you can decide. But, in the interests of my hotel and Lidia, I have a suggestion for you both: while you are still here, I wish to officially employ you as a member of staff at my hotel. You will become resident pianist, in return for your lodging. Food and drink will, of course, be extra. That way, as two employees, you are free to spend time together. Lidia will also be living in when her family moves to Japan, until she finds other accommodation. Perhaps this will make the situation easier for everyone, *n'est ce pas*?"

Harry was so unused to kindness, his eyes misted with tears. "Thank you, Giselle. If that makes things easier for Lidia and yourself, I am awfully grateful."

"*Bonne!* That is settled." Giselle stood up. "You leave in a week for England?"

"Yes." Harry nodded sadly. "Unless . . ."

"Only you can decide, Harry," she repeated.

"I know." He followed her to the door. "Thank you, Giselle. And can I ask you something?"

"Of course."

"If I decide to stay, would you be happy to continue employing me?"

"Harry"—she smiled—"I would be most happy to do so. You are a very talented pianist and make money for my bar."

"Thank you," he said gratefully, and followed her out into the lobby.

Over the next twenty-four hours, Harry wrestled with his dreadful decision. He was convinced, heart and soul, that Lidia was the woman he wanted to spend the rest of his life with; she was the other half of himself, the part that made him better and stronger, his salvation, his love.

He knew everyone else would try to convince him otherwise, citing his traumatic three and a half years in Changi, the mystique of a woman from another world, that it was a passing phase and he would soon get over her. They would tell him he hardly knew her, that they had nothing in common, that it could never last because their worlds were so far apart.

All these things were true, and the logical part of him accepted them. But his soul could not.

Finally, Harry reached a decision. He must return home: it was only fair and decent of him to do that, at the very least. He would tell his family the truth about the woman he had found and his love for her. He would tell his father that, on his death, the estate could be handed over to his cousin Hugo, Penelope's brother. And he would ask Olivia for a divorce.

Then he would return here, to the country that had bewitched him and the girl he loved. He would work as a pianist, free to be himself for the first time in his life. Lidia and he would find a small house together and live with nothing in the way of material possessions, but with honesty, and with true love.

Harry smiled to himself as he entered the lobby, looking for Giselle. If anyone had told him when he arrived here in Bangkok that he would be prepared to give up his heritage, his parents' love, and his wife for the sake of a young Thai girl, he would not have believed them. But now the decision was made, he had never felt so sure of anything in his life.

Giselle was sitting at her desk and gave him a half smile as he walked in.

"You have decided what to do?"

"Yes." Harry nodded. "I'll be taking the passage home."

Giselle raised her eyebrows, then sighed. "Harry, I understand, but I will be sad to see you go."

Harry put both his hands on the desk and leaned toward her. "Giselle, I am going home, because I must do the decent thing and explain in person what has happened to me. But then, as soon as I can, I shall return. So, I would be awfully grateful if you could hold open my job at the bar. I will be gone no longer than three months."

Giselle removed her reading glasses and stared at him in shock. "Harry, are you sure? It is a lot to give up."

"I love her, Giselle, and I can assure you that giving up my heritage will be a blessed relief. I've never been cut out for the job anyway."

"And your wife?" she asked softly.

"I can't live a lie. Is that fair to her? How can I give her what she deserves from me when I'm in love with another woman?"

"You will tell her the truth?"

"Yes." Harry mentally gritted his teeth. "I must. It's only fair."

"You understand how hard it will be?"

"I do. But I'm going to do it."

Giselle's eyes softened as she looked at the determination on his face. "Then I will be glad to welcome you back here when you return."

"Thank you. And now, I must tell Lidia."

That evening, when Lidia had finished for the day, Harry sought her out as she was leaving the hotel.

"We need to talk. In private."

Lidia shook her head. "No, Harry, I must go now. My mother leaves for Japan tomorrow. Tonight, I must say good-bye to her and my brothers and sisters."

"Oh, darling." He knew this would be hard for her. "Then tomorrow?"

"Yes, from tomorrow I will be staying at the hotel." Lidia sighed. "Oh, Harry, my brothers and sisters still think I come with them to Japan. My mother refuses to tell them I do not."

"I'll be here for you," Harry soothed, wanting to take her in his arms, "but we must speak."

Her eyes darkened. "You have something bad to tell me?"

"Bad . . . but also very good, I promise. Lidia, come to my room. I have spoken to Giselle, and she will turn a blind eye, as I am now an employee," he added, desperate to have her alone so he could hold her in his arms as he told her.

"You are employee?" She opened her eyes wide in surprise. "We speak tomorrow. Good-bye, Harry." She waved as she hurried away. "Play well tonight."

"I will," he muttered as he walked back inside, praying he wouldn't lose her once she knew the truth.

40

When he had finished playing in the bar the following night, there was a soft tap-tapping on his door.

Lidia hurriedly came in, checking for prying eyes. She closed the door swiftly, locked it, and ran to his arms.

"My girl, I have missed *this*," he said as he held her close to him. He felt her sigh heavily. He pulled away from her and looked into her eyes. "Have your family gone?"

"Yes," she whispered into his shoulder.

"Was it dreadful?"

"Oh, yes. My little brothers and sisters cannot understand why I am not coming with them. They cling to me and cry and cry." Lidia's eyes filled with tears. "It is such hard decision to make."

"I know, my darling, I know. Come, let us lie down."

He led her to the bed, and as he held her and stroked her gently, tracing her perfect features, she talked to him of her pain.

"Harry, is it right that I must continue to tell a lie to my grandparents?"

"Sometimes, Lidia, you can tell the truth to hurt and a lie to protect. I believe that's what you have done. But it is you that will carry the secret, and the burden of that." Harry spoke with all his heart, thinking he could not tell her about his marriage now, when she was so vulnerable. Perhaps she didn't *need* to know anyway. . . .

A lie to protect . . .

Surely he could go home, do what he needed to, and return to her, free forever?

Harry tried to find the words to tell her what he must.

"My darling, do you believe that I love you?"

She looked up at him, her amber eyes innocent and trusting. "Yes, I do, Harry."

"And do you know that I am prepared to give up everything to be with you? Forever?"

Her eyes saddened suddenly. "No, I do not know this. But I do not care to ask about future before, as I may not want to hear answer. I try to take beauty of each day. That is Buddhist way. If you have something sad to tell me, not tonight, Harry, please," she begged.

"Sweetheart." He held her tighter against him. "I am so sorry to talk to you of this tonight, but we are running out of time. It is a little sad, but it has a happy ending. I promise."

"I understand," she said, knowing she must hear what he had to say. "You talk."

"Well now." Harry took her tiny hands in his and held them tight, like a talisman. "I am going to tell you about me."

Lidia's eyes were full of dread, but she nodded. "Okay."

"You see, in England, I am the son of a lord, which I suppose is something like a prince to you here in Thailand."

Her eyes widened. "You are royalty?"

Harry thought how to phrase it. "No, but my family was given a house and a title many hundreds of years ago by a king, in return for their bravery and support. Where I live in England, we have the grandest house, and many people working for us on our land, farming it."

"Ah"—she nodded—"you are nobleman."

"Exactly. And when my father dies, as his only son, I must take over the responsibilities for my estate."

"I understand."

"Lidia, I never wanted this life. But it is what I was born to, and up until recently, I have accepted it is what I must do."

"Family is everything," she answered simply.

"Well, it is"—Harry stroked Lidia's hair—"and it isn't. When I was in Changi, so many things changed for me. I understand now that this life is very short and can disappear in the blink of an eye. We must make the most of the special things we are lucky enough to find. And I have found you." He looked down at her, drawing her eyes up to meet his. "Last night, when you had to say good-bye to people you love, was it partly because of me?"

In her innocence, Lidia did not hesitate. "Yes, of course."

"Well, in one week, I must do the same. I must return to England to tell my family I no longer wish to carry the responsibility of my heritage. That I have fallen in love with a woman here and wish to return to Thailand, to be with you for the rest of my life."

Her eyes filled with panic and Harry was quick to reassure her. "I will be gone no longer than three months, then I will be back, free to be with you, here."

Harry was used to Lidia's falling silent and expressing her thoughts with her eyes. He watched them closely as they went through a gamut of emotions: fear, sadness, sudden happiness, and, finally, uncertainty.

Eventually, she spoke slowly, thoughtfully. "Harry, you must think carefully about this. Giving up your country and your family and your home is big decision. I know about this. I have done it, but at least I have more here than you will. Perhaps," she sighed, "when you get to England, you decide you wish to stay."

Harry shook his head vehemently. "That will not happen. I cannot live without you," he said simply.

"Maybe I come to England?"

Harry chuckled and shook his head. "You cannot live there, you would not survive. You are a"—he searched for the words—"hothouse flower. You bloom in the heat of your homeland. I would never ask you to sacrifice your native land for me."

Lidia was silent for a while, then said, "But you would do this for me?"

Harry sighed, trying to find words she would understand. "For me it's different. I have been in the Far East for four years now. I am used to the climate and the people." He reached for her hand and squeezed it. "Please understand, it is no sacrifice. It is what I want. To be here with you, to marry you one day, if you will have me. And to watch our children grow up in the land they belong to. Surely this is what you want too?"

"Yes, but"—Lidia shook her head—"it is big sacrifice for you to make. For me."

"Darling," he comforted, "we belong together. And I can fit into your world far better than you could ever fit into mine, I promise you."

"So"—Lidia braced herself, a sanguine expression on her face—"then you must go home. And I will wait until you return."

Harry grasped her tightly, then kissed her.

"I *will* return," he promised, cupping her face in his hands. "Believe me, I will."

"I believe you because I must," she said with a sigh, then smiled. "Now, I would like you to tell me about your life in England. I want to hear who you are."

So Harry held her in his arms and told her about himself, his mother and father, and England. He described the icy-cold winds that blew through one's bones in the winter, and the balmy summer evenings, however rare they were, that made the winters worthwhile. He told her of his school, of joining the army and how much he had hated it.

Then he ground to a halt because anything further would have meant mentioning Olivia. He was now convinced Lidia need not know about his marriage.

Lidia's eyes had grown wide as he talked. "Maybe one day you can take me there. Show me your mother's hothouse and all the beautiful flowers that grow in it. Does she have orchids?"

"No, I don't believe she does."

"Then when you go home, I will send gift of some orchids for her. You can tell her they are from me; from your Hothouse Flower." She smiled.

"Oh, Lidia." Harry could contain himself no longer and kissed her. "I love you, I love you so very much."

She became pliable in his arms as he undressed her, and she rose with the same urgency as he, knowing now how little time they had before he left.

Afterward they fell asleep, exhausted by the emotional roller coaster of their dual existences and the complexities of trying to unite them.

Just before dawn broke, Lidia rose and kissed him gently.

"Harry, I must go to my room before anyone notices I am not there."

"Of course." He pulled her face to his and kissed her hard. "Believe me, my angel, my beautiful flower, I will not let you down."

"I know," she said, dressing silently.

"I love you," he whispered when she turned to leave.

"I love you too," she replied, closing the door behind her.

• • •

In the next few days, as Harry's departure grew closer, they seized every moment to be together. He would meet her on her lunch break, when they could only talk, though the mere touch of each other was a comfort to them both. At night, when Harry returned from the bar, Lidia would be waiting for him in his room. They made love less urgently now, and as Lidia's confidence grew, she delighted in finding new ways to please him.

Harry felt there wasn't one inch of her he hadn't kissed and caressed. He knew intimately every fold of skin, every crevice that made up her perfection. Even though she was little over five feet, her body was in proportion, her upper torso short, her slim hips gently rounded, leading to her long, honey-colored legs and the perfect, tiny feet, which he could fit into his hand.

They would lie together afterward, still touching and stroking, talking languidly of their hopes and dreams for the future.

When she left him in the morning, Harry dozed contentedly. He understood now why the fellows with him in Changi had reminisced on the pleasures of lovemaking. He flushed at the thought of the swift, mechanical coupling he had experienced with Olivia. It was like comparing a bleak January in Norfolk with the warmth, color, and lushness of a day in the sun here.

Harry knew without a doubt he had found what he had been searching for. Up until now, his whole existence had seemed pointless, his recent suffering only amplifying the futility of life. Yet, within weeks, he and his world had irrevocably changed. He now looked to his future with happiness and hope, and having made the decision to return here forever, he felt calm and accepted the pain this would inflict on himself and others.

No longer did he feel every sunrise simply heralded another day to be endured. For the first time in his life, he felt truly happy.

The day before Harry left Bangkok, he braved his claustrophobia and took a tuk-tuk to a street market a couple of miles from the hotel. He bought silks for his mother and Olivia, and, for his father, an exquisite

Chinese pipe, fashioned out of ivory. Then with his last few baht, he chose a tiny silver ring for Lidia; its amber stone would match her eyes.

Harry had already played his last night in the bar, leaving him free to spend his final evening with Lidia. They took a boat upriver to a small restaurant on the opposite bank, its wooden platform stilted so the water slapped gently beneath their feet. By the soft light of Chinese lanterns, Harry took Lidia's hand across the table.

"Darling, I have something for you. It's for me to make a promise to you that very soon I will be back with you forever." He opened the box and placed the amber ring on her fourth finger. "I want to marry you, as soon as I possibly can. Will you?"

Lidia's eyes filled with tears. "Harry, *ka*, you know I say yes." She looked down at the ring, smiled, and held it out in front of her to admire it on her finger. "It is the most beautiful present I ever receive."

That night neither of them slept. They made love and talked of the future and of where they would live when he returned, both relishing each moment and knowing it was their last night together for some time.

"You know I'll write every day, don't you?"

"And I write to you?" said Lidia. "You give me your address."

Harry had already considered this. He reached into his bedside drawer and brought out a piece of paper. "This is where you must write to."

She read it, then stowed it carefully in her basket.

Harry had given her Bill's address. He trusted his young sergeant implicitly; the bond that had formed between them was unbreakable. He remembered the dreadful days before their capture, when Singapore was falling into the Nips' hands and their battalion was surrounded by Japanese soldiers far better prepared for jungle warfare than a few fellows from North Norfolk. Harry had bowed to Bill's superior military instincts as he deferentially suggested the best plan of action to save their skins.

One morning, Bill had spotted a sniper lurking in the thick vegetation. Five minutes later, a hail of bullets had hit the small band of exhausted British soldiers, immediately taking out four of their party. When all had gone quiet, Harry had stood up, dazed, his ears still ringing from the gunshots. Bill had pounced on him and thrown him to the ground, while a volley of bullets meant for him whistled past and hit a banana plant.

"That was a close shave, sir," Bill had breathed, still shielding Harry.

In return, Harry had done something for Bill. When they reached Changi, he had recommended Bill and his gardening ability to the Nips for tending and organizing the ever-expanding cemetery. This placement undoubtedly saved Bill's life. While men were taken away to the north in thousands to work on the Burma railway, Bill had kept his head down and got on with the gruesome job of burying his comrades, and the Nips had left him alone.

Now Harry needed Bill again. He was the only man he could trust to receive Lidia's letters and post Harry's replies. While he was at home, there was no need to hurt Olivia unnecessarily by flaunting his love for another woman, and he could not afford for her to chance upon their correspondence.

Harry let out a deep sigh and Lidia looked at him with concern. "What is it, Harry?"

"Nothing, other than I'm dreading leaving you." He reached for her and took her back into his arms. "At least I'll know that you're safe here at the hotel while I'm away, so that's a comfort."

"Yes, I will be safe and dreaming every day of your return."

Morning came all too soon. When Harry was dressed, he put his arms round Lidia and held her tightly.

"My darling, please believe me when I tell you I love you with my very soul . . . and I will come back for you."

She looked up at him, her face calm. "And I will wait for you here."

41

England
1946

As the early-morning mist cleared and a weak sun broke through the clouds, Harry snapped the locks closed on his suitcase and went out on deck to watch as Felixstowe came into view. The purser had said it would be an hour until the ship docked; an hour before Harry must face the gray shadows of a former existence he barely remembered.

Even though it was May and quite mild for England, Harry shivered in the morning breeze. He had endured an agonizing month on board, contemplating how he should break the news to his parents and his wife. As the outline of Felixstowe appeared, Harry's nerve began to fail him. He knew he must remain calm, determined, and be impervious to any emotional entreaties to stay.

He only had to picture Lidia's beautiful face and her perfect, naked body beneath him, as they made love. No matter what the cost, he could not let that go.

Olivia sat in a dreary dockside café with other nervous wives and parents awaiting the return of loved ones. As she sipped her watery tea and thought how much she hated powdered milk, she wondered whether she would even recognize her husband.

When Bill had returned, Elsie had come up to the house the following day and broken down in Olivia's bedroom.

"Oh, miss, his hair has gone completely gray and his skin sags like an old man. His legs are like twigs, they are, but he's got this huge belly on him, which makes him look like he's expecting twins. He says it's the rice that did it for him, that all the men in Changi were the same." Elsie had blown her nose. "I could cope with that . . . I mean, I'm just grateful that he's home and alive. But it's the way he stares, like he's somewhere else. Like he hardly knows me."

"Elsie," Olivia had comforted, "you must give him time. It's a shock for him, coming home and back to his family in England after three and a half years in that ghastly place. He'll settle down, I'm sure he will."

"I know, but I was so looking forward to seeing him. I haven't slept for the past week with excitement." Elsie had shaken her head sadly. "He doesn't seem that pleased to see me."

"We can't imagine what they've been through, and we've all been told to expect they'll be distressed and confused. It'll be the same when Harry arrives home, I'm sure." Olivia's stomach had churned at the thought.

"It was just that his mum and dad and me, we all saved up our ration coupons to get him a nice leg of lamb for his dinner. It was always his favorite. He hardly touched it, miss, and when we went to bed"—Elsie had blushed—"he rolled over and went straight to sleep. No cuddle nor nothing!"

Even though Olivia had prepared herself as best she could to greet a man who would be much changed, and physically and mentally diminished by his experiences, she was absolutely dreading the moment she saw him.

Forty-five minutes later the ship docked, with a loud blast of its horn.

Harry was home.

Olivia waited in an agony of suspense behind the barrier that kept families clear of the gangplank. Eventually, a straggle of men started to disembark. Olivia scoured the haggard faces, but could not see Harry. She watched as other men were surrounded by their families and tears of joy were shed. Some were in wheelchairs, others on crutches, missing limbs, eyes . . . it was a traumatic sight. From what Sebastian Ainsley had said, Harry was at least all in one piece, although the dengue fever, which had nearly killed him and had delayed his return, would have taken its toll.

Just as Olivia was beginning to fear Harry was not on the ship, a familiar face emerged at the top of the gangplank. To her surprise, from a distance, he didn't look much different. In fact, if anything, the tan he had acquired had only enhanced his looks. He was cleanly shaven, his dark hair combed neatly. In a navy blazer and cream trousers, he appeared more devastatingly handsome than she remembered him.

She left the barrier and walked toward him. She pinched her cheeks furtively to bring blood into them and put her hand to her blonde hair to check it was neat.

As he walked off the gangplank, she called his name. "Harry! I'm here."

He turned toward her, his eyes blank, searching for the voice. Then he saw her and their eyes locked.

Her eyes betrayed her happiness as she walked toward him.

His eyes betrayed nothing as he walked toward her.

When they met, she threw her arms round his shoulders. Harry's hung by his sides.

"Harry, thank God you're home!"

He shook himself from her grip. "Yes, I'm home." He nodded perfunctorily. "Where's the car?"

Olivia felt a lump constricting her throat, but remembering Elsie, she said, "Not far. It's parked about five minutes away."

"Shall we go?"

"Of course. You must be tired." They set off together, Olivia leading the way.

"No, I'm not at all tired. I've just suffered a month's inertia on the ship."

Once Harry's suitcase was stowed in the trunk and he was settled in the passenger seat, Olivia started the engine. They set off for Wharton Park in silence.

Harry gazed out of the window, his head turned away from Olivia. "Everything seems so colorless here after the Far East."

"Well"—Olivia swallowed hard—"at least it's the end of May, which you always said was the best time to be in England."

"Yes. But now I've experienced the tropics, it's not a patch on there, really."

Olivia could not help but be hurt and shocked by Harry's reaction. She knew and understood it would be difficult for him to adjust, but the last thing she had expected was for him to be wistful about the location of his living hell.

"Well, Wharton Park *is* looking beautiful," she replied staunchly.

"I'm sure," Harry replied coldly.

They drove on in silence and Olivia surmised that, although Harry looked normal, his mental state was clearly not as healthy. Perhaps Wharton Park, the home he loved so much, could provoke an emotional response. She steeled herself to accept his oddness, understanding now exactly what Elsie had meant about Bill's being "somewhere else"—it was obvious Harry was too.

Three hours later, they entered the gates of Wharton Park. Olivia glanced at Harry to gauge his reaction, but could not see his face.

"Well, here we are then," she said brightly, "home."

Harry roused himself, then said, almost as an afterthought, "How are Ma and Pa, by the way?"

Olivia was amazed it had taken him so long to ask. "Your mother is in excellent health. Your father—well, he has not been so lucky, unfortunately. He had a heart attack a year ago. He is a little better now," she replied carefully, "but he is unable to work. The doctors said it put too much strain on his heart. Your mother insists that having him in the house all the time puts far too much strain on hers!" Olivia tried to make a joke.

"How miserable for him." Harry looked at Olivia, anxiety in his eyes. It was the first show of emotion she had seen. "He's not in any imminent danger though, is he?"

"Well, one can never be sure with a dickey heart. Right," she said, changing the subject swiftly as they approached the house, "I warn you, everyone is gathering to welcome you home."

She stopped the car and tooted three times. At the sound of the horn, the front doors swung open, and Adrienne ran down the steps to greet him.

"Harry, *mon chéri*! You are home!"

Harry stepped out of the car and walked toward her, into arms that opened wide, pulled him to her, and held him tightly. "Oh, my Harry! You are safe, you are safe home," she whispered into his shoulder. "Let me look at you." She stood back and studied him from head to toe. "*Mon Dieu!* I think you look more handsome and healthier than when you left! Do you not think so, Olivia?"

Olivia, who was standing listlessly by Harry, nodded. "That's what I thought when I saw him."

"I'm well, Mother, really. I wasn't," Harry added quickly, "but I am now."

With Olivia trailing behind, Adrienne put her arm round her son and led him up the steps. She swung back the front door, and there, in two long lines, stood the entire staff of Wharton Park, forming a guard of honor.

As he stepped into the hall, Harry heard Bill shout, "Three cheers for Master Harry! Hip hip—"

"Hoorah!!"

"Hip hip—"

"Hoorah!"

"Hip hip—"

"Hoorah!"

A huge burst of applause and cheering broke out. Harry walked along the line, receiving hearty handshakes and slaps on the back from the men, and bobs from the girls.

"So glad you are home, Master Harry."

"Congratulations, Bill told us how brave you were."

"Glad to see you safe home, sir."

"The house wasn't the same without you, Master Harry," said Mrs. Jenks fondly, standing at the end of the line. "I'll be making the biggest English breakfast you've ever eaten tomorrow morning."

Despite his determination to keep his heart hard, Harry found his eyes filling with tears at the genuine welcome from all these familiar faces.

"Speech!" shouted someone.

"Yes, speech!" added the rest.

"Give us a few words, Master Harry, will you?"

Harry turned back to them and cleared his throat. "Well, what can I say? Other than thank you for the warmth of your welcome. It's much appreciated and it's jolly good to see you all. And thank you for looking after Wharton Park, in what I imagine must have been very difficult times."

Another round of applause broke out. Then Harry glimpsed a

cowed figure shuffling across to him. He realized, with a jolt, that the shrunken old man was his father. Rather than let him struggle any farther, Harry went over to him and held out his hand. "Hello, Father, it's good to see you."

His father smiled at him. "And you, old chap." Christopher used all his strength to pull his son toward him and give him a weak slap on the back. "Well done, my boy! I saw your name mentioned in dispatches. I am proud of you."

Those words were the closest Harry's father had ever come to praising him. They brought further tears to his eyes.

"Bet you're glad to be back, eh what? Hear those blasted Nips gave you boys rather a bad time in Changi. But we saw them off in the end, didn't we?"

"We did, Father, we did."

Adrienne was by Harry's side. "Now, Christopher, I expect that Harry would like to go to his room and rest for a while, after his very long journey." She turned to her staff. "You may go, and I am sure Harry will be round to speak to each of you later."

As the staff dispersed, Harry heard a voice in his ear. "Glad to see you made it back, sir. I was beginning to wonder."

It was Bill. They shook hands and slapped each other heartily on the back.

"Seems a long way away from when we last saw each other, doesn't it?" Harry murmured quietly.

"I should say, sir. And it takes a bit of getting used to, but you'll get the hang of it, I'm sure."

"I'll pop down and see you later on in the hothouse, Bill. There's some business I need to discuss with you." Harry knew he was in hearing range of both his parents and Olivia, so he was brisk about it. "Around five, I would say."

"Right you are, sir. I'll be there, a nice cup of tea for both of us, with milk, I might add." Bill rolled his eyes as they shared a memory of the raw tea they had drunk for three and a half long years.

Harry followed Olivia up the staircase and along the corridor to their suite of rooms. Everything was exactly as he had left it, as if time had not moved forward at Wharton Park at all.

As soon as Olivia had shut the door behind them, Harry turned to her. "Just how sick is my father? He seems to have aged twenty years."

Olivia sighed and sat down on the stool at the end of the bed. "As I told you, he had a serious heart attack. He was lucky to live through it. Remember, Harry, he is sixty, ten years older than your mother. And working at the War Office was jolly stressful for him."

"He looks—" Harry shook his head—"dreadful."

"He has been very ill. But the doctors reassure us that, as long as he takes it easy and receives no nasty shocks to his system, there is no reason why he cannot remain stable."

"I see."

Harry looked terribly sad, so Olivia went to him and put her arms around his shoulders. "I am so awfully sorry, Harry. It must have been a shock for you. I suppose we haven't noticed his aging. But I'm sure that having you home will perk up his spirits no end. He can't wait for you to take him through every second of the campaign in Malaya, and your part in it. He's been talking about it for weeks."

Silently, and out of sheer emotional exhaustion, Harry rested his head on Olivia's shoulder. They stood there for a while, before Olivia said, "Why don't you take a rest? Mrs. Jenks is breaking the habit of a lifetime and won't be serving lunch until half past one, so that you can do so."

"Yes, I think I will." He desperately needed to be by himself, not necessarily to sleep, but to think.

"I know this must all seem awfully strange for you, and rather overwhelming, I should imagine. Elsie tells me Bill still finds certain things difficult, even though he's been at home for months now." Olivia kissed Harry gently on the forehead. "I'm not going to crowd you, darling, but just know I am here if you need me."

"Thank you."

Olivia nodded. "Get some rest." She left the room and walked down the stairs, where Adrienne was waiting for her.

"I have coffee for us in the library. Come, *chérie*, and tell me how you think he seems."

Olivia followed her into the library and sat down.

"Well?" Adrienne inquired. "He certainly looks well, does he not?"

"Yes, he does, but, as Elsie described to me, it feels as though his body has arrived home, but his mind is still elsewhere. I think we must be patient, not expect too much of him."

"Either of us," Adrienne added pointedly.

"Of course," sighed Olivia. "I know that. But I am only human, Adrienne, and what I actually wanted was for Harry to spot me waiting, then race down the gangplank and take me into his arms. I saw some of the other chaps do that."

"You know that is not Harry's way," Adrienne comforted. "Although he was certainly shocked when he saw his father, *n'est ce pas*?"

"Yes, he was."

Adrienne shook her head. "Of course, he knows so little about all that has happened here in the past four years and what is to come. Olivia, you and I have done our best to run this estate, but we need Harry to take charge as soon as possible." Adrienne put a hand to her graying hair. "*Alors!* There are decisions to be made, but only Christopher, or Harry, as his heir, can make them. And I do not like to worry Christopher as he is so frail."

"I know, Adrienne. At least Harry is home now, and all in one piece."

"*Eh, oui.*" Adrienne raised her coffee cup to her mouth. "And I realize we must simply be grateful for that."

42

Adrienne decided it was warm enough to take lunch on the terrace. Christopher insisted Sable bring up a bottle of vintage champagne from the cellar for the occasion. Mrs. Jenks excelled herself, having procured a salmon from goodness knew where, serving it with Harry's favorite béarnaise sauce, new potatoes, and fresh green beans from the kitchen garden.

"I was warned you boys don't like anything too stodgy when you get home," said Mrs. Jenks, pink with pleasure, when Harry found her in the kitchen after lunch and thanked her for the feast.

Olivia sought him out there and suggested a turn around the garden.

They walked slowly, Harry reacquainting himself with his surroundings. Even he had to admit the park looked magnificent, bathed as it was in the soft, mellow glow of a May afternoon.

"So," Harry struggled to make conversation, "you say the house was a nursing home for two years?"

"It was. We had over forty officers at any one time," Olivia explained as they walked round the fountain, which had not played since the introduction of a wartime law to save water. "The old place was full to the brim because, of course, we had the Land Girls to boot. Mrs. Jenks has been a total saint: her experience catering for large numbers of guests stood her in good stead."

"Where did you and Mother and Father live?"

"Oh, we removed ourselves to the East Wing for the duration. Not exactly luxurious, as you know, but it was somewhere to put our heads down. Your father pretended he hated it. He used to give the officers a jolly good telling off for walking through the house in their dirty boots. But, actually, I think he secretly enjoyed it. After all, he was recovering as well, and he was never short of someone to chat with."

"I can imagine. You have obviously been jolly busy while I've been away."

"Everyone has," said Olivia modestly. "But I should warn you, darling, the house is in need of urgent repairs. Having so many people in it revealed its faults. And I rather think you picked the perfect moment to come home. The old place did look pretty grim up until recently lined with hospital beds and medical equipment."

"Jolly nice place to recuperate though, for the chaps who were here."

"Yes, they used to sit on the terrace when the weather was good enough. Some of them didn't make it, of course." Olivia sighed. "There was one particular chap, poor thing had a bullet lodged in his head that had blinded him. I used to read to him as often as I could. Then, one night, when I was reading to him, he died in front of me, out of the blue." Olivia's voice cracked with emotion. "The doctors said the bullet must have been dislodged and that is what killed him."

"Golly, how bloody for you," Harry said guiltily; it had not occurred to him that either Olivia or his mother and father would have suffered particularly during the war. He'd thought of them tucked safe and snug within the secure walls of Wharton Park. But from what they had said over lunch, they too had obviously had a raw time of it.

"Any bombs drop nearby?" he asked.

"A few on Norwich, but, thank goodness, we escaped unscathed here."

"So, any casualties from the estate?"

"Yes," Olivia replied somberly. "We've lost nine young men altogether. I'll give you a list of their names and perhaps you could visit their families. And Mr. Combe stepped on a mine at Weybourne beach only a few weeks ago. You can imagine that Mrs. Combe was devastated."

"Yes. Poor Mrs. Combe. That's a disaster. So we have no farm manager presently?"

"No, we have been waiting for you to come back to choose a replacement. And"—Olivia bit her lip—"do you remember Venetia?"

Harry grinned. "How could one forget her? She's such a character."

"Yes, absolutely up for anything, which is probably why she ended up in France working for some hush-hush organization. Anyway, she disappeared three years ago and we've only just found out what happened to her." Olivia faltered before adding, "She was captured in Paris, tortured and then shot by the Nazis."

"I am so dreadfully sorry, Olivia. I know how fond you were of her," offered Harry quietly.

Olivia bit back her tears. "Thank you. I'm just awfully glad it's finally over. Perhaps life can return to some semblance of normality soon. Now"—she cleared her throat and slipped her arm through Harry's elbow—"I'll show you the kitchen garden. It's about the one thing that's blossomed and grown since you've been away."

She pushed open the door in the wall and Harry spied the rows and rows of well-tended vegetables. It was triple the size it had been when he left.

"This is impressive, Olivia." He could not bring himself to say *darling*. "How did you manage without Bill?"

"I'm not sure"—she smiled—"one just does manage. Jack did as much as he could, and at least it meant we could provide the patients with wholesome food."

Harry glimpsed the hothouse, the sun glinting off its glass, in the corner of the garden. He walked toward it.

"Unfortunately, the hothouse did not fare so well. It was stripped of flowers and came into its own for growing tomatoes. Bill has been hard at work since he returned, restocking and planting, and it's slowly returning to its former glory. I think it comforts him somehow."

"Shall we?" Harry indicated the door.

"Of course, if you would like to."

Harry pushed the door open and was immediately assailed by a strong fragrance that evoked only one thought: Lidia.

For a second, his head spun and he staggered slightly.

"Harry, are you feeling all right?" Olivia took his arm anxiously.

He brushed her away. "Don't!" he said sharply, then regretted it. "Sorry, I . . ." His voice trailed off and he walked away along the rows of flowers. He stopped with surprise in front of a tray of orchids. "I don't remember these ever being here."

Shaken by Harry's brusqueness, Olivia replied carefully, "No, Bill brought them home with him. I am amazed they survived the journey, but apparently Bill tended them every day, and they have positively bloomed since they came here."

"Bill has always had a natural affinity with plants, and I must say orchids are incredibly beautiful." Harry stooped to sniff the fragrant scent, allowing himself to drown in memories of Lidia for a few seconds. He stood upright. "They grow like billy-o everywhere in the Far East, especially in Thailand."

"So Bill tells me," said Olivia as the two of them left the hothouse and walked back toward the house. "Despite the awful time of it you both had, he said it was a beautiful part of the world."

"Oh, yes," muttered Harry, "it was."

After dinner that evening, Harry climbed into bed beside Olivia. And, despite himself, took her in his arms and made love to her. Her body was all wrong: so much more rounded and fuller than Lidia's, her skin a startling, unfamiliar white, and worst of all, she smelled so different. Nevertheless, by closing his eyes and allowing his frustration to fuel his ardor as he slammed into his wife, he could take himself back to Thailand, and to Lidia.

Afterward he lay next to her, guilty and apologetic.

"I am awfully sorry, I hope I didn't hurt you. I am . . . rather out of practice," he lied.

"No, Harry, you didn't." Olivia had taken his violent approach as passion and was amazed and gratified.

"Good." He kissed her on the cheek and then, disgusted with himself, climbed out of bed. "I will sleep in my dressing room tonight. I'm awfully restless just now and often get nightmares. I don't want to disturb you. Good night, Olivia."

"Good night." Olivia blew him a kiss as he walked across the room. "I love you," she whispered, as the door shut behind him.

Harry pretended he hadn't heard and walked through to his dressing room. He sat down on his narrow single bed, put his head in his hands, and wept silently.

In the morning, Harry walked across the park to the hothouse, having been unable to slip away and meet Bill as planned the day before. Bill was nursing his orchids at the far end, his Bakelite radio filling the air with soothing classical music.

He smiled when he saw Harry. "Hello, sir. How was your first night home?"

"Fine." Harry shut the hothouse door behind him. "Sorry I didn't make it down here for that cup of tea."

"Under the circumstances, I wasn't expecting you to. I know how everyone wants a bit of you when you first arrive home."

"Yes." Harry needed to come straight to the point. "Bill, you haven't received any letters for me at your cottage, have you?"

Bill shook his head in surprise. "No. Why should I?"

Harry walked over and sat down on the small stool at the end of the hothouse.

"The thing is, Bill . . ." Harry swept a hand through his hair, not knowing how to begin. "Can I trust you?"

"With your life, sir, as you well know."

"Exactly. And if I tell you the story of what has happened since I left Changi, it *will* be with my life," Harry said emphatically. "I need your help, Bill, but it's a lot to ask of you."

"You know you can count on me, sir."

"I rather fear what I have to say will shock you."

Bill continued calmly watering his plants. "After what we both went through in the past four years, I doubt anything you might tell me will shock me. So, fire away, I'm listening."

"Right then." Harry gathered his courage and slowly began to tell Bill his story. He told him of Thailand, and playing at the Bamboo Bar, and finally of the girl with whom he had fallen irrevocably in love.

"I simply can't live without her, Bill," he ended, relieved to be speaking the words out loud. "And I mean to give up my life here at Wharton Park and return to Bangkok as soon as possible. I was never cut out to be lord and master anyway. And, in the meantime, I've given Lidia your address so she can write to me without Olivia finding out."

He was breathless with emotion and looked up at Bill, who was still tending his flowers. "I suppose you think I am a ghastly fellow to betray my wife and family like this."

"I don't think that at all, sir. I think you've fallen in love. It's not your fault she lives on the other side of the world. As you know"—Bill met Harry's eyes—"my Elsie was all that kept me going in Changi. And if she lived on the other side of the world, I'd go to her."

"You would?"

"I would. Having said that, I'm not already married to another, with the weight of responsibility you have." Bill scratched his head. "Reckon your news will be a rare old shock for your family. Especially with your father so sick. They've all been counting the days till you came home, so you could take over running the estate. Don't know what they'll do if you go, sir, I honestly don't."

"Stop calling me 'sir,' will you?" said Harry irritably. "When it's just the two of us, *Harry* will do nicely." He immediately hung his head. "Awfully sorry to snap, Bill. I'm just rather apprehensive, as you can imagine."

"You must be," Bill agreed with a sigh. "Wouldn't like to be in your shoes, and that's for certain. Anyhow, for my part, there's no problem with them letters you mentioned. Although I'll have to let Elsie know, if they're going to be arriving at our house."

Harry was horrified at the thought. He knew how close Elsie and Olivia were. "Can she really be trusted to say nothing to my wife?"

Bill nodded. "Yes, if I tell her not to. She's the best keeper of secrets I've ever met."

"But surely it puts her in such a difficult position?"

"I'd say it does, but it can't be helped now, can it? And if you don't mind me saying so, I wouldn't like her to see them letters arriving at our cottage from the part of the world where I have just spent the past four years and think it was me who'd got myself a girlfriend. And that you and I had cooked something up."

"No, I can see that. Well," Harry sighed in acceptance, "if Elsie has to know, she has to know. And I am hoping it won't be too long before I can come clean and tell my parents and Olivia of my plans. Even in the past twenty-four hours, I have felt as though I should burst if I don't."

Bill whistled. "As I said, I don't envy you, I really don't. She must be worth it, your girl."

Harry stood up and gave a small smile. "She is, Bill, she is. Right, I suppose I had better be getting back. I will pop in with a letter for Lidia and a few bob for you to post it for me. And perhaps it's best if you bring her letters here and leave them under the orchids over there." Harry indicated a tray.

"If that's what you suggest." Bill nodded sagely.

"Jolly good. Thank you, Bill. Once again, you've come to my rescue." Harry turned to walk toward the door.

"If I could say one thing . . . ," Bill ventured, and Harry turned back.

"Of course, Bill. You know how much I value your opinion. Although nothing on earth could make me change my mind."

"I'm not going to try and do that. I can see it would be pointless. What you feel for her is written all over your face," Bill said softly.

"Good. Carry on then."

"I was only going to say that it's taken me a bit of a time to get comfortable again here. It was thoughts of home that pulled me through, that's for certain. But since I've been back"—Bill tried to find the words to explain—"it sounds stupid, I know, I've missed things about that funny life we made for ourselves out there. And, more than anything, I've missed the place: the heat, the scents of them flowers that grew everywhere, the lushness of it all . . . and the blue sky above us, framing the picture."

They were both silent for a while, lost in the past.

Finally, Harry looked at Bill and gave him a grim smile. "I miss those things too, but it's not all that which is taking me back. I only wish it were that simple," Harry added with a sigh, and left the hothouse.

After Harry had left, Bill continued to tend to the flowers, thinking about what Harry had said and how he would put it to Elsie. He knew she adored Olivia and would not take kindly to betraying her. And, of course, if Harry did as he had suggested he would, Bill had no idea what would become of them all on the estate.

That evening, he told Elsie he needed her to keep something secret.

"Of course I promise not to tell, if you say not to," she said, studying his worried expression. "What is it, Bill? Just get on and tell me, why don't you."

When Bill had explained the situation, Elsie sat pale and motionless, shock on her face. Eventually she said, "You don't think he's really going to do it now, do you?"

"Yes." Bill nodded. "I'm sure he is."

"But it'll be the end of the estate if he does. And of us," she added grimly. "Who's going to run it if Master Harry leaves? There's no one else, and I know from Miss Olivia that things are that bad. The farm needs restocking, the machinery is worn out, and the house needs all sorts doing to it."

"Well, Master Harry said he'd suggest to Lord Crawford that the estate could be handed over to a cousin who's about the same age as Harry."

"That won't be possible. He means his cousin Hugo, but he was killed in North Africa about eighteen months ago." Elsie shook her head. "There's no one else."

"I see." Bill sipped his tea. "I suppose no one has told Master Harry about this yet?"

"No. Well, it's not the kind of conversation you have on the first day home. Although, from what Miss Olivia says, Harry wasn't close to his cousin, so he's probably not even thought to ask. You never know"—Elsie's face brightened a little—"the news might make him change his mind. Surely he wouldn't leave his dying father and his mum alone to run Wharton Park, would he? Because as sure as eggs is eggs, Olivia won't stay here once she has heard the news." Elsie clasped her hands together in despair. "After all them years of waiting for him, and he betrays her like this!"

Bill sighed. "Sweetheart, it really isn't our business and—"

"Yes, it is, Bill!" Elsie was angry now. "Because that fool of a young master has *made* it ours by telling you!"

"Yes. You're right. It's a bad business all round, but what could I do?"

"You could have said no," Elsie snapped.

"Elsie, come now, you know neither of us can refuse when we're asked to do something for the Crawfords. They give us our livelihoods here."

"I'd say this goes beyond the call of duty, Bill. It makes me sick to my stomach, it does! How I'll face Miss Olivia tomorrow, I don't know."

"I'm sorry, sweetheart." Bill moved to give Elsie a hug, but she pushed him away.

"You do as you must, Bill, and pass him them letters. But as for me, I want no part in it and I don't want to talk about it again." She rose from the table, slung her cup into the sink, and went out into the garden, slamming the door behind her.

43

Harry heard about the demise of his cousin Hugo over lunch that day. His father imparted the news in his usual unemotional manner, and although Harry tried not to let the shock show in his demeanor, Adrienne noticed immediately. She reached across the table and put her hand on his.

"I am sorry, Harry. You were fond of him. But there is some good news. Hugo's wife, Christiana, was pregnant before he left for Africa. She has had a dear little boy and they have named him Charles, after his grandfather. You see? Life does go on."

"How old is the child?" asked Harry.

"Almost three now."

Harry's heart sank. A toddler could hardly run the Wharton Park estate.

Christopher yawned loudly and Adrienne immediately stood up and went to him. "Time for your rest, my darling."

"Fuss! Fuss! Fuss!" he complained as Adrienne helped him up and led him to the door.

"When I have settled your father, the three of us will take coffee on the terrace together, *oui*? It is such a beautiful day again."

"Actually," said Olivia, "I have to go to Cromer. There's some final paperwork that needs filling in on my Land Girls. One can't end a war without paperwork, can one? Do you need anything, Harry?"

Harry shook his head. "No, thank you, Olivia."

"By the way," she added, "a Major Chalmers telephoned here this morning. He was checking on your safe return and your health. I said you would telephone him back. The number is written down."

"Right," Harry breathed. "Thought I would have to report back soon."

"Well, I rather think your mother wants to talk to you about all that sort of thing." Olivia kissed him on the top of his head as she passed him. "There is a lot for you to catch up on here, as you can imagine."

Adrienne joined him on the terrace for coffee a few minutes later. Harry thought he might as well get the ball rolling as soon as possible.

"Mother, just how sick is Father?"

"*Chéri*, I think you can see for yourself how frail he is," said Adrienne quietly, passing him his cup.

"What exactly is the prognosis? I mean, Olivia said that if he was careful, he should be able to have a few more years, but . . ."

Adrienne took a sip of her coffee. "Harry, I am so sorry to be blunt when you have only been home one day, but you must know the truth." She sighed and reached for his hand. "Your father is dying. He had a serious stroke not two months ago, which has left him numb down his left side. That is why he struggles to walk." Her eyes filled with tears. "Oh, my Harry, I apologize that I must tell you this so soon, but we have very little time. He could leave us at any moment, and before he does, as his heir, you must speak with him and learn about running the estate."

"I see." Harry lifted his cup to his mouth, struggling to control the shaking in his hand.

"Olivia and I have done our best, but all the paperwork and finances—your father has always taken care of them. There are many matters now outstanding, *mais*"—Adrienne sighed—"there is very little money left in the estate accounts. Olivia and I have arranged the staff wages for the past few months, so I know how very bad things are. *Mon Dieu*, Harry, things could not be worse."

Harry agreed silently with his mother's statement. He cleared his throat and asked, "But how can I run the estate? I am due back in the army any day."

"*Non*, Harry," Adrienne said firmly. "There will be no more army for you. You are needed here, to put the estate back on its feet. We have one hundred workers whose livelihoods depend on you. So you are to be invalided out. Your father has organized this. And I am sure you will be glad of it, *n'est-ce pas*?"

As he sank further into a morass of despair, Harry felt glad of nothing. He resented the way decisions had been made for him. After the strictures of imprisonment, he had just started beginning to make them for himself. He had forgotten that, here, his life was not his own. He opened his mouth to speak but, realizing whatever he said would sound angry and bitter, he shut it again.

Adrienne studied her son's drawn face as he sat silently opposite her, staring off into the distance, his eyes full of misery.

"*Chéri*, I understand how you must feel about coming home to the news of your father's bad health. At least you have the luxury of spending some time with him before he dies. And, Harry," Adrienne comforted, "Olivia and I will help you with the task you have ahead of you. The best decision you ever made was to marry her. I have nothing but praise for her, she has been truly *magnifique*, and I do not know what I, or Wharton Park, would have done without her."

The best decision you *ever made, Mother,* thought Harry bitterly.

He jumped to his feet, unable to sit with her any longer. "I do apologize, Mother. It has all been quite a shock and I need some time alone. I will take myself off for a walk."

"Of course. *Je suis désolée, chéri*," she called after him as he walked swiftly down the steps from the terrace and away from her.

Harry walked fast, his breathing coming in short, uneven bursts. He ran from the cloying perfection of his mother's garden and kept going until he reached open fields, swaying with green-eared corn.

He threw himself down onto the rough ground and let out a scream of agony and frustration. Then he wept uncontrollably, for the girl he knew he would never stop loving and the future he had wanted so much.

Eventually, Harry turned onto his back and gazed up at the cloudless sky.

He could still go *now* . . . just leave . . . run away . . .

He shook his head in despair. How could he? His father was dying. From what his mother and Olivia had said, Harry knew the shock of his disappearance could hasten his father's demise.

"Oh, God! Oh, God!" Harry cried out, his voice strangled with emotion.

He was trapped, well and truly. At least until after his father died.

And then what?

Could he really bear to leave his widowed mother to run the estate on her own—because Olivia would surely not stay to help her once her husband had deserted her? Adrienne simply would not manage. Therefore, to leave would mean destroying not only Wharton Park but the lives of the many loyal workers whose future depended on it.

Harry searched the skies for any possibility of release. Perhaps the estate could be sold? But who, in this postwar era, would have the wherewithal to buy it? And besides, not only would it break his mother's heart but Harry knew she would fight tooth and nail against the idea. She had dedicated her life to it.

The only other possibility was to bring Lidia here to him.

But how could he? How could he divorce Olivia after all she had done, caring for both of his parents and for Wharton Park? Could he really announce that he was bringing a young girl from Thailand across the world to step into her shoes?

Harry sighed, knowing the notion was absurd. Lidia might be many things, but even he struggled to see her as mistress of an estate such as this. Besides, the cold would kill her. His Hothouse Flower would wilt and die.

Harry lay where he was for many hours, watching the dusk fall and, with it, his hope. Fate had conspired to make his plan impossible.

He could not walk away from Wharton Park. Even for Lidia.

But how was he to tell her? How could he write her a letter, informing her that everything he had promised was not to be?

Harry stood up disconsolately and made his way across the fields and back into the park. He decided that, for now, he would tell Lidia only that his father was sick and his return to Bangkok might be delayed. The finality of doing the right thing—setting her free immediately so that she could move on to a life without him—was currently beyond him.

He walked toward the hothouse and pushed the door open. It was deserted; Bill had left for the day. Harry felt his chest tighten as he breathed in the scent of Lidia. He walked down the benches until he reached the orchids. He lifted the pots and found an envelope, rather damp from the moisture of the pots hiding it. His heart quickened as he tore it open.

He choked in despair as he saw Lidia's tiny, neat writing.

My darling Harry,

I get your letter from ship, Ka, *and it makes me very happy. I too am missing you, and I cannot wait for your return. When I feel sad, I think about the future we will have together. And I then am happy. I wear your ring every day, and know it is symbol of our love, that one day we two will marry in front of both of our Gods.*

All here at hotel is well. We get some new linen and pillows for all the rooms, and have less blackout. We have many new guests now so Madame very happy.

All your friends here send best wishes to you, and everyone says they miss you playing piano in Bamboo Bar.

Please forgive my bad English writing. I am still learning, and hoping to get better. I am yours for eternity, Harry, Ka, *your*

Hothouse Flower.

XXX

"Oh my love, my love . . ." Harry groaned, cradling the letter to his chest. "How can I live like this? How can I live without you?"

He slumped onto the stool and reread the letter, thinking surely death would be preferable to the way he felt now. Just then, he heard footsteps and the door opening at the other end of the hothouse. Seeing that it was Olivia, he swiftly hid the letter in his trouser pocket as he stood up.

She walked toward him, her face a picture of concern.

"I have been looking for you everywhere, darling. Your mother said you had taken yourself off after lunch and she hadn't seen you since."

"No. I needed—some time," he offered weakly.

"I am so awfully sorry, Harry. I gather your mother told you the truth about your father."

"Yes, she did." Harry was glad to use this as an excuse for his red eyes and the heartbreak that must be written on his face.

She tentatively opened her arms to him. "May I hold you?"

Harry did not resist her embrace. He needed to feel the physical comfort of another human being. He cried like a baby against her shoulder. She soothed him gently, telling him she would be there, she loved him dearly and would help him as much as he needed.

Harry was lost in his grief, his pain reaching to the depths of his soul.

"I must say good-bye," he muttered. "How can I bear it? How can I bear it?"

"I know," comforted Olivia, wanting to weep for him. "Oh, my darling, I know."

In Changi, Harry had had plenty of practice at merely existing, and over the next few weeks, it was put to good use. He spent mornings with his father in the study that would soon be his, going through every aspect of the vast management task that was the Wharton Park estate. Father and son spent more time in each other's company than they ever had before. But this shared time had a poignancy, as they both knew the reason behind it.

Harry realized he had never appreciated the complexity of his father's role. As he learned what it entailed, his admiration for his father grew.

"The golden rule—even if you have staff to manage such things as the accounts and the farm—is to be in control. You must check the books and take a horse every week to ride across your land. You understand what I am telling you, my boy?"

"Yes, Father," Harry answered, currently flummoxed by a list of figures in the ledger in front of him. Arithmetic had never been his strong point.

"You have to be hands-on and make sure every worker at Wharton Park knows that you are. Your great-grandfather nearly lost this house by being far more interested in the ladies and his port than he was in the estate. The staff ran riot. Remember, a good leader leads from the front, and your army years will have stood you in good stead. I am proud of you, my boy." Harry's father nodded emphatically, as if to make up for all the years he had never said it.

So, in the afternoons, Harry would take a horse and ride across the estate. He learned about the crops they needed for the following year, and machinery that needed replacing. He counted cattle and pigs and visited tenant farmers, noticing some had sneakily extended the boundaries allocated to them on their deeds.

Harry appointed Jim, Mrs. Combe's son, as his new farm manager. The lad had grown up on the estate and watched his father do the same job before him. Jim had no experience managing people, but he was young, bright, and glad of the opportunity. Following his own father's advice, Harry felt it was most important to find someone he could trust.

Late into the night, Harry studied the accounts. It gave him something to focus on, and a reason not to join Olivia in the bedroom before she was asleep. He realized quickly that the estate finances were even worse than his mother had thought.

By the end of the summer, Harry felt he knew every hectare of the estate, how much income Wharton Park could expect from selling the remaining crops and cattle, and what had to be spent on replacing machinery and restocking. Olivia had also pointed out that some of the workers' cottages were in urgent need of repair, but that would have to wait. The big house itself needed thousands spent on it.

Harry had calculated that he would need to borrow ten thousand pounds to start putting the estate back on its feet. It would be two years before it showed any kind of profit and he could begin repaying the loan. It was going to be a long haul.

He sighed and checked the grandfather clock, which ticked quietly in the corner of his father's study. It was half past two in the morning. He thought then, as he did every night, of Lidia and where she might be now. It was already morning in Bangkok. Lidia would be sitting at the reception desk, smiling and charming the new guests . . .

And dreaming of Harry coming back to her soon.

He removed some notepaper from his father's drawer and, as he did every night, penned her a few lines of love. He sealed them in an envelope, ready to give to Bill in the morning. He no longer talked of the future, tantalized her with what could never be, but told her only how much he loved and missed her.

Her letters to him arrived sporadically, but he searched for them every day under the orchids in the hothouse.

Harry sighed as he turned off the lamp on the desk and headed for the door. He felt he had already served a life sentence in Changi; now it seemed he had to serve it again, here at Wharton Park.

44

As summer turned to autumn, and the chill of winter approached, Christopher became too weak to leave his bed. Adrienne sat with him most of the day, talking and reading to him as he dozed, and leaving his side only when either Harry or Olivia came to relieve her.

Then, in December, just before Christmas, Christopher suffered another severe heart attack. He died a few hours later, having never recovered consciousness.

The funeral took place on the day before Christmas Eve, in the small church on the estate where Harry and Olivia had married. It was well attended: over three hundred people came to pay their respects. Christopher's body was entombed in the Crawford family vault, to lie for eternity alongside his forefathers'.

Olivia watched Harry out of the corner of her eye as he welcomed the mourners into the house after the service. His sad, drawn features betrayed his pain; at that moment she thought she had never loved him more. Even though he was still unresponsive and distant, and her attempts to make him talk about his experiences in Changi had failed miserably, he often came to her late at night and made love to her.

She frequently woke to find bruises on her body and felt a dull ache inside her from being taken by him so roughly. At some point she would tell him he needed to be more gentle, but for now, under the circumstances, she let him be. The contact and solace it brought her were too important to sacrifice.

Christmas was a somber affair, although, bearing in mind her delicate nature, Adrienne proved surprisingly stoic about her loss. Perhaps she was helped by having had time to prepare for it and having said everything she needed to say to her beloved husband before he had died.

When the bells of local churches pealed in the New Year, Olivia was grateful. She could only pray it would bring Harry the peace and happiness he so desperately needed.

• • •

In early January, as the first harsh snow of winter fell on Wharton Park, Harry knew he must contact Lidia and break the news that he would not be returning. While the truth existed only in his head, and Lidia was unaware of it and still sent him loving letters, Harry had allowed himself to imagine that being with her was still a possibility, in order to alleviate his darkest moments.

But her most recent missives had an edge of anxiety; she said there was so much to discuss on his return and had asked him tentatively when he thought that might be. He also noticed she was no longer using headed paper from the Oriental Hotel, and a twinge of concern insinuated itself into his thoughts.

Unable to tell her the truth, he wrote and explained that his father had died and he had much to sort out before he could leave to be with her.

Then her letters stopped altogether.

Harry knew something was wrong.

On a whim, he went to the post office in Cromer and sent a telegram to Madame Giselle at the Oriental, asking of her health, but also of Lidia's.

Two days later, he received a reply:

HARRY STOP ALL WELL HERE STOP WHEN DO YOU RETURN STOP LIDIA LEFT SUDDENLY TWO MONTHS AGO STOP NO FORWARDING ADDRESS STOP REGARDS GISELLE

Harry held on to the counter to steady himself. He felt sick, dizzy . . .

Back at Wharton Park, he went to his study, closed the door, and sat at his desk with his head in his hands. He took some deep breaths and tried to pull himself together.

Perhaps Lidia had simply been offered a better job elsewhere?

Harry shook his head. He knew this couldn't be the case: Lidia loved her job, was proud of her work and the hotel, and was grateful for the opportunity Giselle had given her. Besides, she would have told him where she was.

Was she ill?

Harry's heart began banging against his chest.

Was she *dead*?

He slammed his fist down on the desk. He had to go to her, to find her, wherever she was. And help her if she needed him to.

He paced around the study, trying to manufacture a reason that would seem rational to Olivia and release him for the three months or so he would need to find Lidia, explain, and then say good-bye. Perhaps he could tell Olivia that he and Sebastian had discussed business ventures while Harry was in Bangkok, and that he wished to explore them further to bolster the estate finances.

Having settled on this plan, Harry was just about to telephone Sebastian in Bangkok when there was a knock on his study door.

"Damn," Harry muttered under his breath. "Come," he called.

Olivia entered the room, an unusually nervous smile playing on her lips.

"Harry, can I trouble you for five minutes or so?"

"What is it?"

Olivia ignored his abruptness, sure that her news would at last bring a smile to his face. She sat down opposite him and realized her hands were shaking.

"I have something to tell you . . . don't worry, it's the most wonderful news."

Harry stared at her. "Good. Go on then."

"I—*we* are expecting a baby! There, darling. Just what we need after the dreadful few years we've all had."

"Are you sure?" Harry frowned.

"Completely." She nodded happily. "The doctor confirmed it yesterday. I am three months pregnant. The baby is expected in June."

Harry knew he must rouse himself and give the appropriate reaction. "Why, that is the most terrific news." He came round from his side of the desk, reached down, and kissed her on the cheek.

She looked up at him, her eyes anxious. "You are pleased, aren't you, darling?"

"Of course I am, Olivia."

"And this time, I am going to be far more careful. The doctor has advised me, because of what happened last time, to take lots of rest.

So, no more rushing around the estate like a mad thing. Of course, I shall hate every second of the inactivity, but it will be worth it in the long run, don't you think?"

"Of course it will be worth it."

"I'm afraid it's going to mean more work for you though, darling. I'm sure, when we tell your mother, she will be only too happy to help you with the day-to-day running of the house. Once she gets over this dreadful influenza that's so exhausted her. But the spring will soon be here. Oh, Harry," Olivia breathed, her eyes suddenly filling with tears, "our baby."

Embarrassed by her unusual show of emotion, Olivia took a handkerchief from her cardigan and blew her nose. "Sorry. The moment rather got the better of me. I promise I shall not become a weeping sap and irritate you further."

It was then Harry had a sudden glimpse of Olivia's strength. He had offered her nothing of himself in the past few months, apart from occasional lovemaking, which he knew to be savage. He had treated her, at best, with diffidence; at worst, with disdain. And here she was, almost apologetic to be happy about expecting a child because she was worried about his reaction.

In this moment of stark realization, cowed by what he could see as his own selfishness, and loathing himself for it, he knelt down in front of her and took her hands in his.

"Darling, I'm absolutely thrilled. You must take as much rest as you need. And you jolly well deserve it." He took her in his arms and held her for a moment. "When shall we tell my mother?"

"I thought at lunch."

"Have Mrs. Jenks cook something special. We will give ourselves a treat to celebrate you being such a clever girl."

Olivia nodded, glowing from his attentiveness and filled with hope that this could really be the turning point for their relationship, and the one thing that would bring them closer.

Olivia and Harry broke the news to Adrienne, who was still weak from her influenza. She proved to be as thrilled as Olivia had anticipated.

After lunch, Harry took himself off to the stables and rode through the slushy vestiges of the snow covering his land.

He passed a small wood and Wharton Park came into full view. Harry drew his horse to a standstill and surveyed it. For the first time, he drew a sense of pride from its being his. He was now lord and master, and even his mother had to bow to his wishes. And, so far, he hadn't been half-bad at getting to grips with the job.

Now an heir was possible too, maybe even a son to take up the reins when he died, and perhaps other children to come. It was a comforting thought.

Lidia . . .

Harry rested his cheek despairingly against his horse's velvety neck. If life had been different, if *only* it had been different, he would have spent it with her.

But the bald truth was visible in every direction.

Wharton Park was what he had been born to. There was no escape.

His mouth felt dry and tight as the pain of living without her resurfaced.

"Oh, God . . ." he moaned.

He had to accept it, to cease punishing himself and those around him, especially Olivia. She was not to blame for his passion for another woman, and at the very least she deserved courtesy and understanding from him.

First, though, he must find Lidia and set his beloved Hothouse Flower free to live a life without him. But how? With Olivia pregnant and needing rest, Harry knew it was impossible for him to leave her or the estate until at least after the baby was born.

There had to be another way . . .

When Harry finally kicked his horse on again, he had decided exactly what he must do. He rode back to the stables, dismounted, and handed the horse to a groom. By the time he reached the door of the hothouse, his plan was firm in his mind. Bill was there, sitting on his stool, deep in concentration as he studied the roots of an orchid.

He looked up. "Afternoon, your Lordship. How are you?"

"I am well, thank you, Bill." Harry still struggled to remember this title now applied to him. He had associated it with his father for so long.

"No news again today, I'm afraid."

"No . . ." Harry walked toward Bill and watched him for a while as he worked. "And I don't think there will be. She seems to have disappeared."

Bill put his pipette down and looked up at Harry. "What do you mean, she's disappeared?"

"She has left the hotel, and no one seems to know where she's gone. I'm obviously desperate with worry."

"I can imagine," Bill breathed. "I'm sorry. Anything I can do?"

Harry took a deep breath. "As a matter of fact, Bill, there is . . ."

At four thirty, Elsie took a tea tray up and knocked on Olivia's bedroom door. She entered and found her mistress still asleep.

"Wakey, wakey, your Ladyship!"

Olivia stirred and opened her eyes. "Goodness me, is it past four?" she said sleepily, then her face broke into a smile. "It must have been the relief of telling Harry."

Elsie lay the tray beside Olivia. "Of telling him what?"

Olivia turned to Elsie, her beautiful, turquoise eyes shining. She reached for her hand. "Dearest Elsie, now that I have told Harry and his mother, I can tell you too. I am expecting a child. And it's due in June."

"Oh, your Ladyship! That is the best news I've heard for months! It's lovely news, it really is."

"Yes, isn't it? And Harry seemed thrilled too."

"I'll bet," Elsie rallied, trying not to betray her feelings for the new Lord Crawford. As she poured the tea, a sadness suddenly clouded her eyes. "You're ever so lucky, your Ladyship—luckier than me."

"Oh, Elsie, I didn't think. No news so far, then?"

"No. And nor will there ever be. We were married a while before Bill left four years ago, and he's been back a long time now. So . . . well, he took himself off to the doctors last week. And they don't think he can—you know, your Ladyship." Elsie blushed. "The doctor puts it down to an attack of mumps when Bill was twelve. So there won't ever be babies for the two of us."

"Oh, Elsie, I am so terribly sorry." Olivia knew how passionately her maid had wanted a large family. "Perhaps you could adopt."

"Bill's not that keen, and I'm not sure how I feel about it either, but it's early days yet. We're going to let the dust settle and see how we both feel in a few months' time."

"Of course, very sensible."

"Now, your Ladyship"—Elsie put her sadness to one side—"I don't want you to think about me and spoil your happiness. You've been through a lot, you have, and you deserve this good news, you really do."

"Thank you, Elsie." Olivia sat up as Elsie passed her a cup of tea. "And just remember, never give up hope. Life has a funny way of sorting itself out, just you wait and see."

Olivia had just retired to bed that same evening when Harry appeared, sat down on the bed next to her, and took her hands in his.

Twice in one day, thought Olivia happily.

"Darling, if you are not too tired, I want to tell you about my idea," Harry began.

"I am wide-awake, darling, do fire away." Olivia relished that he was involving her.

"Well, I know you are aware of how close the estate is to penury at present."

"Yes, I am." Olivia looked at him. "Have you come up with a way to raise some extra funds?"

"I rather think I have, yes. Of course it's a long shot, but in the few weeks we had together, my father taught me to try and maximize the potential of both the estate and the people working on it. And we have one person in particular who seems to have a rare talent."

"And who might that be?"

"Bill Stafford," Harry answered with a flourish. "I don't know whether you have been down to the hothouse lately, but he really is doing the most marvelous things in there, cross-fertilizing orchids to produce his own hybrids, some of which are quite beautiful. I reckon, if we gave Bill the right sort of help and encouragement, we could start selling the things!"

"I must say, that is rather a good idea. Especially as it would mean so little investment. We might need a couple of extra hothouses at most."

"And, of course, some unusual specimens. Bill's passion—and his talent, might I add—seems to be with tropical flowers, like orchids, and I have suggested he concentrate on those. He insists he needs to learn more. So"—Harry launched into the key part of his plan, hoping he had done enough to convince Olivia—"I have suggested he take a trip to the Far East as soon as possible. There, he can learn about the plants in their natural habitat, and how he could grow them here at Wharton Park. And, of course, bring home as many specimens as he chooses, to start him off."

Olivia frowned. "Surely he won't want to travel all the way back there? Especially with such dreadful memories of the Orient? Couldn't we send him on a horticultural course? Perhaps they run something at the Botanical Gardens in Kew."

"As a matter of fact, it was Bill who suggested the idea. He wants to specialize, become an expert, and be the best at what he does. My feeling is that we should give him a chance," Harry urged, knowing how much hung on Olivia's agreement and support. "After all, he did save my life."

"Well, if that is what you think is best, then, yes, send him. Bill seems to spend most of his time in the hothouse anyway these days, leaving his father to tend the kitchen garden. Of course, I will no longer be able to help Jack, so, perhaps we should replace Bill on a full-time basis, take on an extra chap to do the more menial gardening tasks."

"Jolly good idea," agreed Harry. "The one stumbling block Bill can see with his plan is Elsie. She will doubtless be reluctant to let her husband go when he has only just come home."

"Absolutely."

"That is where you come in, darling. I was hoping you could help persuade her that this is a big chance for Bill to make something of himself, and that she should support him in his endeavor."

"I will do my best, but she won't be happy, Harry."

"Darling, Elsie worships the ground you walk on. One word from you and she will see sense, I am sure." Harry smiled down at her.

Olivia smiled back, blushing at the rare compliment. "I'll see what I can do. What about Bill's passage?"

"I have already contacted Sebastian, and he is happy to organize that for us."

"Well, darling"—Olivia smiled—"you seem to have it all worked out."

When Elsie first heard of the plan from Bill, she was furious.

"What?! Leave me here again, all alone?"

Bill had sworn to Harry he would not mention the real reason he was traveling back to Bangkok.

"I know, sweetheart, but I think I really do have a way with them orchids, and I want to learn more. His Lordship has told me if I manage to produce and sell some special ones in the future, he'll see me right. And we could do with a few more shillings in this house now, couldn't we?"

"Not if it means you off on your travels again," she complained, looking at the clock on the wall. "Anyways, I've got to be off up to the house. We'll talk about it later."

Bill waited nervously for his wife's return. Elsie arrived home with a resigned smile on her face.

"It's all right, you silly man, I'm going to let you go. Her Ladyship had a talk to me today and explained what a good opportunity it is for you."

"Oh, Elsie, thank you, sweetheart." Bill hugged her to him and kissed her forehead.

She looked at the genuine excitement in Bill's eyes and, because she loved him so much, was able to catch it. "As long as it's not more than a couple of months, otherwise I might have to get myself a fancy man to keep me company!"

Bill held her close to him, thinking how lucky he was to have found his true love, right here on his doorstep. "I promise, sweetheart, I'll be back in the blink of an eye."

45

Bangkok
1947

Bill sat in the back of the tuk-tuk, one hand hanging on to the wooden armrest, the other trying to steady his small suitcase as the tricycle careered through the Bangkok traffic. As they lurched round a corner into a narrower street, the tuk-tuk swerved and just missed a woman balancing two shallow baskets of rice, suspended like a gigantic set of scales on a wooden pole, slung across her shoulders.

He closed his eyes, praying this terrifying journey would come to an end soon and this Oriental Hotel would appear as if by magic. He had forgotten all too quickly the intense heat of the Far East; he was parched and soaked with sweat.

"Elsie," he moaned, "why didn't I listen to you?"

To think that, right now, he could be tinkering in his hothouse at Wharton Park, looking forward to his tea of liver and bacon, and later, Elsie's warm body snuggled up beside him. Instead, he was in a countrywide hothouse, with a plate of the rice he had come to loathe as his most likely meal, and who knew where he would end up resting his head for the night? He took comfort from in that his passage home was already booked for two weeks' time. In comparison to his four long years in Changi, a fortnight was nothing.

"I swear, Lord Harry, you'll be the death of me, you honestly will," Bill muttered, as the tuk-tuk pulled up alongside a shabby-looking building.

"Long-Lam Orienten, krub." The driver pointed to it, and Bill breathed a sigh of relief as he saw the small sign above the entrance confirming his destination.

Bill's traveling case was whisked from his hand by a diminutive porter, who led him into the airy hotel lobby and over to reception. A pretty, young Thai girl was sitting behind the desk. Bill knew this was where Lidia had worked, and he prayed he had struck gold instantly.

"Hello, miss. Er . . . I'd like to book a room here for the next two weeks."

"Certainly, sir. It will be one hundred and twenty baht a night, not including breakfast," the girl answered in perfect English.

"Right then," said Bill, not sure what the sum represented in sterling, but knowing Harry had sent him financially prepared.

"Can you sign here, sir, and I have porter take you round to your room. It have a nice view overlooking the river." She smiled at him.

"Thank you." Bill scribbled his name where she indicated, as she reached into a wooden pigeonhole behind her and drew out a large key. "You wouldn't be Lidia, by any chance, would you?"

"No, sorry, sir, she leave few months ago. I am replacement. My name is Ankhana." She handed him the key.

"Would you know, miss, where Lidia is working now?"

"Sorry, sir. She go before I arrive. I did not meet her. You can ask Madam Giselle, the hotel manager, but she not here now." Ankhana rang a small bell and the tiny porter appeared behind Bill. "Have a nice stay, sir."

"Thank you."

Bill followed the porter to his room and, like Harry before him, was delighted by the view of the river from his window.

After a nap and a cat-lick at the basin, Bill set off to find the restaurant. On the shady veranda, he ordered a beer and a delicious hamburger, a delicacy he had discovered—courtesy of the GIs—in Singapore, while awaiting his passage home from Changi. Bill decided he could get used to being treated like a gentleman, with everyone fetching and carrying for you. Yet all he wanted was to find Lidia as soon as possible and get on with the terrible task of explaining everything. Then he could concentrate on searching out the orchids he wanted to ship back to England.

"Two weeks, Lord Harry, that's all you're getting," he muttered into his beer. "Then I'm on that boat home to my Elsie."

After lunch, Bill headed back to reception to see if the hotel manager was in her office.

"Start with Giselle," Harry had said. "She knows everything, and she may well have received word from Lidia since she sent her telegram to me."

Giselle was indeed in her office and came out to greet Bill.

"May I help you, sir?"

"Yes, er . . . ma'am, I'm here on behalf of Lord Harry Crawford."

"Mon Dieu!" Giselle raised an eyebrow. "Our errant British pianist. Well, you had better follow me."

She raised the wooden countertop to let Bill through and led him into her office. "Please sit down, Mr.—"

"Stafford, ma'am, Bill Stafford."

"So"—Giselle looked at him as she sat down behind her desk—"I must presume Lord Crawford will not be forsaking his birthright to marry our receptionist and work as a musician in our little bar?"

"No, ma'am, he won't."

"Quelle surprise," Giselle muttered. "Of course, I was aware he wouldn't, but he was very convincing when he left. I thought"—Giselle smiled sadly—"that perhaps, for once, love would triumph. But, of course, it cannot."

"He was—*is*—in love, ma'am. But he knows now it's impossible for him to uproot, and come here. His father died recently, you see, and he must take on the estate and all the responsibilities that come with it."

"You do not have to explain, Mr. Stafford. I understand completely. And I must presume you are not here to explain his change of plan to me, but to the woman he promised to return to, *oui*?"

"Yes, ma'am." Bill colored under her watchful gaze, feeling oddly responsible for Harry's actions.

"You know she is no longer working here?"

"Yes, his Lordship told me. Do you know where she is?"

"As I informed Lord Crawford in my telegram, Lidia simply vanished one morning about three months ago. I have not seen or heard of her since."

"Was she sick, ma'am? His Lordship is beside himself with worry."

"I do not believe so. She did not look sick to me the last time I saw her. Although there was a sadness about her. . . ." Giselle shook her head. "I think we both understand why that was. She was a most beautiful girl; bright, eager to learn, and an asset to this hotel. I was sorry to lose her."

"Why do you think she left, ma'am?"

"Who knows? One has one's suspicions, but"—Giselle sighed—"I can only assume it was for personal reasons. It was out of character for Lidia. She was always very reliable. And, I thought, happy here."

"Would she have gone to her family? His Lordship said he'd visited them on an island once with Miss Lidia, a day's train ride from Bangkok."

"No, I know for certain she is not there. When she disappeared, I too was concerned. I wrote to her uncle on Koh Chang to ask if Lidia was with them. He replied saying they had not seen her, but he would write to Lidia's mother to ask if all was well. Unfortunately"—Giselle tilted her head—"this uncle seemed unaware that Lidia's mother moved to Japan a few months ago. Lidia stayed behind to continue working here, but, of course, she may have gone to join her mother now."

"Japan?" Bill's heart sank. "Having been a POW in the war, excuse me for saying so, ma'am, but I don't think I could stomach looking for her there."

"Of course. Besides, it is many, many miles away, Mr. Stafford." Giselle leaned across her desk. "I do not know for certain what has happened to Lidia, but I will tell you that if my instinct is correct, Lidia will not have fled to her family. No, that is the last place she will have run to. My belief is she is out there"—Giselle waved her hand toward the window—"in the great mass of humanity that is this city."

"Oh, dear, ma'am." Bill hung his head, the task before him seeming insurmountable. "Where do I start? Did she have friends here at the hotel she might have confided in?"

"I am not aware of a particular friendship. Lidia was a very private person. If she had a . . . personal problem, I doubt she would share it. She would hide away, like a wounded animal."

Bill studied his calloused hands, feeling out of his depth. "Ma'am, I can't go home without finding her, I've sworn to his Lordship I will. Besides . . ."

"Besides what, Mr. Stafford?"

Bill took a deep breath. "If I don't find her and reassure his Lordship Miss Lidia's all right, like, he may decide to come out to look for her himself. He loves her so very much . . . you don't know what torment that man's put himself through because he knows he must do his duty. I swear he'd be here if he could be. And then, between you and me, ma'am, where would we all be back at Wharton Park? Me and my wife, Elsie, along with our parents and a hundred and fifty other souls, plus their wives and kids, depend on the estate for our livelihood. If his Lordship disappeared, there'd be chaos, sure as eggs is eggs. So you see, ma'am"—Bill struggled to be eloquent—"I'm not just here for him, but for me and mine, and the others that need his Lordship at home."

"Yes, I understand how torn Lord Crawford must be. Remember, I witnessed the love between them, and it is a tragedy for both that it can never be. *C'est la vie*, Mr. Stafford," Giselle sighed. "I will do what I can to help you." She tapped her pen on the desk as she thought. "Perhaps you should visit the hospitals, just in case. I have a list somewhere." She opened a drawer in her desk and looked through it.

"I don't even know her second name."

"I can give you that, at least. Here"—Giselle produced a sheet of paper—"a list of every hospital in Bangkok. We had it typed out for relatives of POWs in Burma. This war, so much pain. And see how it still continues?"

"I know, ma'am. Changed me and my life for good and all, that's for certain. And thrown everything topsy-turvy, it has."

"Yes, because in the normal course of things, Harry and Lidia should never have met, but they did, and *pouf*!" Giselle made a Gallic gesticulation. "Look at the mayhem it has caused for so many." She was writing something on another sheet of paper and handed it across the desk to Bill. "Lidia's surname, and a note written in Thai saying you are looking for her, which you can hand to the hospital receptions."

Bill blanched at the prospect. He had seen enough sickness and suffering in Changi to last a lifetime. "I must say, ma'am, I dread finding her in one of these."

"You must start somewhere, Mr. Stafford, and surely it is best to rule them out first?" Giselle stood up and Bill followed suit. She stopped by the door and turned to him. "Lord Crawford is lucky to have such a loyal and faithful friend to travel all this way to help him."

"I am his Lordship's servant, ma'am. I must do as I'm bid."

"No, Mr. Stafford, Lord Crawford has entrusted you with a mission he would only give to a friend, whatever your rank in his household."

"Well then, I only hope I can fulfill it," Bill sighed.

"You will," Giselle said as she opened the door of the office. "If Lidia is still alive and wants to be found, you will."

46

Bill spent the evening stopping every member of the hotel staff he came across and showing them the slip of paper Giselle had given him, but was met with blank stares and head shaking. So the following morning he embarked on the dismal job of visiting hospitals across Bangkok.

As his tuk-tuk hurtled through the sweltering, fetid heat of the crowded city, Bill despaired of ever finding the one person who could bring Harry and himself peace of mind by putting this dreadful situation to rest.

The hospital receptions were surprisingly clean and calm—nothing like the Changi "morgue," as it had been nicknamed. No dying patients moaning in pain, with suppurating, untreatable wounds, and no constant foul stench of human excrement.

By the end of the day, Bill was back at the hotel, sticky and exhausted, but none the wiser as to Lidia's whereabouts.

"Any luck?" Giselle asked, catching sight of him in the lobby.

"No." Bill shook his head. "Eight down, twelve to go. To be honest, ma'am, I don't know if I'm happy I haven't found her, or disappointed."

"Here." Giselle handed him an envelope. "It is a staff photograph of Lidia, taken just before she left. It might help to show it at the hospitals. You never know." Giselle patted Bill on the shoulder. "Better luck tomorrow."

Bill collected his key and went up to his room. He sank wearily onto the bed and opened the envelope to look at the photograph.

The black-and-white face that gazed back at him had the same delicate features of the many Thai women he had seen in Bangkok. Yet a light, a sparkle, in Lidia's huge eyes gave her a radiance, lifting her beyond prettiness and making her beautiful. Bill gently touched the unblemished cheek, wondering if this young girl was aware of the upheaval she had caused him and others, thousands of miles away.

"Where are you, Lidia?" he murmured softly, and laid the photograph carefully on the nightstand by the bed.

After a shower and a change of clothes, Bill was drawn by the music coming from a room near the lobby, and he went into the Bamboo Bar. He ordered a beer and listened to the trio playing jazz. It was not really his sort of music—he preferred Vera Lynn or his beloved classical—but the atmosphere in the bar was vibrant and it lifted his spirits. He tried to imagine his Lordship playing the old Joanna in here—smiling, carefree, and in love—but it was difficult. All that came to mind were the serious, drawn features of a young man with the weight of the world on his shoulders.

A young Thai girl asked if she could share the table with him and he nodded, taking little notice of her as she ordered herself a Coca-Cola. She tried to make conversation with him in halting English, and assuming she was waiting for her young man to appear, Bill answered her questions. Twenty minutes later, when the girl had moved closer to him and he could feel her thigh purposefully brushing against his own Bill panicked. He waved frantically at the waiter so he could sign the check and leave. The girl glowered with disappointment as Bill hurried out of the bar.

When he reached his room and shut the door firmly behind him, Bill realized he was breathing heavily. Even though he had done nothing, he paled at the thought of Elsie seeing him with another woman. There was no one else for him, there never had been, and the thought of hurting her made Bill feel physically sick. He had never understood the attraction of these oriental women; he had watched fellow soldiers throw themselves into the whorehouses of Singapore on their release, when all he could think about was his wife waiting patiently for him at home, with her big brown eyes, sweet freckled nose, and plump white body.

Bill undressed and slid between the sheets, thinking that he and Elsie might not have the money or ease of the gentry they worked for, but they did seem to be blessed with something he now realized was rarer than a black orchid: undying love.

Another sweltering day greeted him, and the humidity felt so tight about Bill's chest, it was as if the oxygen had been sucked from the air. He gulped the cooler air beneath the ceiling fans at the hospital reception desks while the receptionists checked their admissions records for Lidia's name, then studied her photograph and shook their heads.

Bill's quest led him deeper into the city, leaving behind the graceful colonial architecture around the Oriental and the banks of the river. As he rode from hospital to hospital in his tuk-tuk, Bill saw temples painted in rich, bright colors, home to monks who rose at dawn and walked the filthy streets barefoot, holding bowls for the locals to fill with rice. And there were the homeless: cripples with disfigured limbs, women with young babies sitting in the gutters begging, despair clearly visible on their gaunt faces. The poverty was unlike anything Bill had ever seen, and it struck him that, although these poor souls were free to go where they chose, their lives were little better than his had been in Changi.

The more Bill saw, the more he longed for the comfort and relative security of his life and home at Wharton Park. And realized just how blessed he was.

By the end of the day, Bill had visited every hospital in the city, to no avail. He walked back into the hotel, weary and demoralized, unsure where he should try looking for Lidia next. When he picked up his key from reception, Giselle saw him through her office window and came to speak to him.

"I see from your face you have not found her."

"No." Bill sighed. "And I don't know where to look next. Any ideas?"

"Well, I was thinking you could try the neighborhood where Lidia lived before her family left for Japan and she moved into the hotel. She could have gone back there."

"It's worth a try, I suppose," Bill replied flatly.

"I can give you her old address and perhaps you could show her photograph to some of her neighbors, the local street vendors. Maybe someone has seen her . . ."

Giselle's voice tailed off. They both knew it was a tenuous link.

Bill scratched his aching head. "What I don't understand is, why didn't she leave word here for his Lordship to tell him of her whereabouts? She was expecting him to come back and find her, after all."

"We cannot guess why she did this, Mr. Stafford, we really cannot," Giselle answered, despairing for this good, loyal young man who was, despite his lack of culture and education, endearing himself to her more as each day passed.

"Well, thank you for your help, ma'am. I'll try this address tomorrow. My passage home is in ten days' time, and even for his Lordship, I can't stay any longer. I might not have a wife to go home to if I did."

"You can only do your best, Mr. Stafford, and no more." She gave him a short smile and walked away.

Bill had the tuk-tuk take him on the twenty-minute drive to the address Giselle had given him. It was right in the heart of the city, a dark, narrow street lined with tall, wooden buildings that leaned toward each other at strange angles and looked as if a puff of wind would send them toppling over. The smell of food rotting in the gutters was overpowering, and Bill's stomach contracted as he stood in front of the building where Lidia had apparently once lived.

His knock at the door summoned an ancient woman with a toothless smile. Having gathered it was pointless trying to speak to the locals, Bill thrust the photograph in front of her.

She nodded. And pointed upstairs.

"She's here?" Bill's heart skipped a beat. The woman spoke in fast Thai, shaking her head and gesticulating. Bill put his foot on the threshold.

"Lidia? Up?"

"Mai, mai, mai!"

Bill at least knew this meant "no."

"Where is she then? Lidia?" He mimed and gesticulated too.

Then the door was slammed in his face, nearly amputating his toes.

Bill banged on the door for several minutes, to no response. He paced up and down the street, knocking on the doors to either side, this exercise proving equally fruitless.

It was hopeless. He would simply have to return home and tell his Lordship he had failed to find her. If he was honest, it had been a doomed mission from the start. A missing girl, just after a war, lost in a city of millions. And a Westerner, looked on with suspicion by the locals, and unable to communicate with them. He must not feel guilty. He had done his best by Harry, but the fact was, he had nowhere else to look. He would spend the time he had left buying his orchid specimens and would leave for England as planned.

Bill walked slowly down the street, looking for his tuk-tuk driver, who seemed to have disappeared. When he turned the corner, he came upon a large, noisy market. He bought himself a bowl of noodles and wandered aimlessly through the stalls until he spied one overflowing with a wonderful selection of colorful, sweet-smelling orchids. He stopped in front of it to study the plants, many of which he had not seen before.

"Help you?" said a voice from behind the foliage.

Bill squinted through the row of *Dendrobium* and saw a tiny man squatting on the floor.

"You speak English?" Bill asked in surprise.

"Little English, yes." The man stood up and appeared from behind the flowers. At full height, he reached Bill's chest. "Help you, sir? Have many rare orchid here. My family, we bring from our nursery in Chiang Mai. We famous," he said proudly. "Supply royal palace."

"I can see the plants are unusual." Bill pointed at a particularly stunning orange orchid, its delicate, narrow petals covered in darker veins, centered around a white longitudinal crest. He put his bowl of noodles and the photograph down on the trestle table and picked up the plant to study it more closely.

"What is this?"

"That, sir, is *Dendrobium unicum.* It rare and expensive." The man grinned. "It like strong light and dry weather."

"And this?" Bill picked up a plant with gossamer-fine lilac petals. He wished he had brought paper and a pen to write down the names and details of the flowers. This man seemed to know what he was talking about.

"That, sir, *Aerides odoratum.* Grow on ground in forest. Like shade."

"And this?"

For the next twenty minutes, Bill forgot all about Lidia and entered a world he understood and loved. His fingers were itching to buy the entire stall and ship it home to his hothouse. Then he could spend the next few months getting to know each specimen, experimenting with temperature, light, and moisture, and see if he could grow the genus for himself from the original plant, perhaps even cross-fertilize it and produce a hybrid.

"Are you here tomorrow?" Bill asked, wondering how he could

find transport for all the plants he wished to take, and where he would store them when he did.

"Every day, sir."

"I want to ship the orchids I buy to England, you see."

"Yes, sir. I organize. We can send crate to dock to join your ship."

"And I will be here when you pack it and load it," Bill said firmly, not wanting to set sail and find he had been sold five crates of daisies. "I will come back tomorrow to choose the plants and bring you the details."

"Okay, sir. I see you tomorrow."

"Yes. Thank you." Bill turned to walk away, his head still full of orchids.

"Sir! Sir! You forget photograph!"

The man was behind him, flapping the photograph at him.

"Yes, I did. Thank you." Bill reached out for it and saw the man studying it.

He looked up at Bill and smiled. "She very beautiful. I know her."

Bill gulped. "You know her?"

"Yes. She is Lidia. Good customer of mine. She live round there." The man pointed to the street from which Bill had come. "But I not see her now. Maybe she gone."

Bill tried to keep calm and speak slowly so the man could understand him. "Can you find out where she has gone?"

"Yes, easy. My cousin her friend for many year. I ask her."

"Please. As soon as possible. It is very important I find her."

"Why?" The man frowned. "She in trouble? Don't want trouble."

"No, nothing like that." Bill knew it was pointless trying to explain in full so he said, "Tell your cousin to say that Harry is here looking for Lidia. She will understand."

The man thought for a moment. "Okay. But I must visit cousin and take time to find."

Bill produced a note from his pocket and handed it to him. "I will be back tomorrow and I will pay you more if you have news for me."

The man smiled. "Okay, sir. I do my best."

"Thank you."

Bill walked away, hardly daring to hope that such a chance encounter would produce the result he so desperately needed.

47

"I have found her, sir," the flower man informed Bill gravely the next morning.

"Where is she?"

There was a long pause as the man studied his filthy toes. On cue, Bill took two further notes from his pocket and handed them to him.

"I take you there now." The man whistled at the boy on the next stall to keep watch over his own and indicated that Bill should follow him.

"Miss Lidia move now," the flower man explained as he led Bill through a labyrinth of filthy streets. "Her life . . . not good. My cousin say she velly, velly sick. Can't work, can't pay for home."

"What has happened to her?" Bill asked, his heart racing at the thought of what he might find.

"Think you know, sir," the man said glumly. "But I go see her and say Harry here and she velly happy. She say come. You help her, yes? Think she dying."

The flower man had stopped in front of a building, its wooden door half-rotted and patched with planks. As he stepped inside, Bill nearly tripped over a one-legged beggar sitting by the door. He clamped his jaw against the familiar smell of the unwashed and the sick that filled the chokingly hot, airless room. The man led him up some narrow, creaking stairs and knocked on a door.

A murmur answered. The flower man spoke in Thai through the door, eliciting another faint murmur.

"Okay, Mr. Harry. I leave you. She sick. I do not want. Come back when you want to ship flowers."

The man was hurrying down the stairs before Bill could even reply. He took a deep breath, turned the door handle, and walked in. The room was dark, with only small chinks of light coming through the uneven slats of the shutters, the heat in it overpowering.

"Harry?" A weak voice from one corner of the room attracted Bill's attention as he struggled to focus in the gloom. A mattress was on the floor, a small shape lying upon it.

"Harry, is it you? Or do I dream?"

Bill swallowed. He took a step toward the mattress, not wanting to frighten her with his unfamiliar voice until he had reassured her she was safe.

"Harry?"

Bill took another step and another, until he could see her more clearly on the mattress at his feet. Her eyes were closed, her head turned to one side on the white sheet. Bill bent forward and took a moment to take in the perfect, now familiar features. And knew for sure he had found Harry's Lidia.

"Harry, my love," she murmured, "I knew you would come . . . come back for me . . ."

Bill knew he mustn't speak, mustn't break the spell. With a heavy heart, he knelt down beside her and touched her forehead. It was burning hot.

"Harry," she sighed, "I dreamt this. . . . Thank God, thank God, you are here. . . . I love you, Harry, I love you . . ."

Bill stroked her forehead gently, knowing she was only half-conscious, his heart breaking for her.

"Hold me. . . . I so sick, scared. Please hold me . . ."

With tears falling silently down his cheeks, Bill took her tiny, limp frame in his arms and held her, feeling the unnatural heat of infection on her clammy skin.

She let out a small sigh.

"You are here, Harry, you are really here . . . now we are safe."

Bill did not know how long he held Lidia to him. He thought she slept, but occasionally she would jump, perhaps because of a dream or the fever that he could feel burning the life out of her. He had seen it in Changi and knew where it led.

Perhaps he slept too, drugged by the heat in the room, feeling instinctively that so long as he held this poor, broken girl in his arms, she would stay alive.

Eventually, unable to stay crouching any longer, Bill lay her gently back on the mattress. He stood up stiffly and turned to look for any water he could use to moisten her forehead to try to cool her.

Then he heard the sound. It came from the far side of the mattress, beyond Lidia, who was lying deathly still.

In the half-light, the sheet moved, and Bill jumped.

He walked round to the other side of the mattress and saw the sheet move again, and another sound came from beneath it. He crouched down, his heart beating hard against his chest, and tentatively pulled it back.

A pair of bright, amber eyes stared back at him. Then they creased with displeasure, and the perfect miniature mouth pouted. And the silence was immediately filled with the indignant cry of a newborn baby, hungry for milk.

"I had already guessed, of course, the reason Lidia had gone into hiding." Giselle sighed as Bill sat in her office, holding the now-sated baby in his arms. "She was always so slim, but I noticed she had filled out. Here in Thailand, to be unmarried and with child is the worst possible disgrace. But I also knew I could not ask her unless she chose to tell me."

"Thank goodness I found her, ma'am. She was in a terrible state, hardly conscious." Bill took a hefty gulp of the brandy Giselle had poured him when he'd arrived back at the hotel. He noticed the glass shook as he brought it to his mouth. He had seen a lot during the war, but he knew it would be a long time before the past few hours stopped haunting him.

After the shock of finding the baby, its constant crying had dragged Bill from his heat-induced torpor. He took the tiny thing with him and ran from the house, back to the market. The flower man was reticent at first, but the exchange of further notes elicited the appearance of the ancient truck he used for transporting his orchids from the warehouse: it would now take Lidia to the medical attention she so urgently needed.

"It is a miracle you found her when you did." Giselle looked at Bill with concern. "How was she when you left her at the hospital?"

"She was unconscious . . . very sick. I don't know what's wrong with her. I couldn't understand what the doctors were saying, you see. She was on a drip in her arm and oxygen when I left. And, ma'am, when I lifted her off the mattress to carry her downstairs to the truck, there was blood everywhere. . . ." Bill's voice tailed off. "She was soaked in it . . . I mean, from where the baby had come from. I don't know whether she'll make it, really I don't." Bill caught his breath and swallowed hard. "At least she's being taken care of now, not alone in that room."

"Do they know how old the baby is? It looks pretty small to me." Giselle eyed the bundle asleep in Bill's arms.

"Her cord's not dropped off yet, so I'd say only a few days. The doctors checked her over, then handed her to me. I think they thought I was . . . her dad." Bill blushed and looked down at the baby. "I don't know a lot about these babies, more used to calves on the farm, but this little one seems fine and healthy to me. She's certainly hungry for her grub, that's for sure."

"And she's beautiful." Giselle's eyes softened. "Beautiful."

"Yes. She is." Bill's eyes misted over as he glanced down at the baby. "But tell me, ma'am, where do I go from here? What do I do with her?"

"Mr. Stafford, please, I really couldn't tell you. Perhaps for now, while Lidia is so ill, you must take care of her baby. And then, when she is well, decisions can be made."

"Excuse me for saying, but I know nothing about babies. What do I do with the . . . mess she makes? They changed and fed her at the hospital, but"—Bill wrinkled his nose—"I can smell she's not clean now."

"I'm sure we can find some toweling napkins and milk. She can sleep with you in your room—we have a bassinet somewhere in the store . . ."

"And what if Lidia doesn't get well, ma'am? What do I do then?" Bill knew the shock was getting to him. He felt fearful, panicked, and unprepared to be responsible for a newborn.

Giselle sighed. "Really, Mr. Stafford, that is not a decision I can have a part in making. Lord Crawford—perhaps he should be told?"

"No, ma'am, I can't do that. We agreed there should be no contact, in case it was intercepted. If her Ladyship ever heard about this . . ."

Bill cast his eyes down at the baby. "They're expecting one of their own soon."

"Lord Crawford has been a busy boy, hasn't he?" Giselle raised an eyebrow. "*Alors!* It is left to you to clear up his mess."

"I'd put it more kindly than that," Bill replied defensively. "He couldn't help falling in love. And it's clear as the stars in the sky Lidia still loves him." Bill hesitated, a little overcome. "She thought I was Harry, that I'd come back for her, just as his Lordship had promised. I felt right guilty not saying I wasn't and all, but I didn't want to upset her any further. She was that ill. Oh, dearie me"—he gulped—"you're right, ma'am; what a mess, what a bloody mess."

Bill drained his brandy and the two of them sat in silence, lost in their own thoughts.

"It is so very sad," sighed Giselle eventually. "This little one is yet another casualty of the chaos and pain this war has left behind. But, Mr. Stafford, you must think practically. If Lidia does not recover, there are orphanages here who take such children."

Bill shuddered. "Let's hope she does recover. Mind you, then I'll have to explain to her that she will never see his Lordship again, that he is married already, with a babe on the way in England."

"I do not envy you, Mr. Stafford. But I am sure you will handle it well. Please tell Lidia, when you see her, that I send my love. And now I will organize some more milk for that bottle, napkins, and a bassinet."

"Thank you." Bill stood up, the baby in his arms, feeling exhausted from the trauma of the day. "I am grateful for all your help, ma'am."

Giselle followed him toward the door. "My dear Mr. Stafford, we must all do the little we can."

In the following week, Bill had no choice but to learn fast how to care for Lidia's baby. Laor, the cheerful, capable Thai maid who cleaned his room every day, proved invaluable. She showed him how to feed, wind, and change the baby and giggled when she watched Bill fumbling with the napkin pin. He began to know the baby's routine, understanding she cried when she was wet or hungry or had something Giselle called colic—often at five in the morning. He took pleasure in relieving her pain, patting her back until she burped, feeling her tiny body go slack and her little head fall contentedly onto his shoulder. Then he would crawl back into bed, exhausted, and wake only when the baby cried for her next feeding at around eight.

He visited Lidia in the hospital every morning, taking the baby with him. She was still unconscious, her temperature raging, and the nurses looked at him with sympathy as he changed and fed the baby on a mat by her bed. Giselle asked her Thai deputy manager to telephone the hospital and speak to a doctor. Bill learned that Lidia had suffered a serious hemorrhage after the birth. The doctor said the prognosis was not good. Lidia was still bleeding, and infection had taken hold in her womb. She was on powerful medication to stem the infection, but, at present, she was not responding.

Bill sat with her, using the cloth placed in the bowl of water by her bed to cool her burning forehead, but it seemed such an inadequate gesture. Sometimes she stirred, opened her eyes for a few seconds, then closed them. He knew she was unaware that he and the baby were there.

Bill was getting desperate. His ship sailed for England in three days, and he had no idea what he should do if she didn't regain consciousness before he left. He did know, however, that she would be in no fit state to care for her child for many weeks to come.

Laor had shown him how to settle the baby in a Thai-style sling, and Bill set off with the baby in the sling to spend the afternoons with Priyathep, the flower man. Together they visited the main flower market in Bangkok, choosing the plants Bill wished to take back to England with him.

As they trundled through Bangkok's hot, crowded streets, Bill learned from his new friend about caring for and cultivating orchids. He knew this knowledge would prove invaluable. Priyathep's family had been growing orchids in their nursery in Chiang Mai for three generations, gathering them from the mountainous jungles that surrounded their village. Priyathep had promised to ship any new species they found in the future straight to Wharton Park.

During these expeditions, the baby slept peacefully against Bill's chest, only crying if she was hungry or dirty. Bill felt foolish and self-conscious at first, but was surprised how soothing he found the warmth of her tiny body against his.

"She nice baby," Priyathep said one day. "No trouble. You good daddy."

Bill had felt a surge of pride.

"You *are* good, and right beautiful, sweetheart," Bill murmured as he proficiently changed her one night, her amber eyes staring up at him with such trust it made his heart break. He picked her up from the bed and kissed the top of her dark, downy head. He rocked her gently and she snuggled into his shoulder. "What am I going to do with you, little one?" he sighed in despair as he laid her down in her bassinet. She looked at him, and perhaps it was his imagination, but he was sure she smiled, before bringing her fist up to her mouth and sucking it for comfort as she closed her eyes.

With two days left before his ship sailed, and Lidia still unconscious, Bill knew he had to start making plans.

"Do you know of a kind family who would take her here in Bangkok?" he asked Priyathep, as they began the delicate task of packing the orchids into crates.

"No. People here too many babies. Not enough money or food. Mummy die, baby go to home for orphan," Priyathep stated bluntly.

Bill sighed. "Do you know of one?"

"I know, yes, but not nice place, Mr. Bill. Too many baby, maybe four in one cot. Smell too." Priyathep wrinkled his nose. "Baby get sick there and die. No good." He eyed the baby, who was sleeping in a shallow crate lined with a blanket while Bill worked. "No future for her here if Mummy die."

After a sleepless night, Bill went to the hospital as usual and found a smiling nurse by Lidia's bed. She pointed and said something in Thai. Bill saw Lidia's eyes were wide open, looking enormous in her thin, gray face. His heart skipped a beat—he hadn't expected this and was unprepared. Lidia's eyes focused on him and immediately filled with fear.

"Who are you?" The voice was weak and hoarse. "Where Harry? Did I dream he come to me? Why you have my baby? Give her to me!" Her arms struggled toward the baby, tightly held against Bill's chest in her sling.

The nurse turned and comforted Lidia in Thai, then helped remove the baby from the sling and settle her in the crook of one of Lidia's arms.

Lidia fired questions at the nurse and the woman answered while Bill stood by, powerless. He knew the moment had come. He would have served another year in Changi rather than face it.

When the nurse had left, Lidia turned to Bill, her eyes blazing with anger.

"Why you tell nurse you are father of baby? You are not! Who are you? Tell me!"

"I swear, I didn't say that, Miss Lidia. I can't speak Thai anyway. I think they just *thought* I was because I brought you here. I'm Bill Stafford, Lord Harry's friend. He sent me to Bangkok to find you."

"Harry? He is . . . not here?" The fear and anger drained from Lidia's eyes and they filled with tears. "But I saw him, he came to me . . . he held me . . . I . . ."

"Lidia, it was me that came to your room. Harry isn't here. He's in England. I'm sorry, really I am, but there it is."

"No, no, I see him . . . I fight to stay alive for him . . . he came back for us," she moaned, closing her eyes as tears nudged from the corners and down her cheeks.

"Lidia, I—he loves you. He loves you so much. You mean the world to him, really you do."

"Then why he not here now? He promise, he promise me he return to me," she moaned quietly.

"His father died. He has to run his family estate in England. He would be here if he could, I swear." Bill knew everything he said was a feeble, unworthy attempt to comfort a woman who could never be comforted.

"He will come soon?" Lidia asked, her voice no more than a whisper, now that her small burst of energy was spent.

"He can't come here, Miss Lidia. That's why he sent me."

"Then you are here to take us to England . . ."

Bill could see she was fading. "You get some rest, Miss Lidia," he said, reaching for her hand. "I'll stay right here with you. We'll have a chat later and I'll tell you everything."

"He will come. He love me . . . he love me . . ."

Lidia's voice tailed off as she fell asleep.

For the next two hours, Bill sat by Lidia's bedside, his heart breaking at the sight of her reunited with her daughter and dreaming of a future that could never be theirs. When the baby woke, hungry, Lidia slept on; Bill eased her from Lidia's arms, fed and changed her, and put her gently back.

When the sunset cast an eerie, sienna glow through the windows of the ward, Lidia stirred. A nurse appeared with a doctor and indicated that Bill should leave.

Outside, Bill bought himself a beer and a bowl of noodles and sat on the steps of the hospital to eat. Despite his years of suffering at Changi, he doubted he had ever felt so hopeless. And alone.

An hour later, Bill was allowed back onto the ward. Lidia was propped up on pillows, looking painfully fragile, but her eyes were more alert, her countenance calm.

"Please, Mr. Bill, sit down." She indicated a chair. "The doctor tell me you very kind. You bring me here, take care of my baby, and visit every day. He say you good man."

"I've done my best, Miss Lidia. And she"—Bill indicated the baby nestled in her mother's arms—"is a sweetheart."

Lidia smiled down at the baby. "You think she look like her daddy?"

Bill thought she looked just like her mother, but he nodded anyway. "Yes, she does. And all this time, I've wanted to know, what is her name?"

"Jasmine. Her name Jasmine. Harry, he tell me his mother grow it in garden in England. It grow here too. It is beautiful plant with beautiful smell."

"I love it too, miss. And it's a fine name."

"I hope Harry will like it. And you are Bill . . . ? "

"Stafford, Miss Lidia. I was in Changi with Lord Harry. We got each other through, really. . . ." Bill grimaced at the memory. "But, at home in England, I'm his gardener."

"Gardener?" Lidia raised an eyebrow. "He send gardener to find me?"

"He knew he could trust me, Miss Lidia. I'd do anything for him, really I would."

Lidia's eyes softened. "Yes, he very special man. I cannot wait to see him and show him our baby. I understand now from his letters he cannot come here. His father die. So, you come to find me and to take me to Harry in England, yes?"

"Lidia, I—"

"But I cannot go to England now, Mr. Bill." Lidia shook her head. "Doctor tell me there is much damage inside me from baby, I must have immediate operation. Before, they cannot make, as I too ill and they think I die anyway. They say maybe many weeks before I okay. *If* I okay. So, we must wait before I can go on long journey."

Bill swallowed hard. He knew how brave she was being, how ill she really was. "Miss—I mean, Lidia—I . . ."

He faltered and she read the dread in his eyes.

"What is it?"

"Oh, miss, I don't know how to tell you. I'm . . ."

"He does not want me anymore?" Her face was alight with pain.

"No, he loves you, miss, more than anything. It's not that . . . I—"

"If he loves me, everything is okay, so you must tell me, Mr. Bill, what has happened to my poor Harry." She looked at him, her implacable belief in mutual, undying love giving her a stoic resolve that only made Bill feel more inadequate.

"Perhaps I should come back after your operation, when you're feeling stronger. I don't think it's right to tell you now."

"Mr. Bill, I have nearly die. And I may die in operation, or after. Doctor already tell me this. It is tomorrow. There is no time. So, you must tell everything now. Please, Mr. Bill, I must know."

"I—oh, miss . . ."

Lidia reached out a small, shaking hand toward him in comfort. "I see it is bad. I am prepared. Do not worry. I know he love me and that is all that matters. Tell me, please."

So Bill—who seemed to have such paltry inner strength compared to the woman whose life he was shattering—did so. He spoke the words he had dreaded and watched as her face betrayed no emotion, though her hands clenched and unclenched in despair. Then Bill looked at the tiny, precious testament to Lidia's overwhelming love, lying asleep in her arms. And knew he could not tell her the whole story and announce the news of his Lordship's other imminent arrival, far away in England.

"So, there it is. Harry is married, and with his father gone, he has all the responsibility resting on his shoulders. I can't tell you how sorry I am, for both of you, Miss Lidia. He meant to come back to you, really he did, was going to tell his wife everything and ask for a divorce. But even he knows now he can't. He told me to tell you he'll love you forever. Believe me, Miss Lidia, he's right miserable, he is, just like you are. I am . . . so sad for both of you."

Lidia stared straight ahead; catatonic.

"Does he know of baby?" she eventually asked in a whisper.

"No. He doesn't."

Lidia nodded. Bill could see her thinking.

"He cannot have me. Even if I live."

"No, Miss Lidia, with the best will in the world, he can't."

"Maybe he have his child, if he knew?"

Bill knew the answer, but Lidia's face was becoming grayer by the second. "Oh, miss, I doubt it," he replied feebly.

"I want you to ask him if he take our child." She reached for Bill suddenly and tugged his sleeve. "I want you send telegram tonight. Ask him. Please, Mr. Bill, you must. I have no time, I must decide what is best for Jasmine while I can." The urgency was mining all her strength; her hand fell from Bill's arm and she closed her eyes. "I do not matter. I have looked at death already, and maybe it is destiny I will leave this earth soon. But our child . . . our baby . . . should not suffer. Harry will not let that happen. I know he would not. You must take her to him . . . take her to her father . . ."

Bill swallowed hard. He did not have the courage to tell her that what she was suggesting was impossible.

Lidia opened her eyes and looked down at her daughter.

"She deserve a life, Mr. Bill. Even if I live, I cannot take care of her well. Give her what she need. I have no home, or work or money now. I must let her go to England with you. Then she have chance."

"Miss Lidia," croaked Bill, "the babe needs her mum. I think—"

"I think I may die and baby have no one to take care." She kissed the top of Jasmine's head and held the baby's miniature copy of her hand in her own small one. Her eyes, bright with unshed tears, met Bill's. "You take her now, please. It is for best. If I keep her with me longer, maybe I cannot"—Lidia's voice finally broke—"give her away."

She leaned down and whispered to Jasmine, murmuring words Bill did not understand and didn't want to. He knew she was saying good-bye.

Her body shaking with the effort, Lidia attempted to lift her baby up and hand her to him. Bill reached forward and took Jasmine into his arms, as tears rolled, unchecked and silent, down Lidia's face.

"Keep her safe, Mr. Bill, please, keep her safe. I believe you are good man. I must trust in you and her father now, for I do not know if my future is here on earth. But it is not important. Jasmine is future, not me. Please, Mr. Bill, find way to tell me my daughter is safe. If I live, I must know this."

"I will. I'll write to Priyathep, the flower man." Bill's voice quavered with emotion as he uttered promises he had no idea if he could honor. "I'll keep Jasmine safe, Miss Lidia, don't you worry."

"*Kop khun ka.* And tell both of them, I love them, more than stars in sky, and they are blessing on my life from God."

Lidia reached out for the last time to touch her baby, her arm so weak it failed to reach Jasmine and dropped back onto the bed. "Tell them I see them both again. Because"—she looked up at Bill and gave him a smile that lit up her face, granting him a sudden flash of her true beauty—"love never die, Mr. Bill. It never die."

48

One day in April, Bill appeared out of the blue on Elsie's doorstep.

"Bill! Oh, Bill! Why didn't you tell me you was arriving today? I'd have come to Felixstowe to meet you!" Elsie made to hug him, but then saw he was carefully holding something wrapped in a blanket. She eyed it suspiciously. "What have you got there?"

"Let's go inside, shall we, sweetheart?" said Bill wearily. "Then I can put her down and take you in my arms instead."

Elsie closed the door behind him. As he lay the bundle down, it started to stir.

"Oh, sweetheart, I've missed you so bad. Have you missed me?" asked Bill.

Elsie's eyes were still focused on the bundle. "Course I've missed you, but never mind. What is *that*?"

Bill glanced at her nervously. "I decided to bring you home a present. I took a chance it was the right thing to do. But then"—Bill sighed—"I didn't have much choice, as it happened. Go on, go and look at her. She's a little angel, she is."

Elsie walked tentatively toward the bundle, shaking with shock. She peeled the blanket away, and a pair of beautiful amber eyes stared up at her.

"Oh, Bill!" Elsie caught her breath and put her hands to her flushed cheeks. "She's beautiful! Whose is she?"

"Elsie, she's *ours*. I brought you home a baby girl."

"But"—Elsie was so flummoxed she didn't know what to say—"she must belong to somebody? Bill Stafford! I know you and you're not telling me the whole story."

The baby was starting to cry now. "Oh, you poor little mite! Come here." Elsie picked her up and cradled her in her arms, studying the honey-colored skin, the perfect, tiny nose, and the shock of dark hair.

"Hush, hush, little one." She stuck her finger in the baby's mouth to comfort her. "How old is she?"

"Just over two weeks when I left, so about seven weeks now."

"But how did a big brute like you care for her on the ship? He don't know the first thing about babies, does he now?" Elsie said to the baby, feeling herself falling in love, but wanting to be sure she was free to do so.

"We've done pretty well, me and her. She's ever so good, hardly murmurs," Bill said proudly, and Elsie saw the love shining in her husband's eyes.

"Bill Stafford, I knows this isn't all it seems. You'd better tell me fast."

He came behind Elsie and put his arms round her shoulders. "I've done the right thing, haven't I, sweetheart? Just look at her. She's perfect."

"I . . . Bill! I don't know what to say! Really I don't." Elsie shook her head. "You turning up here, bold as brass, with a baby!" Then her face darkened and she felt light-headed with painful emotions. "Is there something you're not telling me, Bill? What did you get up to when you got out of Changi?"

"Oh, Else, my Else!" Bill pulled her face close to his to kiss her. "Don't be so daft! I was back here with you long before this little mite was a twinkle in her daddy's eye!"

Elsie's eyes glazed over and she was reduced to counting the months on her fingers, before a smile of relief spread across her face.

"You're right, Bill, I'm being silly. Besides, we both know you can't be the daddy. But are you sure this is legal and all? No one's going to bang on the door in the middle of the night and cart you off to prison for baby-stealing, are they? And take this little one away?"

"I swear it's legal. She's ours Elsie, our child. And no one is ever going to take her away from us, I promise."

"What's your name?" Elsie cooed to the baby.

"Her mother called her Jasmine. But we can change it if you'd like to."

"Jasmine . . . well, I think that's just right, considering her . . .

Pa"—Elsie tasted the word on her tongue with relish—"grows beautiful flowers."

"And I've brought home crateloads of them too, sweetheart."

Elsie looked up at Bill. "She's a baby from Thailand, isn't she?" Elsie stroked the soft skin of Jasmine's forearm.

"Well, there's a story behind her, and if you'll stop fussing over the babe for a few seconds and make your husband a nice strong brew, I'll tell you exactly how it happened."

Armed with a cup of tea, Bill related the sorry tale to his wife.

"You understand, don't you, that I didn't have no choice? You'd have done the same with her, wouldn't you?"

"Yes, Bill, and you knows I would too."

"Thank God," he breathed, never loving or admiring his wife more than he did at this very moment. "But you know too, that for all our sakes, her Ladyship must never know?"

"Course I do, silly," Elsie murmured, all her pent-up maternal instincts releasing into a warm, contented glow as she rocked her new child in her arms. "And I'll never breathe a word, if it means we can keep this little treasure forever." She looked up at him. "But will you do like this Lidia asked, and tell his Lordship the truth?"

"Lidia's written him a letter." Bill sighed. "It was waiting for me at the hospital the very last time I went to visit her. She was having her operation so I didn't get to see her. She left me an orchid too—said in the note it was special and for the baby to remember her by. No blooms on it yet, but—"

"Oh, Bill, stop fussing about them flowers of yours and tell me what you're going to do with the letter for his Lordship!"

"To be honest, Else, I don't know."

"As sure as eggs are eggs, it'll only stir things up if you give it to him. What if he wants our baby for himself? I'd let sleeping dogs lie, if I were you."

Bill kissed the new mother and her baby. "Tell you what, Else, I'll pop off down the hothouse to have a think."

Bill sat on a crate of orchids, took Lidia's letter from his pocket, and looked at it. He had no idea what it said. It wasn't his business. His eyes still welled up every time he thought about the moment Lidia handed over her baby to him without a word of self-pity, though the pain was visible in her beautiful amber eyes.

As he held the letter in his hands, Bill thought of the passion the lovers had shared and the tragedy of the situation. For all he knew, Lidia was dead. Surely there was no risk if he did pass the letter on? Nothing could be done anyway. His Lordship knew where his duty lay, which was why he had sent Bill to find Lidia in the first place. He would want to know what had happened to her, and perhaps it was best if those answers came from Lidia herself, the woman Harry loved. He might take comfort from having proof of their love living right here at Wharton Park. If he wanted to come down to the cottage occasionally to see his little girl as she grew up, then what would be the harm?

As long as her Ladyship never knew . . .

Harry would never tell her, that was for sure.

Ignoring his wife's sensible advice and simply remembering that he was a mere messenger in this whole drama, Bill hastily secreted the letter in the usual place under the orchids for his Lordship to find.

Then he turned his attention to the crates and started unpacking and sorting his precious plants.

Olivia, who was now eight weeks away from her own child's birth, heard of the new arrival from Elsie that afternoon. She was invited down to the cottage to see the baby and saw the joy in Elsie's eyes.

"She is utterly beautiful," Olivia breathed as the baby grasped her finger and gurgled. "What have you called her?"

"Jasmine, your Ladyship."

"Perfect!" Olivia exclaimed, smiling at Elsie. "I told you life had a way of sorting things out, didn't I?"

"Yes, your Ladyship, you did. And it has, hasn't it? For all of us."

On her way back to the house, Olivia paused outside the hothouse. She had not seen Bill since his return and wanted to congratulate him too on his new arrival and express her admiration for his kindness. Elsie had explained that, in Thailand, many single mothers were too sick or poor to care for their babies, and that Bill had met one such unfortunate girl. When she died in childbirth and her baby was doomed to a grim orphanage, Bill had done the only decent thing and brought the baby home to Elsie, where he knew she would be loved and cherished.

Olivia felt her own baby kick and smiled, secure within the knowledge that her child would not have the same problems as the poor little thing Bill had rescued.

She opened the door to the hothouse and found the floor cluttered with crates of orchids. Bill was not there, but Olivia decided to wait for a few minutes in case he returned. She walked down the rows of flowers, enjoying their wonderful scents, and stopped by the pots of orchids. She picked one up, thinking it would be something beautiful to look at during her forthcoming confinement.

Her attention was caught by an envelope beneath the pot; she picked it up and saw it was addressed to Harry, but with no address or postmark. The writing was unfamiliar, and a small bulge was in one corner of the envelope. Olivia's curiosity got the better of her, and sure the letter contained nothing that Harry would not wish her to see, she opened it.

Moments later, when she had read the few short words three times over, Olivia sank to the floor, panting with shock.

She unwrapped a small wad of paper that had formed the bulge in the envelope and stared down at a tiny amber ring, made for a child's finger.

She swallowed hard to push the lump in her throat back down . . . she would not, could not, cry. This was beyond any relief tears could bring to her.

Olivia tried to make sense of what she had read:

This woman had been deeply in love with her husband. And, presumably, as Harry had apparently asked her to marry him, he with her. He had also promised her he would return to her in Bangkok as soon as he could. When Harry had realized this wasn't possible, he had sent Bill, under false pretenses, to find her. And Bill had come home with what the woman said was her husband's child in his arms.

Bill came into the hothouse.

Olivia struggled to stand up, her knees giving way beneath her.

"Your Ladyship, what are you doing down there? Let me help you."

"No!" She stood and strode toward him, waving the letter at him furiously. "Would you kindly explain to me what *this* is?"

Bill's face filled with horror as he realized what she was holding.

"Your Ladyship—you weren't meant to find it. Please . . ."

"Well, I *have* found it, and if you do not tell me now what on *earth* you and my husband have cooked up between you, I will have you and your wife and that . . . *bastard* off my land instantly! Tell me!"

"Please, remember your condition, your Ladyship, you mustn't upset yourself like this." Bill tried to think quickly. He knew everything was at stake. "It was nothing, really, just a lonely soldier getting confused."

"What? So confused he asked another woman to marry him!" Olivia shook the ring at him. "When he already had a wife at home who had waited patiently for *four long years*!"

"Calm down, your Ladyship, you really must," Bill entreated.

"I will calm down when I know the truth." Olivia was shaking. "Either you tell me, or I will have you *out*!"

"I don't know what she says in the letter, I didn't look . . . I—"

"It says that she loves him, that she will never forget what they had together in Bangkok, and that she 'understands' he cannot honor his vows to her. And that he must take care of her 'gift' to him because she is ill and unable to do so. Oh, *God*!" Olivia shook her head in despair. "And there I was believing he was distant because he was getting over his experiences in Changi. When all along he was pining for some *whore* in Bangkok!" She looked up at Bill. "Is this girl alive? Elsie told me she had died giving birth to my husband's . . . baby." She spat the word out.

"I don't know." Bill found he could not lie. "She might be, your Ladyship, but she was very ill indeed when I left."

"Well"—Olivia ripped up the letter and threw the pieces in the air—"whether she is or not, she is now! And when you see my husband, you tell him she's *dead*. Otherwise, all three of you will be homeless immediately!"

"I swear, I will," replied Bill in desperation. "Whatever you say, your Ladyship."

Olivia paced up and down breathlessly, sweat beading on her brow.

"The child must be taken off the estate at once! At once, do you hear me? She cannot stay here . . . I cannot have my husband's *bastard* growing up at Wharton Park! I will collect her tomorrow morning and take her to—"

"No!" Bill surprised himself with his vehemence. "I'm sorry, your Ladyship, but that child is staying put, with Elsie and me." Bill found he was shaking with emotion too. "Throw the three of us off if you wish, but I promised that poor girl I'd take care of her babe, and that's what I'll do."

"Then you must all be gone by tomorrow morning. Yes, you can all get out! I will not have my husband conspiring secretly with my staff against me!"

"As you wish, your Ladyship," Bill replied, willing himself to recover his calm and say the right thing. "But, with respect, I was on his Lordship's business. And I'm sure he will want to know whether the journey was . . . successful or not. I need not tell him whose the babe is, if that is your wish, but if you make us leave, it would not take long for his Lordship to put two and two together and work out why."

Olivia stopped pacing and stared at Bill silently. "Are you blackmailing me, Bill?"

"No, your Ladyship." Bill did his best to choose his words carefully. "I am stating the facts. Perhaps—perhaps it's best if his Lordship does know the truth. Maybe your Ladyship wants him to know? And account for his actions to you?"

Olivia sank down onto a crate, all the anger suddenly leaving her. She put her head in her hands. "Oh, God . . . what an unutterably dreadful mess."

"Please," Bill coaxed, "you must remember the reason his Lordship sent me to Bangkok; once he was home here, he remembered how much he loved you. And knew he had to stay."

Olivia looked up at him, her face taut with despair. "Don't patronize me, Bill. Harry has *never* loved me! And he never will. He is a pathetic, inadequate, weak man, whom I despise with all my heart." She took a few deep breaths, struggling to compose herself. "At least he's not here. He is in London until tomorrow, seeing the bank. I presume you have not spoken to him yet?"

"No, your Ladyship," Bill said quietly.

"Well, that's something. And he knows nothing presently about the child?"

"No. We had no contact while I was away."

"You swear you are speaking the truth, Bill?" Olivia eyed him.

"I am, your Ladyship. He would have known if he had read that letter, but he won't now, will he?" Bill hung his head in shame. "It's my fault, my Elsie told me it was wrong to give it to him. She's always right, she is," he added, almost in a whisper.

"She is a very sensible girl and you are lucky to have her. She will never say a word about this?"

"Never," Bill replied adamantly. "You know how she's longed for a babe of her own. She'd do nothing to put that in jeopardy."

"No. And, of course, you are right"—Olivia's eyes softened for a second—"this is not the child's fault. So be it. But, Bill, his Lordship must never know. I could not bear him mooning over some half-caste brat down the road, when he has his own child to love . . . even if he cannot love his wife," she added pitifully. She looked at Bill, her composure finally returning. "You must promise me that when you speak to his Lordship, you will say nothing of the child, only that her mother is *dead.* And that will be an end to it. The future of Wharton Park, and all of us who are part of it, is at stake. Do you understand me, Bill?"

"I do, your Ladyship."

"I will speak to Elsie, and tell her I know. I will not be made a fool of by my own maid. And the three of us will keep this secret until the day we die."

"Yes, your Ladyship," Bill agreed gravely.

"Then that is settled." Olivia held up her head and walked past him toward the door. She paused, then turned back to him. "Please know I do not blame you, Bill. You were merely doing as you were bid. My husband, poor fool that he is, has little understanding of what you have done for him. You have been a loyal and faithful servant. And I bear you no grudge."

She gave him a short smile and left the hothouse.

The following day, when Harry returned from London and heard that Bill was home, he excused himself from lunch, saying he was keen to see the specimens Bill had brought back with him. Olivia accepted this excuse, aware of his true motives, but taking some small satisfaction from knowing all the facts herself.

Bill did as he had been asked; he lied for the sake of Wharton Park and all who depended on it. He told Harry that Lidia had died some weeks before he arrived in Bangkok, that he had visited her grave and laid orchids upon it. Then he held Harry in his arms as he wept uncontrollably for his lost love.

When Harry was calmer, Bill mentioned the baby girl he had rescued from an orphanage and said Harry must come to the cottage to see her, when he felt better.

"Of course, Bill, one day soon," Harry agreed, not really listening, then stumbling out of the hothouse, despair leaking from his every pore.

Olivia had not expected her husband to come to her that night, and he didn't. At breakfast the following morning, she was back in control, thinking of her baby and of Wharton Park. But her heart had closed to Harry forever. She watched him at the far end of the table, saw his drawn face betraying his inner agony, and knew Bill had done as he had promised.

Olivia read her husband's grief on his face and found she felt . . . nothing. No longer would she be hurt by his lack of interest in or affection toward her. Instead, she reveled silently in his pain.

Only two days later, she was suffering her own pain.

The doctor was called, and although he did what he could to prevent the onset of Olivia's labor, a few hours later a perfect, tiny boy made his premature entrance into the world.

Christopher Harry James Crawford, heir to the Wharton Park estate, died three days later, after a valiant struggle to hold on to life.

And although Harry tried, once his wife had recovered, to come back into her bed, Olivia had no further physical contact with her husband until the day he died.

49

Wharton Park

I sit in the library, trying to make sense of the story I have just heard. A tragic story of love, deception, and pain—a story of which I seem to be the direct result.

Harry Crawford is my grandfather . . . I have Crawford blood running through my veins. . . . My mother was half-Thai, brought from the other side of the world. . . . Elsie and Bill are not related to me by blood . . . and I am, somehow, but just now I can't fathom how, related to Kit. . . .

Yet, even though the things I've heard have been shocking and revelatory, I find I am calm. This house, Wharton Park, has always been a part of me, yet I have never known why. It is simply the place where I have always felt I belonged. I know now that three hundred years of my ancestors have lived within these walls. Their essence must have soaked into the very fabric of the building.

Wharton Park and the Crawford family—my family—are inextricably linked. The house reaches out, drawing us back, demanding we return. It is as if the house owns us all, and there is no escape. Even a tiny baby girl, born many thousands of miles away, a child who should not have been born at all, was claimed by and restored to it.

My mother, Jasmine, the only direct bloodline of her generation, born illegitimately in the chaotic aftermath of war, never aware of her heritage or legal right to the house, still flourished secretly on its very soil. And, once she was safely reclaimed, she left behind further Crawfords; one of whom, with a dash of fate and chance, now finds herself back within the walls of the house.

The stark truth suddenly dawns on me. But does it comfort or frighten me?

Wharton Park does not belong to the Crawfords.

We belong to it.

• • •

Julia felt the tension in her body, looked down and saw she was clutching Kit's hand tightly. She glanced over at Elsie's gray, drawn face.

Eventually Kit broke the silence. "If I've got it right, Julia and I are technically third cousins?"

Elsie managed to nod. "Yes, Kit, you are."

"And did Harry ever discover that the little girl growing up a few hundred yards away from him was Lidia's daughter?"

"Well, Bill and I kept our promise to her Ladyship and didn't say a word to no one. Harry never set foot in the kitchen garden or the hothouses again. It saddened Bill terrible, it did, that the bond they'd formed between them in Changi was broken. He understood, though, that his Lordship didn't want anything to do with what reminded him of Lidia. I don't believe he set eyes on his daughter for over twenty years. Until one day, when he knew he was dying, he turned up on our doorstep." Elsie turned to Julia. "Your mother opened the door to him. He must have seen then, for Bill always said that Jasmine had grown up the image of her mother. Anyways," Elsie shrugged, "his Lordship came inside, looking like he'd seen a ghost. I think then he knew for certain who she was."

"Must have been one hell of a shock for him," murmured Kit.

"Yes," Elsie agreed, "the poor man was shaking. I had him sit down and made him coffee with plenty of sugar. And even though he was talking to me about wanting Bill to have his Changi diary, his eyes never left Jasmine. She'd just come back from the hothouses, where she'd been painting some of her dad's orchids. His Lordship saw them on the kitchen table and asked her about them."

Tears appeared in Elsie's eyes at the memory, and Kit let go of Julia's hand so that she could go over to the old lady and put an arm round her. "Elsie, if this all too much for you . . ."

"No," Elsie said firmly, "I've started and I want to finish. Anyway, his Lordship asked Jasmine if he could have her paintings, because he liked them so much. She said yes, and then he kissed her and said good-bye. And that"—Elsie lowered her head, swallowing hard—"was the last time I ever saw poor Harry alive."

"It was probably best that he didn't know until right at the end. For Jasmine too," Kit comforted.

"That's as maybe, but I'll not forget the look on his face as he left. He was only forty-eight or so, but seemed years older. He didn't have much of a life, did his Lordship. He and her Ladyship were married in name only. The shock of finding out about Jasmine, then losing her own baby, meant Olivia was never the same again. Even though I loved her, she turned from a sweet girl into a bitter old woman. Harry got no comfort from her, that's for sure. I've often said it; I really believe he died of a broken heart."

"So that's how those four paintings ended up in the Sale of Contents here a few months back?" Kit said with a flourish, looking at Julia.

Julia didn't reply, her mind still in turmoil.

"And Jasmine never knew who her real mother and father were?" Kit asked.

Elsie shook her head defensively. "No. What good would have come of it, for any of us? Oh"—she yawned—"pardon me, this tale-telling is taking its toll." She looked at Julia. "Are you all right, my love? It must be a terrible shock, all this. But at least your mum was your mum and your dad was your dad, even if I'm not your blinking granny. I've always loved you just like I was, mind."

"I know you have, Granny," Julia rallied.

"Well, it was a terrible secret to keep for all those years, but you do what you need to. And that's what Bill and I did."

Kit's thoughts were not clouded with emotion, leaving him free to grasp the ramifications of what he had been told. "But surely this means that Alicia, as your older sister, is more of a direct heir to the Wharton Park estate than I am? Of course, as a woman, she could never carry the title, but she might have a claim to the actual estate."

"No, Alicia wouldn't." Elsie shook her head wearily. "But that's for another time. I think I need some shut-eye." She made to stand up and Kit assisted her.

"Thank you, Kit. You're a real gentleman, a proper Crawford." She smiled, put her arm through Kit's, and he walked with her across the room. Elsie paused in front of Julia, who was still sitting immobile on the sofa. "I'm sorry, my love," Elsie said softly. "I've agonized over whether to tell you or not. But seeing that fate has led you back to Wharton Park, and Kit, I thought it was the right thing to do. I hope it was."

Julia roused herself, stood up too, and put her arms round her grandmother's shoulders. "Yes, it was. And I'm really grateful to you for doing it."

Kit and Julia stood side by side and watched Elsie leave the room.

"Do you think I should go up with her?" asked Julia.

Kit shook his head. "I get the feeling she wants time by herself." He let out a sigh, which turned into a whistle. "Fancy a brandy? I think I could do with one after hearing that lot."

Julia shook her head. "No thanks." She sat down abruptly on the sofa as Kit took a decanter from a cupboard under the bookshelves and poured himself a drink.

"The one question I want to ask Elsie is whether your real grandmother is still alive. If Lidia was only seventeen when Harry met her, and that was in 1945, that would make her, what, eighty now? There is a chance she could still be living." Kit sat down on the sofa next to Julia and wrapped an arm round her shoulder. "Lidia must have really been something for Harry to be prepared to give up everything for her. *And*, my darling, we now know where you inherited your talent for the piano from: your grandfather Harry."

That was a connection Julia hadn't yet made, and she laid her head on Kit's shoulder, thanking God that the blood ties between them were no closer than third cousins. "Yes, perhaps," she murmured.

Kit glanced up at the cracks in the ceiling. "Of course, the moral of this sorry tale is that duty won over love. I feel extraordinarily lucky I'm not in Harry's position. I can understand why he felt he had no choice."

"It's Olivia that I feel sorry for. She knew from the start what had happened, but put the future of Wharton Park above her own feelings. No wonder she was bitter"—Julia sighed—"her whole adult life, unloved and betrayed."

"Yes." Kit took a sip of his brandy. "I'm only sorry now that I didn't pay her more attention when I was here on the holidays. I presumed she was just a dried-up, sour old woman."

"Having lost her own child, it must have been very painful to see my mother growing up on the estate, knowing she was Harry's daughter."

"Life is so terribly sad, isn't it?" Kit sighed and hugged Julia to him. "That's why I'm of the belief that one should seize the day. Now, perhaps, after all this excitement, we should wend our way upstairs?"

Julia agreed, and they walked together to the entrance hall. Julia sat on the stairs as Kit went about the nightly task of switching off all the lights and locking the doors. He came to sit on the stair next to her. "You okay, sweetheart?" he asked, reaching for her hand.

"Yes." She nodded.

"Granddaughter of a gardener one minute, then a lord the next!" Kit teased her gently. "Mind you, rest assured you're not the first, nor will you be the last. I could name you half a dozen aristocratic families with skeletons in their cupboards. Come on, old girl, time you and I were abed. We have a busy day tomorrow." Kit pulled her to her feet and they walked, hand in hand, up the stairs.

They lay together in bed, Kit's arms wrapped protectively round Julia.

"What I don't understand," Julia spoke into the blackness, "is why Elsie didn't insist that Alicia should hear the story too? After all, it's as much to do with her as it is with me."

"Well," Kit stroked her soft hair, "from what Elsie insinuated tonight, I reckon there are a few more secrets to be told."

Julia was up and about early the next morning, preparing Sunday lunch for her family. Elsie arrived in the kitchen just after nine o'clock, shocked she had slept so late. "It must have been the emotion that did me in," she said as she sat down at the kitchen table. "I'm always on my feet by six."

Julia put a cup of tea in front of Elsie. "Well, I'm sure it won't have done you any harm this once. It's nice for me to look after you for a change."

Elsie eyed Julia nervously. "And . . . how are you feeling about what I told you last night?"

"Now that the shock's worn off, as a matter of fact I'm feeling fine," Julia replied honestly. "I mean, it's not as if you were telling me that my parents weren't my parents, is it?" Julia put a hand on Elsie's shoulders, bent down, and kissed her. "And we may not be related by blood, but that won't change how I feel about you."

Elsie reached for Julia's hands. "Thank you, my love, for taking it so well. After all the shocks you've been through in the last year, I was worried it would be one too many. But I thought you should know. I mean, if you and Kit do get wed at some point, there is a blood tie. There seemed something"—Elsie wrinkled her nose as she thought of the right phrase—"*indecent* about not telling you."

"Thank you. I wouldn't worry though, our genes have been diluted through many generations. Now, I've got bacon and eggs in especially for you. Would you like some?"

Elsie glanced at Julia with affection. "You know I'll never say no to a nice fry-up, my love. Is your dad coming to lunch today?"

"I've left a message asking him, but he hasn't called back yet. He's probably sleeping off his jet lag. He only got home from the States last night."

"Julia." Elsie's face became serious. "I want you to swear to me that neither you or Kit will mention any of what I've told you to Alicia until I've had a word with your dad."

"Of course, if that's what you want. Does Dad know any of this?"

"No, he doesn't, and if you don't mind, I'd like to tell him myself. Explain in my own words why I never told Jasmine."

"Of course. Anyway, please don't let it spoil your day," Julia implored. "Alicia, Max, and the children are due here at half past twelve. And they're so looking forward to seeing you."

"And I them." Elsie nodded. She took a sip of her tea. "Silly of me to be nervous about coming back here, wasn't it? Thought it might bring back bad memories, and, instead, it's brought back all the good." Elsie glanced around the kitchen. "It was like a morgue, mind, after Harry died, and her Ladyship rattled around here by herself. I used to dread coming to work. But now there's new life in the place. It doesn't feel *sad* anymore. Of course, what it needed was two young people in love."

Julia blushed and changed the subject. "I was wondering if you could tell me how long I should cook this beef?" she said, pointing to the joint on the sideboard as she cracked some eggs for Elsie's breakfast into a pan. "I'm not really a very experienced cook, but I'm learning."

"Enthusiasm is all you need, my love." Elsie stood up and walked over to the beef. "First of all, I'll show you how to baste it."

50

Just after twelve thirty, Julia saw Max and Alicia's car coming down the drive. She swung open the heavy front door and went down the steps to greet them.

The children flocked around her in the hall, oohing and aahing over the grandness of their auntie's new residence. Julia shepherded everyone through the house and onto the terrace, where Elsie was waiting for them. Julia saw her face light up as her great-grandchildren clustered around her. When Kit came out with a bottle of champagne, he was introduced to the children, and Julia felt a warm glow as she watched the easy way he talked to them.

After a while, Julia left them all chatting on the terrace and went to attend to her beef. Alicia followed her into the kitchen.

"Anything I can do to help?"

"Yes, keep an eye on those carrots and tell me when they're cooked," said Julia, pouring more oil over her roast potatoes. "I'm truly hopeless with vegetables."

Alicia forked a carrot out of the pan and put it in her mouth. "These are perfect. I'll take them off the boil. Weird to see you cooking." She moved the saucepan onto the hot plate.

"I never had time before, but I'm really enjoying learning. Kit's teaching me."

Alicia folded her arms as she watched Julia. "You know, I still haven't a clue how you two got together. There was I, presuming you were back in France, and two weeks later I see you walking down Holt High Street, with Kit Crawford's arm slung cozily round your shoulder." Alicia's voice had an edge. "You might have told me."

"Yes," replied Julia guiltily, "I should have. I'm sorry. I just . . . well, I wasn't sure what to say. It's hard to explain what happened. You might have thought I was making a rash decision."

"And disapprove?"

"Yes, to be honest."

"Julia, after the hell you've been through, if Kit makes you happy, why on earth should I disapprove?" snapped Alicia. "Honestly, do you really think I'm that judgmental?"

"No . . ." Julia shook her head. "I suppose I was just being selfish, wanting to keep it all to myself for a while, see how things worked out before I broadcast it."

"I presume the baby and his, er, girlfriend, have been dispatched now?"

"That, Alicia, is exactly why I haven't said anything!" Julia shot back. "Annie wasn't his 'girlfriend,' and her baby wasn't his. Kit was simply helping an old friend in her hour of need, whatever the local gossips are still saying. People should mind their own business," she added crossly.

"Julia, for goodness' sake, Kit Crawford is the new owner of Wharton Park, one of the grandest estates in the county! He's local royalty and of course he's going to be gossiped about! And you will be too, if you stay with him, so get used to it! And perhaps, if you'd trusted me with the true version of events, I might have been able to stop some of it, at least. But you didn't. Really, I sometimes wonder what kind of person you think I am." The delicate pink of Alicia's cheeks had turned red with rare anger. "And if you had told me, I'd have been thrilled for you, once I understood the circumstances. I think Kit's a lovely man and completely smitten with you. There aren't many men who would have cared for you like he did when you were so sick. I knew how he felt about you then."

"Did you?" Julia was genuinely surprised.

"Absolutely. And I knew you liked him too, but were just too scared and confused to admit it, which I really understand."

"Oh." Julia drained her glass, feeling churlish for underestimating Alicia. "Anyway, now you do know, perhaps we can see a little more of each other?" she said, as a peace offering.

"Yes, that would be nice. Anyway, let's move on, shall we? Is Dad coming today? I know his flight landed late last night."

"I think so, but he wasn't quite sure what time. He told me not to hold lunch for him. I think he really wants to see Elsie."

"Have you told Dad yet about you and Kit?"

"No. You know what he's like, especially after a research trip; his head's still full of flora and fauna. It wouldn't have sunk in."

"And how's Elsie?" Alicia watched as Julia started stirring the gravy. "Has she told you any more of the story?"

"Not really, no." Julia spoke guardedly, remembering Elsie's plea. "I'm sure she will, but she was very tired last night. Right"—she pulled the joint out of the Aga—"I think this beef is ready, don't you? Could you ask Kit to come in and carve?"

George arrived at the house halfway through the beef, looking tanned and healthy. Julia fetched a warm plate of food for him, and as he ate, George regaled the table with his new discoveries from the Galápagos Islands. When they had all finished, he helped Julia carry the plates into the kitchen.

"Darling," he said as he put them down by the side of the sink, "you look like a different person. Or, in fact, more accurately, like the old Julia. I presume it's that attractive young man of yours who's brought about this transformation?"

"Kit has certainly helped, in all sorts of ways," Julia agreed coyly. "I'm . . . much better."

"Well, haven't had much of a chance to talk to him, but he seems like a nice chap. Is there such a thing as a dishwasher lurking somewhere in this kitchen?"

"No. Far too modern a convenience for this house"—Julia grinned—"so I'm afraid it's elbows-in-the-suds time. I'm living back in the fifties here, Dad. Not that I mind. It's such a beautiful old house."

"It is indeed, and I admit, it's an odd experience being greeted at the front door of Wharton Park by my own daughter, and finding my family on the estate once more." He put the plug in the sink and started running the tap.

"Don't worry about that now, Dad, I'll see to it later. Perhaps you could take the pavlova and the raspberries out for me?" She pointed to them on the kitchen table. "Shop-bought, I'm afraid. My newfound talents don't extend to puds yet."

George picked them up and headed for the door, then paused and turned. "So, you being here at Wharton Park with Kit—do I gather this is a permanent arrangement?"

"Who knows? As you once said to me, Dad, I'm taking one day at a time."

"Good girl, good girl. I'm pleased for you, darling, I really am."

After lunch, Kit rounded up the boys to play football, and Julia took the girls on a tour of the house, a situation she had specifically engineered to leave George and Elsie alone together.

"My goodness." Alicia whistled as they walked down the long upstairs corridors, opening doors to room after room. "This is a huge renovation job. The whole house needs a complete overhaul."

"Well, I like it just the way it is," Julia said defensively.

Back downstairs, Julia made coffee and Alicia took the tray out onto the terrace. Elsie was sitting there alone, eyes closed, enjoying the afternoon sun.

"Where's Dad?" asked Alicia as she sat down.

Elsie opened her eyes slowly. "He sent his apologies, he did, said he only got a couple of hours' sleep last night and wanted to get home before he was too tired to drive. He said he'd give you a call later."

"Poor thing, he must be exhausted," Alicia said, unaware there could be another reason for her father to leave without saying goodbye. "Now, shall I pour coffee?"

When Alicia and Max had taken their brood home for baths and bed, Kit nipped out to check something on the farm, and Julia sat with Elsie, watching the sunset from the terrace.

"I spoke to your dad," Elsie ventured eventually.

"Right."

"What you must understand, Julia," Elsie sighed, "is that when you open up a secret from the past, it's a can of worms. I know you've probably heard that many times before, but, my love, it's true. Because they wriggle out and spread themselves in places you never expected them to."

"It must be hard for you to have to do this, but I'm so glad you have, Granny," Julia replied warmly. "Already, there are things I've never understood about myself that are beginning to fall into place. Speaking of which, Kit wondered whether you knew what happened to Lidia. Did she make it through the operation and could she still be alive?"

"Well now," Elsie said slowly, "I'm going to let you into another little secret. Something that even Bill didn't know. You see, when Bill told me how that poor girl had to hand over Jasmine to him, my heart bled for her, it did. Bill wrote to his friend, the flower man, as he'd promised, to tell him to let Lidia know Jasmine was safe at Wharton Park. Not mentioning, of course, she was living with us in our cottage, and not up at the big house with her dad. Lidia wrote back to him a few weeks later, to say she'd survived the operation and was slowly getting better. Well, I thought it would be nice for her to see some pictures of Jasmine, so I sent some to her. Over the years, we wrote to each other, me always pretending I was the nursemaid looking after Jasmine, so she wouldn't get upset, like."

"What a lovely thing to do." Julia smiled.

"Well, how Lidia could ever have thought Harry's wife would accept his illegitimate child, I really don't know. But if it made her happy to think her girl was being brought up a 'lady,' who was I to disillusion her?" Elsie rubbed her nose. "Maybe they do things differently over in them hot countries."

"It did cross my mind that after Olivia lost her baby, she might have thought about adopting my mother."

"Never in a month of Sundays!" Elsie grimaced. "For a start, it would have been impossible for her to pass Jasmine off as her own, Olivia being so fair and Jasmine being so dark, like. But, more important, she would never have acknowledged her as Harry's child. Olivia knew he was in love with Lidia. She wasn't going to have Jasmine as a daily reminder of that love, was she now? However empty her nest remained."

"No . . . you're right. Of course she wouldn't. Do you and Lidia still communicate, Granny?"

"No. After your mum died, I didn't write no more. Couldn't bring myself to tell her. As we both know, mothers never get over losing a child. . . ." Elsie's voice trailed off. "So, in answer to your question, I've no idea if Lidia is still alive."

"No," Julia answered quietly.

"Oh, dearie me," Elsie sighed, "it's no good thinking the past is in the past: it carries on, it does, and by telling you and Kit what I have, it meant that your dad was faced with a decision too. I can only hope I've done the right thing."

"Well, whatever it is, I'm sure we're a strong enough family to take it."

Elsie reached for Julia's hand and patted it. "Yes, my love, I think we are."

51

Three days later, Kit drove Julia to Stansted airport. Julia could easily have taken a taxi, but Kit had insisted. One way and another, they had hardly seen each other since the weekend.

"Have you spoken to your father in the past few days?" Kit asked, his eyes on the busy motorway.

"I left him two messages and he finally called me back yesterday. He's been at Kew, presenting his new Galápagos species to the horticultural powers-that-be."

"He didn't mention the conversation he had with Elsie on Sunday, then?"

"No. And I didn't press it either. He sounded a little distant"—Julia shrugged—"but then, he often does. I'm sure he'll tell me in his own good time."

"You're right. And you've got enough on your plate, sweetheart." Kit reached across and squeezed Julia's hand. "I wish I could come with you, you know. Are you sure you'll be all right?"

Julia nodded stoically. "I've just got to get this over and done with."

"Yes. And . . ." Kit searched for the words. "I want you to know I respect how much you loved them. They won't threaten me, Julia. I really accept that if Xavier was still here, you'd be with him. And I don't want you to be ashamed or guilty about that. I can hardly resent that you've loved others before. Remember, I have too."

The two of them stood awkwardly by passport control. There were things Julia wanted to say to Kit, such as how wonderful he'd been, how happy *she'd* been, and how much she thought she loved—yes, *loved*—him. But she couldn't quite find the words. So, rather than say the wrong thing, she remained silent.

Eventually, Kit threw his arms round her and hugged her to him. "I'll miss you so much, darling," he whispered in her ear.

"I will too," she managed feebly.

He stepped back and pushed a lock of her hair from her face. "Please try to take care of yourself. I know how bad you are at that. And, remember, if you need me, I'm here. And I'll be waiting for you, however long it takes."

Julia nodded, close to tears. "Thank you."

"I love you, darling," he murmured.

"Yes," Julia said, too choked to say any more. Then she turned away from him, gave a small wave, and walked through the barrier.

Sitting on the plane as it prepared to land at Toulon airport, Julia was surprised to find she was thinking less of what she now had to face than she was of leaving Kit. Having spent three hours without him, and with no idea how long it might be before she saw him again, she felt . . . bereft. The intensity with which she missed him had taken her completely by surprise.

When she smelled the sweet, familiar, pine-scented air, a large part of her wanted to turn tail, step back on the plane, and return to the comfort of Kit and Wharton Park. By the time she had collected her rental car and was heading along the scenic coastal route to her home, Julia understood it was hardly surprising she wanted to run back into Kit's arms: what she must face in less than an hour terrified her.

But the sooner it was done, the sooner she could return to him.

She had to say good-bye. And say it alone.

The traffic along the coast road was heavy with holidaymakers. Julia wound her way patiently through the pretty resorts of Bormesles-Mimosas, Lavandou, and Rayol-Canadel, watching families spilling off the beaches and into the busy bars and cafés. The whole of France moved south during August, and there was little point in trying to get anywhere in a hurry.

The winding road began to climb upward, affording wonderful views of the azure sea below. After the hardy baldness of the Norfolk landscape, which Julia appreciated had its own raw beauty, the Côte d'Azur offered spectacular, colorful intricacy. It was rather like comparing a rough diamond to an exquisitely fashioned and polished sapphire, yet they both had their own unique charms.

At La Croix-Valmer, Julia took the steep, narrow road up to the hilltop town of Ramatuelle. As she approached the village, adrenaline began to pump through her. She rarely felt the need for a drink, but she wished she could have one now.

As usual, the roads in the village were packed with tourists, and Julia had to park some distance from her house. She took her traveling case from the trunk of the car and walked along the narrow path to her home, which stood just off the main square. Ramatuelle was a maze of narrow streets and hidden alleys, full of picturesque, ancient stone houses, with bougainvillea tumbling in fat, purple blossoms over the walls.

The village was only ten minutes from the smart beaches of Pampelonne and the resort of Saint-Tropez, so it was more sophisticated than most, with an array of expensive restaurants attracting a chic clientele. Julia loved it best in the winter, when the village was returned to its inhabitants.

She stopped by the wrought-iron gates that opened onto the short path that led to her front door. She dug deep, garnering strength to open the gates, walk up that path, and put the key in the lock. . . .

Any moment now, the door will open. Gabriel will know I am coming and will be waiting at the window with Agnes, ready to run down the steps and into my arms.

I will hold him close to me, smelling his wonderful scent, made up of Xavier and me, and something of Gabriel's own. I will caress his freshly washed dark hair, too long by far for a boy, but I cannot bear to cut it and see the soft ringlets fall from his head.

"Tu es rentrée. Je t'aime, Maman," *he will say, as he hangs on to me like a small monkey and we go up the steps together. Agnes will be there, smiling to see us reunited, and I will sit Gabriel on my lap at the kitchen table as they tell me what they have been up to since I've been gone.*

He will climb off my lap and shyly bring me a painting he has done for me. The paper is stiff under the weight of the clumsily applied paint, but he is proud of it and knows I will be happy to receive it.

We will take a walk outside and Gabriel will hop on his small tricycle, which he will pedal manically around the terrace, showing off his skills to me. Then he will tire and clamber back onto my knee, thumb in his mouth. He will settle down against my breast, and I will feel his heart beating against mine. As he grows drowsy, I will lift him up in my arms and carry him to his cot to lie him down gently. I will lean over and kiss his forehead, loving the feel of his soft skin against my lips. I will stroke his head, murmuring to him of my love, and all the wonderful things we will do together now I am home. As he slips into sleep, he will open one eye to check I am still there.

I am . . . and will be, always.

Julia opened the door to the silent house and prepared to step back into the past. And the pain.

She stood in the shadowy hallway, struck by the distinctive smell that pervades all old houses unlived in for a long period. That the smell was unfamiliar helped her, and she walked to the back of the house and into the kitchen. The shutters were closed against the harsh glare of high summer, so the room was in semidarkness. Julia walked toward the long French oak table, where a note was balanced against a bowl of fresh fruit.

Dear Madame Julia,

I hope you find the house as you would like it. I have stocked the fridge, and there is a casserole on top of the stove. I will be in tomorrow, as usual, at ten o'clock. If you need anything before this, please call.

Welcome home, Madame,

Agnes

Julia plucked a ripe peach from the bowl, bit into its velvety skin, and opened the door that led to the terrace. The old house lay in a crowded, narrow street, yet she was now standing on a hilltop. The magnificent view below was uninterrupted by other houses, the hillside covered in pine trees, olives, and firs, and sweeping down, hundreds of yards beneath her, to the line of shimmering blue that was the sea.

This was where Julia spent most of her time here, sitting under the pergola, draped with bulbous purple grapes, listening to the cicadas, to Xavier practicing and Gabriel squealing with delight from the swimming pool.

Now only the cicadas were here, and she was alone. There was no hiding from the memories. Julia's legs began to give way and she slumped onto a wrought-iron chair.

Only a year ago . . . it felt like a lifetime.

And that day—that dreadful, earth-shattering, life-changing day—had started so simply, like any other. There had been no forewarning, no inkling of what was to come.

A hot Sunday in July . . .

Julia had been catching the midmorning flight to Paris to perform a recital at La Salle Pleyel with l'Orchestre de Paris. She was playing Rachmaninov's Concerto No. 2, her favorite piece. She remembered taking her bags downstairs to wait for the taxi and being happy it was only an overnight stay; she would be back in time for tea with Gabriel tomorrow evening. She always dreaded saying good-bye to him, but comforted herself that it was a good opportunity for her "boys" to spend some time together. When he was at home, Xavier would lock himself away with the piano, becoming irritated if Gabriel disturbed him. So Gabriel had learned not to do so. Julia knew he was wary of his father, whose volatile artistic temperament made him unpredictable.

As it was a Sunday, Agnes was not there to take care of Gabriel, so Xavier was in charge. A conductor friend of Xavier's had invited the two of them for swimming and a late-afternoon barbecue just along the coast. There would be other children there for Gabriel to play with, and it would be good for father and son to spend the day together.

"Maman," Gabriel said, throwing his arms about her neck. *"Je t'aime.* Come back soon. I miss you."

"And I you, *petit ange,*" she replied, as she drew in the smell of him to keep with her while she was away. "Have a lovely time at the party and be a good boy for Papa."

"We are driving there in Papa's new sports car. It goes so fast, *Maman.*" Gabriel wriggled out of Julia's arms and zoomed round the hall making car noises.

"A bientôt, chérie," Xavier said. "Play well, as you always do. I will long for your return." He hugged Julia to him and kissed her.

"Je t'aime, chéri. Take care of Gabriel for me," Julia added as she walked down the front steps.

"I hope he will take care of me." Xavier laughed. Gabriel came to stand by his father and took his hand as they waved her off in her taxi.

In her dressing room in Paris, Julia had rung Xavier on his mobile just before the recital. It went to voice mail, but this was not unusual. They were probably not back from the barbecue yet. She would try again in the interval. Hearing her two-minute call, Julia had switched off her mobile and made her way to the wings.

The faintest glimmer of nerves had flooded through her as she walked onto the platform and took the applause from the audience. Then, when she sat down on the stool and looked down at the keys that would transport her and her audience to another plane, the fear had left her. Her fingers touched the keys, and the first haunting notes of the concerto filled the hall.

When she had finished playing, she'd known the rendition she had just given was the best she had ever played. The audience seemed to think so too and gave her a standing ovation. Clutching a bouquet of bloodred roses, Julia had walked from the stage, elated. People clustered round her, as they always did, congratulating her, showering her with praise, wanting to bask in her unique talent.

"Madame Forrester."

She had heard the manager's voice from behind the group of well-wishers and looked up. His grave face was in stark contrast to the animated smiles around her. He pushed his way through to her.

"Madame Forrester, can you come with me, please?"

He had led her to his office and closed the door behind him.

"What is it? Is something wrong?"

Julia remembered the pounding of her heart as he told her of a call for her from the gendarmerie in Saint-Tropez. He had the number, and the inspector he had spoken to wanted her to call him back immediately.

"Do you know why?" Julia had asked as the manager dialed the number for her, and she'd taken the receiver with shaking hands.

"Madame, I . . . do not know the details. I will leave you alone to talk with him."

He'd left her there, in the office. She had asked to speak to the inspector whose name was on the piece of paper in front of her. He'd answered immediately. And told her what had happened, ending her world.

The car veering off the road on a narrow bend, tumbling down the steep hillside, then bursting into flames, setting fire to the tinder-dry hillside around it.

And somewhere, in the charred, blackened landscape, lay the remains of her husband and son.

A week later, by which time Julia was in England, the French authorities informed her that they had found some remains near the site: the bones of a child aged about two, discovered on the hillside above what was left of the car. Which, the inspector had explained, meant Gabriel had probably been thrown out as the car tumbled down the hillside.

Other, adult bones were nearer the car. The Inspector told her that, because fire removed any trace of DNA, it was impossible to officially identify either of them.

Julia could barely remember what had happened after that first, dreadful call at La Salle Pleyel in Paris. Alicia had arrived—Julia didn't know when—and had taken her home to England.

After two days in Alicia's spare room, Julia had known she could not bear the screams and laughter of Alicia's children. So she'd moved into the tiny cottage in Blakeney, preferring silence to the unbearable sound of what she had just lost.

Julia roused herself, bringing herself back to the present and wiping the tears from her eyes. She knew she was on dangerous territory. She must not allow herself to sink back down by remembering. She had practical things to do here in France—the sooner she did them, the sooner she could leave.

She went back into the kitchen and, adhering to Kit's advice to make sure she ate, warmed some casserole from the stove, then sat down at the table with a glass of wine and forced the food down her throat.

After supper, Julia steeled herself to walk into the sitting room. She sat down at the piano and put her fingers to the keys.

Julia played for them: for her husband and her beloved son. And tried to believe somewhere in her heart that, wherever they were, they could hear her.

Sometime later, Julia opened the door to the bedroom she had shared with Xavier. She took a nightshirt from her traveling case, not daring to go near the wardrobe, where all her husband's clothes would still be hanging, and climbed onto the bed.

She lay stiffly, looking around her. She had always loved this room, perhaps simply because it was hers; a place of refuge and not an anonymous hotel. She studied the painting, which she and Xavier had chosen together from a gallery in Gassin, and saw his hairbrush still lying on the bureau below the mirror.

This was the moment she had most dreaded: the first night alone in their bed, plagued by thoughts of what had once been in this house and was no more. Surprisingly, she felt calm. Perhaps it was simply because she had now accepted that neither Xavier, nor her beloved *petit ange*, would ever be here with her again.

They were gone. Nothing she could feel, or do, or say, would bring them back. The silent house, in which they had lived and loved as a family, was final affirmation of that.

52

When Julia woke the following morning, she was relieved to see it was almost nine o'clock and she had slept through the night.

Agnes, her housekeeper and childminder, appeared an hour later, her eyes full of trepidation as she sought Julia out on the terrace. Julia understood. She stood up, went to Agnes, and put her arms round her.

"Ça va, Agnes?"

Julia could see the relief in Agnes's eyes as she answered, *"Ça va bien, Madame Julia. Et vous?"*

"I am better, thank you. Come, have a cup of coffee with me," Julia continued in French, the language she had always used here, though it now felt strange and unnatural on her tongue.

Agnes sat down uncertainly, as Julia poured some coffee for her.

"Thank you so much for caring for the house. Everything looks perfect."

"It is nothing, Madame Julia. I am only glad to see you looking well."

"I've begun to accept what has happened. I realized I had no choice. The pain will never go, but . . ." Julia ground to a halt. Seeing Agnes, a woman who had loved and cared for her child almost as much as she had, was threatening to overwhelm her. She swallowed hard and steeled herself to talk of practicalities. "There are some things I cannot bring myself to do, and I was wondering if you could help me with them."

"Of course, Madame, anything you want."

"I only intend to be here for a few days, and then I will be returning to England. I am going to sell this house."

"Oh, Madame!" Agnes looked horrified. "But this is your home!"

"I know, but, Agnes, I must. Everything here is what my life used to be. And if that can't be anymore, then I must move on."

"I understand." Agnes nodded somberly.

"I wanted to ask you whether you could bear to clear out Xavier's wardrobe for me after I leave? And"—Julia swallowed—"Gabriel's bedroom? Perhaps you know a charity or a family who might appreciate his toys and clothes?"

Tears came to Agnes's eyes. "Of course, Madame. I know a family who would be grateful to receive such things."

"When the house is sold, I will return for my personal possessions. But I'm going to put it up for sale with the contents included. I think that's best."

Agnes nodded. "There is an old French saying, Madame, that in order to belong to the future, you must accept the past. I will do whatever you ask to help you. I think you are"—tears spilled unchecked from Agnes's eyes—"very brave."

"No." Julia shook her head. "I haven't been brave at all. And if I *was* brave, I'd stay here and still belong completely to them." She sighed. "I've come here to try and say good-bye."

Agnes reached her hand to Julia's. "He—*they*—would want you to move on and find new happiness."

"Yes." Julia offered a wan smile. "I hope they would, and I must believe it."

"Yes, Madame, you must."

Agnes withdrew her hand, drained her coffee cup, and stood up. "And now, if you will excuse me, I must get on with my work. I have left all the bills on the desk in the study for you. Everyone understands that you will pay when you are ready."

"Of course I will. I'll attend to them today and leave the checks for you. Please, thank everyone for their kindness on my behalf."

"*Pas de problem, madame.* We all loved you here. *All* of you," Agnes added, then turned abruptly and stepped back into the house.

Julia spent a long time at her desk, sifting through the post accumulated over the past year. Condolence cards had arrived in a continuous stream since the accident. As she opened them and read the moving sentiments inside, she took comfort from knowing how many people had loved them.

She put the cards into a folder to take home to England, then wrote out checks for the people who had maintained her house in her absence.

She opened a large, official-looking envelope and caught her breath. In it were death certificates for her husband and child, the final affirmation of their nonexistence. The investigation and the case were now officially closed.

Armed with a spade, trowel, and two small cypress saplings, Julia drove the ten minutes to the treacherous bend where her husband and son had met their deaths. She parked in a bay up the road and made her way back toward the bend with the spade and trowel, then returned for the saplings. Standing at the top of the hill, she could see the charred edges of the trees around the bare spot that had been scorched by the fire. But, as she made her way slowly down the precarious slope, she noticed the beginnings of rebirth. The wild orchids that grew prevalently along the hillside in this region were beginning to poke their heads through the still-charred ground, and a small number of new green shoots were visible. Fire refertilized in its destruction, and Julia could only hope the rebirth she saw around her was metaphorically relevant to her too.

With no *X* to mark the exact spot where either of them had died, Julia chose what she imagined was the center of the site and began to dig. It was hard work and hot, but she kept going until she had planted the saplings side by side. She knelt beside them for a while, conjuring the beloved individuals they represented, and celebrating their lives.

"Good-bye, *mon petit ange* and my Xavier. Sleep well. You will always be with me, wherever I go. And one day . . . one day, we will all be together again. I love you both, so much . . ."

Finally, standing up and composing herself, she blew each a last kiss, then walked up the hillside, away from them.

The following morning, Julia felt a lightness, an inexplicable sense of relief that she had faced the worst and been comforted by it. Others had suggested a memorial service to mark Xavier's and Gabriel's passings, and that might be possible now that she had said her own private good-bye. Perhaps this was the moment of "closure" everyone said was so important. Whatever it had been, it was a step in the right direction on her journey toward achieving inner peace to face the future.

Julia now embarked on the next important step: she went to visit the local *immobilier* and explained that she wanted to put her house on the market. The estate agent feigned sadness, but Julia knew that, in reality, he was rubbing his hands in glee at the thought of having the most sought-after house in Ramatuelle on his books.

"Madame, I can pick up the telephone, make one call, and you will have your sale. So rarely do houses like yours come onto the market. You can name your price and I can assure you I will get it. But you must decide if you truly wish to do this. Your house comes once in a lifetime, in this village."

"Completely sure. My only thought is that it would be nice to have a family living there."

"I think I have just the people."

"Good." Julia stood up. "The sooner, the better. The house needs to be lived in and I cannot live in it. I will be leaving in a couple of days. If anyone wishes to view it, Agnes Savoir will have the keys."

The agent walked round his desk and shook her hand. "Thank you, Madame, for entrusting your beautiful house to me. And, please, let me offer my condolences for your tragic loss."

"Merci, monsieur."

Julia left the office and walked up to the sunlit square. The pretty cafés were busy with people taking a late breakfast. Julia found herself a table in the sunshine and ordered a café au lait. She sipped it slowly, enjoying the relaxed atmosphere. She would miss it—the French way of life had always suited her.

It suddenly occurred to Julia that one explanation for her feeling so at home here could be her genetic makeup: Adrienne, whom she now knew to be her great-grandmother, had been French. Julia smiled, taking comfort from links with the past. Human beings were a complex recipe, and she was fascinated to have discovered some of the ingredients that had produced her own uniqueness.

She ordered another café au lait, unwilling to leave this moment of calm reflection after the emotional turbulence of the past few days. She thought about the "other" part of her, the part she knew so little about: it lay far to the east, bathed in the heat of the tropical sun, the result of a tragic love that was only briefly fulfilled. Perhaps one day she would go there and experience the beauty that had so bewitched Harry, but it was not for now.

Her thoughts turned to Kit, and she smiled. He had left her alone in the past couple of days, understanding and undemanding as usual, simply sending text messages to say he loved her and was thinking of her.

Julia took her mobile from her bag, scrolled down, and looked at his message. What surprised her most was the way Kit seemed completely secure in professing his love for her, when she had yet to tell him she loved *him*.

Perhaps she had not been ready.

But now that she had completed the task that—in practical terms at least—closed the book on the past, there was no reason not to say it.

"I love you . . ."

Julia practiced the words on her tongue, and basking in the sunlight, she knew there was no doubt in her mind that it was true.

Back at the house, she went into the study to book online her flight home. She would leave tomorrow, eager to return to Wharton Park and Kit as soon as possible. She wanted to tell him that she was completely his at last, unencumbered, free to be with him if he wanted her, for the rest of their lives.

Her mobile rang and she saw it was Kit. She answered it.

"Hello, sweetheart, how are you?"

"I'm . . . okay, thanks, Kit."

"Good. I must say, it's nice to hear your voice. I've missed you, Julia. Are you taking care of yourself?"

"Yes, I am"—Julia smiled—"promise."

"Any idea of when you'll be home?"

Having just booked her flight, Julia knew exactly when, but decided she'd surprise him. "I'm not quite sure, but I've nearly done what I needed to, so probably sooner than you think." She grinned.

"That's wonderful news!" Kit sounded relieved. "Can't tell you how quiet it's been here."

"Pretty quiet here too," murmured Julia.

"Yes, it must be," Kit replied somberly. "I'm thinking of you, sweetheart."

"Me too. Are you all right?"

"Apart from missing you, yes, I'm fine. Right, I'll let you get on then. Just let me know when you're coming home, so I can kill the fatted calf and set off the fireworks. I love you, darling. Keep in touch."

"I will, Kit. See you soon."

That afternoon, full of sense of wonder that fate had given her a second chance at happiness, Julia sat down at the grand piano and played with joy, rather than pain.

As usual, she lost all sense of time and became so immersed in the music that she didn't notice the sun setting behind her. Neither did she hear the door to the sitting room open. Ending the piece with a final flourish, she looked down at her watch and saw it was past seven o'clock. Time for a glass of rosé, she thought, as she folded her score and stowed it in her case, ready to take it home the next day.

A sudden movement behind her caught her eye. And she turned.

For a moment she stared at him, at the figure framed in the doorway. Then instinctively closed her eyes.

She was seeing a ghost, conjuring an image in her mind. He was not real, she knew that.

When I open my eyes, he will be gone. . . .

She did so. He was still there.

Then the figure spoke. "Hello, my Julia. I am returned."

53

Julia had no concept of how long she stared at him. Still her brain refused to process the messages her eyes and ears were sending.

Because it was . . . *impossible.*

As she gazed at him, she realized that this was Xavier—and yet it was not Xavier. Or at least, not the Xavier she had carried in her head since the day he had died. This Xavier had aged ten years, perhaps twenty; a Xavier who was no longer merely thin, but gaunt to the point of emaciation. A Xavier who had acquired a jagged scar running down the left side of his face.

"I understand you are shocked to see me."

Julia had an inappropriate urge to giggle hysterically at his understatement.

She managed to find her voice. "I am trying to work out," she said slowly, exaggerating her words, "whether or not you are a ghost. A hallucination."

He shook his head. "No. I am not."

"Then . . ." Julia struggled to find the right words, but merely managed a half-swallowed "How?"

"My Julia, there are many things we must speak of, but, please, come to me. Hold your husband, who is back from the dead. And feel for yourself that he is real."

Xavier held out his arms to her.

Slowly, following his instructions, Julia rose and walked toward him.

"Oh, *ma chérie*, my Julia," he murmured, as he took her in his arms. "You cannot know how long I have dreamt of this moment."

The touch of him and his familiar smell confirmed he was no hallucination.

It was all too much. Julia burst into tears.

"I don't understand, I just—don't—*understand*!"

As she slumped against him, Xavier half carried her to the sofa and sat her down, his arms locked about her.

"I know, I know, *ma petite*, it was always going to be a terrible shock for you to see me again. I tried to think how it would be best for you," he said, stroking her hair, "but there was no good way."

"But how?" she cried. "How can you be here? You are dead, *dead*! You died a year ago . . . and if you didn't die, then where the hell have you been?!"

"I will tell you everything, in good time," he soothed. "For now, we should celebrate that we are reunited."

"No!" Julia pulled away from him abruptly. "I need you to tell me *now*! Xavier, tell me now," she implored.

"*D'accord*, you are right. I must tell you. But first, perhaps we both need a glass of wine to help calm our nerves."

As Xavier left the sitting room to pour the drinks, Julia sat completely still, unable to comprehend what had just happened.

"Drink this, *chérie*. It will help," he said, handing her a glass.

Julia didn't think it possible that anything, and certainly not a glass of wine, could "help." But she sipped it as he told her to, if only to have something to concentrate on. "Please," she implored again, "you have to explain to me, Xavier. Until you do, I feel I might go mad. Please."

Xavier took the glass from Julia's hand and put it on the coffee table. Then he put his own, long-fingered hands over Julia's, his eyes never leaving hers.

"*Ma chérie* . . . I have wanted, yet dreaded this moment for so long. I did not know what to do for the best; should I stay away from you forever? Prevent the shock of this instant and protect you? And, yes"—he nodded—"in some ways, it would be easier for me too to stay away. To hide, not face up to the terrible thing I have done to you. But then, I knew I must not run away, I must be brave and face my responsibility as a husband, and as a father."

A sudden, urgent thought came to Julia's head. "Oh my God!" She clapped a hand to her mouth. "Tell me, Xavier, tell me, tell me—if you are alive—is Gabriel—?"

Xavier shook his head. "No, *mon amour*, he is gone, he is gone. I . . . saw him with my own eyes."

Julia withdrew her hand from his. She took a deep breath, garnering every ounce of her strength. "Just tell me."

Xavier gulped down the rest of his wine, then tried to reach again for Julia's hands. She pulled them away. "No! Don't touch me!" She could hear hysteria edging into her voice. "Please! Just tell me!"

"*D'accord, chérie*, I will begin. That day, that terrible day, we left the party at seven o'clock. Gabriel asked me if he could sit in the front of my new car and I agreed. We drove off toward home, with the roof of the car down, Gabriel so excited about being in the front of Papa's sports car. He was screaming and laughing, urging me, 'Go faster, Papa! Faster!' And because"—Xavier choked—"I simply wanted to please him, I did as he asked. I took the bend too fast and swerved to avoid a car coming the other way. I lost control and the car left the road and tumbled down the hillside."

Xavier broke down. "Forgive me, Julia, forgive me . . ." He swallowed. "The car finally came to a halt when a tree blocked its way. I was in shock, and my face was bleeding"—he touched the scar on his cheek—"but I was still conscious. I looked immediately to see if Gabriel was all right, but the seat next to me was empty. I realized he must have been thrown out when the car fell down the hill. I managed to climb out of the car and ran back up the hillside to find Gabriel."

Xavier put his head in his hands. "Oh, Julia, Julia . . ."

She watched him numbly as he composed himself, but said nothing. What could she say?

"I found him," he whispered, "further up the hillside. At first I thought he was just unconscious. You see, there was not a mark on him. But then—Oh! God help me!" he cried. "I lifted him up and his head lolled on his neck like a—broken doll. I knew then he was seriously injured, that the fall had caused terrible damage."

"You're saying his neck was broken?" Julia had to know, she had to know exactly *how* her baby had died.

"Yes. Then I realized his eyes were open . . . wide open, but they were not blinking, Julia, they were not blinking. I checked his pulse and found nothing, shook him, tried to rouse him, but I knew then he was not seeing me anymore, that he was"—Xavier choked, then shook his head. "I cannot say the word."

"You are saying you knew then that Gabriel was dead?" Julia uttered the words for him.

"*Oui, chérie*, he was . . . dead. I sat with him for I do not know how long, holding him in my arms, willing him back to life, but there was no response. And then"—Xavier shuddered at the memory—"I hear a loud bang and saw the car below us had burst into flames. Everything was so dry in the forest, it took only a few seconds for the fire to travel toward me. And—how can I tell you this, how can I?" Xavier sobbed, great heaving sounds of anguish. "I ran. I ran and ran. Through the forest and away from the fire. And"—he let out another strangled cry—"I did not take our little boy with me! I did not . . . take . . . our boy . . . with me!"

Xavier could go on no longer. He put his head in his hands and sobbed.

Julia sat next to him, staring into the distance, willing herself to stay where she was. "Please, Xavier, keep talking. I need to know everything." She could hardly believe the eerie sense of calm that had descended on her.

A few minutes later, Xavier continued, "Every day, I ask myself why, *why*, in that moment, I did not pick up our *ange* in my arms and carry him away with me? I cannot explain . . . I cannot explain." He shook his head manically. "I left him there, alone! Perhaps, it was the shock, the terrible grief . . . *a madness*, that overtook me in that moment. Perhaps it was simply a selfish instinct for survival. But I did it, Julia, I left him there, I left him there."

He was weeping again, but Julia was still unmoved. "So, where did you run to?"

Xavier wiped his eyes and nose on the back of his hand. He shook his head. "Julia, I cannot tell you where I went, but when I had stopped running, when I knew that I was safe from the flames, I simply lay down where I was in the forest and fell asleep, or perhaps I was unconscious. When I awoke, night had fallen. I closed my eyes and again went back to sleep. The next time I opened them, it was morning. And then—the realization—I must come home to you, explain what had happened. But every time I thought of this, of getting to my feet and coming back to you, I found I could not. In the end I did start walking, and I realized I was close to Saint-Tropez, so I went on until I reached the town." He paused and took a deep breath before saying, "Julia, I beg you to understand that, at that moment, I was half-mad with grief. Outside a *tabac*, there was a newspaper. You know what the headlines were that day."

"No. I didn't read them."

"Well, of course, it was you on the front page. They did not have a picture of me yet, but no one would have recognized me that morning." Xavier grimaced. "When I saw myself—with blood caked down my cheek and my clothes ripped—I looked like a vagrant, not the husband of the famous Julia Forrester."

Xavier stood up abruptly and began to pace around the room.

"I cleaned myself a little in the public facility, then bought some water and a newspaper. And read about the accident, about Gabriel and about myself. And I realized that, as far as you and the rest of the world were concerned, I was dead. And in that moment"—Xavier stopped pacing and turned to face Julia—"I knew I could not return to you and tell you the truth of what I had done; I knew you could never forgive me. I had killed our *petit ange* and left him there in the forest to burn." Xavier stood, drained of tears now, staring past Julia. "So, I ran away."

"Where to?"

"I took a boat, a pleasure cruise, that was sailing along the coast. It took me to Nice, where I boarded a ferry to Corsica. I checked into a small pension in the hills and stayed there until the cash I had with me ran out. After that, I spent some weeks fruit-picking, but always moving on, so no one would recognize me." Xavier shrugged. "Perhaps no one would have, but I did not want to take that chance. I did not want to be found. I think . . . I must believe that I was having a breakdown. I could not think rationally; my mind had closed to what had happened. I only existed. Can you understand that, Julia?"

His eyes beseeched her for a response, but she could not give him one.

He sighed. "And then, I suppose, I slowly began to heal. And I started to think again, think not only of what I had done to Gabriel but also of what I had done to you. I had allowed you to believe that not only your beloved son was dead, but your husband too"—Xavier ran his hands frantically through his hair—"and what a terrible thing it was to do to you. It took many months before I found the strength and courage to return to you. But eventually I did. And here I am."

There was silence between them for a long time.

Finally, she said, "How did you know I was here?"

Xavier looked at her, an expression of surprise on his face. "Where else would you be? If you had been away at a recital, I would have waited for you here. Anyway, you were here, *ma chérie*."

"I haven't been," Julia replied impassively. "I've been in England. And certainly not playing the piano." She stood up briskly, needing to be away from his shocking presence. And to grapple with the horrific truth of their son's death. And Xavier's part in it.

She walked out through the hall and the kitchen, and onto the terrace.

As she stood, gazing up at the ink black sky crowded with stars, she wound her arms round herself in a futile protective gesture. And remembered with derision how she had believed life had taught her as much as she would ever need to know about pain.

She had been wrong.

"Forgive me, forgive me . . . ," Julia asked the heavens, as she acknowledged that, of the two of them, she wished it were Gabriel who had been spared.

He killed our child.

No! Julia shook her head. She could not, must not, think that. It was an accident, a moment of irresponsibility, a tragic choice any parent might make during the many years of caring. . . . Besides, it was impossible to know whether Gabriel would have survived even if he had been strapped in his child seat in the back of the car.

He left him there in the forest to burn.

"Oh, God," Julia whispered.

How could she ever forgive that?

What if Gabriel had still been alive?

The thought was too horrific to contemplate. She had to believe he hadn't been, or she would truly go mad thinking of him suffering alone. She had to trust Xavier and believe he was speaking the truth.

And what of his actions afterward? What of his disappearance for twelve months, leaving her to believe he too was dead?

If Xavier had come home and admitted his dreadful mistake, could she have forgiven him? She could not answer.

Julia stopped pacing and dropped down into a chair.

Were the extreme circumstances a valid excuse?

And what of Kit, now Xavier was back?

She put a hand to her forehead. It was too much, all too much. . . .

She jumped as she felt a hand placed on her shoulder.

"Julia"—he crouched in front of her, taking her hands in his—"I am so very, very sorry for what I have had to tell you tonight. I understand how painful it is for you to hear what actually happened. I can never forgive myself. But, please, can you understand, the only reason I have come back is to make amends? Because I know what I did was wrong, and because"—he bent to kiss her hands—"I love you, *chérie*, I love you so much. Can you find it in your heart to forgive me for what I have done?"

Julia looked down at him, at the desperation in his eyes. She stood up. "I can't talk any more tonight. I'm so tired. I need to sleep. Take the spare room for now, please."

She walked past him silently into the house.

For the next two days, Julia stayed in her room, ignoring Xavier's pleas to talk. She had to process the enormity of what she had learned, and she needed time alone to lick her wounds. She slept for hours at a time during the day, then woke in the cruelest, deepest hours of darkness to face the nightmare.

On the third morning, Julia allowed Xavier into the room. He was holding a tray of fresh croissants, jam, and coffee.

"I have brought you some breakfast, *chérie.* I am so worried you do not eat." He put the tray on the bed and gazed down at her exhausted face. "My Julia, I cannot bear I put you through this terrible pain."

Julia watched him pour some coffee and sat up when he handed it to her.

She sipped it silently, trying to rouse herself.

"I'm going back to England," she said flatly.

"Non!" Xavier looked horrified. "Surely, you will not go now? Julia, you are in no state to travel, and we must at least talk?"

A sudden yearning for the peace, calm, and tranquillity she had known with Kit at Wharton Park brought tears to her eyes.

"Xavier, I—" She sighed, unable to voice the tumult of her emotions.

"Julia," he implored, "please, I make only one request of you: I beg you, stay here with me, at least for a few days. Let me love you, help you come to terms with the terrible shock I have given you. If, at the end of that time, you still wish to leave, I will not stop you. But surely we owe it to our *ange*, as his mama and papa, at least to try?"

It was the one thing Xavier could have said to stop her boarding a plane immediately.

"I have mourned him alone for months," she said quietly.

"Then give me the chance to mourn him with you. I need to mourn too. Don't leave me, please, *chérie*. I could not . . . I could not go on."

Julia looked at him and saw the desperation in his eyes.

"All right. I will do as you ask and stay here. For now."

Xavier threw his arms round her, spilling coffee all over the bed linen.

"*Merci, mon amour*. I promise you will not regret it. So, my Julia, what would you like to do today?"

" 'Do'?" she asked, baffled by the very idea.

"Yes, I think it would be good for you to get out of the house, go somewhere away from the . . . memories. We could go"—Xavier shrugged—"and take a walk along our favorite beach, and perhaps have lunch together?"

"I—"

"Julia, please." Xavier studied his hands, speaking quietly. "I understand how much pain I have caused you with what I had to tell, but is there not the smallest part of you that is glad to have your husband back? Did you—mourn me too?"

"Of course I did! I was beyond"—Julia swallowed—"beyond comfort for months. You have no idea of the hell I went through! And when I finally did start to accept and think there may be a future for me, then you walk in and . . . oh, Xavier." She put her head in her hands. "I don't know . . . I just don't know how I feel."

Despite her determination, her tears could not be abated. Xavier took her in his arms and held her, stroking her hair.

"I know, *mon amour*, I know. But I swear to you, I will make amends, take care of you, comfort you through this, do anything to help you. You are not alone anymore. I am here. Surely we need each other?"

"Yes, but . . ." The *but* was so complex, Julia could not even begin to express it.

"I really think it is a good idea to leave the house for a while. If you are not comfortable, I will bring you home immediately. *D'accord?*"

She sighed, too numb to care where she was, just wishing someone could tell her how to stop the awful dragging feeling that had lodged in her stomach since Xavier had told her what had happened to her child. She felt she was mourning him all over again.

"D'accord."

"*Bonne*. But first"—Xavier sighed deeply—"I must go to the gendarmerie and show them that I have risen from the dead."

"Your death certificate is on the desk in the study. Perhaps you should take it with you," Julia said drily.

He looked down at her as he stood up. "You know that I may face charges."

The thought had not crossed Julia's mind. "For what?"

"For dangerous driving or possibly even manslaughter. But I must do this. I will go now. Get it over with. I am frightened."

Julia saw the look in his eyes, a look she knew well: it meant he wanted her to go with him. She ignored it and climbed out of bed.

"I'll see you later," she said, disappearing into the bathroom.

Julia was at the piano, hoping it might offer the solace she craved, when Xavier arrived home. He stepped into the sitting room, a smile playing on his lips.

"Voilà! It is done! When Monsieur the inspector saw a man in front of him holding his own death certificate—" Xavier chuckled. "*Chérie*, I wish you could have seen his face!"

"I'm sure he was shocked." Julia felt discomfited by Xavier's high spirits.

"He doubts there will be charges, as there were no witnesses to the accident. He accepted my explanation without question. Apparently, I am not the first driver to have left the road in that spot. He said there could be a secondary charge of faking my own death, but only if money from our insurance policies has been issued. Has it?" Xavier looked at her with concern.

For once, Julia was glad of her reluctance to complete the paperwork associated with her husband's "death." "No," she answered quietly.

Xavier looked relieved. "So! *C'est parfait!* You cannot be charged either."

Julia looked up at him. *"What?"*

"Do not worry"—he kissed the top of her head fondly—"it is a minor detail, but proves we weren't working in partnership to extract money."

Julia covered her face with her hands and shook her head. "Please, Xavier! We are talking about the death of my—*our*—child, not an elaborate financial fraud!"

"*Pardon, chérie*, for being insensitive. It is only this stupid French bureaucracy. Now"—he pulled her hands from her face—"let me please take you out to lunch? Perhaps it is right to look at the positive as well as the negative, *oui*? And the positive is"—he tipped Julia's chin up to kiss her on the lips—"that I am a free man, back from the dead, and reunited with my beautiful wife."

54

The pretty coastal village of Gigaro nestled on the opposite side of the peninsula from Saint-Tropez. Standing in a designated nature reserve and set back from the major road linking the Riviera resorts, it managed to retain its age-old charm. Its picturesque, open-fronted restaurants dotted along the unspoiled beach were a well-kept local secret.

Xavier walked into La Salamandre with Julia trailing disconsolately behind him. She watched as Chantal, the owner, stared at him as if she were dreaming.

Xavier nodded encouragingly. *"Oui, Chantal, c'est moi!"*

Chantal put her hand to her mouth. "But . . . *Mon Dieu!* I cannot believe what I am seeing! How?"

Xavier put his arms round her. "It is a long story, which one day I will tell you. But for now, could we have our usual table and a *pichet* of rosé please?"

When Chantal left to fetch the wine, Julia looked across the table at Xavier.

"What are you going to say when people ask you where you've been?" she asked, her voice drained of emotion.

"I must simply tell them the truth." Xavier shrugged. "That I was so mad with grief, I disappeared."

Julia gazed at him. A nasty little thought had been nagging at her all morning. She had to say something to him. "You do realize this is manna from heaven for the media, don't you?"

"You are right, my Julia. Voilà!" Xavier slammed his hands down on the table. "I will call a press conference, invite the vultures to come and peck at us for one time only. Yes, that is the answer! We will contact Olav and he can arrange it."

Xavier reminded Julia of a train at full speed; she understood his joy and relief at returning from exile, but could not keep up with him. Press conferences—and the champagne that arrived courtesy of Chantal—were completely beyond her. She could only focus on her child's poor, burning body, alone in the forest, with the fire raging around it. Xavier seemed positively lit up at the thought of all the press attention. She'd forgotten what a peacock he could be.

"Please, Xavier, I can't face the media yet," she pleaded.

"Yes, of course, you are right. My apologies, *chérie*. To use an English phrase, perhaps I am running before I can walk. But how can I help a small feeling of happiness when I am here, looking into my wife's beautiful eyes? *Santé*." He clinked his glass against hers.

"I can't . . . feel happy. How can I, when I have only just learned the truth about Gabriel's death?"

Xavier reached for her hand, and she gave it to him reluctantly. "Julia, please believe me, it was a terrible accident. And I will never forgive myself. But I have punished myself, and you, enough. What more can I do? Tell me, my Julia, and I will do it, I promise."

"Nothing," she agreed with a sigh, "you can do nothing."

Julia was awoken the following morning by hammering on the front door. She walked sleepily into the hall to find Xavier had already opened the door—to a sea of faces, cameras, and Dictaphones.

As flashbulbs went off in Julia's startled face, she darted into the sanctuary of the sitting room, begging Xavier to close the door. She sank onto the sofa, shaking and breathless. Eventually, she heard the door close, and Xavier came to find her.

"Have you got rid of them?" she asked him desperately.

"*Chérie*, I am sorry this has happened so soon, but it cannot be helped, you know that. You are famous and I am your husband. They will not leave until they have their story. So, the sooner we get it over with, the better. I have told them we will come outside in half an hour to give an interview. That will satisfy them."

"Surely it's you they want to speak to?" Julia groaned. "Do I have to?"

Xavier put an arm round her. "You know it is you they really want. You are the one who makes a good photo for the front page. It is the price you pay for being rich and famous, *n'est-ce pas*? Now, I must go and shower." He looked at her, sitting in the ancient, washed-out T-shirt she liked to sleep in. "Perhaps you should too."

Julia did as she was asked and let the photographers snap her with Xavier's arms round her, planting a loving kiss on her lips. When asked how she felt about her husband's miraculous return, she said she was happy to have him back.

What else could she have said?

Soon after they had closed the door on the press, her mobile rang.

"Julia, it's Alicia. Am I to believe what I just heard on the radio? The newsreader said Julia Forrester's husband has been found safe and well."

"Yes, it's true." Julia sighed. "I should have called you, but I was still getting over the shock myself. And I wasn't expecting the story to get out quite so fast."

"Well, if it's true, it's one hell of a story. You can hardly be surprised. I presume that, now he's back, you're staying in France?"

"I"—Julia paused—"don't know."

"Right." It was Alicia's turn to pause. "Have you spoken to Kit?"

"No, not yet."

"Well, I don't like to tell you what to do, but whatever your plans are, it might be a good idea to speak to him. Let him know before he hears elsewhere."

"Yes, I'm sure you're right." Julia could not even go there just now.

"Dad called, by the way. He'd heard too and sends his love and congratulations. So, Julia, are you happy Xavier's back?"

Julia spied Xavier coming across the kitchen toward her, so she said, "Sorry, Alicia, why don't we speak later? I'm inundated here just now."

"Of course. Send Xavier my regards. I'll call you later. Take care, Julia. Bye."

Julia felt a pair of arms round her shoulders.

"How are you, my Julia?"

"Shell-shocked."

"They love a happy ending. . . . *Je t'aime* . . ." Xavier kissed her neck and his hands began to travel over her body.

Julia pulled away from him. "No! For God's sake, Xavier! Don't you understand? This isn't a happy ending!"

"No. *Je comprend.* I'm sorry. I just want to show my love for you."

Julia found she had broken out into a cold sweat. She needed to be alone, away from him. She walked toward the door as Xavier said, "We have been invited to lunch at Roland and Madelaine's, to celebrate my return. Will you like to go?"

Roland and Madelaine had invited Xavier and Gabriel to the barbecue that fateful day.

"No. I'm tired, Xavier."

After a flicker of annoyance in his eyes, he nodded. "Of course. But I think I should go. I will leave in half an hour. I will see you later, *mon amour.*"

"Yes."

Julia walked onto the terrace and slumped into a chair. It was a scorching day, the only demarcation between sea and sky a glimmering line of white heat.

Alicia was right. She must call Kit. It was only fair to tell him herself.

She looked at her mobile and scrolled down robotically to find Kit's number.

What on earth was she going to say?

She shook her head. What did it matter?

Her husband had returned and whatever heartbreak she felt was immaterial. She was no longer free to be with Kit. How strange, Julia pondered, as she found Kit's number, it was her husband who was back from the dead. Yet she felt she had died inside.

When she heard Xavier leave the house, she took a deep breath and pressed the call button.

Kit looked at his mobile on the desk as it rang. He could see it was Julia. He let it ring.

He couldn't face talking to her.

He knew what she had to say. He had heard it all on his car radio.

Kit stared out of the window across the park. He had always accepted that Julia was with him purely because she believed her husband was dead. There was no competition, Xavier was back. He was Julia's husband . . . she was his wife . . .

"Oh, God," he groaned, shaking his head in despair. He should have known it was all too perfect. . . .

For the first time in years, he had allowed himself to give his heart to a woman. With that leap of faith—raising his head over the parapet, while Julia was brave enough to put aside her own fears and join him—he had learned for the first time what it was, truly, to love.

"Where will I ever find that again?" Kit sighed.

He knew he wouldn't. He also knew there was not a single shred of hope that this relationship could be rekindled. Julia was almost certainly ecstatic, as he would have once been if Milla had come back from the dead.

His mobile rang once more. It was Julia again.

He stared out across the park and decided he would prefer not to hear her say the words.

He understood.

"Be happy, my darling," he whispered. "I will always love you."

Then Kit Crawford put his head in his hands and wept.

55

Somehow, Julia struggled through the next few days. As she so often had in the past, she took comfort in the piano. It provided not only welcome hours away from reality but also protection from Xavier's constant attention. She knew he was doing his utmost to show her how much he loved her and was desperate for reciprocation, but that was something that at present she just could not give.

She was, quite simply, numb. Yes, she was eating, sleeping, talking—going through all the motions of being alive—but inside she was a void. A dark, blank space was where her heart had once beaten and allowed her to feel. Kit had helped that happen, but now all that he had given her was gone.

One evening, having spent all afternoon at the piano, Julia poured herself a glass of rosé and went to sit on the terrace. Immediately, her mobile rang. She saw it was Alicia's number.

"Hello?"

All Julia could hear in response was sobbing.

"Alicia, what's wrong?"

"Oh . . . Julia! I—" Alicia's words were drowned by further sobbing.

"Can you try and tell me?" Julia was shocked by her sister's uncharacteristic distress.

"No, no! It's so awful! Can I come and see you in France? I need to get away. Max says he'll take a few days off and look after the children. Can I stay with you for a while? I know this is a difficult time for you, but . . . I need you."

"Of course you can. Is this something to do with Max?"

"It's not Max! I only wish it was. It's *me*!"

"Are you ill?"

"No! I'm not *ill*! I'm perfectly healthy. But—oh, dear, please, Julia—I can get a flight tomorrow and be with you by midafternoon. Could you pick me up from Toulon?"

"Of course I can." That suited Julia anyway, offering an escape from Xavier's intensity. "Is there anything I can do?"

"Nothing, just give me a haven so I can get my head sorted out. I don't want to fall apart in front of the children."

"Call me as soon as you've booked your flight. And I'll be there to pick you up. Whatever it is, I'm sure it can be sorted out."

"No, unfortunately it can't. It's destroyed me and can never be mended. Anyway, Julia, thank you so much. I'll call you later."

Julia was shocked and distressed to hear Alicia so distraught. She was relieved to feel emotion for Alicia: it meant she might one day feel something for her husband again—be it love or hate. Still, she did wonder what on earth could have happened to drive Alicia—so much the devoted mother—onto a plane, leaving her four children behind.

Xavier arrived home a couple of hours later, saying he had met some friends in Saint-Tropez and they had gone on for some further celebratory drinks. He was slurring his words and Julia looked at him with distaste. His weakness for alcohol, and that he never knew when to stop, had been one of the thorns in their marriage. Julia had accused him on numerous occasions of drinking too much, and Xavier would become aggressive and deny it.

Tonight, as Agnes brought their supper out onto the terrace, and Xavier topped up his glass again, Julia decided to say nothing. She lacked the energy for a fight.

"My sister's arriving tomorrow to stay for a few days," Julia said, picking at the fresh red mullet, slow-cooked in cranberries.

Xavier raised his eyebrows. "The perfect Alicia is gracing us with her presence?"

"Don't speak about my sister like that. Something's happened to her. She wouldn't tell me what it was, but she sounded very upset."

"Perhaps she missed one of her husband's favorite shirts from the ironing pile," Xavier snorted.

Julia did not rise to his drink-fueled bait, but changed the subject. "So, was today your last interview?" she asked, referring to the latest with *Le Figaro.*

"It is up to me." He shrugged. "I have many more requests, including an offer to write a memoir. They are promising a lot of money. What do you think?"

"I think we don't need the money," Julia replied brusquely.

"And *Paris Match* wishes to come here to interview us both."

"No," said Julia firmly. "I told you I would do one press call and that would be it. Please don't involve me in any further plans."

"D'accord," Xavier said glibly, and they ate in silence.

After a while, Xavier reached his hand across the table. "You are not happy, are you, Julia? Please tell me why."

"Perhaps I'm still adjusting," she said simply, unwilling to pursue the conversation.

Xavier squeezed her hand, then poured himself more wine. "Yes, perhaps that is the reason. You seem very different."

"I am different. I feel as though I've lived for a lifetime since I last saw you. These . . . experiences change you, Xavier, of course they do."

"But we can make it like it was before, can't we, *chérie*?" he beseeched her. "Oh! The way we loved each other . . . it was so beautiful. We can find that again, I know we can."

Julia sighed. "I hope so, Xavier, I really do."

Later, he followed her to their bedroom and hovered by the door.

"Please, Julia, let me be with you tonight. Let me show you how I can love you and help us both remember how it used to be." He walked toward her and took her in his arms.

Even though not an iota of her desired him, Julia steeled herself and allowed Xavier to caress and kiss her, thinking that perhaps he was right, that it might help her remember.

After they had made love, Julia lay awake next to him. The act itself had been over in seconds, and Xavier had fallen immediately into a deep sleep.

If she was brutally honest, Julia had found his touch and the smell of alcohol on his breath repulsive. How could it be? Before, she had always longed for closeness, for the feel of his nakedness next to her. Lovemaking had been a strong part of their relationship.

But tonight . . . Julia turned over restlessly, unsettled that, while Xavier made love to her, she had been unable to stop thinking of Kit . . . the knowledge that she could be completely herself, that Kit loved her for who she was . . .

Julia checked herself. There was no point punishing herself with what might have been. Fate had decreed it was not to be, and all she could do was try to accept it.

Julia stood in front of Arrivals at Toulon airport and saw Alicia emerge from the baggage hall. Her sister was a pinched, pale version of her former self. Julia walked over and took her in her arms.

"Hello, Alicia. Welcome to France."

"Oh, Julia, it's so good to see you," managed Alicia, before she burst into tears on her sister's shoulder.

"Come on, let's take you home. And then you can tell me what all this is about," Julia suggested gently, guiding Alicia to the car.

As they headed east to Ramatuelle, Julia stole a glance at her sister, who was staring straight ahead, her hands folded tensely in her lap. "Can you talk about it now? Or do you want to wait until we get there?"

"Is Xavier at home?"

"Yes," Julia said quietly.

"Have you spoken to Dad yet?"

"No. I haven't heard a word from him. As a matter of fact, I was pretty surprised he didn't call me, given Xavier's reappearance."

"Perhaps he's had other things on his mind," Alicia muttered.

Julia registered the bitterness in her sister's voice and decided not to pursue it. They drove in silence as the road started to climb upward and the vista opened before them to reveal an azure Mediterranean Sea at its most majestic.

Alicia suddenly put her hand on Julia's arm. "Stop the car here, will you? I need to get out."

Julia pulled over to a bay at the crest of the cliff, which provided parking for those who wanted to enjoy the well-known beauty spot. Alicia got straight out of the car and went over to the guardrail that separated her from the steep drop to the sea below them.

Tentatively, Julia followed her. She stood next to her and leaned over the guardrail. "It is beautiful here, isn't it?" she asked neutrally.

"Dad told me three days ago that I was adopted."

The words shot from Alicia's mouth with a crispness that belied their emotional intensity.

Julia found that her mouth had fallen open. *"What!"*

"Yes, it's true." Alicia's voice was clipped. "I'm adopted. Mum had cancer when she was in her twenties, long before the bout that killed her in her forties. They thought the radiation treatment would mean she couldn't have babies. So they adopted me. So, Mum is not my mum, Dad is not my dad, and you, Julia," Alicia said as she turned to stare at her with blank eyes, "are not my sister."

"No! I—" Julia shook her head in despair, wondering when the shocks were going to stop coming. "Surely this can't be true?"

"It is. Dad showed me my original birth certificate. Apparently, my mother, who went by the name of Joy Reynolds, was a teenager from Aylsham who got herself into trouble. I was put up for adoption by her, and Mum and Dad—or should I say, George and Jasmine—took me when I was two weeks old."

"But—"

"What about you?" Alicia read her sister's thoughts. "That's what you want to ask, isn't it? It's okay, Julia, you're definitely theirs. It's only me who's the cuckoo in the nest."

"But I don't understand, Alicia. If Mum couldn't have babies, how come I came along three years later?"

"Apparently it's common for women who are childless and adopt a baby to suddenly find themselves pregnant. Something to do with the hormones the maternal instinct brings out in them. Max looked it up on the Internet for me last night, and there are hundreds of similar stories. So, don't worry, Julia, you really are of their blood. Sorry if that sounds bitter." Alicia reached out her hand and put it on Julia's arm. "I don't mean to be. It's just that what I thought *was*, isn't anymore. I don't know . . . who I am."

"No," agreed Julia with feeling, "it must be dreadful for you. I'm so very, very sorry, Alicia. And, to be honest, I can't really understand why Dad has chosen to tell you after all this time. I mean, surely they should have done this years ago?"

"I know." Alicia nodded. "I don't think he was ever going to tell me. But he said he had to because of something Elsie told him."

A glimmer of understanding dawned in Julia. This was why Elsie had insisted Julia shouldn't share the story of her original Crawford genes with Alicia. Because, of course, it wasn't Alicia's heritage.

"Anyway," Alicia continued, "it hardly matters why—he *did.* And it's completely and utterly shattered me." Alicia rested her head on her arms and wept. "I feel completely lost."

It was so uncharacteristic of Alicia to appear vulnerable and devastated that Julia struggled to find the words to comfort her.

"I can understand the shock you must feel. . . ."

Alicia put her head up and looked at Julia. "Can you really?" She shook her head. "No, Julia, I don't think so. My family means just about everything to me. It's always come first, always. Remember when Mum died? I tried so hard to look after you and Dad. Even though I was heartbroken too, someone had to take Mum's place and keep the show on the road. I learned to cope. And you know what?" Alicia's eyes blazed. "I've been *coping* ever since!"

"I'm sorry, Alicia, I really am. I didn't realize."

"No, of course you didn't. You and Dad were both lost in your own worlds, then and now. The problem was, you two, my family, were *my* world. I wanted to be there for you both, it was all I had. Dad floated off collecting his plants, then you left for music college, relieved to get away from me—"

"That's not true, Alicia."

"Come on, Julia, be honest." Alicia's voice had a harsh, ugly timbre to it. "You resented me when I was doing my best to look after you. And I think you still resent me now. Me, with my 'perfect' life, always so capable . . . you've felt patronized. I don't blame you." Alicia shook her head. "It was my choice to take on the role. It helped me survive, bury my own pain. And I've been living it ever since. Always being there for everyone—you, Dad, Max, the kids—and now . . ." Alicia was choked with emotion. "I find out it was all a bloody lie! You and Mum and Dad aren't even my real family!"

Julia stood silently, cowed by the force of Alicia's anger and pain. And, far worse, knowing that a lot of what Alicia said was true.

"It wasn't a lie, Alicia," Julia said finally. "We loved each other—*do* love each other—whatever our true blood may be."

Alicia rested her head on the rail for a while, then sighed. "Forgive me, Julia. I've lost the plot, I'm afraid. What a therapist would call my 'coping strategies' seem to have deserted me. I feel like my life has come tumbling down about my ears. Nothing makes sense anymore. Everything feels . . . pointless."

Julia tentatively touched her sister's shoulder. "It's the shock, I promise. It does get better."

"I can't believe Mum didn't give birth to me," Alicia whispered, "just some complete stranger."

"But then, it was the same for Mum."

It was out of her mouth before Julia could stop herself.

Alicia looked up at Julia, her pale face streaked with tears. "What? You're telling me Mum was adopted too?"

Julia nodded. "Yes. That's what Elsie had to tell me. And almost certainly what she told Dad too."

"My God," breathed Alicia. "Did Mum know she was adopted?"

"No, she didn't. Elsie said that, as far as she was concerned, Jasmine was her child and that was the end of it. And I suppose," Julia added softly, "when it comes down to it, that's all that really matters, isn't it?"

Alicia didn't reply. Julia pulled back the blonde hair from her sister's tear-stained face. "I can really understand how thinking you were one thing, and then discovering you're another, can affect you. But it doesn't change anything that really matters. The only difference between Mum and you is that she didn't know, and now you do."

Alicia, calmer now, looked out across the sea and sighed. "Knowing about Mum helps me, somehow. I think I've just got to get used to it emotionally."

"Yes, you have. And I don't want to sound patronizing, but I've had my fair share of shocks in the past year, so I know you just have to give it time."

"Yes." Alicia stared out across the bay. "I told you once that I was worried about how I'd cope with a real problem, like you've had to—and look at me!" Alicia smiled sadly. "I'm a wreck!"

"You're only human, Alicia," Julia said, realizing guiltily she had misjudged her sister. "Don't be too hard on yourself."

"No. That's what Max said." She turned to Julia and smiled. "He's been wonderful, so supportive and understanding."

"He's a lovely man, Alicia. And he worships you."

"The problem is, I'm so used to being strong, and just now—I'm not. It must be a shock for him, after all these years, to see me so frail."

"Perhaps he's enjoying the opportunity to take care of you for a change."

"Perhaps . . ." Alicia reached out her arms to her sister. "I need a hug."

Julia held her tightly.

"Sorry about the things I said just now. I didn't mean them." Alicia's voice was muffled in Julia's shoulder.

"And I'm sorry I never saw how much you were hurting over Mum too. I behaved like a selfish brat when you were only trying to help. Really, you've been wonderful to me, especially recently. I don't know how I'd have coped without you." Julia found she meant every word.

"Well, little sis"—Alicia broke from the hug—"I need *you* now. Okay?"

"Okay."

That evening, Alicia joined Julia and Xavier for supper on the terrace. Alicia had taken a nap when she arrived and seemed calmer, though she still looked pale. Xavier was on his best behavior, and with Alicia's presence neutralizing any tension between him and Julia, they managed a pleasant evening. At midnight, Alicia yawned and excused herself.

"Sorry, chaps, I've not been sleeping well, and I've now had too much wine on a stomach that's been empty for the past few days. Night, and thank you so much for having me." She squeezed Julia's hand. "I'm so glad I came."

Xavier retired soon afterward, leaving Julia to switch off the lights and lock the doors. It was so different to the routine she'd had with Kit, where they always shared the tasks. As she went round the house, she thought about Alicia and how she'd never taken the time to see Alicia's vulnerability beneath the surface. How, when their mother died, Alicia had constructed her life to protect herself from pain. And now the walls had come tumbling down.

Kit had mentioned it once—he had seen who Alicia really was and understood. As Julia climbed the stairs, she wished she'd had his insight. At least now she had a chance to repay Alicia for everything she had tried to do and the care she had shown. She felt a sudden warm rush of affection and love for her sister as she went into her bedroom.

Xavier had obviously concluded, after the previous night's lovemaking, that he was back to being a fully entitled husband and was spread out on the bed.

"Your sister seemed"—Xavier searched for the words—"more human tonight. Although I couldn't wait for dinner to be over so I could have you to myself again, *mon amour.*"

When Julia sat on the bed to remove her clothes, he pulled her to him.

"No, Xavier!" She wriggled out of his grasp, then shook her head. "Not tonight. I am tired."

The following day, Xavier was out unusually early for yet another interview, so Julia and Alicia enjoyed a late breakfast together. Then Julia suggested they make their way down to the quieter end of Pampelonne Beach in Saint-Tropez.

"How completely decadent," said Alicia, as they settled on comfortable loungers provided by the beach bar. "I suppose, if one has to find out one is adopted, it's some compensation escaping to a sister who happens to live in the South of France. Being here with you has really helped. And you're right; finding out I'm adopted probably doesn't make that much difference."

"No, Alicia, I really don't think it does," answered Julia, enjoying the sun on her face. "And I'm so sorry I've been resentful of you, when you were only trying to help me. I always felt you got everything right when I got it wrong."

"I wish!" groaned Alicia. "I've spent the past twenty years being so busy avoiding how I really feel, I don't know now who I am."

"Well, maybe it'll be fun finding out, and perhaps, for a while, you should concentrate on putting *you* first, not everybody else."

"The problem is, I have to be needed. If I let that go, what do I have left?"

"Well, those that love you, love you for who you are, not what you do for them."

"Really? You mean, if I stopped ironing Max's shirts and forgot to make the children's supper, they'd still like me?"

Julia read the twinkle in Alicia's eye. "You know they would. And, sorry to be blunt, but perhaps you'd get more respect from them if you didn't pander to their every whim. And that includes me. You never know, we might even start pandering to you."

"Wow! What a thought." Alicia giggled. "Anyway, I've only got myself to blame. I've always projected this capable image, and, of course, I *am*, Julia. It's my strength. Most of the time anyway."

"Yes, but you're also allowed to be vulnerable and needy sometimes too, like the rest of us human beings. And you shouldn't be afraid of showing it."

"No." Alicia nodded. "You're right. And the way that Max has been since this happened . . . You know, I used to think I married him just because he was 'there.' I thought that maybe"—she bit her lip—"I just needed 'somebody' after you left and Dad was hardly at home. But this has really shown me what a good man he is. And how lucky I am to have him."

"There's always a silver lining. And at least this has shown you that Max is far more capable than you've given him credit for in the past. I doubt any of the kids are currently wasting away under his care, are they?"

"No. They're not. And just now, lying here in the sun, without anyone asking anything of me, I feel . . . wonderful!"

"Good. Then you should do it more often."

"You know what?" Alicia lay back on her lounger and closed her eyes. "I bloody well will!"

Later, over a lunch of fresh mozzarella and tomato, accompanied by a *pichet* of local rosé, Julia told Alicia what she had learned about her own origins. As they drank café au lait, an intrigued Alicia mulled over the details of the story.

"So, our mother was a Crawford?"

"Yes. The illegitimate daughter of Lord Harry." Julia sighed. "Isn't it ironic? She grew up right under her father's nose, and yet she never knew."

"No wonder Dad felt he had to tell me. Otherwise I'd have thought I had Crawford blood running through my veins too. I might have started putting on airs and graces, worn a tiara to breakfast, et al." Alicia grinned. "What's interesting is that surely your claim to Wharton Park is closer than Kit's? I mean, you're Harry's direct bloodline, whereas Kit's just some kind of cousin. If Mum had still been alive, wouldn't the estate have come to her?"

"Alicia," cautioned Julia, "Mum was born on the wrong side of the blankets, as Elsie so sweetly put it."

"It doesn't matter anymore. With DNA testing, it can be proved. I read of a case recently in the *Times*."

"You're probably right, but, as you know, it's the closest male heir who inherits the *title*. Still, yes, I'm sure that if it had been known at the time, Mum would have been in line to inherit something."

Alicia looked at Julia. "Well then, the question is, now I'm out of the equation, are you entitled to a share of the estate?"

"Perhaps," said Julia, taking a sip of coffee. "But it's not something I've had the time or inclination to investigate. And I certainly don't need the money."

"No. You and Kit are, what . . . ? " Alicia scratched her nose as she thought about it. "Third cousins?"

Julia's face darkened. "Something like that, yes. But it's hardly relevant now, is it?"

"Isn't it?"

"Why should it be?" Julia answered abruptly.

"Well," Alicia trod carefully, "little more than a few days ago, you and Kit were together, for want of a better phrase. You looked very happy and—"

"Alicia, if you don't mind, I'd prefer not to talk about it." Julia stopped the thread of the conversation in its tracks. "Xavier has come back, so I'm still a married woman. Whatever Kit and I *were*, is now irrelevant."

"Have you spoken to Kit?"

"As I said, I'd prefer not to talk about it, okay?"

Alicia took the hint and the subject was closed.

56

The following afternoon, Julia drove Alicia to the airport.

"It's been wonderful," said Alicia warmly as they stood by the departure gate. "Just what I needed. I must admit"—she wrinkled her newly freckled nose—"I don't want to go home."

"Well, come back anytime. With or without the family. And remember, just occasionally, it's okay to think about just you."

"I will." Alicia nodded. "Thanks, Julia. I've learned a lot."

"Have you?"

"Yes." Alicia was on the verge of tears. She pulled Julia close and embraced her. "It's a new beginning for me, isn't it? For us too?"

"Yes, it is." Julia smiled. "Take care, Alicia."

"And you."

Julia drove home slowly, thinking about Alicia and hoping the sudden, new understanding and equality in their relationship would continue. And how much she had longed to board that plane to England with her.

She too didn't want to return home. Even though she accepted Xavier was doing his best, and she must continue to give their relationship time, she couldn't control a tension, a discomfort, and an irritation with him.

Worst of all, where once she had felt so much love for him, there was nothing.

Julia parked the car and walked toward the house, taking a deep breath and telling herself that tonight she would do whatever it took to try to make it better. What choice did she have?

She opened the front door to a delicious aroma of fresh meat, fried butter, and herbs. Xavier was in the kitchen, standing over the stove, turning two steaks around the pan.

"Voilà! You are home. I decide tonight I cook you supper and dismiss Agnes. Go onto the terrace and sit down, *chérie*, and I will be out with our drinks."

Surprised and bewildered, Julia did so. She had never seen Xavier cook in their entire married life. He came out with a bottle of champagne and poured it into glasses.

"To us."

"Yes, to us," she toasted back, and they drank.

He came to sit next to her and took her hand and kissed it. "I could not wait for your sister to go, so that we could be alone. I want to tell you I understand how hard it is for you to accept that I am back and to forgive me for my part in Gabriel's death. But I swear, if you trust me, I can make it up to you. Do you believe me?"

"I believe it's what you want, Xavier." Julia felt guilty that nothing he could do or say would remove the numbness inside her. But she had to keep trying. There was simply no alternative. "There's somewhere I want to take you."

"Anywhere, *chérie*, you know that," he answered eagerly.

"I want you to come to the place where Gabriel died. Only the day before you reappeared, I planted two cypress trees: one for him and one for you. I'd like you to come with me to see them."

After a pause he said, "Of course, anything you say."

"I'd like to go tomorrow morning."

"*Bien sûr, chérie.* We will go."

"Thank you, Xavier."

For the first time since his return, Julia fell asleep that night with her head resting on her husband's shoulder.

As always, when they were at home together with no commitments, Julia was up first in the morning. Xavier rarely rose before ten thirty, which she used to full advantage as practice time.

At eleven o'clock, Xavier finally staggered into the kitchen. Julia was making coffee.

"*Bonjour*, my Julia." Xavier wrapped his arms round her. "Mmmm, that coffee, it smells so good."

Julia handed him a cup. "Why don't you go and take a shower? I'd like to leave as soon as possible."

Xavier furrowed his eyebrows. "Where to, remind me?"

"To the place where Gabriel died, where I planted the trees, remember?"

"Yes, yes, of course. I will not be long."

Julia buried her irritation as Xavier left the room. She understood his reluctance to return. It would be as hard for him as it had been for her. But . . . she needed to see him grieve.

Twenty minutes later, Xavier reappeared in the kitchen, fully dressed.

"*Alors!* Let us go."

Julia drove, as she usually had, with Xavier sitting passively beside her.

"I will go to Paris tomorrow to complete the round of interviews, and then it will all be at an end," he offered.

Julia said nothing. She would not let herself react.

"And Olav said yesterday that the publisher will call to try and tempt me into writing a book. It seems I have never been so busy."

Again Julia did not respond.

She parked the car in the bay on the side of the road and they silently picked their way down the hill until they arrived at the two cypress saplings, standing side by side. Julia had brought some water with her and poured it over the saplings.

Half her thoughts were with Gabriel, the other half with Xavier, as she watched him standing uncomfortably next to her. Eventually, he reached for her hand.

"What you have done is something beautiful. It is a place of peace, out of tragedy. Should we, do you think, tear the other one from the ground, as I assume it represents me?"

"Maybe. I—"

Xavier's mobile rang. Julia watched as he took it from his trouser pocket and studied the number.

"*Pardon, chérie*, it is the publisher from London. I must speak to him."

Julia watched as Xavier walked off to take the call.

She looked at the two cypress saplings, then tore the taller one from the ground. She threw it as far as she could, away from the place that marked the death of her beloved son. And her love for Xavier.

• • •

The summer wore on. Julia was well aware of the irony that she finally had the time she'd always wanted to spend with Xavier, but now only longed for the moments when he left the house.

They fell into a routine: Julia practiced in the morning before Xavier woke, then he took over in the afternoon while Julia went to the beach to escape the house and tried to relax. She often found her thoughts drifting involuntarily back to Kit, wondering where he was, what he was doing—wishing fervently she could pour out her troubled heart to him and listen to his calm, wise words of advice.

One evening in late August, Julia arrived home to find Xavier in the kitchen, making a list.

"I think we should have a party, *chérie*. What do you think?"

Julia raised her eyebrows. "What kind of party?"

"A celebration that I am back from the dead, to let everyone know how happy we are. I am writing a list of all the people I wish to invite."

"If that's what you want." Julia found the whole notion crass and inappropriate, but she was too worn down for an argument. "When are you thinking of having it?"

"As soon as possible. Many people will be leaving the Riviera soon; I was thinking next Saturday would be perfect."

"As you wish." Julia took a glass, filled it with water, and went to her study to answer her e-mails.

Saturday night was soon upon them, and Agnes had helped prepare everything in the short time. Xavier behaved like an excited little boy in the run-up to his birthday and tried on three different shirts for Julia's approval.

As Julia dressed and applied her mascara, she felt no such anticipation. Xavier had invited over a hundred people, some of whom she hardly knew. She had confided her misgivings about the party to Alicia.

"But Xavier's making an effort, Julia," Alicia had countered. "There's been so much pain for both of you, why is it wrong for him to celebrate? Granted, there isn't a completely happy ending, but a better one than you had this time last year." After a pause on the line,

Alicia added, "Sorry, darling, but when are you going to forgive Xavier for the fact he lived, when Gabriel died?"

That was two days ago, and even though Julia had found the words difficult to hear, she knew Alicia was right. She promised herself that tonight, even though she knew her heart was closed to Xavier forever, she would make an effort to celebrate with him.

She took one last look at herself and went downstairs for a glass of champagne with him before their guests arrived.

"*Chérie*, you look very beautiful tonight."

Julia let him embrace her.

He took two glasses of champagne from a waiter, standing sentry in the hall with his tray, awaiting the guests.

"To us"—Xavier clinked her glass—"and to new beginnings."

As he kissed her, the first guests rang the doorbell and Xavier went to greet them. Soon the house and garden were full of people, most congregating near a jazz trio playing in the corner of the terrace.

Julia did her utmost to play the happy wife of the newly returned husband. Xavier made an emotional speech at midnight, praising his wonderful wife and the love they shared. He said how devastated they were to have lost their beloved son, but assured everyone there would be plenty more children in the future.

By one o'clock, the party was in full swing and the champagne still flowing. Julia spied Madelaine, who had held the fateful barbecue, tottering over to her, clearly the worse for wear.

"Honey!" Madelaine held out her arms and pulled Julia to her ample bosom. "It's so wonderful to see the two of you reunited," she slurred in her Texan accent. "It was a day I thought I'd never see."

"I certainly didn't." Julia smiled wryly.

"And we felt so guilty, I mean, it was our party they'd been to before the . . . accident."

"You shouldn't," said Julia uncomfortably. "As you said, it was an accident."

Madelaine drew back from her and stared at her with glazed eyes. "Honey, I so admire you. You are so forgiving!"

"Forgiving that it was an accident?" Julia said, a little bewildered.

"Why, yes! We all told Xavier he should stay the night, but of course he wouldn't listen."

"Why?" Julia managed.

"Because, honey, we all knew he wasn't fit to drive. Not that any of us were," she added, swaying unsteadily.

The information slowly began to compute in Julia's brain.

"Are you saying Xavier was drunk?"

"Surely you knew? He told us when he came over for lunch a few weeks ago, he'd explained everything to you. And that you understood and forgave him."

The look on Julia's face must have registered with Madelaine and she clapped her hand to her mouth. "Jeez, I hope I didn't say anything out of church. I mean, we all like a drink now and then, don't we? Look at everyone tonight." She swept her hand around the noisy, drunken crowd. "I bet most of them haven't got a chauffeur home! Anyway, it could happen to any of us. And I'd be the last one to cast stones. You are reunited with the guy you love," she said fondly. "Come and see us real soon, honey, y'hear?"

The party carried on as Julia packed what she could into the one small traveling case she had arrived with. Xavier was on the piano, entertaining the remaining guests with his brilliance.

He wouldn't even notice she had gone until later.

She left her traveling case by the bedroom door, then tiptoed across the landing and into the room she had not yet had the courage to enter. The smell of him hit her instantly, bringing tears to her eyes. Ignoring the many reminders of her little son's life, Julia walked over to his cot.

Lying there on the pillow was Pomme, Gabriel's beloved teddy bear. She picked Pomme up and hugged him to her. Then she went to the small wardrobe and took out one of Gabriel's T-shirts.

As she walked toward the door, she blew a kiss to the memory of what this room had been. Then she stowed her two treasures in her traveling case, walked down the stairs, and left the house.

57

I lean over the arm of my comfortable seat and look out the window at the world below. Even though I've flown constantly, I still marvel at the miracle of it and find it helps me put my thoughts in perspective.

It is almost dark, and from the flight path on my screen, I can see we are passing over Delhi. It is a mass of twinkling lights, indicating the countless lives packed into the space beneath me. Each with its own story to tell, its own tapestry at some stage of being woven. The strength of each of the individual specks of life humbles and amazes me.

The last lights of Delhi disappear as the aircraft moves on over the vast empty tracts of the Himalayas, and the world becomes black beneath me.

Just now, I think sadly, I am the plane, free to cross the world and land anywhere I choose. I only wish someone could set my flight path for me. Just a few weeks ago, I was so sure that, finally, my life was following the right route, but now it has been blown violently off course yet again. Currently, I feel the wreckage is all that remains.

At least I know I have the strength to cope this time. There will be no self-pity for what might have been. I have said a final good-bye to the physical memories of my son, knowing I will carry Gabriel and the pain of losing him in my heart for as long as I live.

And as for Xavier . . . the pedestal I had always put him on has come crashing down. In retrospect, I know it was fatally cracked when he returned and told me his story. The denouement a few days ago only confirmed what I already knew: Xavier is a weak, selfish man who cares for no one more than himself, not even his precious child.

He disgusts me.

I feel no regret for turning my back on our life and walking away from him. I understand it was impossible for me to stay.

And now, once more, I am returning to the past to try to discover my future.

After dinner, I close my eyes and sleep, as the aircraft carries me safely east.

When Julia emerged from Arrivals, she saw her name being held up by a smartly dressed representative. She pushed her trolley through the crowds toward him.

"Welcome to Bangkok, Miss Forrester. I take you to car now, please." The representative took her trolley and she followed him out into the breathtakingly hot, humid air of the city.

Moments later, Julia was ensconced in a comfortable limousine. Her liveried driver attempted to make conversation in his stilted English, but Julia wasn't interested and gazed out the window as the car sped along the modern highway. She was intrigued by the mixture of tower blocks, interspersed with the glinting gold roof of a Thai temple and battered wooden shacks bedecked with wash strung on lines. She thought it strange that, although she had traveled far and wide and had performed in both China and Japan, Bangkok had never been on her list.

The car came smoothly to a halt by the leafy entrance to the Oriental Hotel. As Julia was handed out of the car by a porter, she breathed in the distinctive smell of the city—the sweet aroma of exotic flowers, underlain with a hint of rotting vegetables—and the scent was somehow familiar to her.

When she entered the lobby, a beautiful Thai girl handed her a jasmine garland. "Welcome to the Oriental Hotel, Miss Forrester. I will take you to your room."

"Thank you," Julia said, admiring the elegant lobby with its stunning array of orchids spilling out of a vast pot, and the huge Chinese-style lanterns hanging from the high ceiling.

Up in her room, she opened the door onto the balcony and looked in wonder at the majestic river below, stretching as far as the eye could see on either side of the hotel. It was peppered with boats of all shapes and sizes, and the cacophony of sound was continuous.

Julia ordered some coffee from room service and sequestered herself on the balcony, relishing the atmosphere. She had always loved warmth, could stand the most humid conditions, and the temperature here felt just right.

She leaned over to her left and saw that the Oriental was a small but perfectly formed oasis of calm alongside its more grandiose hotel neighbors. The oldest part of the building, the part her grandfather would have known, was now called the Authors' Lounge, according to the directory she was flicking through. It stood on the riverfront, a hundred yards away from her, beyond the beautifully kept tropical gardens and the swimming pool. Its pretty, colonial façade was dwarfed by the tall buildings around it, but Julia could imagine these as wooden shacks on stilts in the river—just as Harry would have seen it.

When she had finished her coffee, Julia found herself yawning. She delved into her handbag for the address Elsie had given her and stared at it. She needed to sleep first, have a clear head before tackling the last leg of her journey into the past.

She slept for much longer than she meant to and woke, fuzzy-headed, at a quarter to five. She sat on her balcony with a glass of cold white wine, watching Bangkok turn from day to night. Below her, twinkling white lights festooned the trees on the terrace overlooking the river. The terrace was already full of guests having dinner, and Julia realized she too needed to eat. She took the elevator down to the lobby, smiling in surprise that the lift attendant already knew her name, and went over to the concierge desk.

"Yes, madam, may I help you?" Another exquisite Thai girl smiled at her.

"Yes." Julia handed over her piece of paper. "I was wondering whether you could provide me with a car to take me to this address."

"Of course. It is not far away. Would you like car now?"

"No, tomorrow morning, please. At eleven."

"I will arrange it for you, madam. Is there anything else I can help you with?"

"No, thank you," said Julia, and walked across the lobby, pausing to listen to the string quartet playing Schubert in the corner.

She was ushered to a candlelit table right on the riverfront at the far end of the terrace and ordered another glass of wine and a green curry. She glanced around at the elegantly clad guests, listened to the soft chugging of boats on the river, and felt a sudden calm.

Even if she didn't find her grandmother or discovered she was dead, as Elsie suspected, Julia felt glad she had come. This was a special place; if nothing else, it was the perfect setting in which to take stock and think rationally about her future. She felt cocooned by the gentle staff and the tranquil atmosphere of the spot where her own story had begun.

Surprisingly, Julia slept through the night, for once having no need of the pills she always carried with her to ward off jet lag. She took a breakfast of mango, papaya, and rose apple, washed down with strong coffee. At five to eleven, she was being escorted out of the lobby to her car.

Her driver turned round and smiled at her. "This is private address, yes?" He indicated the piece of paper.

"I think so."

"Okay, madam, we go."

She sat in the back of the car, wishing she could have contacted Lidia by telephone to give the old lady some warning that her granddaughter was about to appear on her doorstep. But, with no surname to go by, that had not been possible. Elsie had only ever addressed the photographs to "Lidia."

"You sure it's a good idea?" Elsie had asked, when Julia called her from Paris and said she was traveling to Thailand to search for her real grandmother. "Stirring up more of the past, when you should be looking to the future?"

Elsie might be right, Julia thought, but perhaps she had to go back to her roots before she could move forward.

The car wound its way through the streets of Bangkok, and Julia noticed the driver raise a surprised eyebrow when she opened her window to breathe in the air and the atmosphere. The overcrowded pavements with residents spilling out of their houses, the alleyways filled with food stalls busily serving customers, and the streets themselves packed with cars, ancient buses, and motorized tuk-tuks were cacophonous with activity. A jumbled meeting of East and West, yet so real, so vibrant and alive.

"We nearly there, madam. House is on river, yes?" asked the driver.

"I have no idea, I'm afraid. I've never been here before."

"Do not worry, madam. We find it, okay?"

Julia nodded. "Okay."

A couple of minutes later, he turned off the busy street into a pretty, residential road. They reached the end of the cul-de-sac and the driver pointed to a gate. "This is right *soi* and that is house you want."

"Thank you." Julia made to open the door, but the driver was already there, tipping his gold-braided, white cap as she climbed out.

"You want me wait?" He smiled.

"Yes, please. I don't know how long I'll be."

"No worry, madam, you be as long as you need. I be here."

"Thank you."

Julia took a deep breath and made her way up the path. The house was pretty, built in Thai style, with wooden-clad outer walls, a veranda that ran all the way round the ground floor, and topped with an inverted V-shaped roof that curled up at the edges.

She walked up the steps to the veranda. Finding no bell, she knocked on the front door, waited several minutes, then knocked again, and then again. Just as she was about to turn away in disappointment, the door opened.

A pair of ancient gimlet eyes appeared in the small crack. "May I help you?" the man's heavily accented Thai voice asked.

"Yes, I'm looking for Lidia."

The gimlet eyes surveyed her, then filled with fear. "Who are you? Why you want her?" he asked accusingly.

Julia was wrong-footed by these questions, not wanting to reveal her identity until she had established who the man was.

"I am from England—a friend of Lidia's asked me to give her a message. Is she in?"

The man shook his head. "No, she out. Bye-bye."

He tried to close the door but Julia held it open.

"She will come back?" she asked, unconsciously falling into the man's pidgin English.

The man shrugged through the tiny crack. "Maybe."

"She is . . . well?" Julia wanted to say *alive*, but felt it was inappropriate.

"She is well." The man nodded. "Now, you go away, okay?"

"When she comes back, can you tell her that a friend of Harry's wants to see her. I am staying at the Oriental Hotel in room 1512 and will wait for her there." Julia enunciated the words slowly and carefully.

"Harry," the man twirled the name on his tongue, then nodded. "Okay, I tell."

The door was slammed in her face and Julia went back to the car.

She spent the afternoon by the pool, filled with anxiety that the old man had not understood and would not pass on the message. But at least she knew Lidia was alive. For now, she could do little more except wait and use the time to contemplate her life.

And face up to her feelings for Kit.

Julia knew it was doubtful her marriage to Xavier could have survived after what she had learned about the accident, but as she lay in the heat of the tropical sun, she forced herself to admit that her feelings for Kit had also played a part in its demise. Kit's love for her, his quiet strength and lack of insecurity, neediness, or jealousy, had made her see Xavier—and her relationship with him—much more clearly.

Kit had no doubt marched into her life at an inappropriate moment, when every emotion she felt was muddled. But that she had found such happiness with him—when she was so grief-stricken over her son and ashamed for moving on so soon after losing her husband—was testament to the strength of what they had shared.

She knew it was love. In its purest and most simple form.

In the past few months, she had also learned one of the most crucial lessons of life: everything depended on timing. If she had met Kit under different circumstances, at another moment, perhaps they would still be together now.

There was no going back. The trust had been broken. Kit must feel like a discarded toy, thrown away when a better, shinier version reappeared. She knew that, if the roles had been reversed, she would have felt that. She hadn't even had the grace or the courage to speak to him in person.

No . . . the damage was done and she had to move on. Men weren't everything, and she must stop relying on them to bring her happiness.

Later that evening, sitting on her balcony with a glass of wine, Julia decided she would call Olav and tell him to book as heavy a work schedule as he could produce.

She looked at the heavenly view of twinkling lights on the water and, despite herself, couldn't help thinking she would like to share it with Kit. To tell him how comfortable she felt in this far-flung country, cocooned in this tranquil yet exhilarating setting . . . how she felt she belonged. Like her grandfather before her.

God, she missed Kit: it was as if only half of her were here. Whether or not she was free to love him, it was unbearably poignant because it was another wonderful thing she had lost in the past year.

She drank a little too much wine that night, and allowed herself to cry properly over Kit for the first time since she had been forced to let him go.

Over the next few days, Julia filled in the time while she waited for a response from Lidia by retracing Harry's footsteps, taking trips upriver to see the royal palace and the Emerald Buddha, and relishing their beauty. She took afternoon tea in the Authors' Lounge, studying sepia photographs on the walls depicting the hotel as it would have been when Harry and Lidia were playing out their doomed love affair.

She checked in regularly with the concierge to see whether any messages had been left for her—they had not. She called Olav to let him know she was ready to take on whatever he had to offer. And spent hours by the swimming pool trying to work out where she wanted to live.

She was now homeless, unless she counted the cottage in Norfolk—which she did not. Apart from being completely unsuitable for her needs, it was too painful a reminder of Kit.

Perhaps a fresh start in an anonymous capital was the answer? A sterile apartment that would mean nothing to her, but would at least be a base to return to between recitals.

London . . . Paris . . . New York?

The world, sadly, was her oyster once more.

As she ate her solitary dinner on the terrace, Julia decided that tomorrow she would go back to Lidia's house and try to make contact with her one last time. Then she would leave Bangkok and begin her life once more.

"Madam Forrester." The terrace manager's voice startled her.

"Yes?"

"I have someone here who would like to speak with you."

Out of the darkness, a tiny, birdlike figure appeared, elegantly dressed in Thai silk, her jet black hair pulled up into a chignon, with two orchids fixed to one side of it.

As she came closer, Julia felt she recognized her, though it took a moment for her to realize why: she was looking at many of her own features. She knew this woman must be eighty, but time had drawn barely a line on her honey-colored skin. She had huge, almond-shaped, amber eyes, and Julia could easily imagine how heartbreakingly beautiful she must have been at seventeen.

The woman put her tiny hands together in the traditional Thai greeting of respect and bowed her head. Then she looked up and smiled.

"I am Lidia."

"Thank you for coming to see me." Julia could think of nothing better to say; she was transfixed by this woman who looked so much like herself. "Please, sit down," she added, indicating the vacant chair opposite her.

Lidia did so, then stared at Julia expectantly. "So, you must tell me why you came to my house and frightened my houseboy half to death."

Julia smiled inwardly at this description of the ancient man who had greeted her at Lidia's door. "I do apologize. I didn't mean to frighten him."

Lidia's eyes twinkled. "He tell me he think he see a ghost."

Julia raised an eyebrow. "Really? Why?"

"He think I die in the street while out shopping and come back to visit him as a young girl. Now I can see why. You are so very like me. I think he is confused—how can you be *friend* of Harry's, but resemble me as a young girl? I did not know whether to expect old lady or young."

"I wasn't sure what to say to him. Lidia, do you know who I am?" Julia felt a strange and sudden rush of emotion as she asked the question.

Lidia studied her. "You are too young to be my daughter, Jasmine. So I think you may be . . . my granddaughter?"

"Yes," Julia confirmed, tears pricking her eyes. "Jasmine was my mother."

It was a few seconds before Lidia spoke. Julia watched as she composed herself.

"I am sorry it take me some time to come to you, but you can understand I was shocked when I heard Harry's name. All these years, there hasn't been a day I have not thought of him. Is he still alive?" she asked, hope and fear combining in her eyes.

"No, Lidia, he died many years ago. I'm sorry."

Lidia nodded and put her hands to her heart. "I knew this in here, but still I hope. How did he die?"

Julia shook her head. "I don't know. It happened before I was born. But Elsie, my grandmother—or, should I say, the woman I thought was my grandmother until a few weeks ago—said . . . he died of a broken heart."

Lidia reached into her basket, brought out a handkerchief, and blew her nose. "You must forgive me, it is not dignified for an old lady to cry in public. For all these years, I hear nothing . . ."

"But Elsie sent you photographs of my mother, didn't she? To show you she was happy and well cared for in England?"

Lidia nodded. "Yes. It was kind of her. But, Julia"—Lidia's eyes looked puzzled—"the photographs are sent from Jasmine's nursemaid, Elsie. Why do you call Elsie your grandmother?"

To her horror, Julia realized Lidia had never known her daughter was not brought up by Lord Harry Crawford at Wharton Park, but by the gardener and his wife in their small cottage.

"Lidia, it's a very long story," Julia breathed, "and one I have only just discovered myself."

"I understand it will take time to explain," Lidia soothed. "So now, tell me of your mother. Is she as beautiful as you? Is she here?" she asked, her eyes so bright with expectation that Julia could no longer stem her tears.

"No . . ." Julia shook her head, realizing her odyssey back to the past would be far more complex and painful than she had allowed herself to acknowledge. "Oh, dear. I'm so sorry, my mother died twenty years ago, when I was eleven," she said, instinctively reaching across the table for Lidia's tiny hand.

Lidia held tightly to Julia's hand, her small body shaking with anguish. She murmured something in Thai, then sighed deeply.

"I think," she whispered, "this is not the time to hear the many things you have to tell me. We must talk of them in a private place, for I do not wish others to witness my pain."

"Yes. I'm so terribly sorry to bring you bad news. Perhaps I should not have come to find you."

"Oh, no, Julia, you must not think that, or be guilty for telling me what fate has done to both of us. I have lost a daughter, you have lost a mother. It is life and death." Lidia smiled at her. "And you must remember, Julia, that the bringer of bad news brings the good news too. For *you* are here. And you are part of me, and I of you. And we are sitting together, reunited at last, in the very place where I met and fell in love with your grandfather. There is a beauty in that, is there not?"

"Yes, there is," Julia agreed softly.

The manager arrived with a drink for Lidia.

"*Kop khun ka*, Thanadol. May I introduce my granddaughter, Julia? She has flown across the world to find me."

Thanadol's eyebrows hardly moved. "It is a pleasure to know this." He smiled. "I am hardly surprised: you are so alike. Please call me if you need anything further."

As he walked away, Julia asked, "How do you know him?"

"Oh, I worked here years ago with Thanadol's father. Many of the staff have relations who were employed before them. It is like family, this hotel, and the people in it were here when I needed them."

"How long did you work here?"

"Ten years, until I met my husband."

"You married?" For some reason, Julia was surprised.

"Yes, and again I meet him right here in the hotel. We were together for forty years. I was with him when the last breath left his body twelve years ago."

"I am glad you were able to find happiness, Lidia," Julia replied gently.

"Julia, it was not love. That was only for Harry. But I had a good life with him. My husband was a very successful man, with a big company, which I helped him build. And I loved him for loving me."

"Did you have children?"

"No." Lidia shook her head sadly. "I nearly die after giving birth to your mother. After that, no more babies."

"I'm so sorry."

"Perhaps," Lidia mused, "if I had not been so ill when *Khun* Bill came to find me, I would have kept Jasmine here with me. But," she sighed, "once you have made a decision and there is no turning back, acceptance is the only comfort. I learn many years ago I cannot change fate . . . or other people."

"No," Julia agreed with feeling, "I understand completely."

Lidia stared across the river, lost for a moment in private thoughts.

"Now, dear Julia," she said eventually, "tonight I feel tired, and I think I must go home. How long are you staying in Bangkok?"

"I was planning to leave soon. But I could stay longer, now you're here."

"Then, please, come to my house for lunch tomorrow. We can talk much more then. One question: do I have any more grandchildren?"

It was on the tip of Julia's tongue to tell her that, yes, she had another granddaughter. But, like much else in Julia's life, that was no longer true.

"Just me," she answered simply.

"And you are enough," Lidia replied warmly, "a true gift from God. Tell me, my granddaughter, are you a mother yourself, or do you work?"

Julia ignored the first part of the question and answered the second: "I'm a pianist."

Lidia's eyes immediately filled with tears before she broke into a smile. "Oh, Julia! You know that the first time I see your grandfather he was playing the piano, just over there in the old Bamboo Bar." Lidia pointed to the Authors' Lounge. "And I think that is when I fall in love with him. He came alive when he played. His is a special gift to inherit. Now"—she stood up—"I must go home."

Julia rose from her chair, not sure what form of farewell would be appropriate. Lidia made it easy for her by reaching for her hand, then kissing her on both cheeks.

"Thank you for coming to find me," Lidia murmured. "Good-bye, my granddaughter. We will speak tomorrow."

When Lidia had left, Julia sat for a while, staring at the river. Sometime later, she rose from the table and glanced up to the heavens. And truly hoped that Harry was there somewhere, watching with joy at what had just taken place.

58

The following day, armed with some photographs she had brought with her, Julia took the hotel limousine to Lidia's house. This time, the door was opened to her with a smile and a Thai greeting from Lidia's "houseboy."

"Welcome, *Khun* Julia. *Khun* Lidia wait for you on veranda. I will take you."

Julia followed him through the darkened rooms, shuttered against the strong sun, and onto a wide wooden terrace that reached out into the river on stilts. It was bedecked with large pots of flowers and the sweet smell of jasmine hung in the air, instantly reminding Julia of the gardens at Wharton Park.

A breeze from the river kept the veranda beautifully cool, and small brass bells hanging from the roof tinkled softly as they swayed.

The house stood on a small inlet at a wide part of the river. Boats still skidded and jostled past, but some way away, their hum providing a soft, comforting background noise to this oasis of calm.

Lidia appeared around the corner of the veranda, wearing an ancient "coolie" hat and carrying a tin watering can. Her face lit up when she saw Julia.

"Julia." Lidia opened her arms to her. "Welcome to my home. I am so glad to have you here. Now." She put the watering can down by a tap and indicated a chair at a table set for lunch. "Please, sit down and make yourself comfortable. Can I offer you a drink?"

"That would be lovely, thank you, Lidia."

Lidia's eyes flickered to the door, where her houseboy hovered; within seconds he had put a glass of water and a coconut with a straw in front of Julia.

"I have beer or wine if you prefer," Lidia said anxiously.

Julia shook her head. "This is perfect." She took a sip of the sweet, sticky liquid and smiled. "It's a new taste, but I like it."

Julia was aware how intently Lidia was watching her and she blushed.

"I apologize, Julia, for staring. It is strange and wonderful for me to see the beauty produced from myself and Harry, and my own daughter and your father. Here in my house." Lidia smiled broadly. "I am pleased with the result, you are very, very lovely. You have inherited the best features of your Thai heritage and English height and bearing. And, of course, a beautiful complexion. Oh, Thai women will do anything to appear light-skinned and European!"

"I *want* to get a tan."

This set Lidia into peals of laughter. The sweet sound was rather like the bells that tinkled in the breeze above her. "Yes, all white people cannot wait to make their skin brown. It must be God's little joke. We all want what we cannot have." Lidia's face grew serious and she leaned in toward Julia. "And, Julia, do not be afraid to tell me what happened to Jasmine when she arrived in England. I have worked it out for myself. As the moon hung high in the sky last night, I understood. *Khun* Bill and his wife, Elsie, adopted my baby, didn't they?"

"Yes, Lidia, they did," confirmed Julia nervously. "There really wasn't a choice at the time."

"Did Harry know? Know his daughter grow up so close to him?"

"My grandmother"—Julia corrected herself—"I mean, Elsie, told me he didn't know right up until a few weeks before he died. He came to bring Bill something as a keepsake and met Jasmine for the first time. Then he knew . . . because she was the image of you."

"So my Jasmine did not grow up in Wharton Park, the daughter of a British lord. Instead she grew up with a gardener and his kind wife."

"Yes. But, Lidia"—Julia knew there wasn't a way to shield her from the truth—"Harry's wife, Olivia, was having a baby at the same time."

"I see." Lidia's eyes darkened. "You must believe me, Julia, when I tell you that for the time Harry was with me here in Thailand, he never mention he is married. If he had, I would not . . ." Lidia shook her head vehemently. "It seems both myself and his wife were betrayed by him."

"I can understand how you must feel, and I don't know why Harry didn't tell you. Perhaps he was frightened he might lose you if you knew."

"He was right, he would have." Lidia's amber eyes were angry. "When Bill come to see me here in Bangkok after Jasmine is born, and he tell me this, I nearly die again from the shock. But over the years I understand better." Her eyes softened as she talked. "I have understood it is possible to love two people at the same time."

"No, Lidia, that isn't the way it was. Elsie told me that from the beginning it was an arranged marriage. Harry had no choice but to marry Olivia and try to produce an heir, in case he didn't return from the war. Love was not deemed to be important. Olivia was thought suitable and it was simply his duty. *You* were the woman Harry loved and wanted to be with."

"And what about his wife? Did she love him? Or did she accept the arrangement?"

"Elsie worked as her maid for over forty years and she says Olivia adored Harry." Julia sighed. "It was the real thing for her, which of course made it terrible . . . when she found out about you."

"She find out?" Lidia clapped her hand to her mouth. "How?"

"She discovered your last letter to Harry, with your engagement ring inside it. And a few days later she lost her own baby. According to Elsie, she spent the rest of her life embittered by what Harry had done to her."

"Oh, oh! What pain was caused by our love!" Lidia shook her head in despair. "I feel sympathy for this poor wife. Did she tell Harry she knew about me?"

"Never. She simply closed her heart to him and put her duty to the estate first. Elsie said they both lived in misery for the rest of their lives. In retrospect, it would have been much better if Harry had returned to you and released Olivia. But, of course, there was Wharton Park, which was in a dreadful mess just after the war. Harry had dozens of estate workers who looked to him for their livelihood. Even though Elsie said it broke his heart, he had to stay in England. He really had no choice."

Lidia nodded. "Bill explain this to me when he come to find me here in Bangkok. He was very kind. I think he was very good man. He saved my life."

"Well, I adored him. Every time I went to Wharton Park, I spent most of my time in the hothouses, watching him tend his flowers.

Both my mother and I grew up surrounded by the scents of the homeland we never knew was part of us."

"That is a comfort"—Lidia smiled—"and I send some special orchid with Jasmine, so Bill can grow it for her. It is very rare, only few in world. I spot it one day in flower market here in Bangkok just before Jasmine is born. I know what it is and I buy it for her. I wonder if it flower for him in England?"

"Really?" Julia thought back to the young Jasmine's painting of the rare orchid that George, her father, had spotted. "Yes, I think it possibly did," she whispered.

"And your father? Is he dead too?"

"No"—Julia smiled—"he is very fit. He adored my mother, and they were very happy together. So happy that he has never tried to replace her."

"And does he know of his wife's heritage?"

"Yes, but only very recently, like me."

"I would like one day to meet the husband of my daughter. So you too were an only child?"

"Well, no, I . . . have a sister, but I've just found out she was adopted. It turns out that my mother didn't think she could have children, so they adopted my sister, Alicia, as a baby. She's three years older than me, and it was a surprise when I came along. I don't think my father ever wanted to tell Alicia the truth, but when Elsie told him the story of how Jasmine came to Wharton Park, he felt he had to. Otherwise, she would have believed she too was yours and Harry's granddaughter. But she is still my sister," Julia said emphatically.

"Of course. Now, I think we should lunch, yes?" Lidia nodded to her hovering houseboy, who immediately disappeared inside.

"So, Julia, you are a pianist? Can I hear you play somewhere?"

"Yes, you can. I've played all over the world. I've been very lucky," said Julia modestly. "I was discovered at the Royal College of Music by an agent when I was nineteen. He's helped me build my career."

"Julia, luck does not happen without talent," Lidia chided. "You must be exceptional. And you are still so young. Where do you go after you leave Bangkok? Do you go to play somewhere?"

"No," Julia replied, as Nong came out of the house, carrying a tray with two bowls of steaming soup. "This last year, well, it has brought some—difficult changes. It will be a few months before I play again. And, to be honest, I have literally no idea where I go from here. That's why I came to Bangkok, to give me time to think."

"Well, you must tell me everything, for I can see in your eyes that you are troubled. But first, enjoy Nong's *tom kha gai.* I think it is the best in Bangkok."

After the delicious milky-coconut-and-lemongrass soup, filled with strips of tender chicken, Nong brought out a plate of mango and papaya for dessert.

"So now, Julia, tell me about your difficult year."

"Well"—Julia still had to steel herself to voice the words—"I lost my two-year-old son, Gabriel, in a car crash, twelve months ago. I also thought I'd lost his father, Xavier, but in fact, he walked back into our house in France a few weeks ago. He was driving the car that killed our son, and he vanished after the accident. He said he couldn't face me." Julia's brow furrowed. "And only a week ago, I found out that he was very drunk and shouldn't have been behind the wheel at all. So"—her voice dropped to a whisper—"I left him and came here."

Lidia's eyes grew wide with sympathy, and she reached her hand across the table to Julia. "This is terrible tragedy for you. I, above anyone, know that to lose a child is God's worst punishment."

"Yes. I can't imagine anything worse."

"There is nothing. I know. Your heart"—Lidia clasped hers—"it is empty."

"Yes," Julia murmured, "there is no comfort or relief from the pain."

"No. I too must mourn for the loss of my daughter's spirit from this earth. I feel I mourn for her twice." Lidia sighed. "But even more difficult for you: you must blame your husband for your son's death."

"I despise him for what he did, not only to Gabriel, but to me too," answered Julia, unable to keep the anger from her voice.

"It is only natural you feel this way. But, one day, you must forgive him for what he has done, for your sake, Julia. I learn it is not good to carry such anger inside. It eat you up, destroy you."

"I know, Lidia, but it's so hard in practice."

"Yes, it is. We have both been betrayed by men we loved and trusted. Your husband, he sound like a weak man, but then, many men are. At first, I think Harry is too, but now I see maybe he was not. He must be strong to stay in England and do his duty."

"If it's any comfort, I truly believe, from what Elsie told me, that the decision broke his heart. You really were the love of his life."

"As he was mine. Did you love your husband?"

"Very much, and I believed he was the love of *my* life, until . . ."

Lidia sat forward in her chair expectantly, and Julia felt the color rise to her cheeks as she struggled to explain. "When I thought I was a widow, another man in England was very kind to me. He cared for me when there was no one else. With his help, I began to recover and see there might be a future for me. And us."

"I see." Lidia listened intently. "And where is he now?"

"In Norfolk. Ironically, he's the new Lord Crawford. He lives at Wharton Park."

Lidia stared at her for a few minutes, trying to comprehend what Julia was saying. "But that means . . . ? "

Julia saw Lidia's train of thought and halted it. "No. We're not closely related. Harry did not have any more children after Olivia lost their baby. Kit and I are—we think—third cousins."

A look of relief appeared on Lidia's face. "I am happy to hear that, Julia. I can see in your eyes you feel strongly for this man. Do you love him?"

"I thought that maybe what I felt for him was because he was there when I needed him. But when Xavier reappeared, and I became his wife again, all I could think of was Kit. And, it still is."

"But then, my dear Julia, why are you not returning to him?"

"Because . . . oh, dear." Julia swept her hair off her shoulders, feeling uncomfortably hot. "It's all too complicated. I didn't even speak to Kit to explain that Xavier was back. He had to find out through the media that my husband was still alive. No"—she shook her head, allowing the breeze on her neck to cool her—"I'm sure he would never want me again. I've hurt him too much."

"You must be aware of the irony," Lidia said slowly. "You are in love with Lord Crawford of Wharton Park, and here with me in Bangkok. I think we both cry many tears into our pillow for those that are far away in England. Perhaps"—Lidia shook her head—"it is Wharton Park itself that is cursed. It is like helpless baby, needing to be fed and cared for constantly. It does not think of those whose lives are sacrificed for it."

Julia smiled at Lidia's imagery. "Actually, the estate will have to be sold eventually. Kit has no money to repay the loans on it, and the restoration will cost hundreds of thousands of pounds. Soon the 'helpless baby' will have a new and, hopefully, wealthier set of parents."

"It is hard to think I lose love of my life to a house." Lidia grimaced. "But I understand it is more than that. It is heritage, and it is sad that this will die."

"Yes, because however much pain it has caused, Wharton Park is so very beautiful. Oh, Lidia, I wish you could see it. I've always loved it, since I was a little girl, and I think back now to living there with Kit as some of the happiest few weeks of my life."

"It is in your blood." Lidia nodded somberly. "If you had been a boy, surely—as Harry's grandchild—it would be yours?"

"Perhaps. My sister tells me that these days, with DNA tests, I could make a claim. But I would never do that to Kit," Julia said firmly, feeling it was time to change the subject. "Do I have other relatives here in Thailand?"

"Oh!" Lidia clapped her hands together. "You have plenty! Aunts and uncles, and so many cousins I could not begin to count. Some of my great-nieces and -nephews are very successful," she added proudly. They are university educated and live in Japan and America. Even though I come from a simple fisherman family, we were always clever"—she smiled—"especially my father. He won scholarship to Chulalongkorn University in Bangkok and become successful journalist and political activist. Now, may I see the photographs of my Jasmine?"

"Of course." Julia fished them out of her bag and moved closer to Lidia, so she could explain each picture. "This is my mother at five years old; then this is when she passed her Eleven Plus to get into grammar school . . ."

"She was smart too!" Lidia smiled.

"She was, and this shows her graduating from university, and this is with my father, and then with Alicia, and me."

Lidia pored over the photographs, tracing the face of her daughter at every stage of her short life. She looked up and asked, "How did she die, Julia?"

"From ovarian cancer. Apparently, it's notoriously difficult to detect. By the time they found it, it had spread and there was nothing they could do."

"I see. And Jasmine always believe Elsie and Bill were her parents?"

"Yes."

Lidia's eyes were bright with tears. "I am sure she was loved."

"She was, I promise you."

"Even if she did not have what I thought she would when I sent her to England."

"No, but, Lidia, once upon a time it mattered where in society you were born. Now, I really don't think it does. The old rules have disappeared. And, in fact, because my mother and I weren't encumbered by our heritage, we were free to do with our lives as we pleased."

Lidia nodded. "I understand what you are saying and I agree. Now, even here in Thailand, women are becoming stronger and learning to be independent. And, though I was born in a different time, I married a man who respected me as an equal, we were in partnership and our business leave me a very rich woman. It is not what I expected when I was young; I thought I simply marry and have a family."

"Believe me, in the past year I've learned to take each day as it comes and to expect the unexpected."

"Then you will know, like I do, that anything is possible. And one must always look to the future and trust in God, whichever God that may be, to guide us. I think we have many thing in common, don't you? We both learn about life the hard way, but it make us wise and strong. And now, my dearest Julia"—Lidia smothered a yawn—"I must take some rest. You are welcome to sit here or you come again tomorrow, and we talk some more."

Julia could see Lidia was exhausted. "I will come again tomorrow."

"And as many times as you can before you leave here. We have much to make up for." Lidia rose, kissed Julia on both cheeks, and took her hand. "I am so happy you came to find me."

"I am too." Julia returned the kiss.

59

In the following week, Julia visited Lidia every day. They talked for many hours, each discovering more about the other's life. Julia learned how Lidia had helped her husband build a small silk-weaving business into a multimillion-dollar company, exporting all over the world. Lidia's designs and unusual colorways had been ahead of their time and proved popular in the West. Her soft-furnishing fabrics now graced some of the most beautiful houses around the world.

"Of course, the business gave me what I wanted most—the opportunity to travel," added Lidia. "I sold it when my husband died, and it left me a very wealthy woman . . . but I still miss the excitement of it."

"Did you ever come to England?" asked Julia.

"Oh, yes, and I always stay at the Oriental in Knightsbridge. They give me a good discount! But"—Lidia shivered involuntarily—"I do not like the English weather. Harry called me a hothouse flower and he was right: I could not have lived there. Which is why I always come back to my homeland. This country, this small house where I first live with my husband, is where I belong."

"I wish I knew where I belonged," Julia said wistfully.

Lidia patted her hand. "Julia, *ka*, you are at a point many people reach, where all the signposts telling you where to go next have vanished."

"Exactly." Julia thought how cathartic these days had been, as she learned to trust Lidia and opened her heart to her. The old lady's gentle, wise words had soothed and comforted her. "I will miss Kit for the rest of my life, but I just can't see a way back to him. He would feel he'd never be able to trust me again. Somehow, I've got to find a different signpost and follow it."

"Do not worry, Julia. I know it is already there inside you. Perhaps you simply need a little help to see it." Lidia smiled.

"I only hope you're right," she replied sadly.

• • •

Julia knew her time in Bangkok must now come to an end, and she had to decide where to go next, so that evening she booked herself on a flight to Paris for the following night. Olav was there for a few days, and she wanted to see him to discuss her future. She was also concerned that, having had no piano at her disposal, her fingers would be stiffening, hampering the progress she had made in the past few months. She could rent a practice room in Paris and catch up on the time she had lost.

Unable to face another lonely supper on the terrace, Julia ordered room service and ate on her balcony. She watched the to-and-fro of boats on the river below, enjoying her vantage point for the last time. She knew she would miss the tranquillity she felt in Thailand, from its people and the place itself. But even Lidia, with all the experience of her eighty years lived to the full, could not show her where to put the next stitch in her own tapestry. Julia knew she had to discover that for herself.

She spent her last afternoon by the pool, where many of the attendants now knew her by name. She had called Lidia to let her know she was leaving, and Lidia had insisted on coming over to the hotel for a farewell dinner. She would arrive at seven, and Julia had to leave for the airport by nine thirty.

At six, Julia showered, finished her packing, and checked out of her room. As she walked past the Bamboo Bar and down toward the terrace for dinner, Thanadol greeted her with his customary smile.

"Good evening, *Khun* Julia, how are you tonight?"

"Sad," she admitted, following him across the terrace. "It is my last evening here. Has my grandmother arrived yet?"

"No, she has not. She has asked that you wait for her here." Thanadol indicated a table that was already taken.

As they drew nearer, Julia recognized the figure at the table.

And her heart began to hammer against her chest.

He turned round, sensing her presence.

"Hello, Julia."

"Hello, Kit." Her voice didn't seem to belong to her.

He smiled and indicated the chair opposite him. "Won't you sit down?"

"But . . . what on earth—?"

"Please, for goodness' sake, sit down and I'll explain."

Julia did so abruptly, feeling her legs might buckle beneath her if she didn't.

"There." Kit put a glass of red wine in front of her. "Drink up, don't want you wilting from the shock."

Julia took a large gulp of her wine. "What are you doing here?" she managed.

"Oh, well, you know how it is: thought I'd just pop across the world and visit Bangkok on a whim," he replied, laughter in his eyes. "What the hell do you think I'm doing here, Julia? I've come to see you, of course."

"How did you know I was here?"

"I hardly need to put Interpol on the case if I want to find you, Julia. I mean, your sister does live just down the road from me." Kit grinned. "But, actually, it was Lidia who alerted me to your whereabouts. She gave me a call, suggesting I tip up here before you buzzed off elsewhere. And just in the nick of time, it seems. I hope you don't mind."

The lightness with which Kit was handling the situation was an instant reminder of everything he was. Julia smiled. "No, of course I don't."

"Could I take that one step further, perhaps, and ask if you're actually glad to see me?"

"Yes. I am."

"Phew!" Kit wiped his brow dramatically. "Lidia assured me you would be, but when I was somewhere over the Himalayas, I broke out in a cold sweat, wondering whether this was some weird reenactment of an old woman's fantasy. Which, to be fair, it may well be. There's quite a parallel between her past situation and our current one."

Julia fingered her glass, studying it intently. Her heart was beating so hard she felt breathless. "I know."

"Not really in my line to chase across the world after a woman who happened to have left me. But, under the circumstances, I decided you were worth a punt."

Julia raised her eyes. "Kit, I didn't want to leave you, I . . ."

"I'm teasing you, Julia, there's no need to say any more. Lidia, in her role as fairy godmother, has explained everything. And then she waved her magic wand and there was a first-class ticket to Bangkok on the doormat at Wharton Park. Not a return, I might add, so you'll have to lend me a few bob if you want me to go away."

"Oh, Kit . . ." Julia's eyes filled with tears as she realized Lidia had gone to great lengths to provide her with a signpost. "Sorry," she said, quickly wiping a tear from her cheek.

"Don't be. It really was no hardship, especially in first class . . . but mostly because I happen to love you."

"I love you too," Julia whispered.

Kit drew nearer to her and studied her face. "Don't tell me that was actually a furtive vocal admission of the fact you might reciprocate my feelings?"

"Yes, it was." Julia smiled.

"Right." It was Kit's turn to look down, suddenly unsure what to say next. "Do you really, Julia?" he asked quietly.

"Yes, Kit, I do. I love you . . . horribly, and I've been miserable every day since I last saw you."

"Then your old Thai granny isn't the mad box of frogs I thought she was," he replied in wonder.

"No, she isn't. She's completely in possession of all her marbles."

"Unlike me, who's just made a mad dash halfway across the world, not knowing what reaction to expect. Until now," Kit added softly. He reached for her hand and Julia gave it to him willingly. "I can't bear to fall into clichés, but, God, you look beautiful tonight, sweetheart," he whispered. "And I don't think I've ever been quite so glad to see another human being in my entire life."

He kissed her on the lips, and Julia responded with equal passion.

"While I've got you here, and just in case you disappear again, I also thought I might as well get it all out of the way in one go and ask you whether you fancied marrying me?" Kit indicated their surroundings. "Given the history, can't think of anywhere more perfect to ask you, really."

"Oh, Kit, I'd love to say yes." Julia chuckled at how ridiculous this was going to sound. "That is, just as soon as I've got divorced!"

"Ah, that's not really in the script is it? But hey-ho, nothing's perfect." He smiled at her and rubbed his nose against hers.

Their fingers entwined.

"Oh, by the way, I've brought you a present."

"Really?"

"Yes."

Kit reached beneath his chair and brought up a strange-looking black plant. He put it in front of her. "There. It's for you."

Julia studied the ink black petals in surprise. "I didn't think you could get black orchids."

"You can't. God forgot to get round to them, so Kit gave him some help. Don't worry, darling, all you need do is pour water over it. Then it'll go back to the beautiful pink it was before I started painting it." He indicated the small scroll tucked into the side of the pot. "That fable will explain it. One way and another, I thought it was rather apt."

Julia reached for the scroll, but Kit stopped her. "Read it later, my very own Hothouse Flower, and, please, when you have, don't be getting any ideas above your station. Remember, this is the new millennium, and all the rules governing male and female behavior have changed. Except for one," he added as an afterthought.

"And what's that?"

Kit looked into her eyes and answered simply, "Love."

60

Wharton Park
January

Despite hours of debate at the kitchen table, and weeks spent sweating over reams of figures, Kit finally decided that the Wharton Park estate had to be sold.

"With the best will in the world, we just can't do it, sweetheart," Kit said as they drowned their sorrows with a bottle of wine in the library. "I know it's going to break your heart, but I really can't see any other way. Even with a grant from English Heritage, we still can't afford what needs doing. It's a drop in the ocean."

"I know," Julia replied miserably. "If only Xavier hadn't come back from the dead and wasn't angling for half of everything I've earned, we could probably just have done it." She shivered and huddled closer to the fire. The house was freezing as the boiler had packed up, yet again.

Kit stroked her hair. "Julia, even if you did have the money, there's part of me that's still Neanderthal and would find it difficult if my future wife were providing the funds that Wharton Park needs. And we must think of the house: hand it over with grace to someone who does have the wherewithal to put everything right."

"I know, but it doesn't make parting with it any easier. Wharton Park *isn't* just a house. It's where we met. And it's in my blood. If there was anything I could do to save it, I would." Julia banged her fist on the hearth. "Damn Xavier! The one time in my life I've actually needed all the money I've never spent! I can't believe he's being such a—"

"You don't need to say it," Kit replied sympathetically. "Anyway, I'm going to speak to the estate agent tomorrow and put it back on the market. I'm sorry, Julia, but we really don't have a choice."

• • •

Ten days later, the agent called to say a foreign buyer had put in a bid for the entire estate, at the asking price. If they accepted the offer, the buyer would fly immediately to England to sign on the dotted line.

They both knew they could not refuse the offer.

Julia stoked the fire in the library and arranged a few snowdrops on the table. It was a paltry and reluctant effort to make for the buyer, who was due to arrive in the next half hour.

"Probably some ghastly Russian oligarch and his platinum-haired mistress." Julia slammed some coffee cups onto a tray.

Kit watched her petulance, knowing it was masking her sadness. Losing Wharton Park would be a far greater blow for Julia than for him.

At eleven thirty, the bell rang and Kit answered it, opening the door. A liveried chauffeur was standing behind it.

"Madam is here," he announced, indicating a limousine parked in the drive. "She wonders whether you would escort her into the house?"

"Of course." Kit looked at Julia and raised his eyebrows as the chauffeur returned down the steps toward the car.

"Christ!" exclaimed Julia. "Who does 'Madam' think she is? The queen?"

"Come on, sweetheart, let's grit our teeth and get this over and done with, okay?" Kit squeezed her hand and led her down the steps to the car.

They stood together, waiting uncomfortably by the car door as the chauffeur opened it to reveal the passenger behind the tinted windows.

Julia did a double take and then shrieked in pleasure.

"Lidia! What on earth are you doing here?"

"Surprise!" Lidia stepped out of the car and hugged her granddaughter warmly. "Oh, it is a wonderful thing to be so old and so rich and use both to play magical tricks on people!" Her tinkling laugh filled the still Wharton Park air.

Then, holding on to Julia, she turned and looked up at the house for the first time.

"So, this is Wharton Park. Many times in my life I have imagined it, and yet it is far more magnificent than I dream." She turned to Julia with a twinkle in her eye. "No wonder it won over me! Now"—she tucked her free arm into Kit's elbow—"take me inside and show me around. And then, afterward, I explain everything."

Once Lidia had taken a guided tour of the main parts of the house, declaring herself too exhausted to look any further, they returned to the library and Lidia had her chauffeur produce a bottle of the best champagne from inside the limousine.

"I would like to toast the house that has affected all our lives: to Wharton Park."

Julia and Kit clinked their glasses against hers. "To Wharton Park," they repeated.

"Now," said Lidia, sitting down. "I wish to explain my plan to you. As I tell to you in Bangkok, Julia, my husband leave me very rich woman. And by rich, I mean *very* rich. Of course, before I meet you, Julia, I think I will share this money out among members of my family and the charities I support. But then, suddenly, I have direct heir, so I change my will when you leave Bangkok last time to leave most of my money to you."

"Granny, that's awfully kind of you but—"

"Hush, Julia, let me finish," Lidia chided. "Then, when we speak last week, you tell me Wharton Park is for sale, because you cannot afford to pay off debts or restore the house. So . . . I decide *I* will buy it. It will be mine." Lidia clasped her tiny hands together in glee.

"You want to live here?" asked Kit, confused.

"No, Kit. Julia know how I hate the cold. I will be your landlady. You will live here, and with money I pay you for Wharton Park, I entrust you to pay off debts and oversee the restoration for me. And, of course, this task is also for yourselves and future generations of our family," Lidia added softly. "On my death, Julia, Wharton Park will become yours."

There was a pause, as Kit and Julia took time to comprehend what Lidia was suggesting.

"My goodness! It's awfully generous of you, Lidia," Kit replied finally, realizing Julia was too overwhelmed to speak.

"Well, I think it is good joke"—Lidia's amber eyes sparkled—"that the poor Thai girl, abandoned all those years ago by the owner of this house, buys it for her granddaughter, almost sixty-five years later. Do you not think so too?"

Julia nodded, still stunned into silence.

"It is all very perfect." Lidia smiled happily. "When Julia marry you, Kit, my granddaughter will finally be Lady Crawford of Wharton Park. And the journey Harry and I start together all those years ago will have been completed. Please tell me you think well of my idea?" She looked at Julia anxiously.

Julia finally spoke. "Lidia, are you sure this is what you want?"

"Julia, *ka*, I have never been so sure of anything in my life. Kit, do you feel comfortable about my plan?"

"Lidia, we all know that, by rights, this house should be Julia's anyway." Kit turned to Julia and reached for her hand. "And I'd be very happy to stay and do my bit to help return Wharton Park to its former glory. I love the place too. And I know how much you do, darling," he added, gently reassuring Julia with his eyes. "It really is the most wonderful offer, Lidia."

"All I ask is, occasionally, I may be welcome as your guest here and meet your English family. Your father, Julia, and of course, Elsie, who take care of my daughter with so much love."

"Of course you can," Julia said, "whenever you want. I've told Elsie all about you, and she would so love to meet you."

"So," said Lidia, "there is little more to say. Tell me you agree, Kit, and I can sign all papers before I return to Thailand next week."

"Of course I agree. It's a wonderful offer."

"And you, Julia?" Lidia asked gently.

"I love this house so much, Lidia, it would be very difficult for me to say no." Julia's voice was choked with emotion. "I just can't believe we can stay here. Thank you, thank you so much." Julia stood up and hugged Lidia tightly.

"All this in return for one favor, Julia," Lidia added, taking Julia's hands into her own. "I wish to go back to the drawing room, so I can listen while you play for me, on my Harry's beautiful grand piano."

The three of them entered the drawing room and Julia sat down in front of the piano.

Kit watched Lidia's eyes fill with tears as the opening notes of Chopin's Études fell effortlessly from her granddaughter's gifted fingers.

He realized the circle had been completed, each of them with his or her own place in the story that had spanned generations, reunited here together at Wharton Park, which had itself played such a major role in the tapestry they and others had woven.

All that remained now, Kit thought, was to begin a new circle.

He looked down at Julia and knew that, together, they would.

Epilogue

Wharton Park
December, eleven months later

It is Christmas Eve. I am standing by the window in the bedroom I share with Kit, overlooking the park. The scene outside is not as it is in high summer, but as the sun rises, making the frost glitter on the barren winter landscape, it has its own particular beauty.

I turn away from the window and step back into the warm room, my feet sinking into the newly laid carpet. I admire the wallpaper, hand-painted to copy the original, and enjoy the faint smell of fresh paint.

In the past year, Kit has overseen this transformation single-handedly. I can take no credit, as I was busy on other projects. Wharton Park looks as it did, yet everything inside and out is on its way to being restored, to protect another seventy years of Crawfords, who will play out their lives within its walls. Soon, it will be Kit's turn to follow his own dream, still tucked safely within the walls of Wharton Park, but using his talent and experience to help children outside of them.

I am the new lady of the house. On the day of my marriage to Kit, I wore the necklace and earrings that Olivia, and generations of Crawford brides, wore before me. They are mine now, to hand on to my son's bride when he marries.

As with Olivia, Wharton Park must always play a big part in my life. But I have learned, through stories of the past and my own experience, that everything must have a balance. I will use and appreciate the gift I have been given to nurture and protect my family and my talent, but never allow it to destroy them.

Alerted by the faintest sound, I leave Kit sleeping and pad silently through the bathroom to the small room beyond. This was once Harry Crawford's dressing room, but we have converted it into a nursery. I peep over the cot and see that the perpetrator of the sound is still asleep, his thumb stuck firmly in his rosebud-shaped mouth.

Everyone tells me he looks like me, but I know he doesn't. He looks like himself.

"Today, Harry," I whisper to him, "is a special day for you."

He lies, innocent in sleep, unaware that his family—some of whom have traveled from the other side of the world—are gathering to watch him undertake his first rite of passage as he is christened in the small church on the estate. One day, his last rite of passage will also take place there, and he will be laid in the Crawford family vault and reunited with his forebears for eternity. But his tapestry has only just begun and I can only hope it will contain many more stitches than his half brother's before him.

He does not realize the link he provides to the past and the future. Or the weight of responsibility his privileged start in life will give him. I have sworn to him it will never hold him back from living the life he chooses. Or from spending that life with the woman he loves.

I gather the six weeks of new life gently into my arms, relishing this moment alone with him. After this, there will be little time for me to enjoy him, for I have much to do today. The house is full of guests, here to celebrate Christmas at Wharton Park with us. The tree has been cut from the woods and installed in the entrance hall, bedecked with twinkling lights and the same decorations that have been used for generations.

I kiss his sweet-smelling forehead, look up, and call upon God to protect him, understanding so well that my powers as a mother are limited, and I know I must accept that.

Through the pain and the joy of the journey I have made in the past two years, I have learned the most important lesson life can offer, and I am glad of it.

The moment is all we have.

Acknowledgments

Johanna Castillo and Judith Curr at Atria, for their belief and encouragement. Mari Evans and all the team at Penguin UK, who bought the book originally. Jonathan Lloyd, my agent, who has believed in me through thick and very thin. Susan Moss, Rosalind Hudson, Helene Rampton, Tracy Blackwell, and Jenny Dufton, whose generous support during difficult times got me through.

In Thailand, the amazing staff of the Oriental Hotel, especially *Khun* Ankhana, who generously shared her memories of life in Bangkok in 1945, and Kitima, Thanadol, Lidia, Jack, Laor, and Jeab. In France, Tony and Fiona Bourne for the gin and the forest fire, and Agnes Sorocki for help with my bad French and lifts to the airport.

In England, the fantastic Jacquelyn Heslop and Sue Grix, and Pat Pitt, my typist. The late Jack Farrow, a sergeant in the Fifth Royal Norfolks, whose moving and descriptive diary of life as a POW in Changi helped me to create an accurate picture of the suffering that our brave boys were subjected to.

My mother, Janet, my sister, Georgia, and Olivia, my stepdaughter, who over the years have all encouraged me to keep going. Stephen, my husband, who has taught me so much about life; without his love and support, I would not have written this book. And my children: Harry, who helped me type in edits with such, er . . . grace; Isabella, whose zest for life always cheers me up; Leonora, my sensitive, artistic "mini-me"; and Kit, my chocolate- and Stoke City–obsessed "baby." They are used to a blank stare when they interrupt me to ask me a question, and I am so very proud of them all.

And finally, my late father, whose wanderlust and genuine interest in the world and the people in it I have gratefully inherited.